The Seam

John Kitterman

Copyright 2012 by John Kitterman
ISBN-13: 978-0615666518
ISBN-10: 0615666515

Thanks to Jeff Dalton and Julia Cornelius for the cover photo, and to Christian Breeden for permission to use lyrics from his song "Taboo."

For Kathryn

Prologue

You have been here.

A grove of oaks in the woods west of Pocahontas, in a knuckle of Virginia that juts into the flesh of its separated western sister. Two hundred or more years ago some nameless pioneer family built a long-vanished home in their shadows, the timbers and stones that protected their frontier fires now sunk into the soil below the woodland moss. In the lee of the Appalachians, a half dozen of these ancient trees still form a defensive circle around its absence, like a temple to hope but ultimately to despair, guarding their secret that human life is pitiful and short.

Perhaps you might come across it, the grove, the temple, even the secret, while walking in the woods in the fall. Squirrel hunters stop with their rifles slung over their shoulders and stare. Young lovers bed down in their bags. Teenagers drink beer and paint stones. They see the trees stretching their long arms out of the shadows and into the sunlit opening as if pleading or grasping, and the circle of leaves on the ground, and the sunlight pouring onto them like Zeno's honey, and they imagine: Is this the dream called paradise?

But look closer. Things aren't always what they seem. Can't you tell? There's something buried in that heap of leaves. Something human, or recently so. Dig deep into the thick blanket of red and gold that late October like a mother has thrown over a child's bed, and you will feel it. Be careful. You don't want to be frightened out here, so far from civilization. Just reach your arms around until you touch it. It won't hurt you. Much.

Can you feel it? Perhaps a pale hand, dirty under the nails, but with shapely, paint-stained fingers—an artist's hand? Or a foot, callused from going without shoes—a mountain daughter's? Keep feeling along until you come to

1

the corpse's hair, so well disguised by the leaves, the twig-clotted wisps curling across the broad forehead like carved letters on the stern of a caravel, until finally you come to them—the still wide-open eyes, as relentlessly blue as the sea that once lived within, searching the bare, lichen-painted spars a hundred feet above for any signs of life.

Don't stare into those eyes too long: you might drown. And no one would see you go under. There are no surveillance cameras here in the forest. Only the dead eyes that captured the assault. In the corner of the retina, the gloved fist from above clutching the tire iron. Then the dazed, upside down dragging over railroad ties and rocks. The rape, physical and verbal, below the blind gods who can no longer move their arms. And finally, the slitting of the white throat and the deep scarification of the flesh. With no witnesses, except perhaps those invisible planes that traverse the small heaven overhead.

He is long gone, this Tazewell County Death, back down the twisted remains of a road that merges with a spur of the Norfolk Southern. Back to the city which spawned him. Gone, but certainly not forgotten. In the quiet of the grove you can still sense his presence. Above the dripping of the rock-bound spring that wet the lips of the pioneers, under the moaning of the breeze that kicks up with the first cold front that passes through in November, can't you still hear his triumphant laughter? And her voice, rising from the bed of leaves and up the trunks of the giant oaks that transmit it through their branches like radio towers broadcasting from the wilderness?

Her ineluctable command to any who can hear it, throughout the insulated continent they call America: "Revenge me, you safe and expedient citizens! Revenge your wild, red-haired sister!"

Chapter 1

*I*n the beginning God created the Appalachian Mountains and strung them along the East Coast of the New World like a green necklace around a woman's throat, not really a barrier but more like a beckoning, tempting men westward, toward paradise maybe. Or maybe she has a backbone bent with scoliosis, like a miner hunched underground, tortured more and more out of normal as you climb west and enter coal country, the mountains always pulling you farther and farther into their tragedy as you travel 1-81 from Staunton on down to Roanoke and on to Wytheville and Marion where you turn north and then west into Buchanan County and then to Grundy where I was born and raised. It's about six hours by Trailways if you're lucky from Best Western State Hospital the techs call it in Staunton, where they put you in 4-point restraints and fry your brain if the drugs don't work and you refuse to cooperate. I can't crack the window but I know the air is crisp and blue in the morning light and there's still the thin flesh of a moon in the sky like a communion wafer. Sometimes I see clouds that look like the spaceships which navigate by the mountains or are drawn to the radio telescopes at Green Bank. The military know they're there that's why the Navy jets are always flying over the Appalachian treetops. Farther up are the spy planes watching what we're up to down here, Francis Gary on my mother's side. They can see this bus crawling down the interstate, count the lines on the faces through the windows, the geese taking off from the James.

It's no big thing being locked up. I fried my brain the first time when I was fourteen when I snuck in my boyfriend my father hated after he had gone to bed and we sat on the Oriental rugs of the living room while J.T. drank some moonshine and I watched. I could hear the respirator chugging away upstairs so's I knew he wouldn't hear us, but we didn't make no noise anyway, just talking. Then J.T. pulled out this dirty paper packet and asked me if I wanted to get high. He had on the leather motorcycle jacket he always wore even though he didn't own a bike and his boots were splayed out like a ballet dancer's under the coffee table. I asked him what would happen and he said you'll go

3

on a trip so I said okay and snorted it. Then we opened the sliding door to the patio and went on down to the river and sat on a big flat rock. You could hear the water moving through the rocks in the starlight. Jupiter was the brightest thing in the narrow sky which was milky with scratches like linoleum. J.T. made love to me for the first and last time while I listened to the Levisa moving by my ear and watched the airplanes far and silent overhead cross from ridge to ridge. Later I named my baby Cassie after the stars I saw like a woman on her back with feet sticking in the air. I was that woman but I was also way out in space watching myself conceive among the green diamonds of the Appalachian necklace. J.T. said after he graduated high school he was going to save enough money to move to Beckley where he said he had friends who had a motorcycle shop and he could work there and we could party all the time. I knew he was lying and it was just the crank talking but I didn't care cause it was the future.

That was the first time I fried my brain. When my daddy found out I was pregnant he called me a whore and I ran away but then he relented and said I had no choice because I could not have an abortion. By this time J.T. had left so I said who's going to marry me and he said his friend Dwayne Hostetter whose wife died a year ago was willing and would raise the baby as his own so I said okay. Dwayne was an ex-Mormon Catholic disbarred lawyer who worked now as a paralegal in town. The only thing interesting about him was when he talked about Joe Smith and the angel Moroni and the lost tribe of Israel. I loved that story and wished I had enough in me to believe he would appear in the woods in Grundy. Dwayne was a large, middle-aged man with a small head who disgusted me when he ate because he never stopped talking and he fucked me too every day and twicet on Sunday even though I was with child and never weighed more'n a hundred pounds, I guess. It seemed like he was making up for lost time because his wife had taken to bed for years so he just went at me every day while I smoked weed and stared at the paint peeling on the ceiling in images of demons that cured me of lying on my back. He made me take my clothes off and walk around the room and laughed and said I looked like the Virgin Mary and maybe I did but he hurt me so's I couldn't take it anymore so we drove over to Kentucky to get some pills

4

for the pain. We didn't go to Rite-Aid where they knew me because I was embarrassed; we went to an apothecary friend of Dwayne's who advised me to drink a small glass of whiskey before we did it and it wouldn't hurt the baby. But God forgive me I never could stop with one glass but I had three or four by the time Jay Leno came on and I knew it was time to get hurt. So when the baby miscarried I had no one to blame but myself. Dwayne was hunting with Daddy and I started bleeding and the whole thing just spilled out on the tiles of the bathroom floor like a red tide that washed her up on the beach. I took her and walked through the backyards down the road to the rock in the river where she was conceived and washed her off in the cold water and then covered her with some leaves and said a prayer in a language my momma taught me and laid down on the bank next to her and dreamt I was a-flying up to heaven with her. I didn't need no meth then to fry my brain because it was already on fire.

It stayed on fire too for the next ten years. When Dwayne saw I wasn't pregnant no more he figured something was wrong and left me alone for a while, and I saw my chance and six weeks after I took his crappy car and split. I told my father I was moving away and he didn't seem impressed, just said to keep out of trouble. I guess he figured I was married now and I wasn't his to worry about no more, so I just drove up and down 81 for a while, working part-time here and there, moving in with one guy or another, people always thought I was older than I was, until I turned eighteen for real and settled into a trailer in Montgomery County near Roanoke. Me and Dwayne by this time were officially divorced.

I spent time working in all the following places, in no particular order, during those years: tattoo parlors, Burger King, couple years at a used book store where I mostly read novels, Wynn Dixie, Sal's Pizza, Suicide Girls, briefly, what a joke, Dairy Queen, got my GED, one semester at Hollins as a charity case, also a joke, several nameless laundromats, community college, and more than one Waffle House, but much of the time I was also in and out of Staunton when bouts of mania got so bad I couldn't stand it no more or got arrested and had no insurance. And the suicide attempts were frequent enough that the paramedics knew me by my Christian name. But I always had

5

been a big reader so I didn't mind the itinerant life so much because the remedial jobs left plenty of time for myself, holed up in the trailer halfway up a ridge with no one around but the coyotes.

So this time it was late October and as soon as I got home I picked up my dogs and cats from the old couple across the way where my roommate had left them. She was away somewhere which wasn't unusual because she was always taking off for some rally or meeting that I often went to as well because we were in this environmental thing together but it was strange that she hadn't left a note and the Stencils had said she was supposed to have been back several days ago. Still, it didn't seem too out of character as she was a very hardcore person and could go off on a tangent when she was outraged about something and forget what day it was, so I made some coffee and went for a hike up to the treeline where I had stashed a couple of chairs and could chill out under the stars and keep an eye out for her signs. I lived in a little valley with just a few other houses and I could smell the wood smoke as I lay down in the still deep grass amid the rolls of hay and stretched my sore back from the cramped bus seats. It was almost midnight, an owl flew out of a peach tree down the hill, and suddenly I realized it was All Hallows Eve. The cats were walking around in the woods, one was sitting on a hay round, the dogs were sitting too staring into the eastern distance, when it seemed like they all stopped what they were doing and looked at me. And I stared back at them with a big smile on my face. For just a little while, we were a happy family.

Chapter 2

The face on the screen always unnerved him. Furious and blank at the same time. Like the masked gunmen who inexplicably advertised their homemade videos on YouTube, or posed like Facebook friends with guns too big for their bodies. Seung-Hui Cho wanted to be an engineer of infamy, the first collegiate mass murderer. And succeeded. Elias stared at his laptop. It looked like a pyramid sitting on his desk. History is nearing the end of its human run, he thought. Thirty-two students dead. And the shooter. Even three years later he could still imagine his wife looking up from conjugating a verb, Я умру, ты умрешь, она умирает, мы умираем, and there he is in the doorway, the isolated Asian American with the Walther and the Glock and the extra ammo. He had chained and padlocked the doors. Elias closed the portal gently.

And as if that wasn't enough, it seemed like someone had opened the floodgates. Two years later another psycho killer, this time from China, cuts off the head of a coed he thinks has disrespected him, right in the Tech cafeteria during lunch in front of the other students. On its heels, a couple parked in their car near the AT are murdered by killer or killers unknown. No motive. No clues. Then just this past year, a Tech freshman goes down to a Mettalica concert at UVA with her friends, leaves the John Paul Jones Arena and is not allowed back in, attempts to hitchhike home and disappears. No one saw what happened to her. A manhunt turns up nothing in the preppy college town but her shirt. That was in October. The next spring they find her bones on a farm ten miles away. The owner checking his fences tells the police he thought it was the skeleton of a deer.

Was there a sudden breach in the heavens over the Valley of Virginia? The promised land to waves of immigrants. Had the Cho atrocity ripped an artery leading to some latent pathology and sent it oozing into the local water supply? One sociopath starts a mass infection, a virus turns everyone into cannibals, and no one is safe. Shenandoah National Park is shut down. You can't drive the Blue Ridge Parkway at night. And yet, the new freshmen keep coming and the football team keeps winning and the circles of associations just keep widening. There is no way to tell anymore where reality ends and media begins.

Elias stared into the blue light veining the first frost on his windows and could feel the angst rising in his chest. What had happened to the human race? No other species acted like this. Obsessed with guns. Gorged on chemicals and ideology and the internet. Bent on the wholesale destruction of every other living thing on the planet that couldn't immediately be used to its advantage or stocked on the shelves at Wal-Mart. Was it the Biblical mandate that the world was ours to exploit any way we desired? The triumph of capitalism and self-interest? Or just something in the water, a toxin leached from an underground storage tank? It was probably all of these things. But one thing seemed clear to him. The center of the disaster, ground zero, was here in the U.S., at the heart of the American Dream.

There was no point in going back to sleep now—better to make some coffee and stay awake than return to the nightmare of Cho gunning down his wife and students in cold blood. Even awake, he could hear the 9 millimeter barking like a dog in the distance. Three years ago no one knew what was happening, except for the unspoken instinct that something was badly wrong. In the dream he is standing on the second floor of Norton watching helplessly as Cho walks down the corridor looking into each room like a lost freshman. Elias struggles to help, but he can only wade through the concrete air in slow motion. Then the bland angry face turns to him and Cho points his pistol and he knows he is going to die and wakes up.

A late night reader, Elias moves slowly at 6 a.m. and takes forever to put the coffee on and let the cats out. When it's ready he pulls an overcoat off the chair back and struggles into it with the mug in one hand like he can't figure out what to do with it, curses, puts it down on the counter, puts on the coat, picks it back up and pushes the door open to go get the newspaper. The dogs jump off the back deck into the first pool of early morning light. Acorns form hexagrams from the *I Ching* on the planks. Giant poplar leaves lie like Brigge's discarded faces along the driveway. The three species posse makes its slow way down to the baseball bat-bashed box. On the way back he scans the headlines. It's election day. Had enough of that. The war in Afghanistan is entering its thousandth year it seems, despite floods and invasions and earthquakes. Americans know nothing of this history. In the op-eds he reads that Obama is a communist who will redistribute the wealth and turn this great nation into the Soviet Union.

Then he's back at the house and makes some toast and scans the sports. The World Series is over. Then looks for some funny stories to read to his students. Researchers in Great Britain say alcohol is the most dangerous drug. More socialist propaganda. Which reminds him, pour a shot of kahlua into the second coffee. Elias drinks out of a china cup with saucer, one of the many mannerisms from growing up in a formal household. After a shower he switches to the TV and amuses himself sitting on the bed watching CNN for a while with the sound off, trying to wake up out of his chronic depression. Robin Meade has done something to her hair; he can't figure out what it is, but she doesn't look right. It bugs him. Finally he can't stand it any longer and switches the sound back on. It's bangs, she's got bangs. Apparently she didn't have bangs before, how could he have not noticed this? It bothers him even more. Many years ago his wife would have explained what was different, but she

9

was gone now. He is invited to tweet the show to tell them what he thinks of her new bangs. He cuts the set off.

An hour later he's pulling the twenty year old Jeep onto the road. It's not even 40 degrees and still foggy. At the S curve the neighbor's three Great Pyrenees stand in the middle of the asphalt like a 21st century Cerberus; he slowly drives into a field and around them. Their heads come up to his window and he gives each one a pat as he goes by. These shelter dogs navigate their anabasis of the five miles to the end of the road and back every morning. Miraculously, no one ever seems to hit them, even though half the people who drive by appear to be doing 60 on their way to work in Roanoke.

By the time he gets to Route 8 the car is steering itself and Elias is thinking about the war in Afghanistan while listening to the reports on NPR. He had been there. Not this time. But he knew what they were going through. The first days after 9/11. The minivan-size daisy cutters dropped in the desert; white rays that looked like Pat Robertson's New Age heaven disintegrating human bodies in a slurry of ammonium nitrate and aluminum dust to fertilize Wall Street. Now on the radio they were talking about the Soviets and the Americans collaborating on a heroin bust. Karzai is mad agayne. The Soviets invaded, the Taliban took out the Reds, then we take out the Taliban and get cozy with Putin. Meanwhile the kids in the slums of Star City are shooting smack. Ban, ban, Taliban; has a new master, got a new man. Elias can imagine some guy much like himself, button-down shirt and corduroy coat with leather elbow patches, sitting in a concrete shack in Dallas cyberjockeying those drones for eight hours a day then going home to his wife and kids. How was your day, honey? Did you hit all your targets? Did you make quota?

It's all too depressing and too complex to explain to his students. Why even burden them with it, the sins of the fathers? What Elias would really like to do most Tuesdays

10

and Thursdays is just go down on his knees before the front row and cry into the pajama bottoms and flip flopped feet of the first coed he encounters until the last seat empties in fear and confusion. Somewhere in the back of his mind he actually believes this would be a more effective teaching strategy about what is going on in the world than anything else he has done. How much could he get away with, if the dean didn't find out? Sometimes he forgets where he is and asks the undergrads if anyone has a joint, or, barring that, a gun he can put to his head when he has finished reading the news to them. Then he adds, "metaphorically, of course." He never used to act like this; things were getting worse. What he wants to do is to crawl back into Cho's boyhood tomb in Centreville to see what started it all.

Elias has been depressed for several years now without getting any help. The thought of taking anti-depressants was too depressing to him. At first it was not too bad, just some blank moments and some rage, nothing new considering what he had spent the first half of his life doing—working for Navy Intel. He had had to kill people. Now maybe the ghosts were coming home. Maybe Cho was one of those ghosts, and Katya's death was the way the universe righted itself. What goes around. He had declined the therapy the university offered. Then his mother had to go into a nursing home with dementia. Then a friend died when she fell and hit her head on the kitchen counter. In his middle age death was catching up with him, in a different form than when he was overseas. Not even the quick death. The slow, inevitable decline. Very gradually he stopped socializing with his friends and colleagues in the area and started spending more and more time at home. Sometimes he found himself reading obituaries of people he didn't know. It was an ironic obsession: death comforting life. They made him feel somehow less alone. The TV was his wife now and he left her on all night. He stopped doing his kata and his stomach got flabby. He stopped meditating

11

because all he could think about when he sat still was how bleak everything was and all he could see was her face. It was hard not to. She was buried on the property in the family plot. He walked past her every day and when he did he could see her curled up in her coffin on her side just like she did in sleep. Of course he talked to her. She was irreplaceable. He also fantasized a lot about other women he knew, sometimes his students; maybe that kept him going. When he got too depressed to go to school, he swallowed a couple of Black Beauties. He knew things were getting worse, events were slipping away from him like flotsam on the ocean, but as long as he forced himself to go to work, make the students laugh with his sarcasm, keep his pets alive and empty birdseed into the feeder, then he thought he was doing okay.

Lately however even that was requiring too much of an effort. It was like the world he grew up in had been torn apart and stitched back together. Some days he didn't notice, like most people. But most days he not only saw the sutures, there was something black and oily oozing through them, some infection, so that his whole field of vision, of consciousness, became inescapably contaminated. There was no going back. This was the future. His future, anyway. So on the worst days he put his knuckles to his eye sockets and ground away until he woke up hours later with his head on the kitchen table or his desk at school, blinking like he didn't know where he was. And swallowed a handful of ibuprofen.

On the way home from school that Tuesday he stopped at the polls at the fire station and shot the shit with some of the locals who thought he was an anarchist, which in his heart he was. Living in Floyd County was like going to Wal-Mart after midnight: you never knew what might crawl out of the parkinglot. The sheriff's deputy was talking to an old moonshiner while some old lady in an ancient Oldsmobile just about ran them over when she parked her car without taking it out of gear. Good old boys in overalls and John Deere hats mixed with some tie-dyed ex-hippies. The poll workers seemed to be in a competition over who could wear the most American flags and Elias hung around just long enough to catch up on the latest gossip and predictions. Obamacare was gonna get repealed. Cap and trade was the worstest thing that ever happened in Southwest Virginia. Concealed handgun carry was dead in the water. Hunting season was about to start. Don't forget to wear blaze orange.

After he got home and let the animals out he was suddenly too tired and depressed to eat so he lay down on the couch and fell asleep. At 10 p.m. he was still too worn down to cook and too wired to sleep, so he put the dogs in the Jeep and headed out again, this time to the 581 Waffle House.

Late night drives for food happened pretty often. He needed to hit some anxiety-deadening, blue collar oblivion, and Waffle House was as good a fishbowl as any. You could always count on the good folks there to have something appropriate on the jukebox. Elias walked in halfway through "People Are Strange" and sat at the counter. There were a couple of students in a corner booth, a trucker in another hunched over a short stack, and a young woman a few seats down. He ordered a coffee and stared at the menu, which he knew by heart but he liked to look at the pictures anyway for some unfathomable reason. Maybe it was the weird colors, like stills from an early Technicolor movie. The hamburgers and pork chops seemed to detach from the plastic page and float into the air, where they were replicated by more photos framed inexplicably high up on the walls near the ceiling. Caught in the semiotics of Southern food and sensual music, he almost didn't notice but the waitress and the girl at the counter were discussing what sounded like—to Elias who was half deaf from too

13

many gunshots not wearing his headgear and therefore didn't believe half of what he heard—a reference to Sylvia Plath. I'm imagining things, he assumed, but no, it was Plath herself they were talking about, Lady Lazarus, and her marriage to that bastard Ted Hughes who left her for another woman and turned her last suicide attempt into a success. Then Elias recovered himself a little because he remembered these were probably Hollins students, so he wasn't losing his mind. Still, the business about Plath and Hughes was a little unnerving because in grad school in England he had once dated one of Hughes' girlfriends. He heard the young woman at the counter say, "She found a man just like her father and married him and of course he was a Nazi too." The girl was pretty, in a beat up kind of way: dark hair, lanky. She smoked, like most late night customers, in defiance of the ban. Without thinking, Elias heard himself mutter to his menu, "You do not do, you do not do, any more, black shoe." The girl took a drag and looked over at him, then looked back. The waitress came over.

"It's her birthday next week," he said, by way of explanation.

"Who?" she asked.

"Plath."

Then he ordered scrambled eggs, hold the yolks, grits, and raisin toast with apple butter.

"Living dangerously," the girl at the counter said, exhaling but not looking over.

"Yeah, don't tell my internist I'm lighting up too," Elias responded, and pulled his pack from his shirt pocket.

Then, after a moment she followed with: "You don't remember me."

Elias put away his lighter and swiveled around. It was his turn to stare. She met his eyes and suddenly he saw her in the front row of his freshman comp class at the community college five, maybe six years ago, when he first

14

moved to the area. She had been a blonde then, he thought, like his wife, but wasn't positive. Now she looked like Eustacia Vye. The eyes were unforgettable, very caustic, intelligent, dark eyes, like a couple of batteries that had been cut open, and the eyebrows like black scars. He didn't look away, and neither did she. Then his food came and he started in on it.

"Yes I do."

"Where?"

"Right here in Roanoke. First row, first seat on the far right."

"Far left from where I was sitting."

He turned again to face her and smiled. "You talking geography or politics?"

"Both," she said, slid down off the stool, ground her butt into a plate, and came over to the chair next to him. She had on tight jeans, cowboy boots, a tight thin shirt and a thin black leather jacket. Elias got the weird sensation he always felt when he ran into an attractive coed off campus, in another country where she was no longer a student and he was no longer bound by the Faculty Handbook. It was the serpent pulling somewhere between his gut and his groin, and combined with the late night, the coffee, and the depression, he knew that it meant he was about to get involved in something he couldn't foresee and did not feel up to.

"You gave me an A," she continued, "the last one I got before I dropped out."

"I gave you an A?" he said. "That must have been a mistake." She laughed. But he remembered her essays now, almost never on the subject or in the rhetorical method he assigned, but dark and riveting, the hard core drug life in underground Roanoke.

"You still writing?"

"You could call it that."

"Anybody read it?"

15

"Not really."

"I'd like to see it," he said, stubbing out his cigarette on his saucer, and fishing a couple of dollars tip from his pocket.

He paid the waitress at the cash register, and turned to the girl. "Seriously."

She looked him in the eyes again and asked, "How 'bout now?"

He held her gaze for a moment and she added, "I need a ride."

"Sure," he answered, and grabbed his coat off a chair. "If you don't mind getting molested."

She walked out into the parking lot in front of him without comment, and seemed to know his Jeep with the fading "Free Tibet" sticker on the bumper. The dogs had their heads out the passenger side window, the Jack Russell climbing all over the Lab to get a better view. He opened the door and tried to push them into the back, but she climbed right in with them on the front seat and was immediately involved in a free for all.

"I warned you," he said, getting in on his side and turning the key.

Then she stopped moving and said, "All right, now, get in the back," and snapped her fingers loud and pointed. They immediately jumped into the back seat and sat looking at the two of them. Elias looked back at the dogs and then at her.

"She who must be obeyed," he said.

"I have some mutts myself at home."

"Which is where?" he asked, turning the key.

"Outside of Christiansburg. Just off 81. Is that far out of your way? If it is, say so. I can get another ride."

"No, that's almost on my way. No problem."

She lit up another smoke and opened the window. "I've had a bad day," she offered. "My roommate disappeared and doesn't answer her cell. I filed a report at

16

the police station and then my car wouldn't start, so I had to leave it and hitched to Roanoke to talk to some friends and wound up at Waffle House." She said it all matter of factly, but Elias sensed she was more upset than she let on.

"Your roommate disappeared? What happened?"

"I really have no idea," she answered. "I've been out of town the last few weeks and when I got home she had gone without letting me know where or why. It's not that unusual—she's a member of an environmental group called Mountain Justice. She'll take off sometimes suddenly to do some research or investigate something, but she generally lets me know. This time she didn't."

"Did the police say anything?"

"Waste of time talking to them. They'll give it 48 hours, they said, to see if she shows up. Now of course if she had been twelve or the daughter of some rich guy or a Tech student they would put out an alert and everyone would mobilize to find her. But she's a nobody to them, or worse than a nobody. She's got a record. Multiple arrests, mostly for protesting, but some for drugs. They don't give a fuck what happens to her." She finished her cigarette and rolled the window back up.

They were heading down 81 and Elias felt like he was out in a nor-easter, pushed far down the beach by the chronic depression, but swimming instinctively against the current toward this girl in trouble. He really wanted to get rid of her and go home and go back to sleep, but he also intuitively knew that was the wrong thing to do, probably because when he woke up tomorrow he would feel even more depressed for abandoning her. She steered him to the exit at Route 8 through Christiansburg, and down a few back roads he had never driven. Then she said, "It's the next right," and he swung the Jeep into a deeply rutted, rocky drive that ascended about a hundred feet to a small trailer. Dogs started barking inside and his dogs answered them.

17

She turned to face him and said, "I suppose I should offer you a cup of coffee, but you probably want to get home."

She apparently could tell that he wanted to leave, but he couldn't bring himself to do it.   Her eyes were too searching, her forehead was too broad, her hair was too dark. The engine was ticking and so was the starry universe through the windshield.   The barking dogs were like some kind of Greek chorus to all this. He had the feeling suddenly that he had driven the car in front of a stage, and he and the girl, whose name he still couldn't remember, were already caught in a drama which they couldn't escape, some ancient tragedy.   He got out of the car without answering her, stretched, and looked up.   The heavens were cold and brilliant.

"I wonder who won the election," was all he could think to say.

"Fuck, what difference does it make? Out with the old boss, in with the new boss."

He had to laugh at the 60s reference from the mouth of a twenty something.   "I wouldn't mind some tea if you've got any."

"I've got tea growing ever where," she said.   He wasn't sure he heard her right, but it didn't matter.   She unlocked the thin metal door saying, "I usually leave it unlocked." The dogs were wary of him, until she spoke to them and he got down on the carpet. They were good trailer guard mutts, like she said, but then why did she need to lock the door?   It was roomy inside, sparsely furnished, the windows were still open, and there were plants all over the counters in the kitchen. The TV was left on, just like at his house. The air smelled like paint fumes. She put a kettle on and went around closing the windows. He went over to the small dining table and started looking through the books and papers piled on it.   Articles about mountaintop removal, watershed pollution, American Electric Power, Mason Dixon

Energy, coal mining, mixed in with some books, *The Rainbow, Twilight of the Idols*, and a lot of catalogues.

"Here's your tea." She put a large hand-made mug in front of him with a quart bottle of local honey. "I haven't had time to get any milk." She turned on some music, sounded like Teddy Pendergrass; then she sat down opposite him, pulled off her boots, put on some ballet slippers, pulled her feet up under her and started rolling a joint from a baggie that was apparently left on the table. When she finished she lit it up, toked, and passed it to him. What the hell; he had no classes Wednesday. He took a long drag, and then they just sat there for a moment collecting their thoughts.

"So what do you think happened?" he asked, exhaling. The smoke hung in the air of the trailer for a moment, sweet and comfortable. He relaxed for the first time since he saw her. And he suddenly remembered her name. Of course, Anna.

"I think she's been murdered," she said, and tears started crawling down one cheek. She didn't wipe them away and she didn't really start crying. She just sat there with a streak down one side of her face and calmly drank her tea, as if some truth inside of her was pushing its way out through her eyes but she was still in control of everything else.

"Jesus, Anna," he said. "What makes you say that?"

"I know how these bastards work, and I know Sylvie. She would of called me if she was alive."

"Maybe her cell phone is dead. Or maybe she's been arrested and can't call."

"Maybe somebody split her head open with a axe and she can't call."

"Fuck, you can't think that way. That's too pessimistic. You need to be realistic."

"I am realistic. You don't know." She kept drinking her tea and smoking the joint, passing it to him while he tried to figure out what to say next. Her eyes were closing and she looked like she was going to pass out.

"What about your car?" he said, after a moment. "What's wrong with it?"

"Battery's dead. I jumped it but it still wouldn't start."

"Listen," he said. "I've got an extra battery in my Jeep. I'll take you to your car in the morning." He looked at his watch. "But it's almost 2 a.m. and you look like you need to get some sleep." He started to get up, but she just sat there in a kind of daze. He went around to her chair and asked her, "Are you okay?"

"You have an extra battery in your Jeep?"

"Yeah."

"I haven't slept in a couple of days," she said.

Once again, he wasn't sure what to do, caught in the middle of the night with a girl whom he had only known as a student five or six years ago. Still, he wasn't far from his own house, maybe a thirty minute drive, not long for these parts. She seemed to need him in the house; that was her strange request to him, unasked. He understood she was in trouble, probably it was a way of life for her, and he wasn't sure what kind it was, real or imagined. But he was raised to be a gentleman most of the time, and so he asked her if he could crash on the couch and meanwhile she should get to bed. She didn't respond; seemed almost to fall asleep at once. He caught her under her arm and pulled her up; she was almost weightless, and hung onto him so that he could feel her hair on his face and her body against his. Then he reached down and picked her up in his arms and took her back to the single bedroom while her dogs watched them carefully. She curled right up on the quilt and immediately was asleep.

He went out to check on his dogs in the car; they were curled up too in a pile of blankets he kept in the back. Then he went back in and took off his shoes and stretched

20

out on the couch. There was a cardboard box on the cushions he had to put on the floor. It was filled with surreal pencil drawings of what looked to be dead people, some of them part human and part machine, some of them with parts of their bodies blown away, or the skin peeled away. They looked like they had been killed in battle, but it was a science fiction kind of Armageddon that was pictured: men and women and spaceships with swords and high tech weapons, something right out of Edgar Rice Burroughs. Normally at this point Elias would have started looking around the bookshelves for little metal dragons and figurines of wizards. But these drawings were so realistic, so detailed and anatomically correct, that they looked like they had been drawn from life. And by someone who knew what she was doing. Who was the artist, Anna or her roommate?

He put them back in the box and turned off the lamp, then lay there for a few minutes, mentally exhausted and absolutely thoughtless, in the blue light of the TV. Then he got up and locked the door.

Chapter 3

Wittgenstein asked, "What does it mean to know the mind of another?" On the couch Elias dreamed he was reading *The Blue Book* on the beach with Anna lying nearby in a bikini, tanned and long legged. Then she was climbing onto the couch with him, straddling him and lifting the white sand dunes of her breasts and the shells of her ears. Waves were breaking onto the two of them. He was being carried out into the water but he couldn't take his eyes off her. Then she changed into his wife who floated up from a grave that opened beneath the couch, her face eaten up with bullet holes with worms crawling out of them, and he was afraid she was going to touch him and angry that he was afraid of her. He tried to get away but couldn't; he was in the coffin with her.

That woke him. Or so it seemed. The TV was still on. He was watching a corpse rot in stop-action on the Discovery Channel when religious fanatics drove a plane into the Twin Towers. Then the President's maudlin earnest face took over the screen. He started to talk and Elias looked away. He found himself driving down Route 8 on his way to school, to the police station, to apply for a permit to carry a concealed weapon, an excuse for being out all night, for flying a plane into a building, for being born, for being pure being. An F-18 Super Hornet appeared out of the fog doing Mach 1 and blew over a willow onto the highway. He stopped, got his chainsaw out of the back and tried to cut it up, but it turned into a woman's legs which he stacked neatly between two trees like a German Baptist.

He woke up a second time. Sweating. Anna was sitting on the linoleum kitchen counter with her legs dangling, smoking, watching him. He sat up and rubbed his face.

"Good morning," she said.

"Good morning."

"You look like hell. Did you have a bad dream?" She got up, poured a cup of coffee out of an old kettle, and brought it to him.

She seemed only half ironic. "Yes and no," he said, trying to hide the crazy shit that he knew was seeping out of his depression. "The part that had you in it on the beach was pretty good," he said, taking a long sip. "The part with George Bush not so good. What was in that shit anyway?"

"W. is long gone, darlin'."

"Gone but not forgotten, I'm afraid."

"Apparently," she said, tossing him the Wednesday *Roanoke Times*. Overnight, it seemed, Republicans had taken over the world. He couldn't look at it. She was wearing a long plaid flannel shirt, underwear, and socks, as much as he could tell. She didn't seem to be any the worse for wear. He, on the other hand, had a weed headache, but it would go away.

"So what's the plan?" he asked.

Within a half hour they had walked the dogs, finished off the coffee and some Pop Tarts, and gotten out of the trailer. The sparse lawn was littered in leaves. She directed him to the police station. On the way he seemed to have some déjà vu from his dream. Clouds had moved in and it was sprinkling and colder than it should have been for early November. A pickup truck crossed into his lane then crossed back. A woman in purple robe and slippers lifted the door to an American flag mailbox. Deer carcass on the shoulder. Three dumpsters sat starkly below a timbered ridge. Really early Christmas decorations. Maybe they were year-round.

They pulled into the lot and she pointed out a twenty-five year old Buick Regal that looked like it could have been used as an armored vehicle in Iraq. While he held a small broken umbrella, she propped up the hundred pound

23

hood with a stick and began pulling out the battery with a small pair of pliers she took from the glove box. When she yanked the wires off the terminals the muscles in her forearms tensed like a mechanic's. Then she took the wing nut off the air filter, opened up the top of the carburetor, and pulled a spray can of engine starter out of a pocket and doused the carburetor with it. "Just for good luck," she said, and winked. Then he lugged the extra battery from the back of the Jeep and they hooked it up. It started. She looked happy for a moment. Then she went inside to check on the status of her roommate while he sat in the car with his foot on the gas. Time passed. He couldn't see the dogs in the Jeep anymore the windows were so fogged. Too much time. He cut the ignition. Tried it again. No problem. Then he went inside the station.

She was sitting in an orange plastic chair in the lobby looking straight ahead at a small framed photo of the Republican Attorney General of Virginia on the wall.

"What happened?" he asked, but he knew the answer.

"They found a body over in Bluefield. A young woman. Looks like Sylvie. They want me to go identify her."

"Bluefield?"

She looked up at him. "West Virginia. Hour and a quarter maybe."

"I'll drive you. Come on. Have you got directions?"

She looked at him like he was a moron and he didn't ask again.

They took 81 South down the New River Valley, then 77 North into the mountains, through the Jefferson National Forest and across the Appalachian Trail. Bluefield sat right on the border with West Virginia, a small city of maybe 10,000 he guessed. They found the hospital where they had taken the body and met two police officers who told her she wouldn't want to see it. Just enough to give them some identifying marks. In their blue and grey uniforms they looked to Elias like they were involved in a Civil War re-enactment. She refused and so they took them into a morgue, and unceremoniously uncovered the body lying on a stainless steel table.

Sylvie had red hair with a white stripe running from front to back. There were two or three piercings in each ear, two or three more along one eyebrow, a couple more in her nose, and another through her lip. One eye was swollen shut and heavily bruised, both cheeks were bruised, and there was blood in her hair and crusted under her mouth. Her throat had been cut. That was all they would show. Anna never flinched. In fact, she reached out to pull the sheet farther down but the deputies refused, saying she wasn't a close relative and only needed to "identify the body." They pulled the sheet back up and in a side room she gave a report of Sylvie's relatives, recent jobs, and so forth. They asked about her arrest record, wanted to know if Anna knew anything about the needle marks on her arms. They wouldn't answer many of her questions: where was her cell phone, had she been sexually assaulted, where did they find her? They kept saying the investigation was ongoing, and they could share information only with the next of kin. She kept pressing them, but they stonewalled. Then she got in their face, telling them that she knew what they were thinking: Sylvie was just another meth whore and they could care less what happened to her. But she wasn't. She had been murdered because she knew what the coal companies were up to. "I know all about how powerful they are and how they control the government and the law. Big Coal is the man. Big Coal runs this town," she yelled at them. Elias watched the whole spectacle objectively, sizing everyone up. The cops had been very professional before, albeit unsympathetic to the grief-stricken girlfriend, but at that point they turned to Elias and surprised him by saying "You better keep a tight leash on your woman," and got up to leave.

Anna was still angry as hell; she followed them through the maze of corridors shouting at them and he had to hold her back from pursuing them out the automatic doors that opened onto the parking lot from the ER. They stood there a moment until they realized all the local sick people sitting in the waiting room were staring at them. Thin women with shy, startled children. Elderly mountain people in flannel shirts with the collars buttoned. This seemed to settle Anna down and they walked out into the cold evening air. It was almost dark and had started flurrying again; the snow fell through the street lamps and melted in the hot tears on Anna's face. Elias could not tell if they were from sorrow or rage. As they pulled out of the lot, he caught a glimpse of the two deputies watching them from their squad car parked in a corner.

Chapter 4

He didn't see her again for the next week but he called twice and left messages. Frankly that night and the next day seemed like a movie he had watched before falling to sleep, a foreign film on IFC but set in Appalachia. Familiar landscapes in a different language. While he was teaching his classes he kept thinking about her and seeing her sitting in a desk staring at him with that relentless demand. Now that he was back in his normal world, the world of work and depression, he almost resented her for leading him into her underworld. But he knew better than to think that for long.

On Friday, the *Roanoke Times* carried a tiny story in the back pages. "Local Woman Found Dead in West Virginia." The police suspected foul play and believed it was drug related, but offered no details. The name was being withheld pending notification of family. That sort of thing. Then the next Wednesday there was a brief obituary. Sylvie had been a Tech student two years ago, dropped out to work with Mountain Justice. Most of her relatives seemed to be from Kentucky. Still no word from Anna. On Friday he left his shared adjunct office in Blacksburg and stopped at her place on his way home. It took only one missed turn to find it. The blue Regal was outside with a cat on the roof who ran under the trailer when he pulled up. He knocked but there was no answer and no dogs barking. He was about to leave when he decided he needed to look around. Maybe to ease his conscience. He walked around back and saw her sitting in a chair at the top of the hill behind the trailer, so he started climbing the grassy slope toward the woods while her dogs raised cane until she shut them up. When he got close he could see that she was writing or drawing in a notebook which she quickly closed and put away. She looked tired around the eyes. He sat in the other plastic lawn chair and she passed him her half full can of Yuengling.

The lone sugar maple in the field in front of them was divided vertically, exactly half green and half yellow; tomorrow it would go completely gold. Before he had a chance to say something she said, "I didn't call back because I didn't want to bother you. You've already gotten more involved I'm sure than you had any idea of when you gave me a ride. I appreciate that. But you've got a life and this business is my problem."

She didn't look at him but kept gazing into the distance. It was a nice view from this spot, looking east across the New River Valley toward the Blue Ridge. It was almost twilight, and the rosy blinking light of a plane traversed the sky above the mountains. In the pasture next door a couple of horses watched them with their heads leaning over a wood fence. He could hear the rumbling of a train in the distance.

He took a swig. "Actually, I don't have a life. You caught me on a good night when I left my house for once to go to Waffle House. Normally I just eat in front of the TV." He almost finished the beer and passed it back to her. "So what have you been up to? Any news?"

"Nope. I've just been sitting here trying to figure out what to do next. I did call Sylvie's mom. She says the police told her that Sylvie was involved in a meth ring and was probably killed in a revenge slaying. I told her not to believe it. She also said the police asked if she'd like to have the body cremated, and when she said 'Lord no' they said because the body was badly mutilated and decomposing from being outside." She turned to him. "Did she look disfigured to you? I don't think so. Anyway, she got a local funeral home to pick Sylvie up when they'd finished with the autopsy, if you can call it that. She told me she'd have a closed casket service right away. Actually, this Sunday."

"Where's the funeral?" Elias asked.

"Grundy."

"Where's that?"

"Buchanan County, three hours west of here. Hillbilly country." She pronounced it Buck-cannon.

"Are you going?"

"I don't know," she answered. "I got some things to do."

"On a Sunday? Like what?" he asked.

"You don't really want to know," she said, and pulled another beer out of the small cooler beside her chair. The sun was now below the ridge tops and the air was cooling quickly. He zipped his fleece pullover up all the way and then noticed that all she had on was a light cotton shirt. She didn't seem to notice the temperature drop.

"It's getting cold," he said. "How's about you and I drive over to my place and I'll make some dinner. You can bring the dogs; they can meet mine. And I also have more beer."

"What kind?" she asked.

"You name it," he said. "And lots of it."

"Have you got any good old movies? I'm addicted to them."

"How old?" he asked, thinking black and white.

"You know, seventies and eighties. The young Susan Sarandon and Robert Downey Junior."

"I can do that."

"All right," she said, rolling out of her chair, "but I have to cut out at midnight."

"What happens then?" he asked, picking up the cooler. "You turn back into a waitress?"

"Something like that," she said, picked up a large pair of binoculars he hadn't noticed in the grass next to her chair, and they headed down to the trailer.

"Fuck, how far out from civilization do you live?" she joked, after a half hour on narrower than normal,

29

winding but paved roads. "I mean, I know this is Floyd County, home of the middle class counter culture, but aren't you a little too far from the nearest rescue squad in case you have a stroke or something?"

"I take my cue from Thoreau. He said, 'Don't ask how far you are from town, but how far town is from you.'" He turned onto a dirt road that ran down into a stream-carved valley. She looked sidewise at him, like he was going to kidnap her. "I live under Buffalo Mountain, almost into Carroll County. It's not far from Willis."

"Doesn't ring any bells. But it can't be as remote as Grundy."

He had a cabin in the woods up on the plateau that was Floyd County. It was a remodel of one his grandparents had built a hundred years ago. He started working on it not long after he moved to Southwest Virginia from the coast. He was a lowlander and a bachelor most of his life, but now in middle age when he got out of the Navy he felt some need to move to the mountains and live on his grandparents' land. He took the first job he could get in the area as an adjunct English teacher. It was his second career. The cabin had taken the better part of a year to finish: timber framed, with a new tin roof. Living room, kitchen and bath downstairs, with a bedroom and a bath upstairs, and a small stone fireplace that he had rebuilt from the original that had taken another summer. It was wall to wall bookshelves. He had no mortgage and few expenses, so his pension and the part-time work was sufficient and left him lots of time to be alone with himself. He needed it. He had a lot to forget.

Then he met Katya at Tech. He was wary at first because he was so smitten by her, her blonde hair and Polish blue eyes and the crooked nose. She was thirty-five and had already been through a lot, but she was ironic and even-tempered. Very easy to live with. They had two years and then she was gone. Now another woman was walking around in the living room.

30

The dogs got along: her females and his males. He made some stirfry and they ate in front of the fire and drank more beer. He pulled out his stash and she rolled a blunt, one handed he noticed, and they smoked and talked and watched *Thelma and Louise* for a couple of hours. Where he had lived, different jobs, how he wound up with a Ph.D. He skipped a lot of stuff. He told her about his dissertation, and she told him about learning the tattoo business. He asked her what growing up in Grundy was like, how she knew Sylvie, and what she had been doing since he knew her in community college, but she mostly evaded those questions, so he shelved them. For now. Then about midnight she stood up and stretched.

"What's with the sword?" she asked. It was resting on a stand on the mantel.

"Just something I used to do," he responded.

"Good to know how to gut someone," she said, "should the need arise. Now, I got to go."

They had killed a six pack, plus whatever she had drunk before. She didn't appear to be the least bit high, but he was and he knew he wouldn't be able to sleep.

"Look," he said, "why don't you just sleep here on the couch and I'll take you home in the morning? The dogs have crashed; you should too. You look dead."

"Thanks for the compliment," she said, getting to her feet and pulling on her thick, ripped ski parka, "but I've got some work to do."

He checked his watch but he knew what time it was. "Work?" he asked. "You know there's nothing open in the whole New River Valley except Waffle House and the munitions factory in Radford. But if you'd like some company, I'm not doing anything myself. Unless you're one of those two in the morning Wally World zombies who walk in out of the hills when the rest of the world is asleep to do some shopping?"

She laughed, a stoned laugh, came up close enough to touch him and looked him directly in the eyes. Hers were daring and unblinking. "All right, if you want to get in my life so bad. But don't say I didn't warn you. Dress warm. It's cold where we're going."

"What about the dogs?"

"Leave 'em," she said. "They'll get in the way."

He banked the fire and they left. A half moon had risen and the bare wooded hills were bathed in its light. Now that the leaves were gone you could see homes way back in the trees that all year you didn't know were there. They had been falling so fast you could hear them hitting branches as they descended. Wood smoke mixed with fog hung in the air in every little hollow.

He drove slowly but even so they had to swerve several times for deer and possum caught in the headlights. They stopped at her place where she retrieved a canvas bag, then they headed into Roanoke. She had changed out of her boots into some faded red Converses. He suddenly thought to himself, shit, she's probably got a gun in there, and asked her where they were headed.

"Rail yard," she said.

"Rail yard? What are you going to do," he asked, "hold up a train?" He was still high and wondering how serious he needed to get.

"No," she answered, "I'm going to bomb it," and she pulled a can of spray paint out of the canvas and started shaking it. It took him a moment to get the connection with all the clicking.

"Holy shit," he said, "you're a fucking graf writer. That's wild." He was staring at her, not minding the road. But he didn't get it, why now on this cold-ass night? Her friend had just been murdered. She was feeling bad. Maybe she just wanted to take a break ... "

"Turn here," she pointed, ten minutes later. They had left 581 and without his being aware were moving into northwest Roanoke, the Black neighborhoods, row after row of narrow two story frame homes, many in bad shape, paint peeling, narrow streets filled with low-rider cars with tinted windows and tiny tires. Northwest was separated from downtown by a hundred- yard-wide maze of warehouses and thousands of coal cars, where the Norfolk Southern tracks carved a scar straight through the city. Across from downtown she showed him a small underpass covered with graffiti and they eased into a road running parallel to the tracks.

It looked dangerous out here in the middle of the night. Elias started to feel the old adrenaline surge, and his mind automatically cleared of everything but the task at hand. This was not something he wanted to get into again. She had been right; he was too depressed and didn't really want to know what was going on with her. But it was too late. So he decided to go with the flow.

She turned to face him on the front seat. "Okay. This is a piece of cake. Just remember two things. Don't make any noise—at all. And do whatever I tell you to do without stopping to ask questions. If I say 'Book it' you fucking book it back to the car. Got it?"

He was slightly amused and intoxicated with taking orders from this girl. "You the man," he said. "What do I do?"

"You're my backup. Keep your eyes open around the yard and let me know if you see anyone."

They got out of the Jeep, closed and locked the doors as quietly as possible. Then they hiked down the gravel road a half mile keeping in the shadows of an earthen berm. She obviously knew exactly where she was going, but she kept looking at the railroad cars in the near distance as they walked. Most of them had been bombed, covered with words, tags, cartoon faces, superheroes, messages of all kinds in cursive and print so flamboyant that it took a while to see what they were. It was a kind of hieroglyphics, a foreign

33

picture language, travelling across the state, from the mountains to the coast and back, on the coal trains. Finally she stopped.

"There," she whispered, and pointed.

He looked. "What?" he asked. She was staring, intent and silent. "What?"

"Sylvie," she said.

It was as if she had said "Satan," or "ghost"; a shiver ran up his neck. But he understood. "She left a message," she said. "Come on."

She snaked across the three or four empty tracks gleaming in the moonlight and he followed. The coal-loaded hopper car was much larger up close than he thought it would be, maybe twenty feet tall, and the writing was so far off the ground he couldn't figure out how someone could spray that high. On the side, in green and white outlined in black, there was a convincing rendering of Dr. Seuss's Grinch with a gun and fixed bayonet, lunging forward. He was stepping over the body of a young woman who had a letter in her hand. She had red hair and a frightened look on her face. Surrounding them was a swirl of letters and numbers written so fluidly that they were almost impossible to decipher close up. Anna ran her callused hands over the rusted metal and paint for a minute, as if she could absorb something through her touch. Then she took a can of spray paint from her bag and quickly made an R.I.P. below the girl, then signed something that could have been her name. When she finished she turned to Elias and said, "Let's go." But he had spotted someone moving, a brakeman, a guard, someone walking home drunk. They bent down and got under the train car, out of the fluorescent lights. It smelled like oil and diesel. Whoever it was, they could just hear his footsteps on the gravel. Anna motioned to Elias to grab the struts under the car and pull himself up from the ground. A cone of light flashed under the car, and they could the man's trousers and heavy boots as he walked slowly past. He didn't stop. Elias could feel Anna's breath on his neck. His out-of-shape arms were started to shake from holding himself off the ground so long. He thought he heard breaking glass, then a long silence. Finally a car engine started up, a diesel. The headlights swept the yard as it made a slow, wide turn, then it was over.

A few minutes later they were back at the Jeep. The driver's side window had been smashed. Elias rooted around inside but he knew there was nothing of value except a couple of tools. "They're still here," he said, holding up a crowbar, but she was already climbing in. "Get the hell out of here," she said. He brushed the glass aside, got in and pulled out of the yard, and quickly got back on 581 before he asked, "Who was that?"

"I don't know," she said, "but I can tell you one thing for sure. That guy in the yard was no cop."

"So what? If it wasn't a cop, maybe it was somebody walking home. I mean, he broke into my car."

"Not likely. That was a white guy. Where was he walking to, chocolate city? I spend a lot of time in that yard, and I never seen anyone dressed like that. He was wearing green company pants and hunting boots. And I don't mean he was out firelighting deer neither. He was hunting us; he wanted to know who you were. Now they know about both of us. You need to start being careful."

Elias didn't believe her, but he was pissed off that someone had broken into his Jeep. It wasn't like they were parked illegally. There were no signs. The window was missing and the November night air was freezing now that he was doing 60 on the interstate. "What did it mean," he asked her, "the Grinch and all the writing? What was she trying to tell you? I didn't get it."

"It's code," she said. "The Grinch represents the coal company we've been investigating. It's an in-joke, from the Crich family in Lawrence. Sylvie's sense of humor. She's saying she left us something at the post office in War.

35

It's a town in West Virginia. Something important. We've got to go get it."

"What do you mean 'we were investigating'? I thought this was her thing, not yours."

"We're in it together, but she does most of the legwork. It's a family cause."

"But why didn't she just call you? Why go to all this trouble to write on the train when you can just talk to each other directly?"

"Well, for starters," she answered, lighting a cigarette and passing it to him, "we're graf artists; that's what we do. We're Old School. Graf writing isn't real unless there's some danger involved. Second, cells are too risky. You never know who might be listening in. We had a few occasions where somebody knew something they shouldn't have. Online it's even worse; there's no privacy on the net. Everything about you gets saved and sold to the highest bidder. It's not freedom, like so many idiots believe; it's capitalism run amok. Besides," she added, "most times you can't get the phones to work in the mountains. Some of those places she was staying are not even on the map. The people are too poor to get cell towers."

It was true. He couldn't even use his cell at home, unless it was a clear night. He had a land line for backup. He thought about the graffiti. "Okay, I understand the reference to War, and the letter. But what about the woman? What was she doing there?"

Just as she answered he recognized the face. "It's Sylvie. She drew herself."

It was almost three in the morning and he was starting to come down from the adrenaline rush. The alcohol was making him very sleepy, and the interstate was taking on some surreal qualities.

"Do you want to go on to War now? How far is it? We can stop and put the dogs in the kennel at my house."

36

"A couple hours, but the P.O. isn't open until nine on Saturdays. It can wait."

Chapter 5

That night, exhausted as he was, lying on his bed upstairs he couldn't stop the thoughts and images scrolling through his mind. In less than a week his orderly everyday life had been taken over by a young woman he barely knew. It happened so fast it didn't seem real, or at least it didn't seem consequential. For her, certainly, she had lost a friend, from drug violence apparently, or from some combination of illegal activities, but he couldn't avoid the fact that Anna was not normal, that she was wound too tight, angry as hell, and because of that or because of some meth-related effects she was not being logical and realistic. There was a paranoid flavor to her talk, a defensiveness in her conversation. Of course he was no stranger to the drug culture himself, a product of the 60s, but she was mixed up in the meth and heroin epidemic that seemed to have been raging in rural Appalachia for decades, often under the radar. Still, at the same time she was very self-possessed and systematic in her analysis of things; she could be very convincing. Her talk had the ring of authenticity based on experience, and he wanted to believe her because he wanted her to trust him. But he knew at some point he would have to call her on it if she went too far. Maybe that's why she brought him in. To stop her. He really didn't know.

And now she was downstairs supposedly sleeping on the couch, but he could hear her walking around, thumbing through books and magazines, listening to music. They had become close, or become a refuge at least temporarily, for each other. He liked protecting her from the death that now clung to her trailer, and from the threats, real or imagined, that she endured. But he did not know where this thing was going, how fast or how precipitously. What he did know deep down was that her presence made him forget his loneliness. She was full of nervous energy; even when she smoked a cigarette and offered a laconic answer to a question, she seemed in the grip of some obsession. He figured she saw him as a kind of father figure, and he did not want to disappoint her. But he also wondered what would happen if she came into his room in the middle of the night and wanted to get under the covers and be held. He was strangely committed to her as if from the moment they met. If this is what it took—driving around Southwest Virginia for a few weeks and getting tangled up with some questionable people, to exorcise some demons—then maybe that was his dharma. Maybe it always had been.

Elias got up at seven with the sun, and he couldn't tell if she had just woken up too or had never gone to sleep. But an hour later they were on 460 West heading back to Bluefield, drinking coffee and listening to the news on the radio. He had jury rigged a square of cardboard box over the broken window with duct tape, and he wasn't sure if it was illegal since he couldn't see out of it, but frankly he was beyond caring for the moment. One of the good things about not getting enough sleep. They were listening to NPR out of Roanoke. There was a story about China's state-run coal company, the world's largest, in talks with Mason Dixon Energy based in Richmond, the company that controlled most of the coal mined locally. Apparently the Chinese wanted to invest here, buy mines, to feed their enormous demand. They had already bought up 3.4 billion dollars' worth of U.S. companies, and that was only the beginning.

Anna turned the volume down. She had her boots up on the dash and a coffee cup in her hand with the word "Veritas" on it. The cardboard next to his head was making a ripping sound in the wind.

"What's it been?" she asked, in her manic I-don't-expect-or-need-an-answer manner. "Not even a week since the election, and look what's already happening. The Republicans cleaned house in this region; they didn't want any cap-and-trade deal to stop the good old boys from

39

making more money off of all those black seams running through the mountains. They'll gut the EPA and find a way to stop the carbon capture programs to save corporations money. Then they'll sell out to the Chinese. It's the last gasp of the coal industry. Just like my dad. They've put the people of West Virginia on a black lung ventilator and now they're cutting their losses and bailing. Fuck those people who say we can't blow up the tops of these mountains. Fuck those people who have to drink the black water. Fuck the people who say we can't damn the New River. Fuck anybody who gets in our way, as long as we keep raking in the money. I've heard it all a million times in my life." Then she looked over at Elias. "Do you know what money like that does to people?" she asked. He didn't have long to wait. "It fucks them up. I mean, it corrupts them absolutely. Good mountain people, otherwise decent, God-fearing, hard-working people will turn into the worst kind of abusers—polluters, drug dealers, murderers, you name it. Almost overnight, you lose your soul. I've seen it happen, to the best of families. Nothing corrupts like easy money." She looked back out the windshield but wasn't finished. "It's a disease. It's infected everyone, from the politicians to the police and on down to the local miner who's willing to bash somebody's head in with a baseball bat because he thinks she's trying to take away his job. It's all fucked up."

"And now Sylvie's dead."

She lit up a cigarette and he could see her hands were trembling. She exhaled, and behind the veil of smoke around her face he caught a glimpse of the torment she was going through. He had no idea what to say. What was it she said about her father? Elias knew there was no way they could do anything about the kind of conspiracy she was sketching. If it even was a conspiracy.

"God is dead in this country," she started again. "I have to agree with the Baptists on that one. She used to live in the mountains. But they're tearing them down. They're an endangered species. Instead they've made an altar to coal, just like the one down to the Catholic church in Norton.

"An altar to coal?"

"They made an altar *out of* a big block of coal. Anthracite. It's a tourist attraction. Appalachia's second biggest industry."

He waited a minute, watching the scenery roll by. It was the kind of morning when clouds looked like mountains and mountains looked like clouds. Then he said, "Materialism has killed the native gods that lived in the landscape. Even the beauty Jefferson wrote about—we don't appreciate it anymore. He was a deist; he could understand the rational laws of the universe. But these assholes are Calvinists stuck in some anal retentive stage. For them wilderness is a bad thing, unless you can make a profit off it. The devil lives there. Somewhere in West Virginia or Kentucky." He stopped looking out the window and turned to her. "But let's figure out what happened to Sylvie, and then maybe the other pieces of the puzzle will fall into place."

She glanced at him again like he just didn't get it, but she kept silent. They were in the thick of the mountains soon enough, got off the four lane divided highway and onto the two lane road through Bishop, Squire, and Cucumber that kept him concentrating on the morning traffic. When they got to the little town of War about 10:30 Anna knew right where the post office was, in a two story brick building in a row of businesses along the main street. They parallel parked in front, got out, and stretched their legs. The town was surrounded by ridges which blocked the morning sun, and the sky was milky with a thin layer of clouds. Inside the post office was dark, one of the fluorescent lights was out, and Elias looked at the photos on the walls while Anna went to the window and rang a bell.

A middle aged, platinum blonde woman emerged from the rear of the building, more made up than Elias

41

would have thought possible from a public official. She looked at Anna and then over at him with a blank expression. Wary of strangers, Elias thought.

Anna said, "Good morning Mrs. Hurley."

The woman did a double take.

"Well as I live and breathe," she said slowly, "if it ain't Diana Jassey come back from the dead." She stopped, seemed momentarily to have surprised herself with that statement. Then she slowly came around from behind the counter. "Lord child, let me have a look at you." Mrs. Hurley surveyed Anna from top to bottom, touching her hair and her clothes like she really was making sure she was real. "What have you done to your hair? Last time I saw you you was a blonde. Now you've gone back to your momma's coloring. Still wearing those cowboy boots though."

"Mrs. Hurley used to cut hair," Anna said to him by way of explanation.

"Still do on the side. Post office is only part-time now. Town's going under. Pretty soon I'll be watching TV all day like everybody else."

"This town's been going under for fifty years," Anna said to her, and lit a cigarette.

"You got that right," Mrs. Hurley said, removed the cigarette from Anna's mouth, took a long drag off it herself, and went over to the door and flicked it into the street.

Anna stared at her. There was a moment of silence.

"I'm expecting a letter."

"I figured you was," Mrs. Hurley said. "I got it right in the back," and she disappeared for a moment. When she returned she said, "I heard about Sylvie. I am so sorry. I know that girl had a rough life, but she should'a never come to such a pass. It tore me up to hear about that drug violence," and she handed Anna a large manila envelope. "She was a right smart girl, both of you cousins was smart, going to college and all. But she got into a bad crowd."

42

She seemed about to continue but Anna said, "Thanks Mrs. Hurley. Well, we got to be going. It's been nice seeing you."

"Ya'll headed over to Grundy?" she asked, looking at the two of them. "Isn't the funeral tomorrow?"

"Yes mam," Anna said. "I believe it is."

"Well, give my condolences to Ruthey and Joseph, and the whole family. Is she going to be buried in the family cemetery?"

"I don't see any reason why not," Anna said, and Elias detected some anger under the politeness.

"I just mean I heard she was kind of messed up, her body. That maybe Ruthey was going to cremate her. And also on account of the bad blood between your dad and ..."

She was interrupted by an elderly man in overalls pushing his wife in a wheelchair through the heavy glass door. Anna quickly said goodbye, Elias too, and they walked out to the car. As he adjusted to the bright light, he had a strange sensation. Something about the conversation with Mrs. Hurley seemed to have shifted the ground beneath them, as if the town had changed while they were in the post office. Under the mountains War's main street had taken on the character of a Western movie set. Elias had an uncanny feeling, as if he had stepped back in time and half expected men in dusters with pistols in their pockets to stop them and demand to know their business. But there was no one on the street, except a couple of young men passing by in a green pickup with a deer carcass sticking out the back. It occurred to Elias that this might be the first day of hunting season.

He lit a cigarette and turned to her. "Sylvie is your cousin? You never told me that."

"Second cousin. I told you we grew up together," she said. Then she cursed under her breath. "Come on, dude, drive. Let's get the hell out of here before I have to hear anyone else talk down about her. Rumors are as thick around here as a swarm of gnats. These people got nothing else to entertain themselves with."

"She seemed genuinely friendly and glad to see you. A little nosey maybe. But why did she act like you had died and been reborn?"

"Probably she was thinking of Sylvie. We look a lot alike, 'cept for the eyes." She was right, Elias thought; it was just that Sylvie' face was so beaten up that it was hard to recognize the resemblance. "Besides the fact," Anna added, "that we both had a reputation for being wild."

"So where are we headed now?" Elias asked, about to get in the Jeep.

She gave him a bit of a twisted smile. "How'd you like to see Grundy? It's only another forty miles. Not even an hour's drive. Although the way you drive it might take longer."

"Maybe you ought to drive," he said. "I'll enjoy the scenery."

"What scenery?" she asked and began to move around to the other side of the car. "It's nothing but one coal mine after another."

They exchanged places and took off. Anna turned west off Route 16 onto 83. She was right. They zigzagged down hollow after hollow, and coal mines every few miles like pueblos high on the cliffsides, and processing plants with miles of conveyor belts overhead like giant snakes on legs, and black holding ponds for the slurry. In ten miles they had left McDowell County, West Virginia and had entered Buchanan.

"What about the mountaintop removal?" he asked. "I haven't seen any."

"Normally you won't. They don't like you to see them. They're up high. You got to know where to look. Just imagine the biggest hole in the ground you can, big enough for several Super Wal-Marts with acres of parking lot. Then think of it as a complete wasteland. No animal

44

life.   No plant life.   No topsoil.   Nothing.   That's mountaintop removal."

"Wal-Mart is already a wasteland," he said.

"You got that right."

The envelope was lying on the dashboard. "What about the package? Aren't you going to open it?"

"You open it," she said, and pulled a small open-bladed knife from a sheath he had never noticed in her boot. "And while you're at it, pull these things off me. We're in West by God Virginia now and I can drive better barefoot."

He yanked off her boots then slit the envelope across one end. A small object wadded up in newspaper and wrapped in tape fell into his hand. They looked at each other: there was nothing else. He pulled off the paper and there it was—the cell phone. Small and gold like some leaf fallen from the golden bough of a totally mechanical civilization.

"Maybe this will answer some questions," he said.

"More than likely," she replied, "but I don't want to look at it now. I've got other fish to fry here in a minute. Just put it in my backpack, will ya, until we get back to Blacksburg?"

Thirty-five minutes later they arrived in Grundy. Elias was a bit taken aback. He had half expected a picturesque old mining town nestled in a valley, like Telluride. It turned out Grundy was in a valley all right, but the river that had carved that valley had apparently also flooded the town so repeatedly that they finally had to move it. It seemed to be sitting under three separate cliffs, as if it had multiple personality disorder, and it was watching its former selves across the conjunction of two rivers. They had blasted away the mountains to make more room, sheared them right off, so that you could look up and see all the strata, millions of years of geological time. Elias felt like he was down at the bottom of a strip mine, buried in another era.

For all its isolation, there was a brand new Wal-Mart, not yet open. But it looked different from any big box Wal-Mart Elias had ever seen. At first he couldn't figure it out. Then he realized what it was. It was three stories. Two stories of parking garage with the store on top. There was so little flat land they had to build everything straight up.

This was one of the selling points for mountaintop removal. It struck Elias that they wanted to just level West Virginia to solve its economic problems.

Anna drove to the funeral home, two brick buildings right on 460. It was a little after eleven, and there were only a couple of cars in the small lot. She switched off the ignition and turned to Elias. "There's no way in hell that I am going to attend that funeral tomorrow, or see my family. It'll just get in the way of what I've gotta do to find out who killed Sylvie. You don't know my kinfolk; they're a mess. I'll spare you the details. But I do need to see Sylvie. If you don't mind going in with me, I'd appreciate it. Not that you haven't already done too much for me." She pulled her cigarettes out of her pants pocket, flipped one half out, thought better of it, and put the pack on the dash.

Elias said, "You already saw her in Bluefield."

"Just her face. I need to know what they did to her," and she opened the door and got out.

Inside the funeral home was another world, just a threshold away from the raw mining town. There were expensive rugs and old lamps everywhere. No one seemed to be around at the moment, but there was a message board on the wall: Sylvia Presley. Parlour 1. Visitation hours 2-5 PM. Anna took him by the hand and they walked down the silent corridor to number 1. It was a large room, and filled with flowers. The dark wooden coffin rested on the far side, closed. Anna said, "Watch the door," walked over to the casket and raised the upper lid. She appeared to be examining Sylvie's arms. After a moment she closed it and

46

pulled the lower lid up. It wouldn't stay by itself. She looked over at Elias and he came and held it.

Sylvie had on a green silk gown; it looked like something you'd wear to a ball. "It was her senior prom gown," Anna said, as if she could read his thoughts. "Her mother must have kept it." Then she pulled it up to Sylvie's waist and they looked at her legs. They were white and stiff; she was wearing stockings. It was very strange seeing her just from the waist down. There was something dark on her upper thigh, and Anna rubbed at the makeup that had been placed there. A deep bruise started to appear. She kept rubbing and more arose from the pale skin. Then Anna took a hold of her panties and pulled them down. They both looked, Elias against his will. He instinctively reverted to the old military objectivity, but Anna gasped and recoiled and grabbed his arm hard. Even with the reconstruction that the undertaker had done, Sylvie's vagina was a torn up mess. There were stitches all around it, like short railroad tracks leading nowhere, and inside her panties they had stuck gauze in case any liquid seeped through. There were also what looked to be burn marks on her abdomen. And then there were the red cuts that spelled out the obscene message: "psycho bitch." It was not a pretty sight, like some redneck version of "In the Penal Colony." Elias wanted to cry for her but knew he couldn't.

He heard Anna say softly under her breath, "Somebody's gonna pay for this." Then she pulled the panties back up, dress down, closed the bottom lid, and opened the top part again. "Look," she said, holding up an arm, downy with light brown hair. "See these tracks." Elias bent over and looked closely. "The marks on her arms; they're needle marks all right, ceptin' she didn't make them. These were added after she was dead. See. Somebody just jabbed her a few times to make it look like she was a junkie." She gently laid the arm back on its satin pillow, then leaned over and gave her a kiss on the lips. Elias did the same on her cheek. Then they closed the lid and left.

On the way out they ran into a tall young man in a dark suit who recognized Anna. Before he had a chance to ask her how she was doing she pulled him aside and began grilling him about the autopsy report. Had he seen it? Were the police aware she had been raped and mutilated? Did he see the needle marks on her arms when she was brought in? He seemed overwhelmed at first with her questions, then broke down and stammered that he was "freaked out" by the way she looked, then switched gears again and started getting defensive, saying he was told she had been involved in a drug gang. Anna wasn't letting him off the hook, kept badgering him, until he told her they had both seen a lot of their high school classmates become meth addicts, and a lot of them had ended up the same way. Sylvie wasn't the first and she wouldn't be the last.

"She was raped, you asshole, and butchered. And I'm sure you know who was behind it," Anna shouted at him and then walked out the doors into the sunlight. Elias continued to look at the guy.

Then the young undertaker said to him, in a confidential tone, "See if you can talk some sense into her. Even in high school she would sometimes go off her rocker and start claiming people were out to get her. Her cousin was murdered by the drug dealers she was involved with; that's what the police told us, and whatever else they did to her was probably punishment for something."

Maybe he was twenty-five, and really didn't know anything. He had a sallow, pimpled complexion and looked like he belonged in one of the caskets. Perhaps it was the only job in town. Elias said, "Drug dealers just pop you in the head; I've seen it a hundred times," and he made the sign of a gun with his hand and pointed it at the other's head. "That wasn't a drug dealer; that was someone who hated women."

48

And he walked into the parking lot where Anna was leaning against the car, smoking.

Chapter 6

They stopped and had lunch at a diner on 460, cheeseburger for her, grilled cheese for him, then Anna fell asleep. They didn't get home until twilight. Daylight Savings Time had ended and the days were suddenly shorter and filled with winter light, but right now the weather was so mild it seemed like Indian summer. They went to her place first where she got some things and he used the bathroom. She started her car and let it run for a few minutes. While he was brushing his teeth with a toothbrush he found lying next to the sink—did it belong to Sylvie?—and some Burt's Bees organic toothpaste, he found himself staring at an open shelf of plastic prescription bottles, a long row of them. The first one he noticed read Lithium Carbonate 300 mg. The next one was Seroquel 200 mg. He didn't look to see whom they were for, but he recognized the Lithium: it was for bipolar disorder, what used to be called manic depression. He made a mental note that Anna didn't care to hide anything if she left her meds out in the open, then he spat in the sink, and walked out.

She followed him in the old Buick and when they got to his place the dogs ran around the yard in circles like maniacs for five minutes when they let them out of the kennel. A half moon was rising through the poplars behind his house and the forest looked like it was on fire. Then they went inside and Elias made some pasta while Anna got the wood stove going. Twenty minutes later they were sitting on the floor eating and drinking Dos Equis, trying to keep the mutts out of the food. Anna pulled Sylvie's cell out of her back pack and flipped it open. The battery was dead so Elias hooked it up to his charger. In the menu under "Contacts" there was a long list of names and numbers that apparently had some meaning to Anna. She scrolled through the list.

Then she clicked on "Recent Calls," then "Received," and scrolled through that list. Two numbers kept getting repeated. One was local, in Blacksburg, 540 area code. The other was an 804 area code.

"Where's that?" Elias asked.

"Richmond, I think. Sylvie was dating a law student from Richmond. That might be him. She didn't tell me much about it, which was unlike her, but I just figured she didn't want me getting any wrong ideas. Anyway, look: there are outgoing calls to those numbers as well, most in the last few weeks."

Then she switched to "Photos." At first Elias couldn't make out what he was looking at: it looked like a text message. Then he realized it was a photo of some sort of text. Apparently Sylvie had been snapping pictures of some documents spread out on a table or desk. It was hard to see what they were exactly, so they loaded them onto Elias' laptop. On the screen the images came up clearly: they were the pages of a ledger or journal of some sort with handwritten entries with words written in some language that Elias didn't immediately recognize, ten or fifteen pages in all in tiny script. It looked like some eastern European dialect, but it wasn't Cyrillic. There were words like "nos" and "tup," "mikta" and "maxkana kasit." Maybe it was written in code, he thought. He Googled some of the phrases and got nothing. Anna had a strange look on her face as she bent over him and the laptop, fearful but placid at the same time, as if she were asleep and having a bad dream. "I don't know," Anna said, as if she could read his mind again. "Sylvie must have thought it was important if she took pictures of it and left it at the post office." Then she turned away.

When he opened up the "Videos" menu the first thing they saw was a young guy talking to Sylvie who apparently was holding the phone camera. They were in what looked to be someone's office or library, and he was sitting behind an ornate desk in front of a big window, laughing and talking. He was going on about his family. Boasting. They were rich. Very rich. And powerful. Then he moved away from the desk to a large leather couch, still talking, gesticulating wildly, and sat down and invited Sylvie to join him. He had a drink in his hand. Elias could hear Sylvie's voice: it sounded like Anna's, the same southwest Virginia accent and the same blue collar diction, but softer, and less sardonic in the laughter. The young man looked to be in his twenties, attractive, dressed like a preppie in a button down shirt and V neck sweater with a polo player logo. He seemed to be intoxicated; in fact, as the conversation continued he was actually slurring his words at times. He kept asking her if she didn't want another line, why didn't she want a line, or maybe she wanted him to slam her. The camera focused on the desktop where you could clearly see five or six lines of white powder, and then he picked up a piece of aluminum foil, put some of the powder on it, and came around the desk and offered it to her. He held a lighter under it until some vapors started to rise then cupped his hands around them and inhaled, then held it out to the camera, to her, in closeup.

Anna suddenly got up from the desk. She had a pained look on her face. "This is fucking nuts," she said. "That guy is a sociopath and she's getting high with him."

"Do you know him?" Elias asked.

"No, but I know the look."

Sylvie started asking him about what kind of influence his family had, she didn't believe him, she thought he was just exaggerating. She laughed at him, said he was always trying to impress her to get in her pants. Then the guy seemed to shift gears and get antagonistic. He said, "You don't even know what the fuck I'm talking about. Enough fucking power to buy anything they want, including people," and he took a drink. Sylvie said, "People ain't hard to buy off; they'll sell out their friends for a speedball, where

52

I come from. Or you want somebody messed up, that's just a couple hundred dollars."

He laughed in the camera. "Fuck, I'm not talking about hundreds of dollars to get some lowlife to suck your dick; I'm talking about hundreds of *thousands* of dollars to buy people to vote the way you want them to, or to cover your ass with the police when you need some problem to go away. That's real power. My family works behind the scenes; they make this company what it is." Then he started pressing her again to get on the couch with him. She kept making excuses and asking more questions but he wasn't taking no for an answer and the next thing Elias and Anna knew he had grabbed her by the wrists and violently pulled her down. The phone fell to the floor and all they could see was the ceiling, where a chandelier threw arabesques of shadows. They could hear them moving around on the couch for a minute, then a hand reached out and closed the cell.

Anna shut the same cell and stood up. She was agitated, and started walking around the room talking. "This guy I'm almost positive I've seen before. I'm pretty sure it was at an MTR protest. He was in the group of mine company execs who were trying to get to a meeting. That was back in May I think. In Richmond. I remember him because he didn't look like one of the politicians or one of their goons. Probably a family member. I'm guessing this is the guy that Sylvie was hooking up with and that explains a lot."

"What does it explain?" Elias asked.

"Well, first it explains why she didn't tell me anything about him. She probably knew I would object. And second it explains who killed her."

"Object because she wasn't supposed to be dating one of the enemy?"

She shot him a dagger. "Because it was too dangerous. You don't know these people, what they are

53

capable of. Who they know. They have a Board of Trustees that would make you piss in your pants." She started ticking them off on her fingers. "Past head of the NSA. Past head of MISHA. A general. Couple of CEOs and billionaires. You think I'm joking when I say we don't talk to each other on the phone? Why do you think we use the trains? These people can get into your life, they can get into your brain, change your DNA. Do you think those pigs at the morgue didn't get your license plate number? Do you think they don't know where I live, where *you* live? More than likely they know we're here right now, and they know we've got Sylvie's cell, although she might have sneaked that by them." She stopped to light up a cigarette and blew the smoke into the fireplace. "They've got satellites that can see right into your living room. Which reminds me, have you got a gun on the premises?" She looked at him like it was a perfectly normal question.

"MISHA?" he asked.

"Mine Safety and Health Administration. They're in bed with the coal companies."

Elias was thinking he needed to placate her. "You know," he said, "we really ought to take this information to the police. They can't all be corrupt. What about the Tech police?"

She laughed like he was a complete moron and took another drag. "Campus cops?"

He tried something else. "What if I talk to my colleague in the Criminal Justice Department? He used to be a commonwealth's attorney. He'll know whom to go to, or at least set us on the right track."

She was watching the oak pop and burn. The room smelled sweet like the smoke.

After a while she said, "Do what you want to do. Just keep in mind that we're talking millions, maybe billions of dollars at risk here. Sylvie was right when she said you can get a man killed for chicken scratch. If somebody

54

decides you and me are in the way, screwing up some deal or exposing some congressman on the take, then they will show up in our backyard. I've been intimidated before, but when they killed Sylvie they crossed the line. Whatever she did, she got to them." She threw her butt into the fire, stood up and announced, "Now I've gotta go to work."

Elias looked up. "Work? Damn, it's ten o'clock. I thought we were in for the night."

"You're in for the night. I'm off to Waffle House."

"But you've got to be exhausted, what with everything you've been through." He said it, and immediately felt like a father, and the role made him uneasy, the way he was beginning to feel about her.

"I slept in the car, remember?" she said. "Besides, I don't need much sleep."

He could relate to that. "Hold up," he remembered. "Let me copy that info from the phone. If anything happens to it we need a backup." She handed it to him and he loaded the data onto his laptop.

Meanwhile she gathered up her things and then left, giving him a kiss on the cheek on the way out. She was right, Elias thought. She could probably go without sleeping for the next week, wired into some inchoate anger that she seemed to have been born with, but now let loose with the murder of her cousin. He had no real fear for himself; twenty years in the military had bred it out of him. And a lifelong analytical habit made him too skeptical to believe anyone, much less the government, was looking for him. He simply wasn't that interesting. But he was afraid for Anna; she was in over her head—possibly with this mining company or more probably with some drug dealers—and he would have to watch over her without letting her know. He had dealt with many enemies of the government before, but he didn't know much about local crime. Or vendettas. To some extent he believed the locals were amateurs, but he knew they could be crude and unpredictable, so he was going to have to think differently.

"I'll call you," she yelled from the front yard. "Don't forget to lock your doors."

He did.

Chapter 7

But it was Thursday afternoon before she called, five days later. He should have spent the remains of the weekend getting caught up with some school work. It was almost Thanksgiving break and he was behind, which was unusual because he didn't have much of a life, but he kept getting distracted every time he picked up a stack of papers or a textbook. He was obsessive about watching the news, but it was infuriating trying to understand what was going on in the world according to CNN during the day. The media were such idiots. Or rather the public they pandered to were idiots. Elias had a sense that most of what he watched was just an appearance. Full of sound and fury, it eventually lulled him to sleep. Meanwhile, shit was happening everywhere all over the global village. Afghanistan, Iraq, China, India—almost overnight they all seemed like colonial outposts of a network of power brokers that was messing with his life right here in Southwest Virginia. People were getting killed here, people he knew, for the very same reasons they died anywhere. Tens of thousands of people were starving to death in Somalia, photos of mothers with bleeding feet holding their emaciated babies out toward the camera, but about all he could find on CNN was Kim Kardashian.

He was in his office at Tech grading freshman comp essays when the phone rang. "It's me," she said. "The insane woman you're sorry you gave a ride to."

Elias started to laugh, as if she had emerged from some hillbilly slasher film, but there was a serious tone in her voice which stopped him. He had not called her, though he wanted to, because she said she would call him. He didn't want her to think that he didn't think she knew what she was doing. It was complicated, and he wanted to keep it simple, if at all possible. But he had driven by her place, twice. Once her car was gone, once there were several cars parked in front.

"How're you doing?" he asked.

"I'm okay. It's been kinda crazy for me, of course. How're you?" She spoke fast.

"Grading papers," he said. "My brain has turned to mush."

"I'm sure you said the same thing when you were grading mine."

"Yours were interesting."

There was a short silence. "Why don't you come over if I'm so interesting?" she asked. "Even Zarathustra came down from the mountain eventually. Didn't he? That is, if you're not doing anything. If you can't that's perfectly cool too, so don't pretend you've got to listen to all the fucked up crap that's going on in my life ..."

"Are you cooking?" he interrupted.

"If you can call it that."

"Okay, it'll be about an hour. And I talked to that guy I know," he said.

"Oh yeah. I know. Save it for when I see you," she said, and hung up.

When he got to her trailer she was inside moving some pots and pans around on the stove. There were no barking dogs and he asked why. "I just got home. They must of ran off," she said, "while I was at work. They do that sometimes; probably chasing a deer. They've been known not to show up for two or three days. Why don't you give 'em a holler."

"Sure," he said. He took the beer she offered and went out the back door. The sun was setting and the sky over the Appalachians was rosy gold. He started up the hill toward the tree line but before he had gotten twenty steps he saw something that made the hair on the back of his neck stand up. It looked like there were two animals hanging from the sugar maple in the middle of the field. The tree had shed all its golden leaves, and they were lying in a pool of red sunlight around it, as if it had cried a halo. Elias thought for a second that his mind was playing tricks on him, then he yelled for Anna. She came to the door just as he took off for the tree. She saw him run, looked in the distance, screamed once, then ran after him. From the vantage point of a painter, or a mythologist, or God, the two adults running up the hill to the maple and the hanging dogs would have looked symbolic, or archetypal, or even Shakespearean. But it was not a concept. It was gut-churning disappointment and rage at the human species, mixed with a profound horror at what cannot be changed.

One of the dogs, Gypsy, the smaller one, was still alive, choking and drooling but she knew they were there and was trying to get loose. The rope seemed to be twisted around her collar. The other dog, Gudrun, was limp. But they were too high to reach and too far out on a limb to climb. Suddenly Anna started running across the field to the fence, whistling as she ran. Elias watched her and for a moment thought she had lost her mind. But then he saw the horses in the neighboring field running to her and without hesitation she had swung herself over the fence and taking a few strides had jumped on the grey horse bareback, grabbing its mane in her hands. Then he saw her kick the horse hard in the flanks going the opposite direction and it broke into a gallop, and then a hundred feet later she wheeled and came back straight at the fence, almost in slow motion it seemed from a distance, sailing cleanly over it and not breaking stride on the other side. When she got close to him she pulled back hard on its mane and yelled at it to stop, which it did throwing a cascade of dirt onto Elias' jeans. She was also yelling instructions at him now. The horse was nervous around the twitching dog in the air, but he grabbed it by its halter with both hands and led it directly under where she was hanging. Anna stood up on the horse's broad back, pulled the knife from her boot, and cradling Gypsy with her

59

shoulders cut the poor dog down in one slice. She half fell from her back into Elias' arms. Then she cut Gudrun down, got down off the horse and said, as if she were pleading, "Give her to me, please." She was sobbing, and she took Gypsy out of his arms and into hers and started walking fast downhill toward the trailer. "Take the horse back, please," she said over her shoulder.

Elias hadn't said a word since he shouted, the whole sequence probably taking no more than a couple of time-stopped minutes. He led the grey across the field and down the fence line to a gate, then he walked back up and picked up the soft pile that was Gudrun and carried her down to the house. She seemed at peace, her smooth black skin glowing in the late sun. He elbowed through the screen door and laid her body on top of the washing machine. She wasn't even stiff yet; they must not have been hanging for long. Anna was on the phone, asking someone a lot of questions. The vet. Gypsy was lying on the rug, coughing and trying to breathe.

"We've got to take her to the animal clinic at Tech. Can you come? They're closing but they said they'd wait fifteen minutes until we get there."

"Of course," he said, thinking it was a thirty minute drive.

They shut the door to the trailer and climbed in her car with the dog between them on the front seat. The Buick caught and shuddered as she raced the engine, then they were down the dirt drive in a roar of dust, bottoming out and banging the frame in the ruts, and out onto the highway without checking for traffic like a couple of demons.

The hospital was part of the vet school at Tech. The few staff left were so sincere when they showed up afterhours that Elias tried to remember if people had always been this way on campus, or only since the shooting. He had been here off and on for six years, but all he could recall was from 2007 on. Before that was almost a blank, as if he

60

had been somebody else. Then his wife was alive. And thirty-two students. Still it seemed surreal, this hospital, as if a portal had been opened into an older life.

The clinic was all glass and linoleum but had that sick dog smell about it. There were lots of questions about how Gypsy got hanged, and Anna blamed it on some vicious kids in the neighborhood. She had stopped crying by the time they got in the car, and the tears had dried before they got to Blacksburg, and now that it was clear Gypsy was going to live, she was calm and careful about what she said. Still, they were told to call the sheriff's office because the clinic would have to notify them. So they said thanks and left the dog in their care.

It was Thursday night and Elias didn't have to be back at work until Tuesday. On the drive back to the trailer Anna started talking about the corporate conspiracy that she believed was behind Sylvie' death and now the hanging. She was really wound up and as usual he couldn't get a word in edgewise. She said she had found out who the guy in the video was—Ronald Breedlove Junior, son of the chairman and CEO of Mason Dixon Energy. He was a real sonuvabitch, the dad, she said. Elias had seen him once on TV, a big braggart of a man being interviewed about global warming and not giving in an inch, basically calling the scientists idiots and the environmentalists meddlers. Ronnie Junior had been a student at Tech off and on, apparently where Sylvie had met him, and was now in law school at UVA. Anna said she was sure that this guy had killed Sylvie, or that somebody in the company had had her killed because she had gotten information about the company, probably illegal political payoffs with the election so close and cap and trade hanging in the balance. It was all on the cell once she figured out what the docs meant. What she didn't understand was why they sexually molested her if they were going to pretend she had been killed by some meth dealers—that part just didn't make sense. And also whether

61

they knew about the cell phone, and what was likely to happen next. They killed her dogs as a warning not to continue asking questions about Sylvie's death and not to go to any higher authorities, that was obvious. Thugs had been hanging dogs in Appalachia for years as retaliation, she said. But how much did they know about what information she had? Anna didn't think they knew about the phone; otherwise, they probably would have done something else, something worse to them, but they were not about to stop with the intimidation until Anna was dead or locked up because she was not going to stop looking for the truth and exposing the bastards who did this to her.

By the time they got out of the car she was still talking non-stop, and Elias went inside with her and made them both some green tea. But she had opened a beer before it was brewed so Elias had a beer with her and a tea chaser.

"Anna, listen," he said, in the momentary lull that coincided with her taking a swig. "I talked to my colleague at school: you know, the prosecutor. I didn't give him all the details, but I told him that I knew Sylvie. I didn't mention your name so he probably thinks she was in one of my classes, and I said she was an MTR activist who had been threatened by the coal companies and that the police had maybe jumped the gun on the drug killing and had overlooked that whole conspiracy scenario. I told him I knew her and she told me she had gotten some inside information about the company—which was technically true, she did tell us in a sense in the video, which would have been probable cause for the coal company to have her murdered. I also said that the county cops might have been bought off." Elias realized he was talking fast to keep up with Anna so she couldn't interrupt and start another monologue.

"Did you use the word 'conspiracy'? Because if you did, these lawyers don't like that word. It automatically makes them think you're crazy."

"I don't think I said 'conspiracy.' Maybe. I don't really remember the exact words. Anyway, he took it all in and said it was possible, of course, but he thought it unlikely that a corporation with as much power as the coal companies would take such a risk."

Anna laughed.

"But he did say he would see what he could find out about the murder, the arrest and so forth, even though it was in a different state, and he would get back to me. Meanwhile he said to keep him posted."

She had rolled and lit a joint and passed it to him but he was tired and getting depressed and turned it down. "I don't have your energy," he said. "If I smoke this late I won't be able to go to sleep. Frankly, you probably need to get some sleep too."

"Who's got time to sleep?" she asked, her eyes burning. "I'm not planning on going to sleep for the next week. The alcohol doesn't affect me; I can drink all I want and stay wide awake. And frankly, darlin', I would advise you to think seriously about staying awake yourself lessin' you want to come home to dead dogs and a pile of ashes."

It took a second for Elias to realize what she was saying. Suddenly he felt like he ought to head home. "You mean you think someone would kill my dogs and burn down my house?" he asked.

"It's happened before, and it will happen again. Don't forget we are talking about millions of dollars at stake. These people have got no morals; all they care about is how to keep working that money seam. That's all that matters to them. They don't give a shit about some hillbilly Grundy girl and her liberal English prof. Well, maybe they have to be a bit more careful about you; someone might wonder why you turned up missing. But not me."

Elias wandered over to the stove and surveyed the contents of the cast iron skillet she had been cooking in hours earlier. The chicken looked good even to a vegetarian; he was not that choosy.

"You're no hillbilly," he said, "and I'm no liberal. Let's eat and regroup and figure out what we're going to do next."

She took a last hit and rubbed out her joint in a plate. "You eat," she said, "I'm not hungry now that I have a dead dog on my washer to bury. Actually," she continued, pulling on her jacket, "I'm just not in the mood to plan anything at the moment. I'm going to run some errands . Stay here if you like, or not. But I may not be back for a couple hours."

Elias wanted her to stay but he sensed that arguing with her was pointless, so he walked over to where she was standing, held her by the shoulders and looked in her face. "Why don't you let me bang together a box for Gudrun?" he said. "I want to do that; I liked her. And then we can bury her wherever you want. Meanwhile, you know where I live, and you can call me anytime. Maybe we can eat together tomorrow night?"

He was sure she responded to his offer; he could read it in her eyes. But there was so much anger there, so much hard-edged suspicion just below the flirtation and the wit, as if her eyes were guarding the border of the unknown country of her identity, that she did not succumb to his gentility. She would not waver, not yet, maybe not ever. That was okay, Elias seemed to tell her in his voice and hands; unlike most men, he really did not need anything else from her.

He went home and quickly fell into a deep dreamless sleep, with a little help from his friends.

Chapter 8

Friday he spent doing chores: cut up a few limbs fallen from an oak nearby and stacked them almost reverently on the woodpile, cleaned the gutters, nailed down some loose boards. Winter was coming. Occasionally he'd go inside and take another look at the images on his laptop, but he couldn't make any sense of them. He figured he'd let someone at school look at them next week, but he didn't know who. Then he'd haul on his field jacket again and go back out.

He started doing his kata again. It felt good walking barefoot through the winter woods with the dogs, smashing dead limbs. He went back to the basics of the Seitai-gata: mae, ushiro, uke nagashi, tsuka-ate, meditating in between techniques. His speed and agility returned like parts of his personality he had forgotten about. He could feel the center of his being return to his abdomen, and his hands and feet got tougher.

Saturday he still hadn't heard from Anna. He watched football games most of the afternoon while he graded papers during the commercials. The scores affected the grades. Then he switched to the news channels, which was a mistake. Obama had apparently changed his mind about leaving Afghanistan next year; now he was saying 2014. Elias couldn't believe what he was hearing. That war had been a mistake from the get-go. Al-Qaeda was a criminal organization; you don't invade a country to get criminals. That was massive overkill. It was also an unwinnable war. Trying to force democracy on these tribes was colonialism all over again. There was more bad news. North Korea was saber rattling. The heir apparent looked like an Asian version of the fat kid in Bad Santa.

It was dark now, and Elias was getting restless. Finally about 11 p.m. he gave in to his impulse and drove over to Anna's. The moon was full and the countryside so flooded with light that he could have turned off his headlights. When he got there he saw a Fat Boy and a couple of cars out front and another around back, but he parked anyway and knocked on the door. The Allman Brothers were playing so loud inside that the plastic windows on the trailer were rattling. The curtains were closed. Then someone turned the music down and a man's face appeared in the diamond door window. He had small, scrutinizing eyes and a full beard.

"What you want?" he said through the door, almost in a grunt.

"I'm Elias. Friend of Anna's."

The man stared at him some more and then looked back into the room for a moment. Then he said, "Uh huh. Elias. Come on in, dude, and join the party," and he opened the door.

There were maybe seven or eight people in the small living room and kitchen, not counting Anna who was sitting at the kitchen table with a glass pipe in her hand staring at him. She looked wide-eyed and thin; the veins in her arms were sticking out more than usual. Gypsy was lying on the linoleum at her feet, wearing a foam neck brace.

"Come on over here, darlin'," Anna said, and he walked over and took a seat. "How 'bout a beer?" she asked and leaned back in her chair, deftly opened the refrigerator door behind her one handed, pulled out a long-necked Bud, and slid it across the table to him. He thanked her, and she just kept staring at him. Her eyes looked abnormally large, then he realized her pupils were just very dilated.

"What?" he asked.

"Nothing, darlin', just looking," she said.

"Okay," he said, and took a swig.

"You look so serious," she observed, critiquing him. "It's Saturday night. Time to party. You remember going to parties, don't you? Centuries ago? When you used to have

66

fun?" and she flicked open her lighter and held it under the pipe until fumes started to appear from whatever was in the bowl, then she inhaled them. Then she said, "Just fuckin' with you, darlin'," and exhaled. "You ain't that old. You still look good. And you know I love you," and she kind of slid out of her chair and eased around to his side of the table and before he had time to know what she was doing leaned over and kissed him on the mouth, soft and wet. He could feel her hair falling across his ears and cheek. Then just as quickly she was back in her chair, smiling at him. Elias was a little shocked, and pleased, but he chalked it up to the drugs and alcohol and decided not to make much of it.

Everyone else seemed to be paying them no mind. There were four guys and three women. One of them he recognized, Sylvia Plath from Waffle House. There was a couple on one couch, kind of slumped over each other, in close conversation. He had very long hair and a full beard, turning grey, and was wearing a tie-dye shirt and jeans. She also looked like a hippie. There was another couple leaning against the kitchen counter, talking. The beefy guy with the squinty eyes who answered the door, and a woman with very close cropped hair and a face that looked like a sidewalk, lined and rough, though it was hard to tell if she was out of her thirties. They all seemed older than Anna, except for the two clean-cut guys and the girl who were hanging around in the doorway to one bedroom. They also were smoking something Elias didn't recognize, probably meth or heroin he guessed, but he wasn't sure. He knew it wasn't weed. He didn't object to it; he just hadn't done any speed for an awfully long time, and he was satisfied with the beer. For now.

As if she had read his mind again, Anna asked, "Would you like a little hit off the white dragon, darlin'?"

"What is it?" he responded.

"Just some homemade crank," she said. "Guaran-goddamn-teed by our very own doctoral candidate in chemistry to contain only the purest ingredients. None of that fucked up lithium shit you normally get. This is the real McCoy, darlin'," and she pushed the pipe across the table.

Elias looked at it and thought seriously about joining in. He was depressed; it would feel good. But some part of him thought better of it. No one here was in control, and considering the trouble that had been dumped on Anna and himself, someone, he figured, needed to stay sane. He looked in Anna's wide-open pupils and saw what he thought was the same need. So he demurred.

"Suit yourself," she said. "You know," she added, taking another hit, "our boys over in the Middle East are doing the same shit. I don't know what they call it—black beauties or whatever—but it's all crank of some sort. Keeps 'em wide awake for days at a time so's they can kill more people. Then they get used to it, come back home to West by God, and start right back in on it. Hell, it's the poor man's cocaine, the redneck's crack. Just like moonshine; when they made it illegal and put all the local folks who'd been cooking it for generations out of business, it went underground. You know, there's stills all over the place in these woods, just like the meth labs."

"Every third trailer," someone said.

Elias got another beer out of the fridge. It was true. He knew all about using speed in the military. And there were the remains of a still in the woods behind his house. "Most of the drugs we take for fun started with the military," he said, sitting down again across from Anna. "The Germans and the Japs made a lot of meth during World War II. It's been said that Hitler had his own personal stash. Probably what kept him going at the end. I don't know whether that should make you feel any better or worse for using it. Probably neither," and he pulled a joint out of his shirt pocket and lit it.

The party kept going like that for the next two hours. The beer bottles kept adding up on the table and there was no sign that anyone was slowing down. Elias talked with some of the others. The scary butch woman in the kitchen turned out to be very smart and not at all as hard core as she looked; she was a nurse in a clinic. Elias got along with her famously, and with the chemist. They talked about Tech, the graduate programs, the football team, the shootings, the mysterious murders. It was a pretty normal scene, all things considered; that is, Elias thought, not your usual redneck meth madness. Still, he knew that it was an escape for Anna, maybe for the rest of them too, and she wasn't, in the best sense, being herself. Not once had she brought up Sylvie, or the documents, or the dogs, except to show him the lacerations under the fur on Gypsy's neck. She was coy with him too, at times ignoring him completely while she talked and danced with her friends, then staring intently at him from across the room.

After one of those occasions she strolled over to him when he was talking to the nurse and pulled him out into the living room. "Come on and dance with me," she pleaded. "You haven't danced with me all night." She had put some R&B on the stereo. They both had beers in their hands, and she started dancing very sexy in front of him, on her own. She had on jeans and a tank top that stopped about six inches above her abdomen, revealing a small tattoo. At first he couldn't make it out, then he saw what it was: "Sylvie," inside a heart. Anna saw him staring, was smiling at him, danced up closer, and started rubbing her body softly against him. She had no bra. Elias wasn't sure where this was going, but after a few minutes of off and on contact she took him by the hand and moved towards the bedroom. A couple of people had left; everyone else was in the kitchen, smoking around the table. It had to be three o'clock in the morning.

"You're very sexy tonight," he said."

"I'm part black," she said, and winked.

She was so close to him in the semi-dark of the bedroom door that he couldn't help but kiss her, this time open mouthed.   She grabbed him hard on the ass and pressed her body against him. Then she pulled back.

"This is crazy," he said.

"I know," she replied. "Normally I'm not that attracted to men. Must be the teacher-student thing. Once you see somebody like that, the feeling never goes away."

"That's not what I meant," he said, softly. "You're in some serious fucking trouble. Your cousin is dead. Your dog is dead. Your life has been threatened. And what do you do? You get high."

"It's just a temporary escape," she said. "Like sex. What's wrong with that?" And she ran her hand down the inside of his leg.

"Normally, nothing. But this isn't a normal situation. You said so yourself; these are some fucked up rich and powerful people who could be out to kill you. Tonight. Tomorrow. You don't know. You've got to keep your wits about you. Don't take any chances. You need to …"

"Shhhh," she said, putting a finger to his lips.   "It's okay.   These are my homeboys; they ain't going to let anybody sneak up on me. This party's been going on since Friday, and it'll keep going on until I'm ready to get even. So don't worry about it. You can't control it anyway. Just relax. It's going to be okay."

"You relax," he said. "I can't." He was right. It felt like he was getting pulled into something too intense for him at the moment.   Besides, he was beginning to feel the old weariness, the old depression, inundating the edges of his consciousness like a rising black tide. His wife's murder, the abysmal losses.

He managed a smile. "I'm going to go on home. I'm an old guy, remember? I can't party all weekend like you all. As long as you're safe—that's all that's important right now. I care about you; you know that. I don't want to see you get in a worse jam."

She gave him a twisted smile. "Do you care about me?" she asked. "I'm a screw up. Don't care too much, or you'll regret it."

"I doubt that," he said, kissed her on the forehead, and went to retrieve his coat. Then he said goodnight all around; she was still in the bedroom doorway, and he was suddenly out in the cold night air. The wind had scoured the sky clear of clouds and Orion had marched out of the eastern forest. The New River Valley spread out below between the Appalachians and the Blue Ridge like the fertile crescent in Iraq, just before the war began. Elias jumped in the Jeep and drove as fast as he could, watching for deer on the way home.

Chapter 9

That was Saturday night, November 20. Elias didn't hear a thing from her for the next two days. Then on Tuesday, Thanksgiving week, he got a phone call mid-afternoon in his office. It was Anna. She was in jail and wondered if he could bail her out.

"What happened?" he asked.

"They burnt my goddamn house down, is what happened," she said, as if she were calmly taking a drag off her cigarette. In fact, Elias could hear her smoking when he spoke. But she was not calm. "I went to work last night and when I got back the fire department, the cops, the FBI, the whole fucking government was there going through my shit, the goddamn motherfuckers every last one of them. Do you think they had any sympathy for the fact that the coal company had just burned my trailer to the ground? No, they busted my ass for producing with the intent to distribute. They think I burned down my own fucking house! What do they think I am, some redneck idiot? They're all in this together. They know where we live, where we work, when we're gone. They've got satellite surveillance and X-rays that can see through the fucking walls. They are out to get me and everything I come in contact with, which means that you are not fucking safe either and you must be crazy to even want to take my call." She took another drag. "Thank the Lord I took Gypsy to work with me or she would have been burned up too."

"What about the cats?" he asked.

"The cats? Oh, the cats are feral. They can live through anything."

"So why did they arrest you? Just because your house burned down? I don't understand," Elias said, trying to calm her down.

"Hey? Are you listening to what I said? It's a conspiracy. Yes, I know I'm not supposed to use that word, especially on the goddamned jail phone, but let's call a fucking spade a spade, shall we? They burned down my fucking house, they waited until I left and they burned it to the fucking concrete, and they made sure their fucking minions, the goddamned local redneck sheriff, would put 2 and 2 together and get 5." Then Elias could hear her yelling at somebody on her end, "That's right, you illiterate half breeds, I'm talking about your fat ass." Then he could hear them coming for her and a struggle to get the phone away from her. Anna yelled, "Keep your fucking hands off of me or I'm going to lay you out," then there was more cursing and more yelling and suddenly the phone was banged down loud and went dead.

He immediately started going through his checkbook and credit cards, not really knowing what he could use, but vaguely remembering doing this on several occasions twenty years ago in the middle of his own wild years. He thought of calling a bail bondsman but instead he just got some numbers from the phone book and headed over to the Montgomery County Regional Jail. He knew where it was because he had worked with some black student activists, the Zulu Nation, who spent time there counseling inmates.

As soon as he walked into the waiting room the first person he saw looked like a construction foreman, dressed in Carhartt jacket, Western hat and jeans. Of course, a bondsman bailing someone else out, so Elias talked to him about Anna. Her bond was set at ten grand; it seemed like a lot, and the bondsman agreed: "There's a bad meth epidemic in this area and they're sending a message to all the wannabe dealers. But generally first-time bond's around twenty-five hundred. She must of been here before." He had his own portable electronic card swiping device, and they were done in a few minutes of paper work.

But the wait for Anna to be released took quite a bit longer. Apparently she had been ranting and raving since they brought her in, hadn't slept, and was in isolation at the moment. They didn't think it was safe to release her until she calmed down. Somewhere deep down in his gut Elias felt the smallest slithering of the worm of suspicion, but he couldn't make himself believe that the affectless policewoman he was talking to through a plexiglass window could be part of some large conspiracy which included coal company CEOs and the like. He was too much the product of his middle class background to question the law: despite the military, his temporary association with the Zulus and people like Anna, and the daily revelations in the newspaper, he had too much Kafka in his unconscious, too many literary paranoid fantasies to believe Anna over the police. Still, all this went through his mind in a few seconds and then he announced to the officer, "It's okay. I'm her doctor. I can deal with her. She has bipolar disorder with a secondary schizo-affective diagnosis. She just went off her medications for a while. Once she gets back on her lithium and Serequel all the cursing and antagonistic behavior will go away," he said, and he gave her his business card from Tech which gave his title without any particular discipline. "I can guarantee it," he added, smiling.

He really hadn't intended to deceive her, but the spiel came out almost unwilled. He simply believed that he knew what was best for her, and it was not jail. He was in fact a doctor, of course, just not of medicine. But why should he have to say that?

The woman seemed to respond to this jargon-laden rant, maybe because he was still wearing a coat and tie. "You better hope you're right," she said, "or else you're gonna have your hands full. That lady has got a mouth on her. I could call her a few choice names but it wouldn't be professional," and she got up with a huge set of keys in hand and left her post. Ten minutes later she was back with a deputy and Anna in plastic cuffs. Elias prayed that she would stay silent until they got out of there, but it was not to be. As soon as she had signed the release form and been given her belongings—including the folding knife and the straight one she appeared to carry everywhere in her boot—she lit into them with a litany of curses and observations about their parents that he thought for sure they would put her back in lockup, but apparently they were used to her language and simply warned her they would keep an eye on her as Elias took her by the arm and half dragged her into the parking lot.

"Keep a fucking eye on your jobs, you shitheads; you won't have them for long when I get finished with you," she yelled back at the metal door as it slammed shut. A nervous pedestrian hurried into her SUV. On the third floor some inmates hollered down at her. "And fuck you too!" she yelled back. Then they were in his Jeep.

On the ride back to his place Anna kept searching the radio for music she wanted to hear. Never seemed satisfied with anything she found, so for the next twenty minutes they listened to five to ten second blasts of DJs, commercials, and songs until Elias thought he was going to go insane. He tried to find out what had happened at the trailer.

"Nothing happened," she said, lighting a cigarette. "Have you got a joint? The bastards came in and torched the place, like I told you, and then they arrested my ass as soon as I got home."

"But why did they arrest you?" he asked.

"Well of course the po po planted the shit that they needed for evidence. You know, the ammonia, soda bottles, the empty ephedrine packs. Hell, they didn't even need to do that: I had enough engine starter and batteries in the trailer for the cops to make a case. They were just being thorough. Overkill as usual, the stupid rednecks. Another meth lab blown up and burned to the weeds, another drug dealer put behind bars. It's the oldest cover in Southwest Virginia." She was talking very fast and staring out the window she had put down when she lit up. It was a mild afternoon now, two days before Thanksgiving. She was quiet for a brief moment while she smoked, then flicked her butt out the window and rolled it back up. "As for who were the motherfuckers who tried to kill me, I would venture to say the same goons of course who hanged my dogs and who have been watching us since Sylvie got some shit on them. Mine company thugs, but now they're high tech. They probably have known about us for months, me and Sylvie, not to mention the whole Mountain Justice crew. Where we live, where we work, where we shit, where we fuck, and everything in between."

Then she turned to look at him. "So how was your day? Until the psycho bitch showed up? You probably don't want to hear about all that, now do you darlin'?" she said and got a strange look on her face, Elias thought, like she was sexually aroused and angry at him at the same time. For a remarkably pretty girl, she looked really bad. Her hair was dirty and lank, she had dark circles under her eyes, and her skin had a smoky pallor. She was thin as a bicycle. She couldn't sit still, and she started picking at the skin on her arm distractedly, like she didn't know she was doing it. On the ride she drank one and a half containers of bottled water.

They stopped at the animal shelter to get Gypsy, who had lost her foam collar and looked worse than Anna if that were possible.

"What about your medications?" he asked.

"What medications?" she said, obliviously.

"The medications I saw in your bathroom, for bipolar disorder." She was staring at him like he had just quoted from her diary. "I told the deputies I was your doctor; they wouldn't have let you go with me otherwise. I figured you didn't care if I knew you were bipolar or else you wouldn't have left them out in the open," he said, looking at her for a reaction.

"Whatever the fuck," she said. "When you're mentally ill the whole world eventually will know. I'm surprised you didn't tell them you were Sigmund Jesus Fucking Freud." She thought for a moment, then turned to confront him. "What's it going to be then, Eli, you want to be my shrink or my lover boy? You got to make up your mind because you can't be both, you know. If you're my shrink, you get to act like an asshole as long as you don't cut off my Xanax, and if you're my boyfriend you can do whatever you like as long as you don't act like a fucking asshole. But there is no in-between."

"How about if I just be your friend for now, and we'll let the future sort out the rest, okay?" he said, and impulsively leaned over and gave her a kiss on the cheek, almost running off the road in the process. They were halfway to his cabin on a two lane switchback. He could see the setting moon out of the corner of the windshield.

"Easy boy," she said. "I think you want to be my boyfriend. Just don't try to play doctor with me. I know every trick in the DSM IV."

When they got to his house the first thing he asked her to do was contact her psychiatrist, tell him what happened, and get a refill on her scripts.

She gave him a look. "Ten minutes later and you're already trying to control my life," she said. But she did it anyway. "The problem actually is not with the doc, it's the pharmacy," she said, holding the phone in one hand and a beer in the other. "They don't like to refill until it's time. But I think they'll do it. And now that I have done what you asked, how about you get me another beer and let me roll a J to celebrate being out of jail?"

So they talked for a couple of hours on the rug in front of the fire with the dogs. Or rather, Elais listened while Anna ranted. He made some pasta, and she crashed around midnight in mid-sentence describing her addiction to old movies. He put her in his bed, cleaned up, and fell asleep himself under a blanket on the couch.

But it was a short sleep. At 3 a.m. he woke up to the sounds of her banging some cupboards in the kitchen. When he found her, she had half the contents of his refrigerator on the counter and seemed to be in the process of constructing some kind of huge, postmodern sandwich. "Anna, you hungry?" he asked, jokingly. Then he noticed: her eyes were closed, or almost. She was apparently sleep walking. He wasn't sure if he should wake her so he went over and took her by the arm to lead her gently back to bed, but she pulled away violently and yelled at him, "Stop it!" Then she went back to making the sandwich. He watched her for a while, and so did the dogs, sitting by the counter patiently and following her every move. She would periodically spill something on the floor and they would eat it. The whole scene looked like some kind of kitschy Norman Rockwell painting, except for the fact that Anna, dressed in a pair of his pajamas, was bipolar and coming off a five-day meth binge. He decided the best thing to do was to let her continue. Maybe she would go back to bed afterwards. So he stoked the dying fire, sat on the couch and read his old UVA alumni mags while she putzed around in her unconscious state. It was incongruous, the prep school PR and the manic girlfriend. Then she started talking aloud. He couldn't make out what she was saying, but he had the creepy sensation that it might be something important, something he needed to decode, to know, about her or the trouble she was in. He got a notepad and pen and went back into the kitchen to watch her more closely and listen. Her amanuensis. She had made a mess of the food and was leaning back against the counter eating with her hands off a plate and now mumbling incoherently, the dogs at her feet. She seemed to be slowing down. Once again he tried to move her upstairs; this time, she went along with him, carrying the plate and shuffling her feet.

When he got her to the bedroom she got under the covers with the plate on her lap. The TV was on CNN and the blue light invaded the room. For a moment she looked more peaceful, then she turned over after a minute and threw her arms around her pillow like a bombed Iraqi clutching his dead child on the bloody pavement. She started saying whole sentences in Standard English. This nocturnal monologue seemed to center on a scene at church, because she kept repeating some words from the Book of Common Prayer and made references to a priest, but really he couldn't make out the details. She must be Catholic, he thought. He had watched her take her last dose of nighttime medications she had stashed in her backpack: a massive amount of pills just to be able to go to sleep: tranquilizers, sleep aids, and anti-psychotics, but she apparently was still passing through the valley of mania. He was amazed that she could stay awake when the meds she had taken would have knocked out a horse. She was twisting and turning between the sheets now, struggling no doubt with the amphetamine withdrawal, and Elias wondered if maybe he hadn't made a mistake bringing her to his house instead of a hospital. Interspersed with the angry tone of her religious rambling he could hear some foreign words; he thought maybe they were Latin from the liturgy, but they didn't sound like any Latin he was familiar with. They were earthier, chanted kinds of sounds, alien words and yet somehow he had a feeling he had heard them before. Probably in some old research he had done. After a while she became silent and appeared to be sleeping again, so he went back downstairs.

Twenty minutes later she came down the stairs again. This time she had taken off his pajamas. He started to get up and take her back upstairs, but he was for a while so fascinated with what was happening that he forgot. All she had on were some panties. Her body seemed to be telling him who she was. Her breasts were small, conical, with wide aureoles. On the small of her back was a tattoo that read, "Absolute power corrupts absolutely." Her naked body was thinned from the drug use, but Elias could see the well-defined muscles in her arms and legs, and the overall impression was of strength and grace, in spite of the shuffling around. For the next hour or two she stayed busy, all the time without seeming to open her eyes. First she put on some R&B. Then she smoked a roach left on the coffee table. Then she spent about twenty minutes in the bathroom doing god knows what. "Break up to make up, that's all we do. First you love me, then you hate me, ..." She made coffee, really strong, five sugars, six creamers, fed the dogs, then swept the kitchen, but first, put on more music, the Chi Lites, no, the Commodores, no, more Stylistics: "You Make Me Feel Brand New." How did she know what she was choosing? Was it habit, or some unconscious impulse? Did some laundry, whites mixed with colors which he sorted while she wasn't looking, then cleaned the counters. Suddenly she stopped in mid wipe, turned around and looked in his general direction, and said, "Stop watching me; I feel like you're guarding me." Eyes still closed. Like he was having a conversation with a manic dead person. Then she got on the phone to order some clothes for a wedding, except that Elias could see she had not entered any number: she talked to phantom sales reps at LL Bean, Victoria's Secret, and J. Crew, ordering shoes, shorts, dresses, skirts, tops, bathing suits. More coffee, three sugars, six creamers; "We're running low on creamer," she said. "Can you go to Minute Mart?"

Next she set up the ironing board and did some laundry, but the iron was not plugged in. She dusted. Mopped. Started a grocery list for next week. More music: The Floaters—"Everything happens for a reason!" she announced. Then she apparently changed her mind. "No, the Four Tops. No, GRACE FUCKING JONES!!! Pull up to the bumper, Baby!" Finally she danced over and sat down in a chair and started flipping through all of the Christmas catalogs he had gotten in the mail the past month, looking, apparently, for more things to order: Athleta, Garnet Hill, Sundance, Free People, Title IX, Williams-Sonoma, all the companies his wife had ordered from. She pulled a new Vanity Fair out of her backpack and started ear-marking pages. She tried to call her psychiatrist to make an appointment, got the machine and left a message. She chewed some gum and drank the rest of the bottle of wine left on the hearth. She smoked some more pot and wrote in a notebook. When Elias looked at it later it was illegible, but she had drawn tortured faces in the margins, young women whose bodies were twisted and broken. Then she switched from R&B to Sarah McLachlan ("Angel," that's a good sign, isn't it, he thought). She put on the DVD of *The Last Waltz* and started giving herself a blind pedicure and nail painting on the couch.

It's quite possible that Elias, though caught up in her world from the first moment he saw her again at Waffle House, didn't actually fall in love with her until this moment. There was something about watching her go through the motions of beautifying her feet, her callused, muscular, high arched feet and then painting her nails with some imaginary polish she asked him for that conjured up a lost childhood, hers and his, that leapt the years between them and bound his heart to hers in chains. She fell asleep in the act, her head nodding onto her shoulder. Then she woke up again at 6:30, moved to the couch next to him, and watched skateboarding & surfing on Fuel. Finally at seven, as sunlight was filtering through the apple trees and into the east windows, she made coffee again, part decaf (that was an excellent sign), took the dogs out, brought him some coffee, and went to bed again. "Honey, how do you like me now

…?" she asked him with the covers pulled up to her chin, before falling off to sleep.

Later in the morning he was reading the paper in bed next to her when she opened her eyes, sat up suddenly like a corpse in a coffin, and announced, "Take this needle from my veins; I'm beautiful enough without the drugs." It was 9:30 because the TV was on and people in suits were clapping for capitalism while the Stock Exchange bell rang. They even had Santa Claus on to get the market going, his red cheeks puffing up Christmas purchases. Elias said softly, "Anna, wake up, you're dreaming." Then she opened her eyes, startled, saw him and scrunched against the half-dozen or so pillows she had flattened in the throes of sleep. She told him she had been dreaming she was talking to Billy Crudup and Samantha Morton in a scene from *Jesus's Son*. This was one of her favorite movies, she said, along with about fifty others that she could watch whenever they came on, and Billy Crudup was possibly her favorite actor, mainly when he played Steve Prefontaine in *Without Limits*. She was talking very rapidly considering she had just awakened.

Anyway, apparently she and Billy and Samantha were shooting up together in a small motel room, and she had glanced into a mirror on the wall and had suddenly become afraid that she was losing her looks and nobody would love her anymore. She laughed about it but Elias thought there was a plaintive edge to her laugh. Then he looked past her relentlessly guarded face and anxious eyes, past her talking and gesticulating, and out the window and into the almost ruined orchard filled with sunlight. He could feel himself dissociating from her mania for a moment. He tuned her out, mostly, for his own sake, and for some reason started thinking about that scene at the end of the movie when Fuckhead, what his friends called Crudup's character, peeps through an Amish woman's window while she is singing in the shower. He is apparently drawn by her voice, like Odysseus to the sirens, and while she's brushing her hair near the window, he actually reaches in and touches her. That is, he reaches in and touches her THROUGH THE CLOSED WINDOW! That's really the only completely miraculous thing that happens in the movie, which is after all called *Jesus's Son*, so you expect something transcendental. Of course he was a heroin addict, and probably hallucinating, but that didn't matter. It was Elias' favorite scene, something about the way Crudup's hand just goes right through the glass like it just wasn't there, or it was made out of plasma, or placenta, like it's perfectly natural that he can reach through without breaking the membrane.

And Elias wondered if anyone might be looking through the window at them, at that moment. And he wondered what kind of person it might be—someone like Billy Crudup, an innocent wandering through a landscape of mental illness, drugs, and poverty, or more likely some white-collar sociopath like the guy who occasionally ripped off his newspaper. And then he started thinking about the idea of Jesus coming back to take a look around. Even Jesus' son. Would we recognize him? What would he think when he looked in at them, Anna lying in bed in her oversize pajamas and him in his T-shirt? Would he take pity on them? Would he take pity on Anna and take away her sorrows, her nightmares, her illness?

Probably not.

And then Elias caught himself; he was day dreaming, as he was wont to do in bed looking out the window into the trees. But this was no dream; there probably was someone out there watching them in bed, and it sure as hell wasn't Jesus. So he got up and lowered the blinds.

There was another bombing on CNN, this time in Afghanistan. In the darkened room the images flickered from the TV across the screen of Anna's affectless face. He could see Kandahar on her cheekbones and Humvees racing across her forehead and again he was mesmerized. He looked at her again, looked at her agitated eyes that he had never been able to penetrate, knowing that behind them she had just walked off a bright Hollywood movie set into the dim confines of his little bedroom in the country, and he suddenly felt sorrier for her than he ever thought possible, and for the second time in as many hours he fell in love with her again, and before he knew what he was doing his hand was hanging in the air, just hanging there for a moment in the space between them, as if it didn't know what to do, caught between two countries, illness and health, and then he touched her face, lightly, beneath her sleep-mangled and sweaty hair, and without saying another word she looked straight at him, as if he were some sort of lesser but by no means impotent god, turned over and went back to sleep, with Iraqis fleeing from her eyes.

This time she slept for twenty-six hours, except to use the bathroom, once again without opening her eyes. When she woke up late Thanksgiving morning, she seemed herself again, but when he asked her how she felt, she said, "Like I woke up under a car." She took a shower, made some eggs, grits, and raisin toast, a Waffle House breakfast; he walked the dogs and got the paper. It was balmy out; the forsythia, fooled into thinking it was summer again, was blooming, a yellow tunnel down to the road. He read the headlines: conservatives were upset that the Pope had mentioned that prostitutes might wear condoms to prevent AIDS in South Africa. When he mentioned it to Anna as she was setting the table, she went off.

"The fucking Pope ought to be taken out and horsewhipped for all the stupid shit he says. The whole Catholic Church is a fraud, a fucking fraud. It's all about power; they got it by lying to people two thousand years ago, and they are not about to give it up, no matter how many people die of AIDS, no matter how many kids get abused, no matter how many billions of people are born on a planet that cannot sustain them. It just doesn't matter. All that Christian ideology is bullshit, and they know it, but they won't admit it as long as they can fool some of the people all of the time." She was vehement. Elias agreed with her, mostly.

"Where did that come from?" he asked, a little later. "The pope is actually telling people to wear condoms. It's a revelation," he joked.

"Where did it come from? My father's Catholic and he beat it into me; that's where it came from. I still feel guilty for some of the shit that's happened to me, even though I know it wasn't my fault. When they brainwash you when you're a kid, there's no escaping the effects. That's all I have to say about it at the moment. Now eat your breakfast before it gets cold."

"Yes, mommy," he said and pinched her ass as she put the plates on the table. Immediately it felt strange to him that he was acting sexually towards her. Because she seemed to vacillate between two personalities, one flirtatious and the other more businesslike, removed from him by age or temperament. This morning he was unsure which she was, but he couldn't stop himself from touching her. For comfort. His or hers?

"I need to go to a meeting," she announced. "I assume my car is in the impound. Can you give me a ride to get it?"

"A meeting?" he asked.

"An NA meeting. Narcotics Anonymous."

He considered that for a moment. "Can I come?"

She looked at him curiously. "Are you trying to play doctor again? Because if you are, you can forget about it. I don't think you have a medical degree, no matter how you conned them at the jail." Then she lit a cigarette. "Thanks for that, by the way," she added, and exhaled.

"My pleasure," he said. "No, really, I'm just interested. Read about them, never been to one." She looked unconvinced. "Besides," he said, brandishing his table knife with a deft little kata in the air, slashing it back and forth, "it's not safe to be out alone. We need to watch each other's back. Remember?"

"Can't argue with that," she said.

"But will they let me in? I mean, don't you have to be an addict to attend?"

"A dollar and some lip gloss will get you in, darlin'."

"No, seriously."

"Seriously? You just need a desire to change. Anything about you need changing?" She checked him out, from head to toe. "I don't think so."

They hung around the house and watched the end of the Macy's parade. It lacked substance, they agreed, compared to the old days. Then football games and old movies until about six when she suddenly walked over to her backpack on the floor, picked it up, and dumped the contents all over the coffee table in front of him. Cigarettes, lighters, perfume, keys, journals, spray paint, pocket knives, her cell, crackers, nail polish, a thin sweater, two paperbacks (*The Human Stain* and *The Will to Power*), pens, change, a couple of bills, and a screwdriver, all in a heap.

"I'm impressed," he said, smiling.

She wasn't. "That's all my worldly possessions you're looking at," she told him, "except for what's in the car."

He had completely forgotten; she had lost everything in the fire. No meds, of course, but also no clothes, no furniture, no plates, no music, no books, nothing. He felt like an asshole. She needed something clean to wear so she could go out, but she didn't want to ask.

She was standing over him as he sat on the couch immersed in her backpack pile, and he glanced up at her. She had a woebegone look on her face. He didn't know what to say. Finally, "I got rid of everything of my wife's. Couldn't stand looking at it. But what's mine is yours," he said slowly. "Really. Anything you need, just help yourself. Check out the closet in the bedroom, and the chest of drawers. There should be some shirts in there, and jeans. Whatever you like." She started up the stairs. "I like women in men's clothes anyway. Marlene Dietrich!" he yelled after her. "It's the German in me."

An hour later she sat in the Jeep in an old pair of his trousers with the legs rolled up and a plaid flannel shirt hanging loose and open at the neck down to a wife-beater. She had switched from her cowboy boots to some old Chuck Taylors he hadn't worn in years. She had big feet; they fit her pretty well. She always sat with them up on the dash.

It was a nice night and they enjoyed the ride into the city. Anna asked, "So how long did I sleep?"

"Couple of days, off and on."

"Did I do anything weird?"

"Like what?"

"Like take anything apart, or wash all your floors."

"Yeah, as a matter of fact you did do some house cleaning. And I found a flashlight in the refrigerator."

"I must have been looking for something."

"Yeah. Like Diogenes with the lights on."

"It's the Halcyon. It's a hypnotic. But at least the manias are good for something. Just don't ever take me shopping when I'm having one. You'll regret it."

The meeting was in old southeast Roanoke, at a huge community church on the main street. It took up half the block. The NA group, her home group, she said, met in the basement. They arrived just as things got started, took a couple of folding chairs and joined the circle. After some readings from the Twelve Steps and Twelve Traditions, people took turns talking. It was Thanksgiving, of course, and the topic was gratitude. Everybody there, it turned out, had something to be thankful for, despite their myriad addictions, financial and relationship problems. Some of the narratives were tragic, Elias thought, some were funny. All were lucidly honest. It was a strange phenomenon for him, being in a group of strangers who were sharing heartbreaking stories of mischief and woe. He had been trained to block them out. Mostly street people, but also some professional types and a few students. He felt oddly like he had wandered into a Puritan church about four hundred years ago, except that an angry God had been replaced by a benign higher power. The same sins. The same sinners.

Anna didn't say anything.

After they had joined hands and recited the Lord's Prayer, a couple of people came over to ask Anna how she was doing. Apparently they had heard about the fire, and they knew about Sylvie. She told them the police had set her up and had killed Sylvie. Astonishingly to Elias, they completely took her side, even saying the same thing had happened to someone else they knew. They sympathized with her, recommended some lawyers. It was as if either they were crazy or he was; as if a door had opened there in the hallway of the dark church basement between his daytime world of civilization with all its history of law and justice and their underground world of persecution, pain, and conspiracy.

They stopped to get something to eat at one of the few pubs open, and it was pushing midnight when they finally left I-81 and were climbing back up through the woods and onto the plateau above the New River Valley. As they started the turn into his driveway, Elias saw what looked to be a green pickup pulled off the road at the next bend, and noted it. Not unusual during hunting season; just the same it was nighttime and he was suspicious after all the talk. Then, almost to the house, he saw them. Two men just in the bare woods a hundred feet off, moving through his headlights as they came around a slight curve. "Look!" he said to Anna. They were out of sight in a moment down the hill. There was no space to turn around; there was nothing he could do but back up, and by the time he got down to the road the truck was gone. He pulled over, got the long, heavy Mag-Lite out of the glove compartment and sent the beam into the woods. Then in the gravel on the edge of the road Anna found a Bic lighter—that was all. After searching some more they drove back up to the top, let the dogs out of the kennel, who were barking like banshees, and walked the perimeter of the cabin. Nothing. Just the two men and the pickup. Nondescript: ball caps, camouflage jackets. Could have been firelighting deer, could have been about to set fire to his place; there was no way of knowing for sure, but in the context of everything that had happened in the past few weeks Elias was not going to take any chances. The threats which had overtaken Anna's life were now more tangible to him. Even Sylvie's viciously mutilated body, he had reasoned, was the work of some vicious meth dealers. But the men in his woods, who were they?

Anna had cut on the deck light and was standing at the window. "They're not going to come back tonight," he said. "They know we saw them. But tomorrow we'll have to break out some hardware." She gave him a funny look but didn't say anything. "What do you think they want, and what do you think we should do about it?" he asked, reasoning on some level that maybe she knew something she wasn't telling and that perhaps she had some idea of how to stop any more violence. He didn't say it, but he was thinking drug violence.

She lit up a cigarette, something she always seemed to do before she lay something heavy on him. "I think they want to get rid of us. I don't think they give a good goddamn whether we burn up along with the house or not. These people can cross right over from threat to murder if you look at them wrong. They, or somebody like them, killed Sylvie, made it look like it was drug-related, killed my dog and burned down my home. Isn't that enough to prove that they won't stop? I think they don't know if Sylvie got something on them or not, probably not, but they are going to destroy everything they can and hope that if she did take something they destroyed it too. Which reminds me," she said, exhaling a plume of smoke, "where's your computer?"

Elias whirled around and looked over at his desk. The computer was gone.

"Fuck!" he yelled. He opened all the drawers and scanned the bookcases, then went to the back door and checked it. Locked. "No wonder the dogs were going nuts," he said. "I thought they were just outside, but somebody must have gotten in here and grabbed the computer right before we pulled up. Probably one came in and one stood guard. Fuck! I can't believe it." Then he went to the back door and examined the lock from the outside. It had been tampered with, but not much. Somebody knew what he was doing. Meanwhile Anna had bolted upstairs and came down a moment later with a laptop in hand. "At least they didn't get the laptop," she said.

"But I haven't transferred Sylvie's video and photos to this one. They've got them."

"I know," she said. "That's bad news. But I've still got her cell phone. I never let it out of my sight." And she pulled it from her backpack. "Here," put it on your laptop and make some copies."

He transferred the data for the second time and they looked at it again. The video was easy enough to understand, though not legally damning, but the language or code that the handful of documents were written in was too difficult to untangle. They stared at it without comprehending.

"It could be a made-up language," he said, and sounded out a few words. "It almost sounds Indian," he said. "Native American, I mean. But I wouldn't know where to go about finding out. Next week when I'm back at Tech I'll see if there is anything in the library."

Anna looked tired. "Come on," he said. "Go to bed. We can work on this tomorrow." And he began to unroll the sleeping bag on the couch.

"No," she said. "You sleep upstairs with me. When I take my meds I can sleep through anything, and I don't want to be asleep if those goons come back." And she pulled on his arm.

"They're not coming back tonight," he reiterated, but he left the lights on.

Chapter 10

The next morning was sunny and warm again, and after breakfast Elias dug through a downstairs closet until he came up with a large boot box. He took it over to the coffee table where Anna was reading the *New York Times* and took out two pistols, a .32 caliber semi-automatic Luger and a long barreled .22 revolver, along with several boxes of bullets.

"The Luger was a present from my father-in-law when I got married," he answered to Anna's unasked question. "He didn't want his daughter to be unprotected. And the .22 I inherited from my father when he died; he used it to shoot squirrels out on the farm we owned, although I never actually saw him kill any. Anyway, I haven't shot either one in years, but they look okay to me."

He disassembled, cleaned and oiled, and loaded them, ritualistically. Then they went outside into the woods, and he set up a few beer cans on some fallen limbs against a hillside. Forgot the headgear. What the hell, they're not that loud. He took the .32 in one hand and rested it butt down on the other, sighted along the barrel, and squeezed the trigger. He knew it wouldn't hit anything far away. The boom sucked all the silence in the universe down its snubbed hole like an animal rooting up the garden. They were plunged into a stopped explosion, as if they had dived into a pool and were holding their breath underwater. Everything around them for a few seconds seemed to move in slow motion. Even the buzzards appeared to be painted on the sky. Elias swallowed hard and the world was born again.

Of course the can was still standing.

"You have to relax," Anna observed. "Your technique is fine but your hands are moving slightly. That shot hit the dirt just an inch to the right. You need to relax your shoulders, let them drop, like they tell you in ballet class."

He was a little amused that she was giving him instruction, but he tried not to show it. "Did they teach you to shoot while you were in ballet class?" he asked.

"In Grundy," she said, "it's considered bad manners if you don't know how to shoot," and raised the longer barreled .22 and smoothly knocked over every can, one after the other.

For the next week that was their routine. When Elias got back from school in the afternoon they would fire off a few rounds just before dusk. At least if anyone was watching them they knew they were armed. Meanwhile he pored through books at the library: hundreds of entries on Native Americans but next to nothing on native languages. The ones he did find had similar words and sounds—especially the Cherokee—but nothing matched exactly. Of course he wasn't even sure the code was a native language. Maybe the writer had made up the words based on some native tongue. They weren't written languages anyway. He also talked to his prosecutor colleague again. He had examined Sylvie's autopsy report and compared it to what Elias had told him and he said the two accounts didn't square. They were sitting across from each other in Sigmon's office at Tech. The semi-retired prosecutor at times affected a back woods speech that belied his relentless train of reasoning and go-for-the-jugular attack.

"The coroner's report doesn't say nothing about the words you described. It just says she died of multiple stab wounds. What did you say they were? Something bitch?"

"Psycho bitch."

"Right. That's unusual, and, I have to say, suspicious. Either somebody's incredibly inept over there for leaving it out, or someone left it out on purpose. I don't know these people, so I haven't called them to discuss this situation, but I know people who know them. I have to say that in my experience drug-related murders don't generally involve leaving these kinds of messages, and combined with the lacerations you described around her vagina, in my opinion it sounds like a sex crime." He paused for a moment to retrieve something on his computer. "I also found out something else. She was a student here, part-time, in 2007-2008. Normally if a Tech student dies, even a former part-time student, and especially a murder case, the media covers it pretty heavy. And we've had several murders and disappearances since the massacre. For some reason this one didn't get any press. I'd like to know why."

"I'd like to know too," Elias said. He cleared his throat. "There have also been a few other things that have happened that I haven't told you about. I won't go into all of them, but Sylvie's cousin, another former student of mine, had her trailer burn down a week ago in a suspicious fire, and then a few days later I scared off a couple of guys who had entered my house and stole my computer."

"What's the connection?" Sigmon asked. "I don't get it."

"Well, Anna, the cousin, and Sylvie were living together in the trailer, and apparently they were both involved in this activist organization, Mountain Justice, that's protesting mountaintop removal. Also, since her house burned down, she's been staying at my place. She's got no relatives in the area so I'm putting her up temporarily. I think it's possible that whoever murdered Sylvie might want to get to Anna as well."

"Why would they want to murder Anna? If the first girl was killed for sexual reasons, why would they target her cousin? And if the murder was not personal, then what was the motive? Because they were protesting against the coal companies? I'll grant you that some of these mining people are second generation hillbillies, but that's not a good enough reason for a corporation to be involved in a capital crime."

"I know, I know," Elias explained. "Maybe Sylvie found out about something illegal that was going on, and they murdered her for that. But I can't prove it ... yet. Anyway, if we assume that Sylvie was murdered to keep her quiet, that means that there could be a coverup, and the sheriff's department and the coroner and so on could be involved." Elias had swiveled in his chair and was looking out the window at the campus. Students were crossing the quad bathed in mid-afternoon mountain light. He paused. "Frankly, I have to tell you that it's pretty threatening to think that the police might be involved. It means I don't know whom to go to for protection, for the girl."

"It's also pretty unlikely that this is a conspiracy. Generally the simplest explanations are the most likely. The first girl was involved in drugs, or had a psycho boyfriend, and the other events are just coincidences. Once you start thinking there is a conspiracy out there and you are the target, then you start seeing connections everywhere."

"I understand that."

"Still, there is a history of rural sheriffs getting caught up in the drug business; it's happened in Montgomery and the surrounding counties. And there's even a longer history of the coal companies hiring people to do their dirty work for them, like stopping the unions and intimidating people to sell their land. Though I haven't seen anything like that in a while; most of those methods are outmoded today. Everything is high tech surveillance and political power brokering now."

"Maybe it is political," Elias said, turning back around to face him..

"What do you mean?"

"I mean, maybe what Sylvie found out was that the coal and energy companies were buying politicians. After all, we just had a very contentious election. Emotions are running pretty high; a lot of people in Southwest Virginia are out of work. And there is big money involved in whether or

95

not these environmental restrictions, cap-and-trade, will be enacted. Very big money."

Sigmon pulled on his beard. "My daddy was a country lawyer. He used to say that in coal country money is black, not green, and every politician claimed he just had a little coal dust on his hands. I'm not saying you're right, but you bring me some proof that there is something more going on here and we'll take it from there. Meanwhile, I'll do some nosing around. But I can't go investigating the sheriff's office without any evidence. Now, if you can get the murdered woman's next-of-kin to ask for an exhumation of the body, we can at least find out what happened at the coroner's office, and if I let the media know there is an investigation into her cause of death and that she was a Tech student, we might scare some folks out of the woods."

Elias got up to leave. "Thanks, Bobby," he said. "I'll get back to you."

"What about those prowlers?" he asked, as Elias started out the door. "What if you're right and they come back looking for the girl?"

"I've got a gun," he said. "Two, actually."

"Just make sure you shoot the perps inside the house, not out," Sigmon said.

Chapter 11

Four days later a bombshell, this time on the front page of *The Roanoke Times*. Elias read the headlines as he trudged back uphill Saturday morning through falling snow after retrieving the paper at the road. Another dead girl, another Tech student. Her body had been hidden in the hollow trunk of a tree, where some local bear hunters found it, in the Jefferson National Forest just north of Blacksburg. They had been interviewed by the media. They said the coed had been "butchered," folded up like a pocket knife into a two foot space. And they said she had words written in blood on her: "psycho whore." The paper spelled it "w ----," and said it rhymed with "ore." That stopped Elias in mid paragraph. He finished the article back at the house reading it aloud to Anna. When he put the paper down and looked over at her—she was sitting cross legged on the floor drinking coffee next to the lab—no reaction. There were also statements from the sheriff's office—clearly a different one than had handled Sylvie's case—to the effect that there was nothing to connect this crime to any others at the moment, the investigation had just begun, that they were not releasing any information about the woman, including her name, except that she went to Tech.

"What do you think is going on?" Elias asked her, increasingly suspicious that she wasn't telling him everything.

"I have no idea," she said between sips. "But it sure as hell sounds like the same guy."

"This is really weird," he said, staring at the taped off crime scene in the forest. "Who knows what happened to Sylvie; who knows the message on her abdomen?" He ticked them off on his fingers. "The people who killed her, the sheriff's office and the coroner's office, the funeral home people in Grundy? That's it, isn't it? Why would they murder someone else the same way when they took so much

97

trouble to keep Sylvie's murder a secret? ... I don't get it. And who is this latest victim? Is she in Mountain Justice? Is this another coal company murder? Or another drug murder?

"They're fucked up crazy," she answered. "Who knows their motives? All we need to know is that they're killing people, and at the bottom of it it's all about money, the root of all evil."

"Cupidity," Elias said, without looking up from the front page.

"What?"

"Never mind," he said. He folded up the paper and watched her. "It looks to me like they want us to believe this is a sex crime, unless of course Sylvie's murder was a sex crime, and this is a serial killer with nothing to do with the coal companies." She looked askance at him. "But ...," he added, holding up a hand, "but, if both murders *are* part of a conspiracy, then they're trying to make it look like there is a serial sex murderer, as part of the coverup. And maybe the police are linking them to the other Tech murders. ... That's what I think, for now."

"The police," she reminded him, getting up off the floor, "don't even know about Sylvie, except for the scumbag sheriff's office that got paid off. The Blacksburg police, the Virginia Tech police, are out of the loop. Assuming they're not on the coal company payroll too, then they think *this* is the first mutilation murder. Sylvie is still unrelated, drug-related, just like my arrest for making meth. It's all bullshit. The only way to get the truth is to find it yourself. Old school." She looked pretty angry and upset; she had stood up and started pacing as she spoke. Elias thought maybe she was getting manic again. Maybe he shouldn't be reading the paper to her.

"Look, Anna," he said, "there's really nothing we can do about it now, unless we go to the police ourselves and tell them about Sylvie and what we think happened to her. But

Sigmon is looking into that, and he's going to make the connection between her and this girl they found in the tree. So it's probably best for us to just wait and see what happens."

"You can wait to see what happens. I've got a dead cousin and a dead dog that need some revenge." She was talking and walking around while holding her coffee mug, spilling some as she made a point. "You can be removed and objective all you want; it's not happening to your family. And you don't know half the shit that's behind all this. You've got to be from Buchanan or someplace like it to understand."

"You're absolutely right," he said. "I'm just along for the ride. But meanwhile, it's Saturday, it's snowing, and we can't do anything about it."

"I need to get out," she said suddenly.

Elias wasn't sure what she meant. "I need to get out too," he said. "Why don't we take in a meeting?"

She stopped pulling on a sweater in mid movement, with just her head through the top, and looked at him suspiciously. "What—you've been to one meeting and already you're some kind of authority on what I need?" she asked, sarcastically. Then she pulled on his coat. "I need the meetings. You don't." And she went out the door into the snow with the dogs.

Elias continued reading the news. After ten minutes he put the paper down, got another coat out of the closet, and walked out into the new snow. There were only a couple of inches on the ground but it was still falling. The sky was not as gray as earlier; it didn't look like they would get much. In fact, there were already sizable rifts in the clouds where deep blue was visible like eyes in an ashen face. Anna was sitting in an old Adirondack chair in the yard smoking a cigarette watching the cardinals pulling sunflower seeds from the feeder hanging in a pine, the only red in a world of green and white. Above her, Buffalo Mountain was

99

obscured in the snow, just an impression of a dark mass humped in the sky. Elias surveyed the scene: the field, covered in leaves and briers and dead grass, was still mostly brown, but the snow settling into the paths the deer made through the meadow and apple trees created a Google Earth map of his property, seen from his elevated position, a kind of palimpsest of animal roads through the landscape. His eyes followed one line of snow through the couple of hundred feet of field from the surrounding woods right up to his house. Hard to believe, he thought, that the deer come so close. You would think the dogs would scare them away. Musing on this sight, but not considering the implications too seriously, he wandered over toward where the path came up to the house. "What the hell," he thought, or perhaps even said aloud. The snow revealed an otherwise undetectable wear in the grass that followed along the edge of the eastern half of the house, with wider spaces at the windows, especially looking onto the livingroom and the downstairs bathroom. The evidence was clear.

He walked back around to the front and called Anna.

"Now what?" she asked.

"Look," he said, pointing at the snow trail. "There's a direct line from the woods to these windows. Somebody's been spying on us. I can't say how long, but I would guess at least a week to leave this track."

She walked around the house with him, stopped at the bathroom window, and looked in for a while. "He could have watched me take a shower," she said, matter of factly. But Elias heard the sharp anger just under the surface.

"It's hard for me to believe the dogs didn't bark. Maybe we had music on. Or maybe the water running blocked the noise."

"Maybe they're just stealthy devils," she said. "Mountain men, used to sneaking around in the dark at night."

"More than likely," he said.

100

A gust of wind blew some snow off the trees and momentarily obscured their vision. Then he could hear in the western distance a sound he recognized immediately. Like the coming wind on the edge of weather. But it wasn't the wind, it was a plane flying fast and low, diving down through the cloud-rent. One of a pair of Navy and Air Force jets that flew over the area almost every day. Unusual with the snow, but they would be ahead of the front in a few minutes. Those guys could fly anywhere. As they cruised over the house, one at a time, the twin Pratt and Whitney engines created a roar that felt like it could lift the roof off the cabin, or suck them up into its vortex like a surfer locked into a wave. They made a noise like ripping cloth, as if the fabric of time itself had torn.

It was impossible to talk during a flyover, much less think.

"Jesus," Anna said, her hand visoring her eyes, as the first plane disappeared beyond Buffalo. "I know I'm still coming down from a mania, but it looked to me like that jet waved at us just then as it flew over."

"Waved at us?"

"Well, you know, with its wing."

"They fly over here every day," he replied. "They use the mountains for training."

"But can he …"

Then the second one drowned them out.

"They're F-18's, Navy jets from the Strike Fighter Squadron in Virginia Beach," he continued, when the noise diminished. "I used to live right down the street from the runway. You can tell because of the V-shaped tail. Most of the ones we see are F-15's from Seymour Johnson in North Carolina. They've got the perpendicular tails. They've been flying this VFR for years, especially since 9/11. They're getting their mountain training for Afghanistan."

"VFR?"

"Visual Flight Routes. They're training for low level mountain flying."

"Aren't they really low?"

"Yeah. They're not supposed to go under 500 feet."

"How do you know so much about these planes? Weren't you in the Navy?"

"A long time ago. When I was your age." There was a pause in thought and mood, paralleled in nature, as the jet noise slowly vanished over the mountains.

"What about the spying?"

"The spying? Yeah, well, strictly speaking, it's not spying if we know they're there. Anyway, I say we forget about it and drive to Roanoke and take in a movie. It'll do us good to get away from this situation for a few hours. Get some perspective, then come back and figure out what we're going to do next."

She looked at him sideways like she always did when she was trying to ascertain his motives. "You mean escape from reality for a few hours," she said.

"It's okay to escape from reality," he countered. "You said so yourself. It's just a construct. What's not okay is to escape from what's real. Even if we could."

"Sometime you're going to have to explain the difference to me. I still don't get Lacan. But as for those bastards who peeped me through the window, they're going to pay," she said, and they walked in from the cold, the dogs shaking snow all over the stone threshold.

That night they couldn't decide on which movie to see at the Grandin, Anna arguing for the documentary *Inside Job* about the bank bailout and Elias opting for the Valerie Plame flick, *Fair Game*. So they compromised and saw *Love & Other Drugs* instead. As it turned out, the romantic comedy hit closer to home for both of them than they expected. The young woman in the film, dark like Anna, was fighting early onset Parkinsons, and the Viagra salesman she loved had to choose between taking care of her for the rest of her life or going on his own way once he found out how sick she was. After the movie they sat in a booth in a little bar around the corner crowded with late night locals brought together by the early snowfall.

"If she wasn't so beautiful," Anna said, "he wouldn't have had to think about it. He would have been long gone. Not to mention she wouldn't have been such a psycho bitch."

Elias ignored the second part. "But if she wasn't so beautiful they would have never been attracted to each other in the first place. Their physical beauty was equal. He had to decide based on something else. His love for her was not just physical."

"Of course," she said. "But still, most of these decisions are based on looks. They're not as altruistic as Hollywood makes them seem." She blew a smoke ring. "If you weren't attracted to me, you wouldn't be here right now. Admit it." Everyone in the bar was smoking like crazy, apparently oblivious of the signs, or maybe it was a snow-caused anarchism.

"Of course. It's a natural law, probably beyond our conscious control." Then he added, changing the subject, "You know, you look like Anne Hathaway."

She raised one eyebrow in disbelief, only confirming the resemblance.

"Yeah," she responded. And you look like Jake Gyllenhal."

Elias had to laugh. "No, seriously," he said. "I mean it; you've got the same dark features. And the tough exterior, just like she had in the movie. And you don't want to lose your independence." They had drunk one Dos Equis and now were sipping on another to chase a Bushmills. He was watching her long fingers trace some patterns in the water on the tabletop.

"It's not just an exterior," she said. "Not a front, an inky cloak; it's the real thing, even by your definition. It goes

103

down to the bones." She paused. "Look, what good does it get you being soft? And why would anyone want to give up their independence? That's all we've got going for us, when it comes right down to it. Life is nothing but subjective experience. Windowless monads. Give that up and you might as well be dead, or good as dead—brainwashed."

He looked at her somewhat astonished, as usual. "Jesus, Anna, where did that allusion come from?" he asked.

"Comes with the territory."

"What territory is that?"

"Coal country," she replied, almost too softly to be heard in the noisy bar.

"You learned Leibniz in coal country?"

She laughed so hard she choked on her beer and started coughing.

"Philosophy 101, stupid. I actually read the books."

"What the hell happened to you that you became a pessimist at such a young age? What are you, anyway? Twenty-six, twenty-seven?" he asked.

"Twenty-five."

"Okay, so in twenty-five years you mean to say you've never been in love like these two guys in the movie, never once transcended your windowless ego and taken a leap of faith into another person? Trusted somebody enough to let your guard down for a while? I find that hard to believe. You seem like a really caring person to me." He was sincere, although he was never sure he sounded that way.

There was a moment of silence in which the rest of the bar seemed to have disappeared or receded into the distance. "I loved my cousin," she said. "And look where that ended."

Elias suddenly realized he was going down a dead end street. This girl in front of him was no ordinary human being. And she wasn't his student anymore either. It was getting so that every time she opened her mouth or looked him in the eye he took another step toward the brink of something. Commitment? Or a train wreck? He was in the same situation she was.

He changed tack. "What year were you born?"

"Nineteen eighty-five."

"Jesus Christ. I was already out of college and in the Navy. You're half my age," he said, lighting a cigarette. "I'm robbing the cradle. Doesn't that bother you? Not to say that there's anything going on. But just hanging out with me, staying at my house? It's hard for me to fathom why you would want to do that when you could be with your own friends."

"If you want me to move out, just say the word," she said, "and I'm gone."

"That's not what I'm saying, and you know it. In fact, it's just the opposite. I like having you around. It's good for me. I'm just pointing out that this is not a typical romantic comedy, even if you do look like Anne Hathaway." He paused. "By the way, wasn't that Shakespeare's wife's name?"

"I don't know," she said, "but it was kind of strange to see the two of them together again like in *Brokeback Mountain*."

"That's another good example," he argued, exhaling smoke, "of what I'm trying to describe. Two gay cowboys—think what it took them to admit how they felt about each other. They had to risk everything to be together, even for just a week every year or two. They kept up an appearance of heterosexual normalcy just so they could be together in the mountains where they wouldn't get hunted down. Brokeback Mountain was utopia for them."

"There's no such thing. And look what happened to them," she observed drily. "One gets killed by some homophobes and the other ends up living by himself in a trailer."

"But," Elias said, stubbing out his cigarette, "but, there is some hope at the end. The Heath Ledger character agrees to go to his daughter's wedding. He agrees to get involved in her life."

"Yeah," Anna said. "And Heath Ledger is dead too."

How was he supposed to respond to that? "Can you imagine," he said, half-jokingly, "if those guys had been miners instead of cowboys? What would have happened to them in Buchanan County?"

"They would have been buried under the overburden on some MTR site and never seen or heard from again," she answered through a thin veil of smoke.

"Mountaintop removal is, literally, a brokeback mountain," Elias observed.

"Five hundred and counting," Anna said.

They downed the last of their whiskeys and got up to go. It was after 1 a.m. and the streets were deserted. The snow had apparently ended, for the moment, but it was windy and cold, and they put their arms around each other as they walked to the car. She stopped to look in the window of the Roanoke Ballet Theater and he remembered her analogy when they were shooting.

"Did you take dance classes?" he asked.

"You'd be surprised," she said.

"In Grundy?"

"I told you you'd be surprised."

"How about your parents? I've known you for a month now and you never mention your parents. Are they still alive?"

"My dad is. My mom died when I was a kid."

"What does he do for a living? I know you said something about him when we were driving over to War. Does he work in the coal industry?"

"You could say that," she said.

They were at the car, and when they got in she immediately turned on the radio. They drove up Bent Mountain and down 221 South toward Floyd, listening to a late-night bluegrass show out of Blacksburg. Then, for no apparent reason, Elias decided to get on the Parkway. The speed limit was only 45 but there was no traffic anywhere and he could go as fast as he wanted as long as he didn't hit any deer. The two lane mountain road curved through cattle and Christmas tree farms higher and higher and then dove into woods so dark and deep you forgot you were only twenty miles from the city. This section hadn't been ploughed yet, and hadn't had enough traffic to keep it clear, but in 4-wheel drive it was no problem. A pleasure really. At this height snow had started falling again off and on. A national treasure, the Parkway, almost to his front door.

There was no moon but the new snow in the Jeep's headlights threw the fences, firs and oaks into three dimensions as they cruised by. They had already slowed down several times for a raccoon and a small herd of deer when Elias noticed a vehicle some distance behind them. It was too late for most county people to be out, and too early for the newspaper. Then, a few minutes later, in a short straightaway in the woods, he saw the flashing blue light and swore, immediately thinking of the broken window, still unfixed weeks later.

"What is it?" Anna asked, and turned to look back.

"Cop car," Elias said. He started to slow down. "Or probably a ranger."

"Don't stop," she urged him, putting her hand on his arm. "I've got a bad feeling. You don't know who it could be."

He continued to slow. "It's the police, Anna," he said. "I've got to stop." And he pulled over onto the grass at the edge of the road and left the car running. He cut the overhead light on and began looking through the glove box

107

for his registration, while she continued to stare intently out the back window.

"I don't think it's a sheriff's car," she said, very apprehensive. "Looks like the light is on the dash. Please, it's not far to your place; let's just keep going," and she attempted to put the car back into Drive.

"What, are you crazy?" he said, and stopped her. "It's probably my broken window, or a taillight, or who the hell knows what." And then he thought, he had to get out of the car because the officer wouldn't be able to see him through the cardboard of the window. They didn't like you to get out normally, but he had no choice. So he unfastened his seat belt, opened the door, and stood up in the road.

Immediately he realized Anna had been right and stopping was a mistake. In the headlights of the other vehicle he was momentarily almost blinded, but he could distinctly see two men on the snow-covered road walking toward him with shotguns about a hundred feet back. And they weren't in uniform. Without pausing to think he jumped back into the Jeep, threw the transmission into Drive, and slammed his foot on the gas pedal. The radials gripped the snow pretty hard and they dove back onto the pavement, fishtailing just a little as he straightened out.

They heard a boom behind them and then nothing. She looked back.

"What's happening?" he asked, cooly. He had reverted back immediately to his military training, as if the past twelve years had never happened.

"They're coming," she answered, just as cooly.

He was already going twice as fast as he normally would on this road in the snow, maybe sixty. "Is your seatbelt on?" he said as he fastened his. He could see the headlights behind him, maybe a couple hundred yards; they didn't seem to be catching up.

"It's on," she said.

Elias figured it was about six or seven miles to his turnoff, and then another three to his house. If they could get there ahead of the vehicle they could get to the guns, or maybe the other car would even stop by then. His brain was computing every conceivable means of escape and communication, but he knew there were few houses between here and his, they were far off the road, and people were wary of opening the door to strangers.

"Reach in my pocket and get the cell. See if it works," he said.

It didn't. Out of range or interference from the snow. Meanwhile, he was going too fast, just on the edge of control, but if they caught up with him and managed to shoot through the window or hit the tires it could be disastrous. He was losing some traction on the curves but not enough to skid out, and going as fast as he could on the straight stretches. At some point he became aware that the radio was still on; some fast-picking banjo player seemed to be doing the soundtrack for their car chase, he thought, not surprised that he could make such an observation in the middle of a crisis. He was flashing back to some similar episodes in his life, but he brushed them aside and focused. He did not actually think they were in a potentially fatal encounter; some part of him watched what was going on as if it were a movie in which he knew more than the people chasing him.

They almost overshot his turnoff onto Buffalo Mountain Road. He had to swerve hard and drifted across the snow a few yards. When he straightened out and looked in the mirror he could see that the car behind them had definitely gotten closer. They must be professionals, he thought, or desperate. It was a race now for the finish line; every time Elias came out of a curve he looked back and saw the lights behind him in the middle of the curve. The road was rougher now, and more twisted, but he knew it well. He was up to sixty in between the turns, in a wooded area, the tree trunks flying by, a mile or so from home, when suddenly Anna yelled, "Look out!"

He saw the buck almost the same moment she did, up ahead on the right half of the road. In a kind of freeze frame of almost supernatural clarity he could see its uplifted head, white throat, and antlers. He had only a second to consider if it was going to stay put or move when he nudged the wheel to the left and went around it with only a couple of feet to spare. But even without jerking it, the suddenness of the maneuver at that speed threw the Jeep into a violent fishtail. He gripped the wheel hard and tried to maintain control. They seemed to go up on two tires and it looked like they were going to flip, but they came back on all four only to leave the road on the right side in another fifty yards and dive down an embankment between the trees toward a small stream. A heavy jolt or two bounced them hard up the backbone and the car came to an abrupt stop. Just as they had a sense that they were okay they heard a thud in the distance, an organic sound, and then maybe three seconds later a deafening crash, metal against trees. Once the noise subsided, for another few seconds it was as quiet and peaceful as if they were Adam and Eve in the primeval forest. Then the radio seemed to recover from the shock, and the bluegrass started up again.

"Are you all right?" he asked her, putting his hands on either side of her head. She looked okay.

"You have a cut on your nose," she said. He looked in the mirror; it was nothing. He must have hit the steering wheel. His bag hadn't deployed.

"We've got to get out," he said. "Can you open your door?"

Both doors worked; it seemed the Jeep had not hit anything unmovable, just a few small saplings and underbrush. They stood up in the snow, then started to climb the embankment, pulling themselves up several feet by holding on to brush with their gloved hands, and just as their

110

heads cleared the level of the road they could see the other vehicle on the far side and back a ways partly smashed in between some trees, and the buck flattened against the hood and windshield. The headlights were still on, and there was a light on in the car as well. It looked like the deer's antlered head had gone straight through the windshield and gotten wedged into the driver's side, and they could see the remains of a human face behind the antlers.

Then the passenger's side door opened and a large bearded man stepped out with a gun.

Elias grabbed Anna by the arm and they jumped back down into the trees, sliding and lunging through the briars and limbs to the stream and without stopping clambering across the rocks of a shallow spot ten feet across and up the bank on the other side. They had their boots on and they could get some traction but the snow made everything slicker and it didn't feel like they were moving very fast. There was a small ridge on the other side and they started up it as quickly as they could when they heard a loud boom behind them from the shotgun and this time the crack and splintering of a tree trunk ten feet ahead. Elias looked back but couldn't see anyone; it was darker now that they were well into the woods, mostly pines which gave some cover, but the snow made everything brighter, and, he realized with a shock, meant that they could be followed by their tracks if the guy knew what he was doing. They kept climbing without stopping or talking, just the sounds of their heavy breathing, to the top where they suddenly found themselves on the edge of a Christmas tree farm. Hundreds of symmetrical dark green pyramids of varying sizes placed at regular intervals like chess pieces on the snow. Now they could hear some crashing below them and they started running on mostly level ground across the clearing to another treeline on the far side. The Christmas trees were six to eight feet tall, enough to hide them momentarily but not for long, they knew. They were moving through the

111

maze of firs and pines when Elias saw a small shed ahead and stopped suddenly.

"What are you stopping for?" Anna yelled at him.

"I know where we are," he said. "My house is just over the next ridge." He was looking for an opening in the woods ahead while she looked behind them. Then Elias spotted a man, a different man, coming out of the trees much farther off but ahead of them, with a rifle.

"Fuck!" he cursed under his breath and ducked down, pulling her. "There's another one."

"Another what?"

"Another guy with a gun," he whispered. "Come on, this way. We've got to get back into the woods." He grabbed her hand and they started crossing the tree farm in a different direction. "I know where we can hide," he said as they ran, crouched over.

"I don't want to hide," she said, panting. "I don't want to be hunted down and killed like an animal. Let's stand and fight these sons of bitches." She had pulled out her pocketknife and held it, unopened, in her now bare hand.

But they kept moving and in a half minute they were back in the trees again, headed in a right angle to the direction of his house. They got up a little higher, and stopped to look behind. One of the men apparently had spotted them and shouted to another on the other side. They could see him just below them in the clearing, not far away. He had a full black beard and was dressed in camouflage. The guy in the car.

They kept climbing. Now they were at the top of another ridge, in a slight depression. There were some exposed boulders in a kind of hollow filled with pines and oaks, and Elias guided them to some rusted and broken tanks almost invisible between the rocks.

It was an old moonshine still. Three or four large vats split and half buried in the snow and earth.

"They'll see us," she said. "We can't hide here. They'll come right up to us and shoot us. Let's get out of here."

"I know," he said. "But they're in front of us and behind us. We can't outrun them, they'll shoot us, but we can take them by surprise from here. You're going to have to trust me on this. I know what I'm doing. We just need to even up the odds, maybe get one of their guns." And he looked around and picked up a couple of wrist-size branches on the ground, swung them against a rock. One broke, he threw it away; the other didn't. Then they walked over to one of the barrels lying on its side, stopped, and Elias stepped into the barrel as far as he could, then backed out and climbed over the top, lifting his body off the metal to leave no visible sign. Following his lead, Anna swung her legs over the vat to avoid the snow, and stepped on some rocks on the other side. Then they crouched down behind a twin oak, leaving no imprint behind them. To someone else, it looked like their tracks stopped, then went into the barrel. She had her three inch blade out; he had a four foot oak branch in his hand. "Let me make the first move, but if we wind up on the ground, go for his neck," he whispered, "or cut the tendon above his heel. Otherwise, any fleshy spot will do."

Their pursuer was right behind them; they could hear him coming up through the trees, breathing heavily, coughing. The wind was starting to kick up on top of the ridge, and the last of the waning moon suddenly broke free from the scuttling clouds to throw the world into a dance of light and shadow.

There was a strange smell in the air; Elias couldn't place it. It smelled like ..., like dirt. A musky dirt odor, strong and sharp, underneath the clean snow smell.

Then the bearded man appeared, just fifty feet away, a shotgun cradled in his hands. His clothes, his hat, were covered with snow where he had fallen. He looked almost

113

comic, but his face was dark and scowling. He hardly stopped to look around the top of the ridge, but came forward, following their tracks in the snow, across the hollow. Then he saw the still and stopped. He raised his gun, and Elias steeled himself for whatever was going to happen. He tried to stay calm, watched his breathing, and he thought he could hear Anna's heart beating next to him through his jacket. He had his heavy stick in both hands now, the right just ahead of the left; Anna's knuckles were white around the knife handle. The bearded man slowly walked up to the large vat, tried to peer into it, but it was dark and mostly blocked with wind-drifted snow. Then he seemed to smile, they could see teeth, and he tapped the barrel of his shotgun sharply against the metal tank. The clanging was so much louder than anything else up there on the ridge that it must have carried a quarter mile in the wind. He reached into the front pocket of his camouflage jacket and pulled out a phone, flipped it open with one hand, and started to speak to someone, while he kicked the rusted tank with one foot trying to knock the snow away.

This was the moment Elias had been waiting for—to take him by surprise. It sounded like the guy said, "I got them hiding in some old still …. Can you hear me?" Then he started to look in again while he was talking, when it happened.

Something huge and black rushed out of the open end of the vat, hitting the bearded man square in his chest and knocking him flat on his back. It was growling and he was screaming and the gun was lost and the animal, the bear, was mauling his face. It took a moment for Elias to realize what was going on—there was so much noise and confusion with the snow flying, but the man was down and the gun was on the ground. The black bear must have been four hundred enraged pounds, relentless in attacking the intruder of its sleep den. The man struggled to get out from under it but he was helpless, as if he were a swimmer drowning in fur

114

and trying to get to the surface. They could see his face covered in blood, screaming, his clothes and flesh ripped open, just twenty feet away, for the better part of a minute.

Then the screaming stopped. The bear dropped the lifeless body from its jaws, prodded it, and listened. And in the wind-swept silence it rose up on its hind legs, snorted in the air, and turned around to face the tree they were crouched behind. The snow glistened in its fur as it growled again, horribly wild and loud, showing its yellow teeth. And the smell Elias had noticed before came back to hit him full in the face: the stench of acorn-fattened, earth-covered bear rising up like it was the embodiment of the wild. He thought about climbing into the oak but the lowest branches were too high up. There was really nothing to do but run, and he was about to grab Anna's hand when she suddenly stood up, broke her tree cover, and stepped out in full view of the animal. There was an instant of what could only be called recognition, when Anna and the bear looked directly at each other, then she yelled like a mad woman right at the beast. It sounded to Elias like "You-kay-yay!" Like some kind of cowboy exclamation or deranged Confederate scream. And she kept screaming it, first at the top of her lungs, two or three times, like she wanted to get its attention, and then, slowly, lower in volume.

Elias was amazed—at her, and that the bear just stood there, snorting, growling, blood and saliva still dripping from its mouth, the lifeless mangled man at her feet. He thought Anna was somehow trying to scare the animal, startling it with her screaming. The five foot four girl and the seven foot man-slaughterer. Anna kept repeating it, only now it was not a warning, not a verbal attack or threat, but something softer, more like a command, or even softer than that, like an appeal, or an acknowledgement.

Like a bear in a circus, the animal sat down on its haunches and stopped growling.

If she had walked over and patted the bear on the head, Elias could not have been more surprised. She turned to him. Her eyes were blazing like black suns. Her face was flushed and her hair was blowing in the breeze. She looked like some supernatural being, or goddess, there on the mountaintop, in the snow beneath the oaks. "Come on," she said. "It's okay. She won't bother us."

He was dumbfounded, but there was no time for thought; there was still another hunter out there, so they started down the backside of the ridge, hand in hand, glancing behind periodically to see if anything was following them. Elias knew exactly where he was—it was no more than a few hundred yards now to his house. Maybe the other guy had given up when he heard the screaming. Maybe the bear would get him too. Down they went, into the deep meadow that bordered his property.

Twenty minutes later they were inside the house. No sign of the other man, or men. Elias immediately went upstairs and retrieved the guns from under the futon. He also unlocked a hidden closet behind the fireplace where he stored other weapons, just in case. The dogs were wild to get out; they must have heard the gunshots, sensed the danger. He thought about leaving, then remembered they had no car.

He called 911 on his land line and told the emergency operator there had been a car wreck, injuries, and a bear attack. He didn't say anything about the chase and attempted murder; something told him not to go into that on the phone, not yet anyway. He just gave her his address.

It took about a half hour before they heard the first sirens in the distance. They were coming from the opposite direction from the wreck, then up his driveway and to the house. A middle-aged Patrick County sheriff's deputy, closely followed by a young Floyd County one. He met the officers, gave them directions to the wreck, told them the

116

general location of the dead man, then decided to go with them. Anna wanted to come too so they both got into the back of the Floyd deputy's car. At the road they stopped for an ambulance just turning into his driveway; it backed up, and all three vehicles took off down Route 787 heading east. It was about a mile back to the cars, around a couple of curves. Elias explained on the way that they had been driving home from Roanoke and there was a car behind them, and that they had just barely avoided a deer in the road, and the second car had run into a tree.

A minute later they rounded the last turn and drove up on the wreck. The Jeep was almost out of sight off the left side of the road, the lights still on.

They got out of the police cruiser. The lights from the two sedans and the ambulance lit up the forest like a disco. There was even music. Elias thought he must be punch drunk from exhaustion and the chase, but then he remembered the radio in the Jeep was still playing. Early morning bluegrass. Ralph Stanley. He reached in and cut it and the lights off.

When they looked farther down the road on the other side, there was no wrecked car.

"What the hell," Elias said to himself, but Anna heard and understood.

"You said there was another vehicle?" the Patrick County officer asked, as they trotted the fifty yards down the road from the Jeep.

"It was right here," Elias said, stopped and pointed. "See, here are the tire tracks, going right off the road." Then he moved down into the trees and a moment later found the dead buck. "Here's the deer they hit," he yelled back, and the deputy followed him into the snow-heavy brush to take a look.

"Apparently, they were able to get out and drive away," he said, looking at the ruts in the snow. "The 911 call mentioned injuries," he said, looking at Elias. "Do you think

117

you might have been mistaken, or were there other people in the car who might have gone to the hospital?"

"There were definitely other people," he said, and told the officer about the man with the gun. At this point the EMT crew and the other officer were standing around watching and following the conversation. As Elias started telling his story he realized it probably sounded pretty strange even to these first responders, used to emergencies and unbelievable domestic disputes. He stopped himself with their flight up the hill.

Then the Floyd County deputy started questioning him. "So you and your daughter were driving home with this car right behind you. You almost hit the buck and go off the road. The other vehicle hits the buck and goes off the road. Then you see a man with a gun get out of the car and immediately start running? Is that correct?"

"She's not my daughter," Elias said. "Just a friend. And the man looked menacing, with the gun in his hand. We assumed he was dangerous, and we were right. He took a shot at us. Then he followed us through the woods, and a bear killed him up on the mountaintop."

The deputy conferred with the older officer. At that point a state police cruiser showed up, another ambulance, and another sheriff's car. There was a group of about a dozen men in uniform talking with each other, pointing, talking on their radios, for maybe ten minutes while others took his and Anna's drivers licenses and asked them a few mundane questions.

One of the deputies came back from his cruiser and asked Anna to sit in the back of his sedan, where he asked her questions about her arrest. They wanted to know if he and Anna had been drinking or using drugs. They took a breathalyzer sample and asked permission for blood. Of course they had been drinking but Elias was pretty sure he wasn't over the limit. He looked at Anna. She said, "Sure, what the hell. Go right ahead. Cut my wrists while you're at it." And held out her arm to the EMT. Then they questioned them about what they had been doing that night, did they get into any altercations, did they owe anyone money, and so on.

Finally the older sheriff asked Elias if he could take them into the woods to where he said the bear attack occurred. They made Anna stay in the car; she didn't like it, but she had started talking to one of the techs whom she apparently knew.

"Better bring a stretcher," Elias said.

Two of the officers pulled out their heavy flashlights and along with two of the medical people followed Elias into the trees, across the stream and up the ridge where they had been pursued an hour before. It was now about four in the morning. The wind was steady, getting stronger by the minute, as a front passed over. The tree limbs were shaking all their snow onto their heads, the evergreens were blowing around, and a few stars were sharply etched in the occasional break in the clouds overhead. Elias was having a hard time finding some of their tracks as they wound their way up the slope, the snow was filling them in so fast. He stopped to look for the bearded man's footsteps, but he didn't find any separate ones, so he just kept going.

Along the way the policemen kept asking him questions. What was his relationship to Anna? Where was he employed? Did he know she was a felon? Had he ever seen her in the company of the men in the wrecked car? Why was she carrying a knife? Apparently they had searched her before they left the road. The Floyd County man was asking most of the questions; he looked to be maybe twenty-five, head shaved, with full lips and large ears. The sheriff from Patrick was mostly listening. He was roughly Elias' age, had a full head of grey hair under his cap, cold, grey eyes. Looked vaguely like Kris Kristopherson.

They made it to the tree farm, crossed to the other side. Up here in the open the tracks were even more covered; in another half hour they would be totally obliterated. They entered the treeline, climbed to the humped peak, and there in the opening, like a sacrificial offering, the twisted limbs of their would-be murderer already half covered with snow and gore. The bear was nowhere to be seen.

"Jesus H. Christ," one of the techs said, when he took a close look at the man's face. "Almost chewed completely off. Look, Donny, his eyes have been ripped right out of the sockets."

Almost immediately the sheriff got on his cell phone but he couldn't get anything in the snow, while the deputy went through the dead man's pockets. They were empty of any identification. Then he picked up the Remington pump shotgun, carefully ejected a couple of shells, checked the barrel, and smelled it.

The others stared at him, and he announced, "Looks like he didn't get a shot off." He looked at Elias. "Didn't you say he took a shot at you?"

"He did. Hit a tree back near the road."

"Uh huh."

Elias was getting more and more suspicious, more and more cautious. "What do you think?" he asked the older sheriff.

He looked back at Elias but seemed to be addressing the other men. "I speculate something happened back down there at the highway," he said, "or before. I don't know what. I don't know if this person knew you or you knew him. Right now I've got a whole lot of questions and very few answers. I do have a few facts. You did wreck your SUV. That's a fact. There is a dead buck down there and it looks like another vehicle was involved in that. I do have some tracks up here; I'm not exactly sure whose though. And the main fact, a curious fact, a dead body with no ID on it. 'Hit does look like he was killed by a bar, but I'll let the coroner decide that. And I've got a gun." He held it out

120

before Elias. "This is not your gun by any chance, is it?" he asked.

"No, it's not my gun." Then, as they appeared to be waiting for him to say more, and Elias was watching the first deputy trying to get his cell to connect, he suddenly remembered that the bearded man had had a phone in his hand when the bear hit him. Where was it? Someone must have taken the gun, or someone else had shot at them back at the road. Did this guy not carry any identification, or had someone already emptied his pockets, and maybe switched guns? But did he get the cell phone? "I don't own a shotgun," he repeated.

"And you say you watched this person get attacked by the bar? Why didn't the bar attack you as well?"

"Anna shouted at it and it left us alone."

"She shouted at it? She shouted something to the bar, who had just chewed this fellow to death, and h'it left you alone?" He pulled a notepad out of his pocket and checked it. "That would be Miss Jassey, the person released on bail for production and distribution of methamphetamine?"

"That's right," Elias said. He didn't bother to puncture the policemen's mocking tone, thinking that maybe playing naïve might serve them well. Besides, he wasn't about to trust someone he didn't know.

There were a few more questions, and then they took out the body. They made an unusual cortege, Elias thought, as they crossed through the rows of Christmas trees. It was cold, very cold, maybe single digits, or at least it felt like it. The wind was gusting twenty or thirty knots now; it blew so much snow around they experienced a whiteout at times. Everything disappeared for five or ten seconds, then there they were again: sheriffs, medics, a dead man without a face, and a college professor, trudging single file between the Christmas trees like the participants in some esoteric,

121

druidical pageant, three weeks early. Then they disappeared again.

Back at the road Anna was talking to another deputy who looked about her age. "Am I under arrest?" Elias could hear her asking. "If not, then my boyfriend's back and we're going home." Elias would have been embarrassed but he knew she was just antagonizing them; it seemed to be her way. Some kind of payback, he figured, but for what he hadn't a clue.

A tow truck arrived and yanked his Jeep from the gulley. The ambulance took off with the corpse, and one by one the sheriffs' cruisers left the scene. He paid the driver with his credit card, and then they were alone on the road. It must have been 6 a.m.; in another hour the sun would be coming up.

"Let's get that buck," she said, and started off down the road.

It took him a moment to realize what she meant. "What?" he said, following her. "What are you going to do with him?"

"Well, one thing I'm going to do," she said, pushing through the dead brush, "is thank him. He probably saved our lives." Elias followed her off the road. There was a thin creek on this side too, maybe just a seasonal trickle. It was iced over, but he thought he could hear the water still running under the ice.

She had found him and was cradling his head. It was remarkably intact, considering what it had been through. Even most of his antlers were miraculously saved —eight points, and wide spread—but two were broken off and glittered with shards of windshield glass. His eyes were open. It almost looked like he was watching her as she seemed to whisper something in his ear. Then she closed his eyes and said, "Give me a hand," and they hoisted him into the air by either end. He was heavy; they had a time getting him up to the road.

"We'll put him in the back of the Jeep," she said. "I know a local family who can use the venison. It's cold and ain't been too long. But I want his antlers for myself. Especially this one right here," and she pointed to the highest one which was stained dark red.

On the way back to the house she said, "So you didn't tell them about the coal companies trying to kill us. Does that mean you don't trust me, or the police?"

"You heard what they said; they think all this has something to do with drugs. Actually, you didn't hear everything they asked me up on the ridge. They had all kinds of questions, the tenor of which was that you were involved in some meth business and these people tonight were part of it. Two dead bodies and they still believe it's a drug war."

He didn't tell her he was thinking the same thing.

"Four dead bodies counting Sylvie and the Tech girl in the tree. But this driver tonight who got gored in the head, he's disappeared. No corpse, no death. I guess they didn't have enough time to get rid of the body on the mountain. Or maybe he was too messed up to carry."

"He was pretty messed up," Elias agreed. "Which reminds me, what the hell did you think you were doing back there screaming at that hibernating bear? And what was it you yelled at it? Sounded like something Bruce Willis might have yelled in *Diehard*. "Yippee Ki Yay" or something like that?"

She looked at him like he was nuts. "You need to get some sleep," she said. "I just wanted to scare it off, just like a bull in a field. Haven't you ever gotten caught crossing a pasture and run into a bull? You just yell at them. I don't know what the fuck I yelled. Whatever came into my head." She was quiet until they pulled into the driveway, as if she were remembering the scene. "And another thing. That bear wasn't hibernating. Bears don't hibernate around

123

here; it's not cold enough. They just sleep for a week or two."

"Hibernating or not, I'm glad that bear woke up when it did, and you knew what to say to it."

Back at the house Anna wanted some coffee but Elias declined and stretched out on the bed upstairs, on his back, fully dressed. In a minute he was out. But he woke up for a few seconds when the sun came up and, half asleep, realized she was stretched out next to him, writing in her journal. The TV was on. She smelled like woods. She had pulled the covers over him, and he turned into her womb-like heat and fell asleep again.

Chapter 12

Noon Sunday she woke him with pecan waffles and coffee. "Were you up all night?" he asked, getting out of bed and sitting in an armchair. His body was stiff from all the climbing, and he didn't understand how she could stay awake after all that.

"Yeah," she said. "It's nothing. I go two or three nights sometimes without sleeping."

"Must be useful when you have to study for a test. Or when you've got some bearded rednecks trying to kill you," he said grimly.

"The phone's been ringing off the hook," she said.

"I slept through the phone?" he asked, surprised.

"You've gotten a slew of messages. There's one from somebody named Sigmon. Says he wants to talk with you ASAP. He's in his office working."

"He's the county prosecutor I told you about, teaches at Tech. When did he call?"

"Maybe ten. Then the Floyd sheriff's office called and they want you, us, to make a statement. Really, to grill us some more. Also Channel 10 news called and tried to interview me over the phone but I told them to go fuck themselves."

"Real nice," Elias said.

He got on the phone after he ate.

"Damn, Elias," Bobby said, "what the hell is going on? You've got a dead man on your property, killed by a bear. You've been shot at? And now you're living with a woman accused of making meth. The media is going to have a field day with this. Anything else?

"Who said I was being shot at?"

"It's on TV."

"It's on TV? Jesus H.," then he stopped himself—the bearded, chewed-up face swam into his consciousness,

125

and the whole night before. He started to explain the details but then thought better of it. "I can't talk on the phone," he said. "How about if I come to your office? How long are you going to be there?"

"Can't talk on the phone? What, do you think someone has your phone tapped? You're not getting paranoid, are you?"

"I'll tell you when I come by," he said. "First I've got to give another statement to the people in Floyd."

"Okay, if that's what you want. I'll be here until two."

One thirty that afternoon Elias rapped on the half-open door in Durham Hall.

"Come in. Come in," Sigmon said, getting up from his desk and coming around to shake Elias' hand. A moment later he was rubbing it with his left.

"You don't have to squeeze the life out of it," Sigmon said, laughing. "Is that how you killed the bear?"

"Sorry," I've been out of it all day. ... It's from kendo," Elias said, taking a seat in the comfortable leather armchair and leaning back.

"Is that Japanese?"

"Yeah. I was stationed in Japan for three years. Picked it up there."

"Army?"

"No. Navy. And the bear isn't dead. Anna scared it away. But we're very lucky not to be."

"How'd she do that?"

"She yelled at it."

"Yelled at it?"

"Yeah."

"Maybe it has something to do with her pheromones. Anyway, tell me everything that happened. Including the parts you didn't tell the sheriff."

So Elias spent the next half an hour narrating again the events of the previous night, beginning with the flashing

126

police lights on the car behind them. Sigmon listened patiently, occasionally asking for clarification.

"Did the sheriff over in Floyd have anything else to tell you this afternoon?"

"Actually, he did say they had identified the dead man already from some tattoos. I had no idea they would be that efficient. But apparently he had a record and they searched the database for the tats."

"It's hard to escape the law with all the technology we have on hand today."

"Anyway, he wouldn't give me the name, but he said this guy had been arrested a number of times before for drugs, possession and distribution, assault, and some other stuff, spent time in prison, Red Onion, and was not somebody to get on his bad side. Also, he lived in McDowell County, West Virginia. You know where that is?"

"Sure," Sigmon said. "Coal country." Then he added, "Red Onion? He must be quite a piece of work. That's one of our supermax prisons, only for level six criminals. You know, terrorists and murderers."

"I hear they're building prisons over in Kentucky on reclaimed mountaintop removal land. The politicians claim it's good for the economy—creates jobs."

"You still think you're caught in the middle of some kind of coal company conspiracy, don't you?"

"Maybe," Elias said. "Some of the time. Although the police seem to be convinced that it's all drug related."

"It does make a lot more sense," Sigmon said. "Everything that has happened so far can be explained by the local methamphetamine trade, without any need to bring in any conspiracy theory. Good for the movies; bad for law enforcement. We know there is a network of meth labs in the region, and distribution. There are some very big boys involved, many from out of town. I've prosecuted quite a few of these cases myself. The young woman who was murdered, she was most likely involved in the drug trade somehow, maybe even unwittingly, and perhaps the murderers sent a message by marking her body. Although I still have a problem with that one. Anyway, maybe they raped her as well to send a message. Now we know the people who have been chasing you and the cousin, the people who killed her dog, and this ex-con who ran into the bear—they're mostly likely related, most likely all drug dealers and enforcers. Probably members of an outlaw motorcycle gang. We have a few here in the valley. And the cousin is a meth addict, you said as much yourself. Have you ever been around meth addicts? I have. They're some of the most paranoid people in the business. They believe people are out to get them. They think someone has bugged their house, or their car. Okay, maybe that's not so unrealistic, given that they're breaking the law. But get this; they believe in aliens. I'm not shitting you. I prosecuted more than one poor sonuvabitch who said, on the witness stand, that he had been abducted by aliens and their spaceships were lurking about his trailer. Right here in Montgomery County."

Sigmon stopped to laugh. "Then there's the fact that this woman is mentally ill, another reason not to believe her story. She probably has a history of paranoid delusions and conspiracy theories, I would guess, if you could talk to her psychiatrist." He paused. "She's been locked up overnight numerous times, institutionalized on four occasions for longer, and just got out a month ago from Western State Hospital, two days before her cousin was found murdered. Now, that could be a coincidence, or it could be that both of them are mixed up in the drug trade."

"How do you know about her psychiatric history?"

"It's in her file. I got to read it. She has been diagnosed as bipolar disorder, schizoaffective disorder, and …," Sigmon paused to look at a notepad he had scribbled some information on, "and, of course, the addiction." He had a way of sterilizing the personal out of one's life history so that it seemed like perfectly ordinary public information. Perfectly ordinary, but Anna was not ordinary. Who was?

"As a former prosecutor, I have to say that I think you're in the middle of some drug dealing. As a West Virginia lawyer, on the other hand, I have to admit that this coal business is plausible. I've seen people killed over it.. However," he continued, "there is no evidence linking any of this to the coal companies. Just because the murdered woman was a protester doesn't mean some CEO sitting in his office in Richmond didn't like that and had her killed. That would be a big risk for a corporation, don't you think? The pictures you said she took of some papers—that could be anything. Even if they are coal company documents that doesn't mean they are incriminating. And the video, from what I remember, is simply her boyfriend trying to impress her about how rich he is. He probably just wanted to get laid."

Elias stopped him. "I have to say from your perspective, from an objective perspective, it does look like the kind of drug violence I read about in the newspaper. I can see that. It's like the evidence for the existence of meaning in the universe; it's all rationalized after the fact to make everything conveniently fit together. But you're wrong about Anna; she's not your garden variety addict. I've been around her. She's got an illness, but she's on medication. And she's not delusional, as far as I can tell. The fact is I just can't escape the intuition … there just seems to be more to it. There's too much coordination: Sylvie's murder, the Tech coed who was murdered in the same way, what about her? The spying on my house, Anna's trailer burned down, the attack on us last night—there seems like there's just got to be a mastermind behind it all and I can't believe that some local meth dealers are intelligent enough to do all this. It's just not a plausible narrative. And what's the motive? Why send all these intimidating messages? Don't they just kill people? And that's another question I have. Why don't they just blow up my car or something if they want to get rid of me? Why shoot me in the woods or burn down my house?"

"It's too incriminating to blow up your car. These aren't just local meth heads. This is a regional network. They have professional, hired killers who will make it look like an accident. Your house caught fire; happens all the time around here in the winter. People put their space heaters too close to the laundry or overload the outlets. Then there's the hunting accidents. You got shot by a guy who had a couple of Buds up in the stand and thought you were a deer. Common occurrence. That's why those men were carrying shotguns. Look Elias, you're so caught up in all this you can't see the forest for the trees. You've been harassed and run off the road. Someone tried to kill you. Of course you have a right to be suspicious. But it's not that complicated. The Tech coed, most likely a copycat murder. Or, of course it could be we have a serial killer right here in Montgomery County. I don't know. They're rare. But either way it argues against any coal company conspiracy."

Elias sensed that he had been trying to argue a point he didn't completely believe himself. He stood up and took a deep breath. "It does sound extreme," he conceded, "that these executives would resort to such violence to get their way, when they can just buy politicians and have the laws changed."

"Exactly," Sigmon said. "Traditionally, the coal industry has ruled Appalachia through corruption and intimidation. But times have changed. It's the twenty-first century. You can't get away with that kind of thing anymore. Too hard to hide."

"I always thought the most undetectable crimes were the ones right in front of your eyes," Elias said. "The Purloined Letter syndrome."

"What letter?"

"It's a Poe story. The criminal hides the evidence in plain sight where nobody thinks to look for it."

"Where's it hidden?"

"On the mantel."

"Smart," Sigmon observed. "But that's fiction. Law enforcement deals in fact. I don't think you're going to get very far using Mr. Poe in court, even if he is from Virginia."

On the way home Elias stopped at Wal-Mart and picked up a burglar alarm, the most expensive they had, he could rig up to the doors and windows. When he got back it was dark, and Anna was sitting at the kitchen table holding her meth pipe. The three dogs had her surrounded and all four of them turned toward the door when he came in, but no one moved.

"What's going on?" he asked.

"As you can see," she said, "I've had a slip." And she took a hit.

"A slip or a fall?" he asked.

"Chill out," she said, when she had exhaled. "I'm not going to try to seduce you again," and she gave him a look out of the corner of her eyes.

"Not what I'm worried about," he said.

"Oh really? Then tell me what you are worried about. That I won't seduce you?"

Elias gave a grim laugh. "Maybe," he said. "But if I were you, I would keep a clear head when someone's trying to kill me."

"If you were me," she said, "you'd always have someone trying to harm you, which is why you'd be hitting on this pipe," and she took another.

"Not to mention the fact that they're going to start drug testing you every week now as a condition of your bail."

"Another good reason to get high," she said.

He gave up, took the alarm system out of its box, and started hooking it up. A few minutes later she closed her works in a zippered bag, took it into the back somewhere, and came out to cook. Food.

When he asked if he could help, she stopped, cast iron skillet in hand, and looked him in the eyes. Then she looked out the window into the night trees. Elias stared at the flexed muscles in her forearm as she spoke, and noticed a rash just inside her elbow.

"I want to apologize," she said. "I know I shouldn't be using, I know it can fuck me up, I know it could get me arrested again. It's just that I've been in a hypomania, as I'm sure you're no fucking doubt aware, and I'm not quite ready to come down from it yet. I don't need to get depressed right now, because when I get depressed I can't do anything: I can't work, I can't read, I can't deal with the arraignment, all I can pretty much do is sleep and watch television. I'm just good for nothing. And my attitude's not too great either. You sure as hell don't want to see me depressed. So I take a little hit now and then just to keep the buzz going until I can get through this nightmare." She looked at him again. "Does that make sense, or are you just going to stare at me?"

"Yeah, sure," he said. "But don't be so judgmental. Maybe I think you're the same human being whether you're in a mania or in a depression. Maybe I'd like you just fine either way."

"Yeah, but I don't like me." And she slung the skillet back on the fire like a short order cook.

The next day was Monday, still windy and frigid. They decided to hike up to the ridge to look for the lost cell phone. Elias stuck the .32 in a side pocket of his ski parka. It was difficult climbing; the snow was frozen over so hard that some places you couldn't get your boot through it and you just slid down to the next sapling. "Slicker than a minnow's dinner," Anna said. The tall poplars seemed to be walking up the ridge with them, peering over the tops of the other trees like long-legged Giacometti people.

When they reached the top, they were surprised: no bloody mess. The snow had completely covered up all evidence of the struggle, short as it had been. They hadn't thought to bring a shovel, so they had to get down on their hands and knees and kick and punch through the icy crust and feel around in the snow like they had lost something underwater, until fifteen minutes later and about ten feet out he came across it. Of course, this was evidence, and Elias was sure he would hand it over once he saw for himself what was there, but at this point he didn't think anyone knew what was going on any better than himself.

Then they both stopped what they were doing and listened. They had heard something make a deep thud. There it was again. Then a rasping, like a saw. They didn't see anyone. Elias pulled the Luger out, snapped the magazine out of the handle, and checked the cartridges. Looked good.

"Stay behind me," he told her, which lasted about two seconds, then they walked out to the edge of the woods into the Christmas tree farm. It was much prettier in the daytime without the shotguns and the corpses. A half dozen men were working on the trees, a Mexican work crew with their hatchets and cotton hoodies and fingerless gloves in the freezing temperatures.

Each group stared at the other. "Felice navidad," Elias shouted and waved, forgetting he still had the Luger in his hand. They looked at him like he was a rabid coyote, not the baby Jesus. He put the gun away. "Lo siento senores. Mi novia y yo caminos en los arbros. Habamos desde la colle." One of them waved back with a machete, and they returned to their frigid work, as silent as if they were wearing brown masks.

133

"Out for a fucking walk in sub-freezing temperatures, with a gun," Anna said. "They must think we're some crazy gringos," and she punched him in the ribs.

Back at the house, they checked out the cell. Motorola, from Verizon. There were quite a few contact numbers. Area codes all over the map. Anna got out Sylvie's phone and compared the numbers as Elias read them out. There were two matches. One was a 434 area code; Elias thought it might be Charlottesville. On the dead man's phone there was no name, just the initials RBJ; on Sylvie's it said "Ronnie." The other number was an 804; there was no name on either phone for that one.

Nothing on the videos. But lots of photos of unknown buildings, homes, automobiles, then there was Anna's trailer, from various angles, her car, other cars in front, Elias' Jeep, and last, his house, again from all perspectives. There was a photo taken through the bathroom window of Anna getting out of the shower. She didn't say anything. Anger caught in his gut to see the verification that their movements for the past few weeks had been watched. Of course he had seen the tracks in the snow, but now he was seeing what the enemy saw, what possibly the murderer had seen.

"Wait a minute," he said. "Go back to that photo of my Jeep."

Anna scrolled back. The window was not busted. He looked more closely, got out his magnifying glass to scrutinize it.

"Damn, Anna," he said. "That's a train track in the background. That picture was taken when we were in the railroad yard in Roanoke. Remember that guy who walked past us? It must be the same guy."

"Stands to reason," she said. "Lord only knows how long they've been watching me and Sylvie, and you just walked right into our little conspiracy. Sorry darlin'. I told you that first night not to get involved."

"I don't blame you," he said. "I blame Ted Hughes."

"Oh yeah," she said. "I forgot about him."

Then she casually picked up Sylvie's cell and entered the first number, the 434 one: "Ronnie." There was no answer, so she texted: "Need 2 C U, ASAP." Then she used the other phone and tried the 804 number. A man answered. She said she wasn't sure if she had the right number, but she needed to speak to someone in security at Mason Dixon Energy. There was silence. Then the man asked, "Who is this?" Anna said, "I have some information about the man who was killed by the bear." "Who is this?" he demanded to know. "You know," she said, "the man who was following Anna Jassey around and killed her dog. The man who burned down her home. The cocksucker involved in killing her cousin, you goddamn motherfucker …, " and he hung up.

She looked at Elias. "That asshole definitely knew what I was talking about. He didn't act surprised at all by the bear story. Did you hear him?"

"I heard you scare the crap out of him. Now he knows we can connect him to the man who tried to kill us. He probably had no idea that anyone had found his phone; now he knows it's you who found it."

Elias started pacing around the living room. "I'm not so sure that was a good thing: To let him know we have the phone." He stopped in front of the front door sensor he had rigged up, jiggled it, listened to the alarm go off, then suddenly turned around. "Who do you think he is, anyway?"

"Who do I think he is? I think he's some corporate exec at MD. Maybe the head of security, maybe an employee, maybe the fucking president. Who knows? But the point is, they know we know, so they're going to start bugging out."

"Yeah, but what do they know we know—really? The sheriff's office doesn't think this is a conspiracy, just

135

some kind of drug payback. We've really got nothing to go on. There's no reason for them to be afraid."

"Elias, they're already trying to kill us. Kill us! You think they're not scared we're going to expose their corporate schemes and shut them down? That information Sylvie got could be a disaster for them. They could be looking at prison and financial meltdown."

He sat down on the couch next to her. "Anna, what if that guy on the phone was not some energy company CEO but rather a drug dealer who hired that ex-con to do all those things to you? Maybe he has a vendetta against you and Sylvie. Maybe she crossed him and he's taking it out on you. We really don't know who's behind all this. We have no absolute proof."

Her eyes flashed and she started to say something, then she got up and went over to his desk and pulled the phone book out of the bookcase. "Look," she pointed, "area codes and time zones. Here's 804; what does it say?"

"Richmond," he said. "But that covers a large area."

"Richmond is the headquarters of Mason Dixon," she said. "I think we can assume we've hit the jackpot with that phone call."

Elias rubbed his forehead. "You know, most of me agrees with you. It's just that it sounds so implausible, it's hard for me to wrap my brain around it. I think maybe we've watched too many movies and TV cop shows to know what's real and what's not anymore. It's like the fantasy has taken over." He stood up. "Fuck it. We'll just have to be careful, be safe, protect ourselves and see what happens next. At least the police know that somebody is out to get us, even if they think it's a drug dealer."

"Even if they think we're the drug dealers," she corrected him.

"Even if. It doesn't matter because they'll be watching us, and we want the police watching us."

"You want the po po watching us," she said. "I don't want those little shits anywhere around me."

"Okay, they can watch me. And you stay near me. Meanwhile," he said, "meanwhile, I've still got exams to give and grade this week, somehow, in the midst of all this craziness, so I've just got to keep my head screwed on straight."

"Good luck."

Chapter 13

A couple of days later Anna announced she needed to do a meeting. She had been stuck inside with the doors and windows locked while Elias was at school. He didn't ask, but he assumed she had been using off and on, although he didn't know where she got the stuff. He was apprehensive that the cops would bust her, maybe bust him too, and she was going to have to take a drug test soon. She didn't seem to care, and frankly, if she didn't care, then Elias didn't either. It was her problem, she was an adult. But that was just a momentary justification; he really did care, and he didn't want her to lose her bond and go back to jail, even though he reasoned she might be safer there than at his house. The alarm system was in place, she had the guns and the dogs, and he called her often, but based on what had taken place already, he knew whoever was after her was dangerous, organized, and not likely to give up.

She said she could go alone, but Elias didn't think that was safe. "I need *you* to protect *me*," he kept telling her. "You shoot like you were born with a gun in your hand. And you look like you know how to use that knife too."

"I would have cut that bastard up on the ridge. You told me to go for his neck and cut his—what? His ankle?"

"The Achilles tendon," he said. "It would disable him. Like Paris did at Troy."

"What's the other ankle called—the Iphigenia?"

"That's pretty good," he said.

"Just didn't want you to think that all us hillbillies was illiterate." She smiled. He hadn't seen her smile that much since the harassment started, except when she was high, which somehow didn't seem like her real smile. She had a very provocative mouth, he thought; there was something particularly alluring about her teeth, something he couldn't quite figure out.

138

So they drove over to Floyd and ate at Oddfellas. There was a young group of musicians called James Justin & Company playing local bluegrass. Elias knew a couple of them from school. They hung out together for a while, Elias had a beer, then they drove 221 north fast down Bent Mountain into Roanoke and hit the meeting a quarter after eight. They had been listening to music, feeling pretty good, ready for anything. It was a second Wednesday of the month speaker's meeting at the same church, Anna's home group. The folding chairs were now arranged in rows and there was a well-dressed obese woman, about fifty, who had just been introduced. She spent the first half hour talking about her childhood—it was really horrifying. Her parents were alcoholics; she had to pretty much grow up by herself. She was the oldest, and by the time she was ten she was actually taking care of them and her siblings. Her father could get abusive, but mostly toward her mother. She had no other life, it seemed, and then she was raped when she was twelve by one of her parents' friends. After that, the only road to pleasure was through eating, and then later through narcotics, heroin being her drug of choice. She said that she probably would have stayed a junkie her whole life, except she got pregnant. She stopped using for a while, had the baby, and began to get her life together. Then she slipped. She went on a bender, and while she was passed out one night with the baby in the bed with her, she accidentally rolled over on it and smothered it in her sleep. She woke up to find it dead. She was arrested, of course, and spent two years in prison. But she got clean inside, started going to NA, and here she was, at thirty-seven, putting the pieces back together.

That was the gist of it, just a summary. It was almost impossible to sit through it without crying or leaving the room, but nobody left. Elias felt pretty numb. He had seen a lot of horror but it had been his job. And he mostly was able to bury it deep in his head. He kept looking over at

Anna out of the corner of his eye; she was expressionless but her right hand kept twitching. And she must have gone to get coffee three times.

"That was unbelievable," he said in the car when they left.

"Speaker's meetings are always the best," she said. "Every addict in that room has a similar story to tell. Just as tragic. When you hear them it just tears you up."

"Have you even told your life story?" he asked.

"No, darlin'. Those people generally have a year or more of being clean. They've been through all twelve steps, sometimes twice. I've never made it past step two."

"What's step three," he asked, "that's so terrible?"

She took her cigarette out of her mouth and said, "Made a decision to turn our will and our lives over to the care of God as we understand him."

He thought about it for a moment. "I could see how that might be a problem for you."

They stayed up late. First they watched the news. There was nothing new on the Tech student found in the tree. They kept saying it didn't seem that it was related to the previous Tech homicides, the one in Charlottesville and the one near the Parkway, not in modus operandi anyway. Elias and Anna just looked at each other; they knew what it meant. It just confirmed for him that some violent force in the community had been unleashed with the Cho rampage, affecting the whole student body. Why did he put her in a tree? What was that about? Meanwhile Anna ranted that it was another sign of the disintegration of civilization and the end of the human species. "It's been a long time coming," she said. "And it'll be a long time gone. Won't that be a pretty sight—the natural world scraped clean of human beings."

"You sound like Rupert Birkin."

Elsewhere, Elizabeth Edwards died from cancer. Julian Assange was jailed for rape. The world's environment

140

ministers were still arguing in Cancun about how to slow global warming; at the moment, all cuts in greenhouse gas emissions were "voluntary." In the U.S. people were pushing for more nuclear energy, except they hadn't figured out yet what to do with all that radioactive waste.

They watched three hours of old movies. The second half of *The Miracle Worker*, then *Singin' in the Rain*. She asked him if he knew that Debbie Reynolds' daughter, Carrie Fisher, was bipolar. "Carrie Fisher, from *Star Wars?*" he asked. He hadn't heard that. But the movies kept getting interrupted by an Amber Alert scroll. Some local twelve-year-old had apparently been abducted or run off with her mother's boyfriend, and the mother had been murdered. When they switched to CNN to get the details, they showed a photo of the girl that made her look like she was eighteen: makeup, cleavage, like she was out at a bar. It was alienating, Elias thought. Anna said, "Girls grow up early around here." They talked some more and then maybe two-thirty or three they both fell asleep on the bed upstairs.

He woke up in the night to someone speaking. He had been dreaming that Anna was speaking to him but he couldn't quite make out in the dream what she was saying. He could see her; she had on some kind of necklace made out of animal's claws or teeth. Her hair was pulled back straight and tight and she was naked, he thought, from the waist up, but he couldn't see her breasts. Then he woke up and Anna was sitting upright in bed talking gibberish to him. At first he thought she was awake, but she wasn't. She was talking in her sleep again. Her eyes were closed, like before, but this time she looked terrified, an expression he had never seen from her. She looked like she was about to be put to death. He started to wake her but he stopped because he realized suddenly that what she was saying wasn't all gibberish. In between a lot of mumbling and incoherent English words he heard something he had heard before, or at least he thought he had. Foreign words. He wasn't sure. Maybe he had heard it in his dream.

First she kept saying what sounded like "meta, meta," repeated again and again. Then a moment later she very distinctly said "Wokneedabewan. Leave me alone. " It was so clearly articulated it could have been an English word he didn't know. He wrote it down in the notebook she kept by the bed in her backpack. She started to sound like Pocahontas in that Terrence Malick movie. Then there was more unintelligible stuff and then she started saying, "quaglida, quaglida" over and over, and she acted like she was trying to get out of bed, but she couldn't. Her feet kept getting caught in the covers. Elias was fascinated, but slowly it began to dawn on him where he had heard, or rather seen, these words. It was the language in the documents on Sylvie's phone, the evidence that she had probably given her life to photograph. It was, he figured, some Native American language.

Just then Anna opened her eyes and looked at him and said, again very clearly, "Keleepromarin," and she pursed her lips as if to kiss him. It was almost as if she was teasing him. Had she been awake all this time? Was she gaming him? So he kissed her.

But she pulled back from the kiss with a start, sat up straighter and said, "What are you doing?"

Elias was startled. "I'm sorry," he said. "I thought you were awake. I thought you wanted me to kiss you."

"What made you think that?" The terrified look had fled the rest of her face but stopped in her eyes. Not really herself yet, he thought.

"You opened your eyes, you puckered your lips, you said something."

"What did I say?" she asked.

"Are you awake now?" he asked.

"Of course I'm awake."

"Listen. I know this is going to sound bizarre, but you were talking in your sleep. At first I couldn't make out what you were saying, but after a while I realized it sounded like some Native American language." She looked like she didn't believe him. "I'm not kidding. And what's even more amazing, it sounded to me just like the language in the photographs that Sylvie took. The documents ... from Mason Dixon Energy. It sounded just the same. I've been reading over those words for weeks and I know some of them by heart. I'm telling you, you were speaking in the same damn language!"

She looked completely taken aback, like she couldn't grasp what he was saying. She kept scrunching up the pillows to sit up straighter, as if being more erect would help her understand.

"Do you have any idea what you were saying?" he asked. "Do you know where it might have come from? Maybe you were dreaming. What were you dreaming about?"

"I think I was dreaming about *The Miracle Worker*," she said. People were badgering me to talk properly and I kept trying to but all these foreign words came out, and they kept forcing me to speak properly. Like grabbing my mouth and forcing it into certain positions. I kept telling them to leave me alone, to stop, but they wouldn't. I told them I wanted to go home, to go to bed, but they wouldn't let me leave. They were restraining me." At this point she started to cry, kind of astonishing Elias who had never seen her break down once in the month they had been together, not when her dogs were hanged, not when they were shot at, not when she examined her cousin's corpse. He put his arms around her and hugged her, and she started sobbing uncontrollably, her small body wracked with spasms of emotion. Once again he felt fatherly towards her, when just a moment ago he had kissed her on the lips.

143

She cried for several minutes, and when she stopped the front of his T-shirt was wet through.

"Are you okay?" he asked. "That was a lot of emotion."

"I'm okay," she said. "I don't know where all that was coming from."

"Jesus Christ, Anna, you've been living a nightmare for weeks now. I think any sane person might get stressed out from everything you've been through."

"But I'm not sane," she said, gave him a half smile, and started wiping her face with the sheet. "All right, what the fuck did you say I was saying?"

"I don't know exactly. I wrote some of it down." He got her notebook out and she gave him a little evil eye. "It was the only thing handy. Did you take any Indian language courses in school, even in elementary school? Maybe somebody taught you some words when you were a little kid. Maybe you just forgot it consciously but your subconscious still remembers it. It's really not that unusual." He shifted around and sat right in front of her, face to face. "Listen," he said, "it sounded something like 'eta, meta, wok-nee-da-be-wan, wok-nee-da-be-wan.' Like something Obi Wan Kenobi might say."

She looked at him like he was teasing her. But Elias could see some recognition in her eyes now. She pushed her thumbs into her temples like she was in pain, then closed her eyes and lay back down, then just as abruptly sat back up and said, "No. That's not right. What did you say again? 'Eta, meta?' I can hear the words inside me, I think. It's like someone else is speaking them in my voice. I hear them but I don't know what they mean."

She lay back down again. "It's more like 'metaugh, metaugh, wak niendabewa.' It means ... it means, 'No, no, I'm going to bed.'

"You're going back to bed?"

144

"No. It means, 'I'm going to bed.' I think. It's something my mother used to say. Or I said to her. I must have heard it from her. I'm not sure; it was a long time ago, when I was a kid. Before I went to school. I must have forgotten."

"How about …" he looked at the notebook again, "how about 'quaglida?'"

"'Quaglida?'" She sounded it out with her eyes closed. "'Gwa-gilida' maybe? It means …, it means, 'I want to go home?'"

"Okay. And then what you said that almost got me punched in the face. 'Keeleepromarin?' Sounds like a new drug."

Elias would later swear he saw the blood tiptoe into Anna's cheeks at that moment, maybe the first and last time in years, like a preteen just realizing her sexuality.

"'Will you kiss me?'" she said.

"You want me to kiss you again? Make up your mind, will you."

She punched him in the arm with her knuckle out. "No, 'ke ly pomerin'—it means, 'kiss me.'"

"What language is it?" he asked.

"I don't know. I'm Melungeon, like my mother. It must be Cherokee or Monacan. Occanechee. Maybe Saponi. I don't really know. I just know the words."

"Melungeon? What's Melungeon?"

"It's the name for people who have Indian and Black ancestry. As well as white, of course. Three races, interbred in the hills and hollows of Appalachia. My mother's from Greenbank. That's a couple hours north, in West Virginia. You probably never heard of it either?"

Elias confessed he hadn't.

"It's where they listen to the stars." She reached over for her pack of Marlboros next to the bed and lit up. Offered him one. He took it.

"Thanks."

145

"Bi-wa," she said.

"It's radio astronomy—they have field after field of radio telescopes pointed toward the sky. You can't take a walk without bumping into one."

"Yeah, I know the place, now that you mention it. It's in a long valley. I drove through it once trying to find a shortcut to Snowshoe."

"Pocahontas County. Anyway, my mom and I are part Indian. See ...," and she opened her mouth and pointed to one of her teeth. He was hesitant. "Don't be afraid," she said, "I don't have meth mouth." He looked in. "Shovel-shaped incisor," she said, lisping with her finger in her gums. "It's common among Native Americans."

He understood what she was saying, but he had a sense that he was looking back through time and space into some utterly alien territory, for him. America before the Europeans. Just by staring into her mouth. Then she took another long drag on her smoke. It was passing strange; this seeming conjunction of old world and new. Jamestown and Grundy. Indian and Appalachian. The seventeenth and twenty-first centuries. And made visible and mysterious in the veil of tobacco smoke. He studied her face, rather unconsciously: the lush black lashes and brows, the slightly bulbous forehead and wide cheekbones, the darkly pale skin, the full lips.

"Did you get a good look?" she asked, after a full minute. "See anything interesting."

"Sorry. I'm just trying to take it all in. So these Melungeons, I take it, are indigenous to Appalachia? You don't find them anywhere else? Couldn't natives and African Americans and whites have intermarried all over the continent?"

"I doubt that, but if they did, they probably didn't form a community like they did in the mountains. This goes all the way back to the seventeenth century, darlin'. Back before your time. Freed slaves or runaway slaves, Virginia

146

and Carolina Indians, maybe some of Powhatan's tribe. Mixing it up with the whites on the frontier. They didn't have many laws back then 'bout getting down with the black and red brothers. Hell, there's almost no laws even today in some Appalachia back country."

"You mean to say that these Melungeons were accepted in Appalachia?"

"Hell no they weren't accepted! They were just lying low. We're talking good redneck white people here. Bible-toting, snake-handling white people. You think they wanted blacks and Indians living next door? Some whites are pretty liberal, but some of these locals are one step up from Neanderthal themselves. That's why the Melungeons had to hide out in the hollers, create their own communities. Most of them are down in North Carolina and Tennessee, on the border. No, you didn't ever want to tell your neighbors you're Melungeon. Not in Buchanan County. I don't care who you were. Of course times has changed, as they say. Blacks and whites been mining together for decades, but mixing the races is another thing altogether."

"Well," he said, leaning back on the bed, "That explains some things."

"Like what?" she asked, suspicious.

"Like that encounter with the bear. What's the Melungeon word for bear? I mean, the Indian word?"

"Black bear?" She thought for a moment. "Yukayek? Yutkayek? I think. I must know lots of words for animals. My mother used to take me for walks in the woods when I was a child. We spent lots of time together."

"That's what you called it. It must be coming back to you; something got loosened up in your unconscious."

"Maybe that last ECT," she replied, and blew a smoke ring. "Lightning of the gods. The divine madness."

"What did she die of? Your mother."

"I don't know. She just disappeared one day when I was around nine or ten, and I never found out what happened to her."

"What do you mean she just disappeared? Didn't you ask your father where she went?" He sat up on the bed again.

"Of course I asked him. But he wouldn't say. I was just a kid. My father and I were never close. He didn't give a shit how I felt; he just wanted me to keep up appearances. That's all that mattered to him."

"Is your father Melungeon too?"

At this point Anna looked like she might lose control again. It looked like a war was going on in her eyes, and her mouth was twisted in a grimace around her cigarette.

"Fuck no he's not Melungeon! And don't ever mention the word around his house or he'll slap the piss out of you." She started coughing and Elias handed her the glass of OJ she always left by the bed to take her meds.

"My father's Catholic," she continued. "From Eastern Europe. Yugoslavia or Hungary or some such place. Jassey. Probably changed the name."

"Your father's a Slav? What's he doing in Southwest Virginia?"

"He came over when he was a teenager, to work in the coal fields. He was poor. It was in the fifties; he had nothing. There were lots of immigrants. Not everyone in Appalachia is English or Irish. He'll tell you."

"So what's he doing now? Does he still live in Grundy?"

He could see in the pattern of her smoking that she didn't want to think about her father. It wasn't spontaneous or relaxed, like she was enjoying it. She seemed to be using each inhalation as a kind of chemical mantra, regulating her breathing and her thoughts. Then they would get the better of her and she would exhale in a rush.

148

She looked at her watch. "It's 6:11 so he's been awake for almost an hour. He's had coffee. Read the *Virginia Mountaineer* and the *Wall Street Journal* online. Right now he's probably watching Fox News."

"Is he retired? You said one time he was a miner. What is he—sixty? Does he still work in the mines?"

"I think he turned sixty-one last month. Six decades of sin and damnation. And no, he's not completely retired, I don't think, but he stopped working in the mines when I was a baby. Emphysema. Prelude to black lung. Kind of hard to shovel coal when you're hooked up to a breathing machine. He moved into management. He worked for Mason Dixon." And she took another long drag.

It took a moment to sink in. "He worked for Mason Dixon? Are you kidding me? Anna, how could that be? I've been thinking he was a miner. What did he do for Mason Dixon?"

"I told you," she said. "Management. He ran the operations in Southwest Virginia. I'm not sure exactly what he does now, if anything."

Elias got off the bed and went over to sit in the armchair his father used to have in his den. Facing her. "So you're telling me that all this time that MD Energy has been engaged in a conspiracy, according to you, to kill your cousin and intimidate or kill you, and me, your father has been working for them, that he's been involved in this plot?"

She crushed her butt in the ashtray. "I don't know," she said. "That's one thing I'm going to have to ask him the next time I see him."

"You think your father is trying to kill you?"

"My father's been trying to kill me my entire life." She was looking him square in the eyes without a stray cloud of emotion shadowing her face. "My daddy never loved me and never will. Now I don't want to talk about this crap anymore," she said, and pulled the covers up to her chin and sat staring straight ahead at the TV.

Elias continued to sit in the chair thinking for a minute. "Okay," he said, getting up. "I'll go start a fire and make some coffee." He went to the window. "It looks cold out, there's ice on the car, but not so windy."

Mechanically, he ground some beans, boiled water, and strained it through the grounds. His mind was elsewhere, sorting through everything she had told him. Her habitually laconic answers to his questions were getting them nowhere, frustrating, often annoying, some kind of defense mechanism, that was clear, but what exactly was she defending? Her independence? That seemed to be the primary thing for her. Family secrets? They kept coming out. Or was this whole affair, from Waffle House on out, a complex paranoid delusion, birthed in a mania, fueled with methamphetamines, and shot through with a need to be in control of her life? She was so full of self-confidence that Elias questioned it. He understood it, but he questioned it. She didn't doubt herself; he didn't either, but that was his training. It wasn't normal not to have doubts. It seemed reasonable to ask questions, of oneself, even in the midst of crisis—especially in the midst of crisis, he thought. Now this thing with her father; it was too coincidental. She was trying to get back at her father for something, and the whole conspiracy thing involving Mason Dixon and Sylvie was probably just a story to cover up the real meaning. It was insane; it was textbook. It was the Ted Hughes business all over again. It was right in front of his eyes. On the mantel. Turned inside out.

But it didn't explain everything.

At school that afternoon he called Sigmon and asked him to check a phone number if he could. The 804 number. Didn't tell him anything more except that it looked to be a number Sylvie had called in the past that they couldn't locate and therefore suspected. He also didn't mention discovering what language the documents were written in.

150

"Is she taking her meds?" Sigmon asked. "Your girlfriend?"

"As far as I know." No reaction to the girlfriend bait.

"And make sure she stays clean. She's got a hearing coming up soon and if she fails a drug test they'll lock her back up."

"I know."

"Look at her eyes. When the pupils are dilated, she's using. And check her arms. The ones who inject get what they call speed bumps. Does she drink a lot?"

"She drinks Diet Coke all day long."

"That's from dry mouth. Chronic meth use will cause it. She's probably still using. You better be careful she doesn't burn down your house."

This sounded almost like a warning to Elias, who was becoming increasingly suspicious of innunendo, but he quickly concluded that it was meant as a reminder, not a threat, that he had entered a different country the night he drove Anna home from Waffle House.

"Thanks," he said, "I'll do that," and hung up.

On the way home the Jeep was rattling more than usual. He figured it was from the wreck and when he pulled up in front of the house he got out and got down on his hands and knees and started checking the wheels, like a pilot doing a post-flight inspection. Nothing unusual. Then he looked inside, thinking maybe the noise was coming from there. Something loose. The Jeep was sixteen years old; this had become a monthly ritual. He secured everything in the cargo area, the back seat, the front, and even looked up under the dash. That's when he saw something that didn't seem right. A small metal box, jammed in between the steering column and the heat duct. It was magnetized and duct taped for good measure. He pulled it off, sat in the front seat, and examined it. There seemed to be no doubt about what it was. The only questions were when and who.

151

"Look what I found," he said, coming in the door.

Anna wasn't there. For a moment he panicked, then noticed the dogs were absent too and went out the back door and found her in the yard cutting up the deer carcass which she had strung up from a tree limb. She appeared to know what she was doing.

"Figured I'd do the butchering and save the family I know the trouble," she said, wielding her fixed-blade knife like she was performing in an operating theater with Gypsy and his Lab and Jack Russell following every incision.

"Where'd you learn how to do that?"

"Kindergarden in Grundy."

"Right. So what did you take in grade school, wringing a chicken's neck?"

"No. Driving mountain roads in the moonlight with the headlights off."

"How about middle school? How to make moonshine?"

"No. How to cook meth."

He didn't want to complete the cycle, but he couldn't resist finding out what she would say next.

"I'm almost afraid to ask," he said. "How about high school? How to kill your abusive boyfriend?"

"No," she said, looking up from a pile of entrails. "How to kill your abusive father."

There was a short silence in which Elias could hear some crows cawing above the fir trees bordering the meadow. The sky was pale blue, the sun had sunk half way behind the mountains, casting a golden light over the humped ridges, and the high clouds were rippled like the ribs of a dying god.

"That reminds me," he said. "Look what I found," and held up the tracking device.

She came over to see it as he turned it over in his hands. She had to hold it too in her bloody fingers, as if it were some sort of high tech talisman.

152

"I wonder where that came from," she said.

"I'm guessing the dead bearded guy or one of his cohorts put it under my dash when he broke into the car at the Norfolk Southern station. I've never left it unlocked, so I'm assuming they have been following us ever since."

"Like they don't have burglary tools? These guys can break in anytime they damn well please."

"Maybe he was in a hurry."

"Maybe." And she went over and sat on the ground with her legs spread and started carving the venison lying on a tarp on the ground into steaks. Elias realized then that the dogs hadn't touched the meat and he was amazed.

"I had a little surprise too," she said over her shoulder.

"What?"

"Got a text from Ronnie Breedlove. Says he wants to meet me Saturday night in Charlottesville."

She had her back to him so he couldn't see her face, whether there was apprehension or neutrality in her eyes. Until this morning he had never seen any fear, not until the sleep talking episode when she seemed to be re-enacting some buried childhood trauma, and he doubted he would see it again unless she was asleep. But he had also started to believe that her seeming indifference, her casual, often sardonic way of replying to his inquiries was not the result of objective points-of-view and assessments so much as an almost inbred anger hidden in an Appalachian toughness and wit, like the knife she was wielding now to cut steaks. After it had been put back in its sheath, it could never be wiped completely clean.

The full text read: "Look 4ward 2 meet u alone C-ville Sat nite. Contact when u get here. 10pm."

He didn't like it. There was no way she could safely meet the person possibly involved in Sylvie's death by herself. She was too confident in her own ability to get out of any predicament. Maybe what got Sylvie killed. He kept reiterating the danger. And what good would this encounter do? Did she really think Breedlove was going to confess to a crime?

She was starting to disappear in the gathering dark, which seemed to descend from the surrounding hills and fold them in an embrace. Elias looked up and saw the first sliver of a new moon skirting the southern treetops.

"Maybe we should go inside. You're going to cut yourself."

"I'll be there in a minute."

They were sitting at the kitchen table after dinner when she answered. "I just want to look the bastard in the face," she said, smoking a joint. "Maybe he's too cocky for his own good. You heard him on the video. I'll play it for him. See how he reacts. He's liable to say something. We can record it."

"I still think it's way too dangerous. You're setting yourself up. They've already tried to kill both of us. It's a conspiracy; you said so. He's not in this alone; he can't be. Hell, you may never get to meet him. They might kill you before you even get there."

"I doubt that," she said, exhaling a languid stream of smoke.

He took the doobie from her. "I can't believe we're sitting here talking about this while we're getting high," he exclaimed. "As if we were discussing existentialism or something. It's unbelievable," and he took a hit. At the same time he knew he had done it before. But he was much younger then. Anna's age. He couldn't tell her about that now, but he could warn her. For all the good he knew it would do. The only thing left was to protect her.

"You don't have to go, you know," she said.

"There is no way you are going to Charlottesville without me. We've been through too much together. Also I know the city. You don't. But it's still too dangerous."

"You can't tell me what to do," she said, sharply. "I'm a free agent. You keep acting like this is your shit, but it's not, not really. It's my business and my family, and if I kill this asshole or he kills me there's no big loss to anyone anyway." She had raised her voice and was attempting to stare him down across the small drop leaf oak table his grandfather had left him.

"You're a fucking free agent; that's a fact," he said, raising his voice to match hers. "But so am I, and you can't stop me from going. I have been pulled into this thing, granted, of my own free will, but now that I'm in it I'm not just going to leave it. How can I? How can I go back to my same old routine of teaching a couple of classes and coming home and eating alone and grading papers and getting up the next day and going through the same thing again? I've been shot at, I've had my car broken into, I've seen a dead girl who's been mutilated, I've watched a man get his face chewed off by a bear, I've been interrogated by the police, I've lied to the police to get you out of jail ...." He had stood up at his chair and was shouting now, and he suddenly had a vision of the two of them as if from a distance: it looked like they were competing to see who could out talk or out shout or out manic the other.

"Okay, okay," she said. "I get it. Calm down. You don't have to raise your voice. We're in this together. For better or for worse."

They both smiled at the reference, and she relit the joint.

It was Thursday. They had two days to get ready. Elias called Sigmon again, at home. He hadn't had time yet to get the number searched. Elias decided to confide some more information in him. He needed a third person who knew what was going on, in case something happened. Like filing a flight plan. So he spilled all the stuff he had been holding back: the break-in at the Norfolk Southern yard, the tracking device, Sylvie's phone, the dead man's phone, the documents and the video, and who was involved. Even the fake police car stopping them that night. The text messages. And finally, his discovery—through some online researching and the tech library—that the documents were written in Saponi, a Virginian Native American language. Also a dead one. Supposedly."

"Saponi? No shit? Have you translated them?"

"Not yet. Haven't had a chance."

"Elias, listen. You need to get the law involved in this. It was already complicated and dangerous; now it looks like you're in way over your head. My advice to you would be to contact the state police and tell them everything you told me. These crimes already cover a number of jurisdictions, and they have the authority to investigate if they think that any local sheriff's offices are involved. If you'd like me to accompany you I'd be happy to. And do not meet that suspect in Charlottesville; that's just crazy kind of thinking. That sounds like it's coming from the girl, not you. It sounds delusional. Meth addicts feel super confident; they exhibit what's called grandiose thinking. Don't be taken in by it; you're only going to make things worse." He paused and cleared his throat. "This Breedlove character is probably involved in the meth trade too. The fact that he's related to the energy exec feeds right into her delusions. Don't be taken in. Look, I can't meet with you right away. I have a conference this weekend and I'm flying out this evening. But first thing Monday we can talk to the state police in Roanoke. I'll set up an appointment before I leave. Okay?"

Elias thought it all through in a few seconds and made up his mind.

"All right. Thanks. I really appreciate it. Text me the time or call me and we'll go together. Thanks again, Bobby."

The next thing he did was take the tracking device he had found to a security company in Salem. It was advertised in the yellow pages, where he was surprised to discover there were five pages of "Security Control Equipments Systems and Monitoring" listed in the picturesque New River Valley region. The tracking device planted in his car was called a Spark Nano. It was a real-time GPS tracker that could pinpoint the location of anything within a few meters by triangulating on satellites. Then it sent the data to a computer or smart phone every few minutes, where it was overlaid with maps so you could see exactly where the person or vehicle was. "This one's dead," the guy said. "Been on too long." "How long?" he asked. "No more than a month, depending on how much the vehicle was driven." That seemed to settle it. They had planted it in his Jeep early on, and they had gotten inside. It must have been done when his window was broken at the railroad yard. He asked the guy behind the desk if he could reactivate the tracker in another vehicle, and was shown how to do so. Then he asked him about purchasing another one that could be concealed in someone's clothing. That was no problem either. "This one's really cool," he said. "It's got a panic button on it. Look, it'll send anyone you program into it a text message or e-mail in case of an emergency. They'll know right where you are immediately." Elias was wondering how many people had other people under surveillance on a daily basis. Wives checking on their husbands, bosses checking their employees. When had all this started happening, and why? Because they could? Technology had tapped into that suspicion and paranoia that lurks just below the surface in everyone. It used to just be the military and the intelligence agencies. Now the whole world was under surveillance.

After an hour he finally walked out of the shop with another Nano, 3 by 2 inches, thin enough to be sewn into Anna's clothing. It didn't come on unless it detected motion and would last a month on one charge if it was used no more than an hour a day. It had a lithium battery. She'd like that.

The guy did say the GPS coverage map had some problem areas; it could act a little squirrely in the mountains if the sat couldn't get a good signal. It liked a clear line to the sky, which is why it didn't work indoors. He wasn't planning on her going anywhere with Breedlove, but if she did he could at least follow them in the Jeep. The whole shebang with the monthly coverage and all only cost him several hundred and change.

Which meant she was going to have to drive her car, which they had rescued from the impound and was now sitting behind the house, the 85 Buick with what she called "the heaviest doors in Buchanan County." He would follow her to Charlottesville. They would contact Breedlove when they got there, arrange a meeting place, and he would be nearby. She would also have his Sony voice recorder in her pocket. It was pretty noise sensitive and could record for eight hours. She carried her pocket knife, of course, and the other one she hid in her boot. Elias debated with himself all day Friday whether he should take one of the pistols with him, or even give one to Anna. He had a rifle he hadn't told her about in the trunk. As he lay in bed Friday night—he and Anna had by this time switched roles and she slept on the couch downstairs, because of her insomnia—it dawned on him suddenly that if he was worried enough that she would do something rash, something irremediable, as soon as she saw Breedlove, there was no way he was going to put a gun in her hand to do it with. And he didn't want a pistol himself in this situation. He could not imagine a killer this methodical doing anything violent in a public place, so as long as she didn't take off with him she was safe. Or so he reasoned. Still, he did not sleep much Friday night.

Chapter 14

They left his place Saturday about 6 p.m., figuring the drive would take three hours and they could get something to eat before the meet, maybe at Durty Nellys. Anna was wearing corduroy jeans and boots and one of his flannel shirts a few sizes too big, but it looked right on her. As soon as they started to convoy Elias realized he had made a mistake following Anna, because she drove like a maniac. He actually said that aloud to himself and started thinking about whether it came from the same root as "manic" as he tried to keep up with her on the slowly descending roads from Buffalo Mountain to the New River Valley and I-81. He pushed the Jeep as fast as he felt comfortable with, but by the time he got to Route 8, a good ten miles, he had lost sight of her, and he could only hope she would wait for him at the entrance ramp to 81. He was wrong. She was long gone.

The traffic north and south was horrible, as usual, long lines of 18 wheelers laboring uphill at 50 only to plunge downhill at 75 and overtake all the cars that had just passed them. The rocky gorge at the James River bridge, the cattle farms in the budding moonlight across the valley, the red-lit radio and cell towers on the ridge tops—none of this beauty penetrated in his present state of mind. At the center of his consciousness he was blank, a cipher, but around it swirled a maelstrom of violent scenarios and conspiracy theories to match the traffic. A half hour later at Lexington the highway straightened out a bit and the cars and trucks detached, and when he got to 64 in Staunton and headed east he was free and clear of the madness. He began to relax a bit. His anger at her leaving him behind had mostly evaporated and he was resigned to whatever befell her. She was the architect of her own fate, she wanted it this way, he kept telling himself as he crossed Afton Mountain and descended into Albemarle County.

He stopped first at Nelly's, on the western edge of town, a pub and deli where he had hung out as a student. There it was—the Buick. The small parking lot was packed, so he had to drive down JPA Extended and park on a quiet residential side street. He felt comfortable back in the college town of his youth. A quarter moon was disappearing into a cloud bank overhead; it looked like a golden shark's fin plying the ocean, and as it sank it illuminated the cloud from within, throwing diffused light over the leaf-strewn streets. Students ambled along the sidewalks, returning from the library or heading out to party. Inside, the pub was long and narrow, wood paneled, no windows, mostly a college crowd. She was sitting at the bar drinking a beer and flouting the smoking ban by hiding her cigarette under the counter. He sat next to her and ordered a draft.

"Wa-hoo-wa," she said. Then, when he didn't respond immediately, "Oh my God, he's pissed."

He waited until he got his beer and took a long swig before he answered.

"Well, you're acting like the irresponsible twenty-five-year-old you are and I'm acting like the cautious fifty-year-old I am. I guess you could say we can't escape from our stereotypes."

She sniggered. "I guess not."

"How'd you know where Nelly's is?"

"I've been to Charlottesville a few times. I know my way around."

"You know, technically, you can't lose me. I can track you wherever you go."

"Unless I lose the tracking device in my bra. Which, by the way, I still can't believe you got me to wear."

"The device or the bra?" He had started to loosen up with the beer and their ritualistic communication strategies.

160

"Both. The damn thing is heavy." She turned away from the bartenders and snuck a smoke.

"Actually, even if you take off your bra I can still track your car. You would have to abandon both vehicles to get rid of me."

She looked at him out of the side of her eye as she drank. "My bra's a vehicle?"

"It's a vehicle in at least two ways," he said, drawing numbers in the water on the bar from the cold mug. "It physically carries your breasts, such as they are, of course, and it metaphysically transports your breasts into the minds of others as objects of commodified desire."

She sniggered again. Must be the alcohol, he thought, unless, of course, she got high in the car.

"Fucking academic. What do you mean by the 'such as they are' crack? Are you saying my breasts are too small? You don't like them?" And she arched her back in his face, pushed them together, and looked down to inspect them.

"I love them, as a matter of fact. Both of them. I just mean that you clearly don't need a bra and look better without one. Live free as long as you can." He winked and changed the subject to food.

They ordered subs at the bar. She got the Cavalier, Smithfield ham and swiss with coleslaw and dressing; he got the Sailor, tuna salad. When they had eaten it was about ten, and she sent the text saying where she was.

A minute later they got a response: "Millers downtown on mall."

"Miller's?" she asked.

"It's a bar. Used to be a drugstore. High ceilings. An upstairs. Good music."

"Preppy?"

"It's Charlottesville."

This time she didn't lose him, because he went first. They navigated the Saturday night traffic past the Corner next to the university, and down Main Street along the

161

railroad tracks, then around and up Vinegar Hill to park behind the pedestrian mall. She said she was going to stay in the car and smoke for a while, then come in alone.

Miller's fronted the mall and had some tables outside when the weather was good. Elias went in first so he could take a position near the door and watch what happened when Anna entered. The clientele was an amalgam of the usual townies, some older professional people, a few bar-hopping UVA students and faculty, and often the scions of the old families whose horse farms and estates lined the Southwestern and Ragged Mountains from Gordonsville to Scottsville. It was one large room downstairs with a long bar along the left side, tin ceiling, and a small bandstand up front. Like Nelly's, it was crowded, and he had to elbow his way to the bar where he ordered a coke. There was a band playing he had seen before: a downsized version of American Dumpster. Guitar, drums, and a washboard. The front man, Christian Breeden, was parlaying one of his trademark junkyard tunes, part blues, part rockabilly, part mescaline. He looked and sounded like Bob Dylan had had a baby with Jim Morrison, and he was wearing a porkpie hat and a psychedelic cape while he danced around the mic, occasionally laying it down almost horizontal, threatening it seemed to let it fall into the audience.

Elias nonchalantly scrutinized the crowd until he spotted Ronnie. From Sylvie's cell. He was sitting three or four tables back from the band with maybe five others, good-looking twenty-somethings. The women were dancing in their seats with their arms in the air spilling drinks. They all looked drunk. Except Ronnie. He looked stone cold sober, alert and tense. Occasionally Elias would catch him sending his gaze around the room, especially when the door opened. He didn't seem to notice Elias. He also didn't seem to be listening to the music, or at least only superficially. He looked much the same as he had in the video: clean cut, muscular, Ivy League, athletic. His hair was a sandy red and kind of wavy, but short. He had a thick neck, a pug nose, and squinty eyes. And when he smiled to one of his companions his teeth were long and white as if he'd been chewing on bones all his life. He was tanned, in December, and meticulously dressed in a white button down Oxford shirt, navy blue V-neck cashmere sweater monogrammed with the UVA logo, and khakis. He was wearing loafers in the leftover snow, and no socks. But he still had his gloves on. The others were similarly dressed, like they might have been on the lacrosse team together.

Anna took her time, walked in about twenty minutes later, and like two predators coming upon the same carcass, they immediately headed for each other. She seemed to know where he was as soon as the door shut behind her, and he was halfway out of his seat in the same time. She had changed, from some stash she had in her car apparently. She had on a long grey wool coat they had bought a few days before at Macy's, but she wore it unbuttoned and unbelted in the frigid temperatures so as she moved slowly to their table it swung open. She had tucked the tight corduroy pants into a pair of riding boots, she had switched a turtleneck for the flannel, and she had pulled her hair back in a twist and gotten rid of the stocking hat that made her look a little like a young Ali McGraw. In short, she looked like she had stepped out of one of the J. Crew catalogues lying around his cabin.

Elias couldn't hear a word they were saying in the din but probably neither could they, because as soon as Ronnie had made some pantomimed introductions they sat down and pretended to listen to the music. Elias realized that there was no way the voice recorder would pick up everything they said in there unless there was some digital technique to home in on the words. The two of them were facing forward towards the band, where Breeden was in the middle of one of his original songs called "Taboo," but from Elias' perspective it looked like they were watching each

163

other with a third eye on the side, while the rest of the table continued to gyrate and jump with the crowd. He was so focused on them that he was almost unaware of a few raspy lyrics that found their way into his consciousness: "I'm watching you bleed but it's not from a wound." Then a few bars later he heard, "You've broken my bow and I blame it on the moon." When the song ended Breeden launched into a story that eventually became the next song. Elias heard the words but didn't listen while he watched Anna and Ron. Someone was born in a junkyard, then it peregrinated cross country to the Burning Man Festival, and ended with some small but surreal private epiphany in the desert that perhaps Breeden could decipher but Elias could not.

During one of those breaks in the music Ronnie and Anna got up and, newly ordered cocktails in hand, moved through the crowd and up the stairs to the other small dining area. This made Elias very nervous. He remembered that the last time he had been in here several years ago almost no one sat up there after dinner, particularly when there was music, so if he followed them he was likely to be conspicuous. On the other hand, if there was no one up there, what might happen? Was there a back stairs, another way down and out? Ronnie looked tensely unpredictable, for all his preppy clothes, and Anna, Elias knew, was as ruthless as a cornered animal.

He grabbed a passing waitress and spoke in her ear over the music: "My daughter and her boyfriend are upstairs. I think they're having an argument. Here's ten bucks. Check on them for me, will you, and let me know how they're doing?" and he slipped the bill in her shirt pocket.

"No problem." And after she dropped off a round of drinks and took an order, he watched her climb out of sight. She was gone longer than she should have been— what was she doing, taking more orders, bussing tables?— and he was about to follow her when she reappeared and came straight over to him.

164

"They're having a heated discussion," she said, "but not out of control or anything."

"Thanks," he said. "Is there anyone else up there?"

"There's a couple of other tables," she said, and moved to the end of the bar.

Still, it was nerve-wracking. Elias wondered why he hadn't wired her for sound. They must have sold the apparatus in the security shop; they had everything else. When he and Anna had discussed this meeting before they left his house in Floyd, he had been particularly adamant about her not leaving his sight, and especially not leaving wherever they were to go someplace else. Public spaces, they agreed, were safe enough, but it was foolhardy to take any chances. She had rolled her eyes. She was pushing the limits, as usual. She was too self-confident, or too angry to be afraid. He should have foreseen this happening. He gave the waitress a nod and she went upstairs again. When she came right back down she made an okay sign with her fingers.

The band took a break five minutes later and the people at the table were quickly getting restless when Ronnie and Anna reappeared. The girls were checking their cells for messages. They had been gone fifteen minutes. Then they all stood up to leave.

It was almost eleven. While she was putting on her coat Anna surreptitiously looked at him and mouthed the words "Follow me." He thought she meant follow her to her car, but when they got outside they walked across the mall to a side street and someone used the remote to unlock a Cadillac Escallade. He had a moment of panicked indecision when he realized what she was doing—should he stop her or not, then he turned a corner out of sight and ran the other way to his Jeep and prayed that he could get over to their street before they pulled away. Suddenly he didn't trust the technology; he was a fool, he thought, to let her talk him into this crazy venture, like something on TV. This was real. This preppy jock had the look of a murderer. Stupid, stupid, stupid he kept saying to himself as he turned the key, threw the car into gear and tore down High Street to the end of the mall running two stop signs.

The bar is a bright clearing in the woods a space for truth to unveil itself Heidegger says and there is the truth getting up from a table and I have my hand on my knife and I can see in his eyes that he is the one and I could kill him right now on the black and white linoleum spill his redneck blood in puddles we could drink from on all fours and get it over with who gives a shit what happens to me but I don't for some reason maybe because I know Elias is in here and then it's too late I sit down with these preppy people I have known half my life but the other half is so far beyond them except for Breedlove he's not from here second generation hillbilly miner's son I can smell the molecules of fear and desire like moonshine pressing through his skin as we watch the music rolling toward us like surf get knocked down stand up get knocked down again never taking my eyes off him order a kamikaze get served the words sometimes I speak the words I listen the wave words slap me across my consciousness the old Roman consciousness you've broken my bow you broke Sylvie's maidenhead you rammed that arrogant old cock knife into her and cut that violation into her white chastity I'm thinking I should still kill him right now and then the roar subsides and we get up to go upstairs he says to talk in private I see Elias watching me and I go with him

It's a cave on the second floor feral with bones on the unbussed plates and soiled tablecloths he tried to take my hand as we ascended I scratched the shit out of him he had to tie a napkin around it he thinks this is a game that we are the same and I will either succumb to him fuck him or he will kill me it doesn't seem to matter and then I recognize him now I understand where it comes from now that I can look right into his ice blue eyes across the table he's Melungen his father is and he is that explains the Saponi so this is deeper than anyone knows I sensed something all along but I figured it was just the meth talking he probably knows I am too he says so what did you need to see me about asap the recorder is not on and I say cut to the chase you

166

killed my cousin Sylvie mutilated her and I want revenge the son of a bitch actually smiles his teeth are not Indian or he had them fixed and says so you're Sylvie's cousin she was quite a wildcat must have been that red hair what did you say happened to her and drinks ice water I said you butchered her and I'm going to cut you to pieces now or later his face turns into an alien or maybe a clone of an alien he laughs you're just a piece of shit meth whore with a very fuckable body who doesn't know what the fuck she's getting into so out of your league just like your butchered cousin and I yeah well the joke's on you asshole she got you and your fascist father on video no amount of money's keeping you from going down down down the black seam not to mention that girl in the tree this time he doesn't laugh you've got nothing he says you're a meth whore manic depressive totally unbelievable and by the way will be locked up for the indefinite future if you think you're getting off that drug charge you're really a stupid bitch still smiling he's so cocky just like I figured there are some things he don't know he has instincts but not knowledge so I say so I guess we're checkmate let's blow this bar and go do some real drugs what makes you think I want to continue this evening with you you're not getting anything out of me I say because I have a very fuckable body and I taught Sylvie everything she knew and I smell the desire and the fear behind it again and I somehow know he doesn't know what I am and so he succumbs and we go back downstairs

Elias follows us outside he is afraid for me but he is just beginning to know me he's smart he'll figure it out not afraid of anything but his own guilt about his wife I'll take him past that he won't let anything bad happen to me so I get in the car with these assholes and fools and play their game we drive way out into the moonless country I'm in the back with the girls doing laughing lines off makeup mirrors with rolled twenties the estates flicker by like an antebellum movie Keswick Cloverfields Merifields Rollaway Hill Cismont Rougemont and we turn into a long paved drive between barren oaks and the Caddy rolls to a stop in front of the big house but he takes me to the cottage around back kicks the barking dog the bastard I speak to him he has no soul the others disappear and I'm glad because I don't want anything to come between us Sylvie's hand is on my knife just wait for the right time the mountain rears up as we climb the steps and I feel the cattle scattered across the pasture and there's a snake under the porch as he unlocks the door and turns on some lamps could be a love nest under the right circumstances now a death nest but he doesn't get too close never stops watching me as he pours some whiskey and makes a fire sits on the couch just like with Elias now his back is turned except all he does is remote light the propane everything is different as he sits back down facing me and smiles and so what did you learn back in coal country about sex I know underneath that J Crew you must have cranked hillbillies lusted after in barns and trailers all over Buchanan County tell me all about them and maybe I'll tell you what me and Sylvie did and you can compare but he's not close enough yet I'm going to have to go all the way with this to do it right and so I tell some off the top of my head tales about riding the dragon with lots of guys at the same time and somewhere along his eyes get narrower and the blue goes out of them and he's breathing heavy he takes off his pants you whore you'd do anything for meth whore we're still on the couch but he's closer and while I'm talking unzip my tight cords and pull them down just to my thighs and he lunges forward and buries his head in my panties with his teeth tearing at them and I have the knife to plunge it up to the antler in his neck and he senses the movement and puts up his big forearm and the blade slices his sweater and he grabs my hand with his other and then back slaps me and I bring my knee up but it only gets his chest and then he has me locked down double my weight and laughing now and cursing because I ruined his sweater and the blood is dripping and he's ripping my panties off and got his dick out ...

Elias caught up with the Escalade at the top of the mall, turning onto High Street and heading out of the city, up Pantops Mountain on 250 east past Shadwell, then veering onto 22 north. There were no more stoplights so he could hang back at a safe distance and observe. And there was almost no traffic. They cruised through Keswick doing sixty and went left at the fork onto 231 and then a few miles farther, turned left again into a private road. Elias slowed and could see the lights of a house maybe a half mile away against the Southwestern Mountains. The taillights grew smaller, and disappeared. He waited a few minutes, then decided to park the Jeep in front of a cattle gate a hundred yards down, where the tractors had worn a lane, hopped the wooden fence and struck off across a field at a jog. The moon was setting, and even though the field was open, he was not afraid of being seen. The golden crescent seemed to be resting on a ridge of the mountains like an ark on Ararat. Elias was technically trespassing, but he hadn't seen any posted signs; still, he didn't really know what he was dealing with: the college students looked harmless enough, but Breedlove himself could quite possibly be a murderer. Who knew what he was capable of? Was this his family's estate, or did it belong to one of the others in the group? Were the parents anywhere? Was there a caretaker on the property? The clouds were thickening, and the air was warming; it looked like it might rain in a few hours. He crossed the hay stubble quickly, jumped a fog-caught, snow-melt creek, another fence, and entered a pasture full of cattle. Black Angus. They seemed asleep, dark clots of matter scattered across a gently rising slope, unaware of his presence. Like a phalanx of sleeping tanks. Then one bellowed. Not too loud, but it startled him as he passed within arm's reach, and he wondered if the people in the house could hear, or would notice. He figured not; it was a cattle farm after all, and he had another hundred yards yet to go. But he slowed down; he didn't want to spook them. Angus could get aggressive, great blocks of shadow converging on him. When he got close to the far fence, he crouched down behind a small cypress and checked his watch. It must have been ten or fifteen minutes since they pulled up. He couldn't hear anything, but the lights were on in the main house, also in what looked like a guest house a couple of hundred feet away, and in the barn around back. There were some outside lights as well, but between the pools of illumination

169

the front yard was dark and even darker under the elms and oaks. The driveway made an oval to the front door, and along the inside of the drive ran a six-foot boxwood. Elias crossed the asphalt and entered the yard, circling along the shadow of the hedge, until he reached the front of the house. Now he could see people in the tall windows.

He was apprehensive, but not so much for fear of being seen; it was because he didn't want to let Anna out of his sight for any longer than he had to, both for what they might do to her and, more plausibly, what she might do to them. They had formulated a plan: to record any incriminating information, as Sigmon had advised, that might be used to break open this case, but already Anna was operating outside the plan. It was becoming increasingly clear to Elias that she was more bent on revenge than she was on getting evidence and letting the legal system handle it. She obviously didn't trust the system—maybe for good reason—and was willing to run all kinds of risks to confront her adversary. Part of it, of course, was fueled by her mania, and part by her drug use, but the logic of it seemed to be hardwired into her brain from her family and the whole Appalachian cultural thing. Settle personal disputes outside the law, and what was more personal than the murder of a family member over money?

All these thoughts somehow found their way into Elias' analysis of the situation as he slowly and quietly crept from window to window scanning the rooms of the house, except that he was afraid he had only seconds to stop something fatal from happening. His brain was a computer constantly downloading more data to process. He could clearly hear music now, laughter and talking, moving between the living room and kitchen. He saw all five of the people who had gotten into the Escalade, all except for Breedlove and Anna. These Ivy League kids didn't appear to be any threat, just like his students. He kept circling the house—it was large and brick, with a columned front porch, and several room additions jutting out—until he got to the back. Then, as he was focused on the windows, he heard something behind him, and wheeled around, fully expecting to see Ronnie Breedlove standing there.

Instead, it was a brindled Great Dane, huge in a rectangle of window light in the back yard about twenty feet away, growling quietly. Elias had no innate fear of dogs, but the deep guttural sound, the size of the dog, and the fact that he was only a couple of strides away, made the hair on the back of his neck stand up and his heart pump faster. As he held his breath he could hear The Black Eyed Peas through the window, people talking, and beneath that, a stream running over rocks somewhere down in the pasture. It was a transcendent moment, full of peace and threat. Instinctively, he started walking forward very slowly like Anna probably would, with his hand outstretched, and when he did the dog suddenly stopped growling, turned and loped over toward the cottage, where, as Elias looked behind him, he saw Anna in the window taking off her clothes.

She was pulling off her jeans; he could just see her from the waist up. And then he got a glimpse of someone—Breedlove probably—moving across the plane of the window and then Anna falling backwards out of sight. What the fuck? The dog had moved over to the cottage and seemed no longer threatening, more like he was watching the human to see what he was going to do. Elias felt a weight of emotions tumble through his gut as he approached the window—worry, jealousy, anger, confusion. He trusted Anna but he didn't like the way she was leaving him out, following her own fate. He thought they had a bond, after the last month of being pursued, almost killed, men dying. They had a blood bond between them now. And here she was with Breedlove, undressing, getting down with the man who killed her cousin? Then Elias was close enough to see the buckhorn knife in her hand, and Breedlove's thick arm intercept it, and then he was banging on the stout locked

171

door of the cottage with his fist, and yelling at them to let him in.

The Dane had caught the excitement and was jumping on the door next to him, clawing at it and barking ferociously, tearing the wood into splinters in seconds with his thick nails. Then several other dogs joined the fray, hounds and retrievers from around the estate. Then the people from the house started appearing and shouting questions, surrounding Elias and trying to stop his pounding. And a minute later the door finally opened and there was Breedlove, blood smeared on his sweater, squeezing Anna in a headlock with one muscular arm and demanding to know who Elias was and why he was trespassing on his property and telling his friends to call 911 because the bitch had tried to kill him. Anna was incensed; her jeans down at her ankles, her panties gone, blood on her face and thighs. She was screaming a non-stop torrent of obscenities and threats and demands that Breedlove release her. Elias could see the fix they were in, and he tried to explain who he was, while demanding that Breedlove let go of Anna and grabbing him by the thumb and torquing it out until he had to relax his grip, but the other young men were having none of it, they kept him closely surrounded, and he could hear in the din one of the girls on her cell telling the police dispatcher about a home invasion and attempted murder.

Finally Elias convinced them to let him deal with Anna and he sat down on the couch in the cottage with her while she pulled her cords back up but all the while she's still shouting at the rest of them, calling them accessories to murder and conspiracy and "white preppy trust fund bitches" and she wouldn't stop no matter how hard Elias tried to calm her down. She had apparently been doing something or her mania had gotten worse, or both, besides the fact that she just tried to kill Breedlove and he apparently tried to rape her.

172

Then the police showed up pretty quickly: three cars for starters, and they began separating everyone and questioning them. Elias once again left a lot out of his explanations. He told them that he and Anna were in Miller's when she left suddenly with the others and asked him to follow them, which he did, and he saw Anna and Breedlove struggling through the window. End of story. The other students couldn't add much. But Ronnie told them that Anna had been stalking him for weeks, and once she got him out here where she wanted to talk to him she pulled a knife and assaulted him. They had the weapon, and then an ambulance showed up and the paramedics attended to his cut. He also informed the cops that Anna was on bail for manufacturing meth, that she had an extensive criminal and psychiatric record, and that she told him she was high this evening. Apparently at least one of the Albemarle County deputies knew him, and after they did some checking on their hand-held computers, Elias could see that they were going to take them in. They arrested Anna, put her in handcuffs in the back of a car, and Elias in cuffs in the back of another car, and took them back into Charlottesville to the sheriff's office.

Elias was booked for trespassing and released, but they kept Anna. She signed for them to turn over some of her stuff to him. The police confiscated the knife, of course, but they gave him her cell and the bra with her tracker still hidden it. When he walked out of the building it was five in the morning and his car had been impounded. A light rain had begun to fall and the streets downtown were wet and deserted. While he was being processed he could hear Anna somewhere in the bowels of the station still screaming at the officers and threatening retribution. He felt like they had made a colossal mistake pursuing Breedlove on their own. Now things were clearly worse, and it might take months before Anna got out of jail and came down from her mania. He had let things get out of control by listening to her and believing that they couldn't trust the authorities. Standing there in the rain he realized that Anna was of course very sick, had been sick and using drugs all these weeks, and there was no way he could stop her from making things worse. From that first chance encounter at Waffle House to the present, he had felt a strange attraction to her, to her fierce independence and then her loneliness and victimization at the hands of stupid, evil men. And he had been pulled into her paranoid, drug-induced world by his own depression and loneliness; he had to admit that to himself. He should have been more objective. The bottom line was that he had turned the search for truth about the murder of a cruelly forgotten young woman but stranger to himself over to a mentally ill girl.

He walked around the downtown mall for an hour aimlessly looking in windows, then headed up Main Street to the Blue Moon Diner as it opened and had a coffee and some eggs and toast. A few students came in who had also been out all night, and somehow they made him feel better. It was as if he had travelled back in time to when he was an undergrad at UVA and used to roam around the county all night having fun. Except now he was fifty, his so-called girlfriend was in jail for attempted murder, her cousin had been tortured and killed, and people were trying to kill him. He sat there in a window booth staring at the street, trying to connect the past and the present, his youth and the night's mayhem. There was a section of the Sunday Charlottesville *Daily Progress* on the table and he stared at it absentmindedly reading articles, killing time until 7. One was about the testing of a new weapon called an electromagnetic railgun, used by the Navy to destroy targets a hundred miles away with some kind of invisible force. Another described the recently elected local congressman who had taken a trip to Buchanan County to thank coal miners there who had supported him. They had appeared in his TV commercials attacking his opponent for endorsing Obama's cap-and-trade policy. Then they presented him with a lump of coal in polyurethane mounted on a plaque to display in his Capitol Hill office.

It was time to go. Elias finished his coffee and took a taxi to the impound yard where he picked up his Jeep for 75 dollars and headed southwest to Floyd.

Chapter 15

After the preppy prick in the ER says lock her up in the psych ward the pigs take me across the parking lot and in a back door so no one can see me, a crazy person might disrupt their fucking dream world, get infected, past an old Plymouth faded no-color packed floor to ceiling with grocery bags full of medical records, canned food, thousands of sugar packets and plastic utensils lifted from 7-11, withered house plants, run down at the heel shoes of every kind, coverless paperbacks, boxes of dried cosmetics, a window air conditioner, piles and piles of clothes and blankets, a regular survivalist bunker with a fine dust of cigarette ash on every inch of the upholstery and windows in five seconds I know her life and how badly she wants to keep it under control.

Inside the corridors are cool tranquilizing any pathology the human condition can throw at it shit up the elevator they unlock me and then lock me in a room with inquisition nurse and techs continuously cajoling and threatening medications just knock the bitch out so we don't have to deal with her can I just get a goddamn cigarette I have to get out of seclusion so I take the paper cup while they watch then they take my clothes and put me in a backless gown get a good look and they leave me and I spit out the pills and push them in the gaps between the wall coverings. There's a window up high I can see the tops of trees moving in the streetlight. They won't give me anything to write with but I rave and bang for a while they want me to sleep but they can't give me anymore meds so I get a couple of last year's crap People magazines and start thumbing through wondering where Elias got to is he still locked up in town waiting for me or already heading back to Floyd I don't know can he get me out I doubt it I'm in for 48 or 72 hours until another magistrate comes by for a hearing then send me back to jail or Staunton for another long bout of detox and shock, or maybe just the incessant lithium and anti-psychotics for a few months until they think I'm not going to kill anybody but of course by that time I will have already done it there is nothing standing between me and him except a few thin walls and he knows it as long as I am alive I will kill him and

176

set Sylvie free it's the law of divine retribution and there is no escape from the wheel call it what you will. I looked him in the degenerate blue eyes and saw what he had never even seen himself the brown man the black man his own daddy never told him even while he himself was writing in the language probably not even shamed by his kind just wasn't good for business the mixed blood in the coal mining business anyway always was power went to your head and the worst was the miners themselves when they went corporate and moved uptown or to Charleston and sent their kids away to school but even the innocent got the dust on them descended from the same seam you can't escape the mountains I should know and now he knows that I am forging a new knife to gut the Irish out of that halfbreed and return him to the happy hunting ground of his ancestors ....

 I stop screaming and sleep a couple of hours the day shift lets me out after breakfast but follow me around so I take a Librium just so they know and then they stop and even leave the door open which is a big mistake. I pretend to sleep really I'm watching the clouds wilder willful wavier meal drift Elias called them the afternoon we sat in the chairs under the protection of the buffalo and just stared at the sky before the shit hit the fan. I know they're plotting to destroy my will to keep me from disrupting the status quo toppling those business suits in their headquarters in Richmond just like they topple mountains and bury my baby Cassie and now Sylvie all that I have ever loved taken from me the sons of bitches have always had murder and rape in their hearts since history began and spread their evil seed into the New World just like the Bible predicted because of the greed and power in their pricks all men are like that using every trick in the book even religion even medicine even education all in the service of Satan or Mammom or almost all because Elias doesn't seem that way although maybe I am just deluding myself again but they can't destroy what they don't know nothing about the blood of the wild universe runs through my veins which is so much stronger they really have no idea what they are fooling with so I just have to trust my instincts and never let anyone get that deep.

 I drift into the room across the hall test the windows just screws there's a dime on her counter and a few twists of the forearm I've got it

177

open and shit we're five floors up no roofs below and wander down to the dayroom. The people in here who aren't zombies yet live outside corporate psychiatric headquarters set up their own palisade of rationalizations and other strategies or they go underground working their fantastical seams like miners until their backs or their lungs or their legs run out and they take to the couch and stare into the back of the TV where the men in suits are waiting for them. The techs come like photons every fifteen minutes with their clipboards and pens to see if I am still alive or still dead and go on to the next door and the nurse with the blonde waterfall and the paper cup her breasts pin me against the wall it's Sunday morning how I would like to suckle them like a cub but that will have to wait patience one thing the medical system has taught me I will get out again they cannot keep me behind walls for long. In the afternoon they give me group therapy for an hour twelve people on the acute unit times a quarter hour each times $125 an hour equals $375 for sitting there bored with the depressed students and the obese wives the obligatory sociopath the psychotic new mother the topless addict the black manic two anorexics and the man who had tried to blow his brains out with a shotgun but only managed to blow off his face. Everyone smokes and no one notices.

Time goes by. Late in the weekend double shift they bring in a large quiet tanned to the middle of his forehead man I know in his eyes is as psychotic as the day is long but they put him in a room down the hall by himself and soon enough he starts rolling on the carpet praising Jesus for sending him to heaven and singing hymns then before they can get the meds into him takes off into the dayroom and possessed with superhuman strength the wild gives its followers picks up one end of the slate pool table with techs on his back like devotees and they go juggernauting off down another hall and I catch up with them in a heap on the floor and insinuate myself down into the pile whispering to him to calm down it's only castles burning and the techs are yelling at me to get away go back to your room and so I leave them with the nurse's security pass in my manic hand and then into tiny dancer's room she is smoking in bed and watches me unspeaking as I go over to her kiss her on the lips sit down on the other bed and pull on her cowboy boots and coat and into the deserted lobby swipe the main door I'm gone swipe the

178

elevator and soon I'm out in the streetlights like a bat goodfuckingbye
Five West ....

The dogs woke Elias in the middle of the night. Not barking, they were running around the house, apparently looking out of the windows downstairs. Lying in bed he could hear the Lab moaning or howling like he used to do when he lived at the beach and ambulances would pass by. It was in the teens, the windows were closed and Elias couldn't hear a thing outside as he listened for a minute but a night breeze moving through the oaks. The moon had set some hours ago but when he looked outside in the faint starlight of the wind-blown sky he could just make out a shape slowly ascending the driveway about a hundred yards away. Whoever it was, he wasn't trying to conceal himself. Elias pulled the .32 out of its holster secured now to the back of the headboard, slipped on his sneakers, and walked downstairs in his pajamas where he heaved on his heavy jacket and let himself out the back door, pushing the dogs back with his foot to keep them in and shushing them. They didn't obey like when Anna did it. He made a wide circle around the shed, keeping the dead stalks of the hydrangeas and the now barren forsythia between him and the driveway. He wasn't really thinking about who was approaching, just figured it must be trouble. Then as he scrutinized the shape closer he suddenly realized who it was. Never assume anything, he said to himself.

Anna walked up to the door and knocked, and now the dogs started barking.

"What happened? Did you convince the doctors you were sane?" he said from the shadows.

"Son of a bitch," Anna cursed. "You startled the horsepiss out of me. Why don't you mind your manners when a girl has been out on the road all night? I coulda blowed your head off, if I had a gun."

179

He showed the gun in his pocket as he walked up to her and then wrapped his arms around her thin frame. She felt bone cold through the thin jacket he didn't recognize.

"Is that a real gun or are you just glad to see me?" she asked.

"The dogs were howling; I didn't know who was coming."

"I alerted them when I got to the bottom of the drive," she said, matter of factly.

"Are you okay?"

"I've never been okay," she answered, sitting down on the front porch. "But if you mean am I recovered enough from being raped and locked up to have my wits about me, then yes. The cold will do that to you."

"And spoken with the clarity of someone who has been on the road for twenty-four hours. What did you do, break out?"

"In a manner of speaking."

"Well, come on in. Tell me all about it."

"Just a minute," she said. "You've got to see something. There's always a reason why things happen the way they do."

She led him out to the middle of the yard by the hand, after he had opened the door and let the dogs out to keep them from scratching it apart.

"Check it out," she said, motioning to the northwestern horizon. He gazed into the distance for a while, seeing nothing but a couple of airliners moving between Perseus and Cassiopeia. Then a spark fell across the void, followed by a second, into the hump of Buffalo Mountain. In the course of maybe five minutes, he saw a dozen more embers leave their brief curved trails, like the points of a firestick waved by a mischievous god child.

"It's a meteor shower. I've been watching it the last couple of hours as I walked up the parkway."

180

She had hitchhiked from Charlottesville, down Route 29 South all the way to Danville, as she explained it, with a few irregular side trips, then west on 58 after she had warmed up in a couple of bars, all the way to the Blue Ridge, and then the last few miles on foot, into the falling stars. She was cold and hungry, but uncomplaining as usual, and seemingly all right.

"I could use a smoke," she said. "Bummed my last one from a farmer in Patrick County hauling hay to his cows. Must have thought I was an apparition."

"You look a little frayed around the edges, but none the worse for wear."

"You mean me or this coat? You can blame that on a coke-head stripper. All they give you in the crazy house is a gown and some booties. Had to borrow the rest. And what's worse: they took my knife, the goddamned pigs. Always arresting the wrong people."

"Don't worry about your knich," he said as they walked into the house. "I'll make you a new one; there's plenty of antler left, and I've got a piece of steel with some history that I've been saving that will work well for the tang."

"For the what?"

"The tang. I'll explain later. Do you want to eat or go right to bed?"

"I've got to take a shower, then eat, then maybe I can sleep."

"Okay. I'll stoke the fire while you bathe and then we'll have some eggs and tofu."

"Sounds very Floyd County," she said and disappeared down the hallway trailing her clothes.

An hour later he was tucking her under the flannel sheets in the guest bedroom, but she seemed to be having a hard time calming down. Elias didn't know if it was the bipolar, or she was just agitated from 24 hours of hitching. She had missed a few doses of Lithium being locked up, she

181

told him; they had only given her some anti-psychotic meds to attempt to knock her out, but apparently she had tongued them. She kept kicking the blankets around with her skinny legs so that now she was lying uncovered in her socks, underwear and one of his Nantahala T-shirts. She looked like an open pocket knife. The heat from the full wood stove had ascended up the stairs and through vents in the ceiling and the temperature in the bedroom was pushing 80.

"Is it too hot for you?" he asked, standing over her and pulling the dogs off the bed. "I can close the vents. You look like you're not going to sleep anytime soon."

She had a scheming, randy look about her eyebrows. "I know what will help me go to sleep," she said, reaching up and drawing her fingernails down the inside of his forearm. "All these fireworks have made me horny."

"Fireworks?" She did look very seductive in that underwear, he thought. He pointed. "What does it say on them: 'You Want What?'"

She turned her rear end toward him and put one hand behind her head, striking a pose. "They're Victoria's Secret for college sluts. 'You Want Me,' it says, and it's not a question."

Staring at her on the bed like one of his students in her dorm room Elias suddenly realized they had gone so far over the top with their flouting of the law that he was starting to take for granted that they could continue on this way without getting caught, as if here in the bedroom in his cabin deep in the woods under the mountain's shadow they were protected from all human traffic, from all rules and regulations, all human activity whatsoever except nibbling at the erotic edges in the sylvan scene of a goddess's inviolate bower. And he caught himself. It was as if he had been drugged for the past few weeks and had just woken up to the future. And it was filled with courtrooms and holding cells and fines.

"We need to talk first," he said to her with a serious face. "They're going to come looking for you. You know that. Probably here. Probably today. This isn't just another psychiatric admission, remember, that you have escaped from. You were arrested for attempted murder. Attempted murder, Anna. And you were already out on bond for the meth charges. The next time they pick you up they're taking you directly to jail, not to the hospital where apparently you know how to get out. They could show up here anytime."

He paused for a moment because she was looking at him curiously; he couldn't tell if the cracked light in her eyes was anger or lust, or maybe something else, some wild light that was beyond anger and lust, something he couldn't really fathom but was beginning to get used to. She was like some animal he had found with a broken leg in the woods to nurse back to health, and now she was torn between staying with him in a domesticated state or running back into the forest. He was fascinated by her wildness, her independence of all customs and rules that were such a part of his life and training. His own outlaw streak had been tempered by the military, or at least it was at times justified by them; he did hate the many stupid laws that trumped when the two clashed, but he was still not sure how much of what she did was part of her nature, part of the natural world, or whether it was simply a chemical imbalance. Was she untamed, or was she mentally ill? Probably, he thought at last, it didn't really matter in the long run; she was what she was.

She slowly sat up in bed on her knees, so that they were about at eye level and stared at him for a few seconds without speaking but with a half smile on her lips, then reached down and pulled up her T-shirt over her head and let in fall on the bed. He looked at her breasts; as he already knew, they were small and the aureole was very wide and dark, the color of Indian tea against her bronze skin. "We can talk in the morning," she said. "You always worry too much. No one knows I'm here, and besides, the dogs will let us know if anybody shows up, and I can hide out in the woods. You don't know me. I can make myself invisible." She took his left hand and put his fingers one at a time along with her own, into her mouth, and then she took them out dripping with saliva and moved them to her right breast, where their two hands, as if one, started rubbing and twisting her nipple until it stood straight up, like a caterpillar erect on a mushroom. Then she moved their hands to her left breast, and then down and across her flat stomach into her panties where they curved into her vagina. All the time she kept looking into his eyes, except when his would stray across her body. Their fingers began to move up and down over her hardening clitoris and still she wouldn't turn her face away, and as they continued the rhythm in and out, falling and rising, with their entwined fingers, Elias began to be drawn into her eyes, into the pleasure that was rising inside of her, like he was falling into a river rushing downstream. He was in the rapids of her eyes, he could feel the tension in her little body rising up from her feet through her bony legs and the muscular flesh of her ass into his hand and her hand, together pulling up in her wave after wave of tension to crest and collapse in her eyes. A couple of minutes later she started to climax, licking her lips and then leaning her forehead into his chest like a cantilevered balcony and softly nuzzling his own nipples she began to speak into his breast some of those ancient woodland words that he still did not know the meaning of but was beginning to understand ...

After she climaxed she collapsed into a heap like burned logs and then he got down on his knees beside the bed and pulled her thin legs apart like a compass and began to gently use his tongue on her. He felt like a wolf gorging himself on his prey, except that she had asked him for it, had willed it in him. She smelled and tasted like the local sourwood honey, and he felt like he could feast on her slowly and contemplatively like this for hours, like he might sit in front of the andirons all night watching the sticks burn and sputter in flames. The dogs kept nosing his face and he had to push them back several times. But finally he got up on the bed and slowly pushed himself inside her, holding her in his hands while she arched her back, and then a minute later she turned over so that he could enter her from behind. It was a little disconcerting to be staring at her tattoo while fucking her—did he have absolute power or did she, or maybe it was simply a warning—but he got used to it, accepted it. At the end he was so much inside of her that he suddenly opened his eyes and felt like he was seeing through her eyes, seeing himself from her eyes turned to look at him behind her in a closed loop, as if he had entered her from one end and risen as a different kind of being from the other, and was mating with her like two animals might mate, oblivious of themselves and each other, oblivious even of the insane material world around them, blinded by the fierce forces that united everything in the creative act. And through that evolutionary window he saw their two physical bodies transformed at last from their animal nature into godlike beings, as if the two of them had bypassed all sense of humanity, passing the seed of immortality and death before they fell apart into the bedclothes and tumbled almost instantly into a dreamless dream.

"Are you on any birth control?" he asked when they woke up several hours later to full slatted sunlight across the bed. The dogs and cats were curled into the covers in their habitual locations.

"Jesus Christ, what a question. I was raised Catholic, remember?"

"I thought you were a pagan, suckled on outworn creeds."

"I'm a Catholic pagan, all right? What could be more natural than the rhythm method? Fuck those artificial hormones." She turned onto her back, filched a cigarette out of a bedside pack, coughed once, and lit it. "Don't

185

worry. I don't want to get pregnant any more than you do. Can you imagine what the baby would be like with all the drugs I'm taking?" She thought for a minute, exhaling smoke rings toward the ceiling beams. "No arms." Ring. "Or three arms." Ring. "And hyper. Hyper as hell. Never able to relax and enjoy life. Just trying to survive it. Lithium babies. They take a licking and keep on kicking."

Elias was only half amused; her sense of humor was grimmer than his. He got out of bed and cracked the window. It was windy and clear, and so was his consciousness. He felt certain that the police would come looking for Anna, despite what she said the night before. He still believed that the authorities would have to take her illness into account when assessing her charges, and that she would most likely wind up back in Western State for a few weeks, or maybe months. After all, what had she really done up to this point? She might be able to beat the meth charges; the evidence didn't indicate any meth had actually been made or distributed. There was, however, evidence that they had been attacked, including the corpse of a convicted felon. So she was in a state of distress. Then the attack on Ronnie Breedlove could be explained either as self-defense, or even a paranoid delusion based on her conspiracy theory about her cousin's death. All things considered, Elias reasoned that the best course of action might be to turn Anna in and have her throw herself on the mercy of the courts. He could get her a good defense attorney, and maybe by the time she got released from the hospital a report on the attack and the mutilation deaths would have come out and things would have settled down.

He turned to speak to her but she forestalled him.

"I know what you're thinking by the way you've been looking at me, and you're wrong. You think they'll put me in the hospital and all these problems will just go away. But there's bigger forces at work here than the psychiatrists and the judges. These people are out to kill me, don't forget. Or

186

at the very least, they want me locked up for a long, long time. You—you're just going to get discredited: getting bamboozled by a drug-addicted paranoid maniac can't be very good on your resume." She paused to inhale. "I'm telling you, they've got a plan and lots of money. This isn't just about you and me and Sylvie makes three; this is about billions of dollars in energy money if they can get the EPA off their backs. What was the coal company in China you read offering?"

"Thirteen billion."

"You think they want a couple of local hillbillies gumming up their plans? Thirteen billion can buy a lot of politicians and po po. There's probably a giant black seam under every one of them mountains in West Virginia and Kentucky, just waiting to be dynamited into kingdom come. And the good country people of Appalachia, why they want those iPads and Cadillacs and Jack Black just like the next guy. This ain't about terrorizing the environment; this is about self-determination. Just give us our $20 a hour jobs hauling coal and you can do what you want to these mountains."

Anna had gotten up out of bed during her speech and started picking up her clothes which were scattered all the way down the hall and stairs. Elias listened to her as she walked around the house, apparently having forgotten or not caring whether he could hear her. After just a few hours of sleep she seemed to be as wound up as when they were separated two days ago. She was ranting something about the Breedlove family, their name, mixed up with her own multi- race origins along with the political machinations of every wealthy person in Appalachia, the desires of the working class, together with the demands of the global economy. In the bits and pieces he could catch it sounded like all the guests on Bill Maher had started speaking at the same time.

She had gone into the kitchen and was feeding the animals, so he put on some clothes and went down to the road to get the paper. It was chilly, in the teens, and blustery, but the cold felt good. The wind was trying to rip the last leaves from the trees. As he was reaching into the box a county sheriff's car went by; he waved with his free hand without looking. The car didn't slow but its presence seemed ominous so he walked quickly back up the drive to the house. Anna was unconcerned, of course. Just a coincidence. She had made coffee and was watching the cell phone video again on the computer, along with the documents. She grabbed the paper while he made some breakfast.

"We've got a lunar eclipse coming on the 21st. Coinciding with the winter solstice. First time it's happened since 1638."

"The year Anne Hutchinson was banished by the Puritans."

"And we might even get a red moon."

"What's that?" he asked.

"When the atmosphere is right, the eclipse blocks all the light from the moon except the red spectrun. They call it a blood moon." She loudly turned the page. "Speaking of which, looks like the Republicans are going to keep the tax cuts for the rich. Millions are out of work, the country's in debt, and the rich just keep getting richer."

"Obama has to compromise to get anything at all accomplished."

"Compromise or cop out? He got voted in by the people who wanted a change. Not the same old same old."

"Politics means working slowly to a consensus. It's the only dialectic when you have just two viable parties."

"It's a puppet show and Wall Street is always pulling the strings."

"That's probably true," he admitted, handing her a bagel and cream cheese. "Even the recession probably won't

188

change anything, not really. Look what happened when they didn't find WMD's in Iraq. Bush still got re-elected. America is not progressive. Never has been. We've always been pro-business and anti-poor. As if everything in life depended on the economy. Capitalism is our religion. We've always exploited the natural world, just like men have exploited women, just like the Europeans exterminated the Indians."

She bent her head back and looked up at him from the computer. Upside down, her face had an alien effect: her mouth became her eyes, her eyes became her mouth. Her eyes opened in a big smile. "Not quite exterminated. There are still a few of us heathens around, causing trouble." And she reached back and pinched his nipple.

"Here's what we're going to do," he began.

"Oh Jesus, here it comes," and she rolled her eyes.

"I have a tent we'll set up in the woods, and a mummy bag good to zero. When the cops come looking for you—and they will," he said, waving off her objection—"you can hide out up on the mountain until they realize you're not here. There's a nature area up there I'll show you. You'll like it."

"And then what?"

"And then what?" Elias realized he had not thought through his plan.

"What happens after they stop looking for me, which they never will, of course, because Mason Dixon's CEO knows we, or at least I, have the goods to bring him down? Do you really think he's going to let this die? Come on, professor. He's out to kill me. It's either him or me. This is a battle to the death, and I'm planning on getting him before he gets me."

Elias was afraid to say what he thought—that the conspiracy theory about Mason Dixon was probably just another of her paranoid delusions, maybe even fueled by the guilt over her drug use, which may have somehow led to

189

Sylvie's murder and mutilation. That was, of course, what Sigmon thought, and he had years of experience to draw from. Or her guilt about her father. Elias had what with her? Six weeks maybe of first-hand observation? On the other hand, he couldn't see himself turning her in. No way he could do that. He would have to try and help her to see through her own illness. Demonstrate, somehow, that she was wrong in her thinking.

"Here's what *I* am going to do," she began. "I'm going to get me another motherfucking knife, and I'm going to find that evil Melungeon son of a bitch, gut him, and send his soul back to hell where it came from. Then I'm going to bleed him and skin him and take those relics to Sylvie's grave so she can have a proper sleep."

"Jesus Christ, Anna. You sound like a Viking. Blood payment and all."

"That's right."

"Well," he said, shrugging his shoulders. "You can't skin him what a regular knife. You're going to need something with a broader blade."

"I know what a skinning knife is."

"Tell you what. How about a compromise? Let's set up your tent in case the cops come by and then we'll work on your blade."

"I'll tell you what. How's this for a compromise? I'll hide out in the frigging woods until I'm ready, then you take me to Charlottesville so I can get my car."

"What are you talking about? You can't get your car. They'll arrest you."

"I'll get someone else to get it for me."

"Like who?"

"Like some wino living on the street."

Elias reflexively made a scoffing sound through his nose.

"What? You don't think I can get my car out of hock?"

190

"What are you going to use for money? It's at least $25 a day. And I don't think they'll take a credit card. Besides, you're going to have to show some ID."

"Don't you worry your privileged ass about me getting my car from the yard. Have you ever had your car impounded?" She didn't wait for an answer. "No, I didn't think so. I have, many times, and I'm sure I'll have many times more." She was starting to get worked up, and angry. "And you don't even need to drive me. I can hitch back to C-ville just like I got here, no problem. And I can drive myself to Richmond."

"Richmond? Why do you want to go to Richmond?"

"Because that's where the sonuvabitch is, him and his coal mining father."

"How do you know they're in Richmond."

"Because it's Christmas break. I just looked it up on the UVA website. He's done his dirty work for daddy and now it's time to reap the rewards. And there's also an unscheduled corporate meeting this week. Something's going down. Believe me, they don't usually hold unscheduled meetings. I got a text on Sylvie's phone from Mountain Justice. They're going to protest. So the whole damn clan of mountain rapers will be there, getting drunk on their profits and going to Christmas mass, and the mountain defenders will be there too, calling them to account. Including me." She paused. "Including us, if you want to come."

"And you're just going to walk into their meeting and assault the lot of them?"

"Something like that. You can always count on a redneck to get right to the point."

Elias understood that there was no contravening her, outside of turning her in to the police. He was coming around to the idea that if she could confront her demons in a relatively controlled setting, maybe she would see her own delusions for what they were and get back to normal, wherever that was. Lacan called it traversing the fantasy.

191

See it for what it is, acknowledge it, live it, and then go on. His mistake in Charlottesville had been to leave her alone with Breedlove and his crew; he should have intervened when they left Miller's and put a stop to the impending violence. He couldn't leave her alone now, that was a given. On the other hand, feeding into her delusions might be just as bad. He decided to try one more strategy.

"I still believe the best way to deal with this is through evidence and the courts. We have the documents, we have video of Sylvie's rape, we have proof that someone was trying to kill us, not to mention your house being burned down and your dogs hanged. And most importantly, we have an ally in Sigmon, the ex-prosecutor. He can get us heard; he can make a case to have this whole thing investigated by the state police. I think that's a much more logical and practical way of resolving this problem than attacking the head of Mason Dixon Energy, which is just going to get you in more hot water, and probably not do a damn bit of good."

Anna turned her chair around and stared at him with a look of benign contempt.

"Does this prosecutor believe me that there is a conspiracy, or does he just think I'm some whack job who needs to take her meds? Tell me the truth. I'll know if you don't."

She drilled to the heart of the matter, Elias thought.

"He believes some of it, not all of it."

"He probably believes less than you do, which ain't saying much. He's not going to pursue this 'problem,' as you call it, like a pack of coon dogs with a full moon. No, he'll make a few phone calls and then the whole thing will collapse. Yes, there's plenty of evidence, but it has to be interpreted, and who do you think is more inclined to interpret it the way it really happened? Me, who is the victim, or the state police, who like all the other cops are being paid by the government which is run by the politicians which are paid by the corporations? You've got to just ignore the whole history of Appalachia to think that the justice system is going to do right by Sylvie."

He gave all she said time to sink in. Her words seemed to animate the very furniture in the room, echoed by the wind blowing outside. Even the dogs were watching them and listening.

"I think you're overstating the case against the legal system. And you know, because you've told me so yourself, that you have a tendency to see things in a slightly paranoid light, because of your illness and the effects of taking methamphetamines for so long."

She gave him an evil look when he said that, but then she smiled.

"'Slightly paranoid' is putting it mildly," she replied, lighting another cigarette from the one she had just finished. "You haven't seen me yet in a full-blown paranoia, and I hope you never do. It's not a pretty sight." She paused, reflecting. "I know I have a history, and there's really no reason for you to believe me, but I know what will happen if I let this go." She moved over to the couch and lay down with her feet up on the cushions. "Breedlove will get away with murder, his father will continue to exploit the land for whatever he can to pad his retirement plan, and basically things will just go on in the same old same old. But you certainly don't need to get any more involved. You've done more than enough for someone who barely knew me until a month ago. I never asked you for your help; you offered it freely, and for that I have to love you a little. But there's really no reason for you to get involved any further; it will just damage your career getting mixed up with me. I am trouble. Always have been, always will be. I have no career, so it doesn't matter what I do. I'm ill, and that's never going to change. Whether I go to Richmond or not, either way I'm just going to wind up back in Western State eventually." She continued to look at him as if she expected him to refute this last statement.

Elias sensed she was both right and wrong, but he also knew there was nothing he could do about it. Maybe it did all come down to love—maybe he just needed to let her know someone did care, he cared, one day at a time, and let the cards fall where they may.

"I guess then I'll just have to love you back a little, and do my best to keep you out of jail and the hospital."

"You have no control over that."

"I know. But it's in my nature to try."

"Do what you have to do," she said, getting up.

He pulled an extra flashlight from the junk drawer, dug the sleeping bag and tent out of the attic, carried everything out the back door and was starting to lead her into the woods when she put an arm on his to stop him.

"Better if I do this by myself. Then when the cops come, you can tell them you don't know where I am without lying. Otherwise, you'll be aiding and abetting."

"I'm not worried about that."

"I know, but I am."

While she was gone, Elias went around to the backside of the shed where he had built a small brick and stone fireplace. It looked like a barbeque, which in fact it often was, but the rest of the time it was a forge where he liked to make things for the property—latches, hinges, andirons—and knives and swords. He had spent nine months while he was stationed in Japan hanging out with a swordsmith he met in his kendo class. Not long enough to be an apprentice. He didn't pretend to know what he was doing: the craft was far too skilled and ceremonial. But working with the metal and the fire relaxed him when he was stressed, a kind of natural meditation. During the hours at the forge he felt a sense of tradition and even timelessness. In the winter surrounded by snow, in the summer heat, it soothed him. Besides, it was practical. Real Japanese katanas were not cheap, and he needed everyday blades for his workouts in the woods when he would practice turns and cuts, attacks and counterattacks. He wasn't about to use the one he had on the mantel; it had cost him an arm and a leg. It was held in reserve for special occasions.

He pulled off the tarp covering the forge and took a long look. It had been some time since he had made anything, maybe a year, maybe two. Too depressed, he guessed, to get motivated. He got some kindling burning, then larger pieces of cedar and oak, then he loaded the bottom with coals, went back into the house, and sat down at the computer screen with the photos of the documents from Sylvie's phone. It was an odd juxtaposition, switching from the Japanese way of thinking to the Saponi. He had saved the texts on several jump drives which he had put in different places, including his office and his safety deposit box at the bank, with notes explaining what they were, in case the computer was stolen, his house was burned down, or anything else might happen to him. He really didn't think any of these things would happen, but he was certainly very cautious and wary now compared to his previous life before Anna arrived on the scene. Living in Floyd the last decade he had forgotten all the horrible things he had done in his youth. Now he was starting to think like he had those years in the Navy.

Anna had managed to translate a good deal of the documents, but they still amounted mostly to names and numbers with no relevance to anything on the outside. If Elias could take them to an accountant in the mining business, maybe he would know, or to a prosecutor, or possibly even an investigative journalist who covered mining, but he felt he didn't have enough hard evidence to convince anyone of a conspiracy that involved murder, torture, and cover-ups. Maybe he had enough to scare someone, as Anna suggested. Maybe old Breedlove was scared enough to use violence to stop them. They were old school, Elias

195

remembered. The father was from rural Southwest Virginia; he had grown up in the business. Underneath the corporate veneer, probably there was a hard core blue collar mountain man who was used to solving problems physically. He was ruthless, used to getting his way. Maybe the fact that he felt threatened now was an advantage that they had over him. He was coming after them. On the other hand, maybe now that Anna was wanted by the police, all he had to do was wait until they locked her up, in one place or another.

An hour later she showed up, brushing snow off, trailing the dogs. She came in the back door, closed it, and stood in front of the woodstove in his castoff L.L.Bean jacket.

"Something's cooking," she said, pulling off the thin driving gloves she liked to use with the bare knuckles.

He turned around from the computer screen to face her. "What do you mean?"

"You've got a fire in the bar-bee. What'cha making? I'm cold and starving."

He smiled and stood up. "I'm cooking your knife. I've got some good pieces of steel I've been saving; they just need to be shaped and given a tempered edge. Come on, I'll show you."

She forced her blue lips into an exaggerated pout. "Can't we just cook some Portabella burgers and get the knife at the hardware store?"

"Shut up and learn something," he said, kissing her cold face and opening the door.

He led her out to the large shed and over to one wall under a work bench where various pieces of metal were hanging from nails and hooks. He pulled out a drawer in the bench crowded with small knives, blades, and other gleaming pieces, rummaged around for a moment, and selected several.

"We're going to blend two metals, iron and steel. These scalpel blades are surgical steel. They're left over from

196

World War II when my father liberated them from the Navy. They're too small for our purposes, but we can combine them."

"Liberated them?"

"Well, he was the medical officer on a tender, the Xanthus, and got hold of all sorts of interesting things when the war ended in '45 and they were one of the first ships in Japan. And this hunk of rebar," he added, pulling an L-shaped piece of metal off the wall, "is from the Berlin Wall. A buddy of mine in Germany sent it to me as a souvenir, knowing I liked to make blades. It's always good to have some metal with some history inside it. The old smiths believed blades took on the character of the men who made them and the metal they put in them. The spirits. So it was important to be in the right mood, the right frame of mind, and to observe the necessary rituals, the pieties, when forging a blade that was capable of destroying someone."

He looked her in the face. "Are you in the right mood?"

She laughed. "You're serious?"

"Of course."

"No you're not."

"Yes I am."

"Well, when it comes to destruction, I'm always in the right mood."

They seemed to be in a staring contest.

"There was this one guy named Muramasa, back in the fourteenth century, who apparently was a very fierce, angry swordsmith. Everybody was afraid of him, but they wanted his blades because they were so lethal in combat. But the blades he made possessed his spirit so much that they had a reputation for cutting their owners."

He was still looking at her, and she raised an eyebrow.

"That's the kind I want. A wild knife. One that can't be controlled."

197

"Okay," he said, moving outside. "As long as you understand that to be most skillful using your knife, you and the blade need to become one." He stopped and fluidly carved the air in a semicircle with his arm. "You move, it moves. It is no longer a separate entity, but an extension of your arm, your mind, your soul. Which means, you have to understand yourself to understand the blade. Okay? For example, what happened when you tried to stab Breedlove?"

"The motherfucker caught my knife on the way down and it only wounded him."

"That's not a good sign. You probably weren't fully into the moment."

"You're right, I wasn't. He was trying to rape me at the time."

Elias paused. "Okay. So we'll weld the two metals, just like the knife will be welded to your arm. But the blade, especially the cutting edge, will mostly be comprised of the surgical steel, and the rebar, which has a good amount of iron in it, will mostly be the body of the sword and the handle, the tang."

The hardwood and coals had been burning for two hours and were red hot. He took some heavy gloves from the wall, gave her one, and then placed the scalpels and the rebar in two sets of tongs and handed one set to her. "This is the ritual part. You're the blade, I'm the handle. I guide, but you do the cutting. Now, lay the tongs in the fire. Do you want to be on top or bottom? Or is that a stupid question?"

He pushed his tonged rebar deep into the coals, and she slid the scalpels on top of it.

"I thought so."

"Now what?"

"When they get hot enough, we start pounding them on the anvil. It's good exercise. You've got the forearms for it."

She flexed. "That's from holding the reins. I can lead too."

He felt her arm and whistled.

"How long will it take?"

"Well, normally it takes months to make a good katana. You've got to fold it innumerable times, repeatedly immersing it in water and oil, shape it, then you have to temper the edge while the blade is covered in clay, dousing it in the fire and warm water, then you have to rub it in oil and polish it with special stones. Then of course you have to put the handle on it."

"Like I said, how long will it take?"

"In your case, since it's just a knife, maybe a week."

"A week! Fuck you! There's no way I can wait a week! I told you, there's a meeting in Richmond this Friday. They're after me; there's not much time left. They're going to lock me up, you know. Then how am I going to get even?"

She was suddenly agitated but Elias kept his composure, staring into the fire.

"The Japanese call it *adauchi*," he said. "Revenge for the slaying of a clansman. It was considered justice to the medieval warrior, a way of restoring balance. But there was another kind of revenge, an excessive, selfish form that was more concerned with ego than with justice."

She pulled her steel out of the flames and studied the glowing metal as its acrid smoke rose up into the low clouds. He threw on some more cedar.

"How can you tell the difference?"

"You have to ask your superior. Usually the shogun."

She turned to face him with the smoking tongs in her gloved hand, the muscles in her arm ridged under the weight.

"So what do you think?" she asked. "Do I have a just cause, or am I a selfish, bipolar bitch?"

"I'm not your superior."

199

"But you are my temporary aider and abetter, my sugar daddy, my keeper, my …, what did you call it? … my handler, my…tang? That's it, you're my tang. Maybe I should drink you."

"Your handle, not your handler."

"But aren't the two words related? You do handle me, in more ways than one."

"Sort of. But the way I envision it, we are the two parts of this knife. You are the blade, the cutting edge, and I am the handle. The point is, we are both combined into the same instrument, just like the iron and steel are welded together."

"Then who is the handler? Who uses the blade?"

"Ah. That's the great mystery, isn't it. What do you want to call it? Nature? God? Karma? Maybe justice would be the most apposite word in this case. Who knows what forces are coming together in these acts. What causes were at work for us to meet at Waffle House that night? Or what were the agents behind Sylvie's death? Maybe it was Breedlove …

"It was definitely Breedlove. He said so."

"He told you he killed Sylvie?"

"Not in so many words. He kept suggesting it, and I could read it in him."

"Well, who knows what caused this guy to become a killer. Was it his father? His upbringing? Obviously he wasn't born that way."

"He could have been born with an evil spirit."

"Okay, he could have, but then you have to ask where did that bad soul come from? What was the reason for it? You see, what I'm getting at is that there are an infinite number of causes for everything that happens; you would have to trace causes back to the beginning of time to know where to put the blame. In fact, such blame putting is pointless. Most people just settle for a certain point, really arbitrary when you think about it in the whole span of time, and start there. Because if there are an infinite number of causal events, then really there is no cause. Everything is causeless. It is simply what is happening in this very moment."

"So nobody's guilty of anything?"

"Guilt is just the wrong word to describe what happens. Call it ignorance. We are ignorant of the larger context of our actions, ignorant of what made us, what forces act on us, and so we do stupid things. Some of them are so stupid as to appear evil, but evil implies that you know what you are doing is wrong. Why am I depressed most of the time? Why are you bipolar? Did God or nature make you bipolar? Was it your parents, in their genes? Was it environmental, just chance? No one knows the answers because the causes are way too complex."

"So you're saying that you don't believe in free will? That's ridiculous. People know when they are doing something wrong. Especially when they do it to kids who are too young to resist."

"I'm saying that free will exists only insofar as you know what you are doing. Most people haven't a clue. They have very little free will. That's why in the Gospels Jesus said that the truth will make you free. It was right after he stopped them from stoning the woman who committed adultery. He knew that her accusers were just as guilty as she was, or rather neither they nor the woman really knew what they were doing because they were ignorant of God, of the truth."

"I thought you were a Buddhist or something."

"I'm not a Christian or a Buddhist. I don't belong to any organized religion. I'm just quoting a text."

She looked at him curiously, maybe even with a stain of malice, he thought. "Then we should punish people for stupidity," she said with finality and returned her tongs to the forge.

201

Just then the dogs started barking. Anna shushed them and in the silence that followed they could just make out the crunching of tires turning onto the gravel of the driveway a half mile off. Before Elias could say a word, she sprinted to the house, disappeared into the kitchen and emerged in a few seconds with a large bag of granola in her hand. "I told you to feed me, but you wouldn't listen. Come on Gypsy. We've got to hide out in the woods. Just send the dogs to get me when the pigs leave," she yelled as she ran across the yard and into the trees. His dogs started after her but stopped when she turned abruptly and pointed back to the house.

He walked inside and quickly gathered up whatever of hers was lying around, including the bathroom towels which he threw in the washer on the way downstairs. But her coat was lying on a chair in the livingroom—the one she had gotten from the girl in the hospital—he had to cram that into a small hidden closet he had built into one wall next to the chimney when he was renovating. Then he let the dogs out the front door just as the sheriff's car pulled up.

Actually it was two cars, a county cop and another late model sedan. The driver was the same young deputy with the shaved head who had interrogated him the night of the bear mauling. Elias couldn't help thinking he looked a little like Eminem in a police uniform, and he smiled. The man riding shotgun was inexplicably a state policeman. Two men in coats and ties emerged from the sedan and stood by their car while the officers talked to Elias.

Eminem said, "Are you Elias Kraft?"

"Of course I am. You were here just a week ago when those men tried to kill me. What can I do for you?" And he stretched out his hand.

The deputy took it reflexively and asked, "Do you know a Diana Jassey?"

"Like I said, you just interrogated both of us."

"Do you know her? Is she your girlfriend?"

It seemed to Elias that the deputy was being much more formal than necessary, considering their recent run-in and the general affability of almost everyone in the county, government employees included. He could only explain this by the presence of the other men.

"I know her but she's not here."

"When was the last time you saw her?"

For some reason he had not anticipated this question. Lying was something Elias almost never did. He had had to lie in the military—it was inherent in his job—but ever since his discharge it was as if he was attempting to make up for his unethical youth. He could rationalize prevaricating and eluding the truth in intellectual language for an ethical reason, but a direct false response to a question was hard to do. On the other hand, he felt the breach of neighborliness in the deputy's unfriendly manner and he was especially suspicious of the other men who were leaning against their car talking to each other and seemingly ignoring the others.

"Who are these other people?"

The deputy looked around like he wasn't even aware there were people with him.

"This is Lieutenant Bondurant from the Christiansburg office of the state police, and these other men work for Mason Dixon Energy Company."

Bondurant, a black man, stepped forward to shake Elias' hand, but the other men did not move. Elias felt compelled to size them up more closely and walked over to them.

"What do you two do for Mason Dixon?"

"Security," the older one said. He was a bull-necked guy with bristly blonde hair who had put on maybe thirty pounds of fat since playing high school football. Elias noticed tattoos on his knuckles and another creeping up what was left of his neck from his white shirt collar, which he looked uncomfortable wearing buttoned. The top of the tattoo just visible looked like a pitchfork. The other man looked the same, just a slightly smaller version. Elias thought they could even be brothers.

"So why are you here?"

"They're here because of threats made against the company and its personnel," the state trooper interrupted. "By the woman we are looking for, Miss Jassey. We have a warrant for her arrest and the authority to search your property. I believe you said she is not here. May we take a look around?"

"I have no problem with the police here if you have a warrant, but I do not want these other gentlemen in my house or anywhere on my property."

Despite the court orders and the authoritative tone of voice, Elias liked the look on Bondurant's face; he sensed that he was not all that happy himself with the entourage from Mason Dixon.

"You fellas wait here, while we go inside," Bondurant said, and he and the deputy followed Elias inside the door. While he made some coffee, they walked around the downstairs and upstairs, just a cursory examination to prove that Anna was, indeed, not there. They asked about an attic and Elias showed them the trap door and pulled down the stairs so they could look there. They never asked about a cellar. When they got back down to the kitchen he offered them coffee, which they declined, then he took them out the back door to the shed where the Mason Dixon men were standing around the forge.

"I thought I asked you to wait at the car."

"You did. But we got cold and saw the barbeque smoking," said the younger man, smirking. Then he turned to Elias. "What are you cooking, Mr. Kraft? Looks like your tongs done caught fire."

"It's a forge. I'm making some tools."

He showed the policemen the inside of the shed, and escorted them back around to the front. Bondurant thanked him for his cooperation and the deputy reminded him that aiding a felon wanted by the police was a crime. He said they might have to come back repeatedly while they worked on this case, and he told Elias to call the Floyd County office if he should hear from Anna.

Before they left the older Mason guy came over and shook Elias' hand while he looked directly into his eyes, leaning forward at the same time and speaking softly: "We ain't fools. We know the bitch is around here. And you can believe we'll be watching." He punctuated his remark by shaking Elias' hand a lot harder than was necessary, clearly trying to cause some discomfort or pain, and Elias responded in kind. In about ten seconds of squeezing they quickly reached a stalemate between the other's weight advantage and Elias' muscular forearms, with neither seemingly inclined to let go, but by this time the cops were in their cruiser and watching through the windshield, and the security guy had to get back in his vehicle. Elias couldn't resist quietly saying as he walked away, "You're not as tough as you think you are." It was as if now that he and Anna had slept together the night before, he was feeling not only protective but competitive about the defense of her honor.

No sooner had they disappeared behind the trees down the driveway than Anna emerged from the woods, where she had been watching them.

"Jesus, Anna. Don't take any chances. That was the sheriff's office and the state police. And two thugs from Mason Dixon. I think I've seen them before, but I can't say where. They're definitely out to get you."

"Unless I get them first."

It was growing dark and they went back into the house to eat, leaving the dogs outside to keep watch. Then they returned to the forge and Elias started working the red-hot metal, banging the scalpels and rebar into one mass, next into a rectangular length which he folded over and banged again. When he got tired he would hand over the hammer to

Anna to shape for a while. Between the two of them the contours of a knife began to appear in the firelight over the course of an hour. It was satisfying work, Elias thought, under the stars. It was twenty degrees, the wind had died down and the coals bathed them in a pool of heat. But soon it was time to go in for the night.

They followed this routine for the next two days: sleeping, eating, working at the forge. Elias made a couple of sweeps of the perimeter of his property each day, looking for signs of anyone spying on them, but didn't see any. Meanwhile, Anna was getting increasingly hyperactive and agitated. He asked her if she was still taking her Lithium medication, and she confessed that she wasn't. She needed an edge, she said, and she didn't want anything to blunt her focus or interfere with her high energy level. The more hyper she got, the less reasonable she seemed to get either to his requests that she take her meds to calm down some or to his suggestions of alternative ways to deal with the Breedloves. She slept only a couple of hours Tuesday and Wednesday nights, between five and seven with the TV going full blast. She said she slept in the tent where she would go during the day when the arguing between them began to escalate or the dogs started barking, but Elias doubted that. She was unhealthily thin, and although she more than once made some lewd suggestions to him, they didn't have sex again after that first time. Elias slept soundly even though he was pretty worried: once he closed his eyes, the phenomena of this frantic life disappeared completely and he fell into unconsciousness quickly. But every time he woke up, there was Anna reading a magazine or watching the tube, and chain smoking. The bedroom was filled with overflowing ashtrays.

Late Thursday afternoon the knife was almost finished. Elias had tempered the edge with repeated firings and quenching so that a wavy, smoky-blue band appeared along the blade. Anna had sawed off another piece of the antlers hanging from a rafter and Elias had cut it on his jigsaw so that it fit the tang, secured in place with a single screw on either side. Now they were taking turns polishing the steel with some small stones he had brought back from Japan and cloths impregnated with oils he had ordered. Each time Anna thought it was done he would hold it up to the light and announce that it was "not quite there yet."

Finally he looked over the whole knife carefully, smiled, and handed it to her.

"So, what's the plan?" he asked. It had started snowing early in the morning and except for a five foot circle melted around the forge, the world was white.

"The plan is," she said, running a long index finger along the edge, "to gut Breedlove like a rabid fox. And then do the same to his daddy."

He looked at her closely in the diminishing light. The sky was still thick with clouds and the snow seemed to be changing over to sleet. He had been so preoccupied with finishing the knife he had not looked up for hours. Her eyes were burning with her mania, and while he studied them, as if in synch with his thoughts, a snowflake landed in her lashes, melted, then another drifted onto the glistening blade she held in her hand. It was very quiet. The frigid air seemed to hold its breath while the snow fell, and a deeper silence could be heard beneath it as some sleet began to ding against their clothing and the roof of the shed.

"Don't look so worried. I'm not really going to gut him. I'm just going to persuade him to confess."

Elias was not at all sure where her exaggeration ended and her reality began. "That was your plan last time. It didn't work."

"It did work. He told me what I needed to hear. I just didn't get it recorded."

"And why was that?"

"I forgot to cut it on."

"I thought you told me he didn't explicitly confess to killing Sylvie."

"He didn't deny it."

Elias shrugged. "So where are we? You talked to him. He didn't admit to anything. Then you left Miller's with him and his crew. He tries to rape you. You stab him and he calls the cops and you get arrested. And now what? We're going to drive to Richmond and do the whole thing again? This time as soon as he sees you he's going to call the police and this time you won't be able to get out of a locked ward. You know, you really aren't thinking through this at all. You're really just going to make things worse, more unmanageable."

"I am thinking about it, all the time. I just don't have the blind faith in the fucking legal system that you do. This isn't really about me, and especially not about you. Who gives a rat's ass about what happens to me? This is about power. This is about getting away with murder. Do you really think that the son of the Mason Dixon CEO is going to go to prison for killing an environmental activist, a college dropout, and a drug user?"

"Yes, I do."

"Get real, Kraft. What have the po po done so far? Jack shit. If I have to go to prison to bring a little justice to the world, that's just the price that's got to be paid. But at least I'll be happy knowing I took down the bastard that killed my cousin. You didn't lose a loved one. You don't have a debt to pay. You can't really understand what I'm going through."

She was so intense that he wondered if he could reach her at all. "If you get locked up for the rest of your life, I *will* lose someone I love."

She looked at him with a frustrating mixture of vulnerability and resolve, as if she had let him enter a room in her heart, but it was a very small room, and he was immediately locked in it. She would do what she wanted, or had to, outside that room. He could only observe and pick up the pieces. Later.

"That's just sentimental nonsense. You've only known me a month."

He ignored what she said. "Besides, I saw what they did to Sylvie too. I have been a witness to this horror, and I want to see the bastard pay just like you do. And then he tried to rape you as well. But the question is, which way is more likely to make them pay? You think you can just walk up to someone and kill him, and order is restored in the universe? Believe me, I know; it doesn't happen that way." As he said this he heard his words from the distance of knowing they weren't completely true, at least not based on his own experience. He had walked up to people and killed them, and it had seemed the right thing to do, at the time. But now he knew that politics, not a moral order, is at the root of the act, and by politics he meant the desire for personal power.

"Elias."

"What?"

"There's something you got wrong."

"What?"

"Breedlove didn't try to rape me. I let him think I wanted to sleep with him. It was the only way I could get him to let his guard down so I could stick my knife in his Melungeon heart?"

"Jesus, Anna."

"What?"

"Nothing. You're just so hard core. It's okay. I just wonder sometimes where the real you ends and the out of control you begins."

"You just don't know me very well."

"Not yet."

She looked up at the sky, licked the snowflakes from her face, laughed, then kissed him and pushed her cold tongue into his mouth.

209

"Well, let's hit it," she said.

"Hit it? What, now?"

"Hell yeah now."

He looked at his watch. "It's almost five and it's still snowing."

"All the more reason to get on the road. Come on, you've got a Jeep. I've seen you drive in the snow. You know what you're doing." He didn't say anything. "Look, we leave now, stop and get something to eat on the way, it's four hours to Richmond, we'll be there at eight, crash with some friends of mine, get up early and go to the protest."

"The protest?"

"The Mountain Justice people. They always protest at these meetings."

"That's probably exactly where the police will be looking for you."

"They've got more important things to do than look for me. Like busting some greens for trying to stop the rape of the country."

"Can't we just go to Breedlove's house? Confront him in private and see what happens."

"I don't know where he lives. He's unlisted."

He thought quickly, knowing that she was going with or without him. Once again, he seemed to be balancing on the knife edge of his feelings, and of her bipolar disorder. Let her go, with the likelihood she would end up dead or in jail, or stay with her and possibly go down with her. It was an ethical decision, really. Give up his desire and walk away from the whole affair, like a month-long dream, or give in to his desire and plunge into the dangerous unknown. But was his desire really to go with her? Maybe his desire was to stay safe, return to his normal quiet life of grading papers and listening to the wind. He was so ambivalent that he relaxed into a default meditation, his intuition seemed to sink into a cleft in the dilemma, and he followed it, finding his own route.

210

"I've got a better idea. We eat here. I'm hungry. Then we leave real early in the morning. You drive, I'll sleep. You can't sleep anyway, and if you drive we'll get there in three hours instead of four, and we can go right to the protest."

She kissed him again, her way of agreeing, and they went in out of the snow.

Chapter 16

He made them scrambled egg whites and cheese, grits, fake bacon, and a pecan waffle. Most of hers went to the dogs. She packed everything they would need in a duffle bag and a backpack: the voice recorder, tracking device, hard copies of the documents from Sylvie's cellphone, cigarettes, a large thermos of coffee, toothbrush and paste, a couple of days' worth of clothes for the two of them, his medications and hers. She put the .38 in a zippered pocket but he took it out. She also hid something in a baggie which he saw her stash in her jacket. Elias figured it was meth, probably, or weed, or both, and if they got caught they would face prison time, but he wasn't sure how to stop her. She hadn't been doing much meth, if any, since she got back from Charlottesville; Elias thought maybe she had run out. But she was smoking plenty of dope. He still couldn't fathom how she would need to get high while she was already in what she called a hypomania, but she kept telling him that she needed it so she wouldn't lose focus. She hadn't slept much for a week now, and she seemed to think that she would crash if not for the stimulants.

He let it go, like everything else.

They sat in front of the woodstove watching *The Last Waltz* and playing poker for hours. At 3 a.m. they put the dogs in the pen with plenty of food and locked the house up. There was a rift in the clouds and it had stopped sleeting.

"Let me drive to the parkway," Elias said.

When they got into the Jeep, instead of heading down the driveway, he drove across the yard and into the adjacent field of stubble, poking out of four inches of snow.

"Where are you taking me?"

"It's just a little trick."

"I don't like surprises," she said, and gave him a look.

"I don't either."

He hadn't turned on the headlights, but he had no trouble seeing with the snow on the ground. On the other side of the field he eased the car across a dry seasonal creek bed and into the woods on a narrow track that was almost invisible now that the moon was sinking below the ridge tops. It was an old logging road that ran at an angle up one side of the mountain, but after a minute he took a fork and headed back toward Buffalo Mountain Road.

"It's the only other way off of my property. Sometimes I take it if there's a tree down on the driveway and I'm in a hurry. I want to check and see if there's anybody watching the house. Only take a second."

He stopped in the treeline before climbing onto the road and got out, not closing the door for fear of making any noise. Walking in the last of the moon shadows he made his way back under the trees to the edge of his property, then forward near to where the driveway cut through the woods, and stopped abruptly when he heard a motor running. It was almost imperceptible, but unmistakable. Then he saw the flare of a lighter. Moving slowly so as not to snap any branches underfoot, he advanced another fifty feet or so until he could see the outline of a car pulled off the road just at the beginning of his driveway where it was flat, before the culvert started. It looked like the sedan the Mason Dixon men had driven but he couldn't be sure. It definitely didn't appear to be a police vehicle. He could make out the outlines of two people inside, but he could not hear them even if they were speaking. He wanted to get closer to verify the car, maybe hear them speak, possibly even confront them for sitting on his property, but he knew he couldn't. That would be crazy. He wondered if they sat there round the clock, or if they ever approached the house. The dogs would have heard them, no doubt, now that they were left outside at night. They were concealed just far enough away to be undetected. And most likely they weren't there in the daytime or he would have seen them when he got the paper and the mail because the trees were bare. You could see a couple of hundred feet into the winter woods. No, they were night creatures. He was a little afraid that they might do something extreme, like burn down his house, but he figured they would only do that if they thought he and Anna were in it. He wondered if they might try to harm his dogs, like they did Anna's. Were these the same guys? Did they know the ones who were killed the last time, the man mauled by the bear? For a long moment he thought, why am I leaving my house unprotected to drive to the state capital on a wild goose chase, a fool's errand? He hated the thought of going away while they were here. He crouched on his knees in the snowy brush undecided if he would even stand up again, much less drive to Richmond. Then he felt a hand on his shoulder and jumped up, almost cursing aloud. It was Anna. Jesus, she was quiet. Must be the snow, he thought.

He put a hand to her mouth and motioned with the other that they should backtrack. He followed in her footprints back to the Jeep, but before they got there she turned.

"Who is it?" she whispered.

"I think it's the security guys from Mason Dixon. I'm guessing they just sit out here at night thinking we might go somewhere."

"We could slash their tires. It doesn't make any noise."

"No, no. no. It's too risky. Let's just get out of here."

"What if they ... ?"

"It's okay. I know what they're capable of, but I think once they see the car is gone they'll leave too. What I'll do is I'll call the neighbor as soon as it's light out—he gets up early—and ask him to bring in the paper. He's done

214

it for me before when I had to go out of town. He can check on the house and the dogs."

"Dirty sneaking sons of bitches. This is what they get paid for—intimidating people."

They got back in the Jeep, didn't close the doors until they were down the road. Elias decided they shouldn't travel by interstate, figuring the state police had his license number. So when Anna took over she got off the parkway on Route 8, took it south to Route 40, and headed east all the way across several counties until she picked up 360 into the city. It was a circuitous, nerve-wracking couple of hundred two lane miles in the wet snow, but they talked the whole time, drinking coffee, smoking weed, and listening to bluegrass and classic rock on the radio until they entered Richmond a little after 7 a.m., the city that tobacco built and the capital of the Confederacy.

They crossed the James on the Mayo Bridge just as the sun was coming up, casting the highrise corporate buildings downtown into a murky glow. The streets were almost deserted; the bad weather had followed them from the west and scared off the commuters, turning Friday into the start of a three-day weekend. It was still sleeting here, and the roads were slick. It occurred to Elias that there may not be a protest that day, or even a board meeting.

"It's pretty dead."

Anna drove with one hand gripping the wheel and a cigarette in the corner of her mouth. "A little snow won't stop these people. They're dedicated MTR opponents; they're used to worse conditions, standing outside all day in the mountains of Appalachia, or what's left of them. Hell, they like the cold."

He was thinking about the Richmond conservatives who had now taken over the state government and represented his supposed interests in Congress. Most of them were his age, or younger. What happened to his generation, he wondered, that had caused such a rupture in beliefs? The children of the sixties? What happened to the revolution? These were the people who had copped out of it, never really understood the principles. Sometimes he thought you could just divide people into two groups: those who got high and those who didn't. It used to be don't trust anyone who doesn't drink. Which really meant don't trust anyone who can't relax, who has no interests other than making money. Now it was don't trust anyone who doesn't smoke, because drugs were still against the law and they would use that to lock you up and silence you. Elias thought it was about freedom. Most people were just afraid of it. Drugs had always opened up his mind. They had a religious purpose. But his generation had become secure in their own increasing wealth and they had of course surrounded themselves with like-minded people. They lived in safe neighborhoods and they all had private health care. They were cut off from the lower classes, the blacks and the immigrants. They didn't want to change anymore. In middle age they had rebelled against their own revolution.

Anna took a left on Cary and parked in a plowed but almost empty lot between phalanxes of banks. They got out, crossed Main Street, and headed into Capitol Square, surrounded by courts and the capitol building itself. Here, Anna said, they would rendezvous with the Mountain Justice group at nine.

She promptly lay down on her back on a bench under the Washington Equestrian Monument, her head under her backpack, with the hood of her parka pulled up but the sleet wetting her face. Didn't seem to mind. Elias wandered around the square, looking at the statues of the eminent Virginians: Jefferson, Patrick Henry. Stonewall Jackson, of course. Even Edgar Poe himself made it, looking very intense under the low grey sky. When he got back Anna was asleep. Couldn't do it at home, but here in public, in the snow, between the state capitol and the federal

216

court, wanted for attempted murder, she looked like a child on a school tour taking a nap with crystals of ice forming on her cheeks and in her lashes, protected, as it were, under the gaze of the other revolutionaries. The lights were on in the offices, but there didn't seem to be anyone around except for an occasional VDOT truck passing by.

Not long after he started meditating nearby, Elias saw through half-closed lids the first of a ragtag assortment of young men and women showing up carrying signs and musical instruments. Stop Poisoning the Water. Black Gold=Corporate Greed. 500 Mountains and Counting. A Bargain with the Devil. By 8:30 there were fifteen or more, dressed like hikers in ponchos and jeans, the guys long haired and bearded, the women with bandanas. A couple of them started playing music under an improvised tarp in a tree, banjo and a fiddle, a local variation of "This Land Is My Land" it sounded like to Elias, with some made-up lyrics. Anna kept sleeping. Finally an older couple arrived, in their sixties, the woman stout with a fierce gaze and beatific smile, the man lean and grizzled and grey-bearded. The woman looked over the group, counting heads and giving instructions for a few minutes, then she seemed to take notice of the waiflike immobile form nearby. She walked over to Anna and looked down at her face. Studied it.

"Anna? Is that you, Anna Jassey?"

Anna opened her eyes but otherwise didn't move. "Who else would it be, Miss Hale?"

"Lord have mercy, you gave me a start. You look like Sylvie so much, it's uncanny."

"Must be the eyes."

"That's not true. Sylvie's is blue. And her hair is red. But otherwise you could be sisters."

She sat up and swung her legs off the bench, yanked down her hood from which her hair tumbled out like crows from a tree, pulled a cigarette from her pocket and lit it. Then she stood up and stretched like a cat in the snow.

217

"Look here, Aaron. It's Anna Jassey. Honey, you here to give us a hand? Cause we sure could use your painting skills."

"Yes mam. And I brought a friend." She waved to Elias across the square and he came over.

"Elias, this is Miss Sharon Hale and her husband Aaron; they've spent a lifetime keeping the coal companies looking over their shoulder."

"And vice versa," Mr. Hale said. "Glad to have you aboard."

Elias noticed the anchor on Hale's forearm. "Thank you, Chief. I'm a Navy man too."

"Takes one to know one. Where at?"

"All over. Norfolk. Yokohama. Helsinki. You name it, I've been stationed there."

"I was in Vietnam. When I got out in '75 I kept heading west until I got to the mountains, and I ain't looked back."

"Same here. Just thirty years later."

The musicians were still playing to keep everyone warm. The sleet was easing up but it was only in the 20's. The bluegrass seemed to create its own atmosphere in the empty square, a little bit of Appalachia kindled in downtown Richmond.

"Anna," Mrs. Hale said, "can you tell us what happened to Sylvie? We heard she died, but we don't know how. The papers didn't say nothing, and the cremation was so fast we didn't hear about it until it was over and done with."

"Cremation? What cremation?"

"They cremated her body I heard because it was so disfigured from her being out in the woods and all."

Anna immediately started pacing and shouting obscenities in the square. Everyone stopped what they were doing and watched her.

218

"That stupid motherfucking cunt! How much did they pay her to not bury her own daughter! That goddamned idiot!" No one got in her way; everyone seemed to know, from experience or intuition, that doing so would only make things worse. Anna was in a fury, and the demons needed time to get out. For a full minute she raged in the sleet until she calmed down and sat back down on the bench.

Then Elias and the Hales and the other protesters moved over and formed a tight knot around her. "She was murdered," Anna said, quite calmly, although Elias knew some of the sleet on her face was really tears. "The police and everyone else said she was involved in drugs, but that was just a lie to cover up the truth. It was the coal company, Miss Hale. They killed her because she found they had bought enough police, judges, and politicians to get any bill passed they wanted and to keep everyone out of their way."

"Well you know Anna, coal always has been in bed with the legal system. But if there is bank records, payments, and can be proved, then you need to take that to the gov'ment."

"You think the assholes who run this state now are even going to look at what we have? Every day the politicians are giving speeches about how badly we need coal to help the economy. Hell, they don't give a damn about Appalachia. Just re-election. 'Scuse my French, Mrs. Hale. And from earlier." Anna's voice was sounding agitated again but she was trying to restrain it.

"That's okay, sweetie. We can talk about this later. Right now we got some marching to do." She turned around and seemed to embrace the Mountain Justice members with her arms. "Okay everybody. It's that time. This here is Anna Jassey and her friend Eli. Most of you don't know her, but you knew her cousin, Sylvie, who is no longer with us. Anna is a artist so if you need some work on your posters she can help. In a few minutes we're going to walk on down Franklin Street ten blocks to the Jefferson Hotel, passing the Mason Dixon building on the way. So we'll stop there for fifteen minutes and make a speech or two, then proceed on to the hotel and set up shop. I didn't have time to get a permit; this meeting was called at the last moment, so we might run into some problems. I doubt it, cause it's nobody around this morning, but if we do, just remember the procedure and let me and Aaron handle it."

A few more young people had arrived by then, making about twenty in all, and a couple of them pulled rolled poster board out of their packs and a staple gun and proceeded to draw on them with magic markers. Anna took an extra and stapled it to some wood stripping, then pulled out a couple of spray cans from her backpack, changed the nozzles to fine points, and started working. In ten minutes she had drawn and painted a woman lying on her back on the ground, arching her body up to the sky, as if she were offering herself, except that the woman looked like a mountain, a denuded mountain. The woman's breasts, abdomen, and womb were sliced off, there was a monstrous digging machine on top of her removing her entrails in huge bucketfulls, and her blood was running into the surrounding valleys off the sides of the poster. It was altogether a very disturbing picture, rendered in exquisitely realistic detail in reds and greens and black. It reminded Elias of the drawings he had seen in her trailer the very first night he went there. The rest of the company had gathered around her as she worked, and watched and waited in silence as she took her time to finish.

"I told you she could draw," Mrs. Hale said. "Now let's go speak the truth to power, and tell the world what's happening in the mountains."

Mr. Hale leaned over to Elias as they headed west down the sidewalk. "Mister, I wouldn't take my eyes off of this one if I were you."

"I hear you," Elias said.

They marched two or three abreast meeting almost no one along the way except a few cars and some commercial vehicles. One honked at them. Lots of puzzled stares through closed windows. In fifteen minutes they saw the Mason Dixon headquarters. It was a squat, dirty building that looked like a Neolithic altar or tomb that took up the whole block. Either by design or by cosmic correspondence, it had in fact the appearance of an aboveground mine, sooty with decades of coal dust raining from the clouds overhead blown all the way from Appalachia, and the acid rain out of the smokestacks of the old coal-fired electric plants, etching its signature into the walls. It was a dank and chill building, Elias thought, remembering the Poe statue. As if death had reared itself a throne.

In front of the main entrance Mrs. Hale gave a speech, the history of the coal company's exploitation of the people and land for profit, how all the money seemed to flee the counties where the coal was mined, and how in the last twenty years leaving holes in the ground wasn't enough, now they had to do their dirty work right out in the open, blowing up the mountains that had been there for millions of years, more than 500 mountaintops removed, or twenty-five a year. Based on that number, she calculated that in fifty years by the time these kids in front of her were her age, more than another thousand would be gone forever, effectively changing the skyline of West Virginia, Kentucky, and Virginia in less than a century what it took God a hundred million years to make. It was the people's birthright, these mountains, but the coal companies and their paid politicians thought they owned them, and were even trying to make it sound like the country needed them to be destroyed, for the economy. It was the biggest fraud in the history of a fraudulent nation, she said, and Americans were fools to be taken in. The land couldn't be successfully reclaimed because they had to put the overburden back in the same order it had been blasted off, and that was too

221

expensive. And the people who lived there were just getting poorer and sicker. Even the creek she had been baptized in, she said, was now too polluted for a service.

By the time she had concluded a small crowd of passers-by and office workers had coalesced in front of her, and Elias noticed a gauntlet of men in ties behind her in the doorway, conferring with each other, taking pictures, and occasionally disappearing into the innards of the building. As soon as she stopped speaking one of them walked up to her and asked if she had a permit. When she said she did not he asked her to leave immediately and he got on his cell.

"That's it," she said, and they moved on down the sidewalk towards the Jefferson.

When they got to Adams, across from the hotel, the cops were waiting. They pushed on anyway, crossing the street, and immediately one of the officers confronted them, asked for a permit, and ordered them to disperse. A few of the protesters yelled demands for the board not to conduct their meetings in secret. What did they have to hide? Then they started playing some more songs, but otherwise they obeyed the police and split off into two or three groups walking around the hotel, each one too small to be in violation. Part of the plan. A camera crew had pulled up to the curb from a local television station and Sharon and Aaron moved over to talk to them.

As soon as he had seen the cops Elias yanked Anna aside and told her it was too risky for her to be out in the open; there was more than likely a bulletin for them to be looking out for her anywhere near a Mason Dixon meeting, and it would be stupid to get arrested here.

"You're paranoid," she said, but didn't move.

"I'm realistic, that's all. Look, they don't know me, and I probably don't look like a Mountain Justice guy."

"You got that right."

"So what I'm suggesting is why don't I go into the hotel and scout around. See what I can find out."

222

"Find out about what?"

"I don't know. Find out if there is even a meeting in there. How long it's going to last. Who's there. Maybe I'll see Breedlove himself. The CEO, I mean."

"Suit yourself," she said, lighting another cigarette and sitting down on the curb in the slush.

Elias opened his parka. He was wearing a button down blue shirt and khakis and his hiking boots. He figured he could pass for a Richmond businessman on a snowy day. Or a tourist here for the weekend. The Mountain Justice groups had made their way around the hotel and were heading back over in his direction, so he left Anna on the sidewalk with a last minute injunction to "not wander off." "I'll call you," he said. On his way across the street he absentmindedly pulled something out of his deep coat pocket; it was a crushed orange and blue UVA tie tangled up with the remains of a joint. Providence, he thought, threw the roach into the street and automatically pulled the tie into a Windsor, flattening it as he made his way through the front doors. Nobody paid him any attention.

The Jefferson was a magnificent old hotel, like a Renaissance palace. Elias entered from Main Street into a two story rotunda lobby with a mezzanine running around it. He decided against asking any questions at the main desk; maybe he was paranoid, but there didn't seem to be any reason to make someone suspicious, especially with the cops still hanging around out front. He wandered through the first floor and some of the side rooms, looking for any signs or notices of meetings. There were a few, but nothing about Mason Dixon, and he didn't observe any activity at the conference rooms. There was a bar and restaurant, T.J.'s, and a few high-end shops. He took the stairs up to the mezzanine where there were a couple more conference rooms. Outside of one of them he noticed a man standing by himself stiffly in a suit who did not look like he belonged there. In fact, he had his hands crossed in front of him and

223

he was looking up and down the hall. Security. Elias waited at the far end reading a brochure he had picked up, then joined in a group of people talking and heading in the man's direction. When they passed he glanced over and sized him up. Six foot. Two hundred pounds. Affectless. But out of the corner of his collar, the top of a tattoo that looked like a trident.

Elias continued walking past the coat check and into another sitting area and stopped. This was definitely the meeting. He reflexively started to light a cigarette, then remembered where he was and called Anna.

"I found it. There's a security guy outside."

"Where are you?"

"Mezzanine. The meeting's in the Jefferson Room. I'm nearby."

"I'll be right there." She ended the call before he had time to say no, don't take the chance. She was constantly disregarding his plan, even their agreements. There seemed to be no way to stop her.

Elias started pacing, anticipating a scene, or worse. It was 11:30, the weather had broken, and the lobby below was starting to fill with a lunchtime crowd and visitors checking in for the weekend. When Anna appeared on the stairs, she had a couple of the Mountain Justice people with her who had managed to slip in side doors. Then some more approached from another direction asking which room held the Mason Dixon meeting. Before Elias could respond, he saw the security guard notice them and slip inside the Jefferson Room, only to emerge a moment later in front of the members of the board itself, six or eight of them being hustled en masse in the opposite direction. Suddenly things seemed to get out of control, as the young people converged on the board members asking questions about what they were doing and demanding that the public be informed of what was happening to their mountains. More security and a policeman from downstairs moved to block the protesters, as the knot of people, like two dogs locked in combat, slowly made its way along the mezzanine toward the stairs. The TV crew, meanwhile, had made its way upstairs too and was pushing into the crowd. People were shouting, starting to shove; Elias was afraid someone would get hurt. He kept to the perimeter of the crowd, keeping his eyes on Anna who was lost in the thick of it, when he caught sight of a familiar face, or at least one he thought he recognized though he had never seen it in person.

It was Ron Breedlove Senior. Elias had scrutinized the face so many times on the Web and in YouTube videos that it was strange to apprehend it just ten feet away. It was as if Seung-Hui Cho had appeared in the hotel; there was an uncanny element in seeing the man in the flesh, as if evil had been made incarnate. Maybe he had been handsome as a younger man, with the ambitious self-centeredness that his son possessed, but now he looked to Elias like a hillbilly Hitler: he had a small bushy moustache and tiny, piggish eyes, short hair too black to be natural, and pockmarked oily skin, but his barrel chest filled out his suit, and his thick arms and legs gave him an imposing, threatening mass, like a mountain denuded of life. He was, in effect, a solid embodiment of coal itself, just like his building down the street.

He had a face, Elias realized later, that could never understand beauty. And now he was angry; he yelled over the crowd at his men and the police.

"I want these people out of here! Now! This is a private meeting. They have no permit to protest. Arrest them! And get the media out too. There is nothing to film here."

Meanwhile the whole crowd had arrived at the elevators and the security from Mason Dixon and the hotel managed to get the board members on it. The protesters were pushed back and the doors closed. Elias had extracted Anna from the throng by the back of her parka; she didn't like it and was fighting against him but he was too strong for her and managed to get his arm around her and walk away from the commotion. The rest of the group was chanting "Stop Raping the Mountains" to the TV camera while being escorted down the flight of stairs from the mezzanine to the lobby.

She was furious again. "What the hell do you think you're doing? You can't stop me if I want to talk to somebody! You don't own me!"

"Anna, you were on TV! Do you want to be on the six o'clock news? You're going to get yourself arrested if you keep acting like this."

"I don't give a fuck who sees me! I've got nothing to hide. They're the ones who committed murder and torture. Whose side are you on?"

"I'm on your side, of course. That's why I'm trying to protect you."

"I don't need protection. I thought I made that clear. I never asked you to look after me."

"Too late for that. Look, be reasonable for just a second." He had her up against the wall of a nook. "Breedlove was here. Did you see him? You want to confront him, right? You don't want the police to grab you, do you?"

She seemed to get a grip on the situation and calmed down.

"I saw him but I couldn't get close to him."

He grabbed her hand. "Come on. I have a plan."

She shook loose. "What plan?"

"Come on, let's go. The police are going to be back in a moment. I think I know how to catch up with Breedlove." They ducked into another elevator at the other end of the mezzanine. Elias punched the button for the parking garage and turned to her.

"Look. They didn't walk to the hotel and I doubt they're going to stick around for lunch with the media here.

They're probably headed for their cars. We can see where they're going."

"But you forgot our car is ten blocks away. We'll never be able to follow them."

"We don't have to follow them," he said, and held up the tracking device he had in his pocket. "All we need is to attach this." As he was telling her all this, some part of his mind was also thinking, "What am I doing? Trying to impress her? I'm just giving her another opportunity to get arrested. I'm only making things worse."

But it was too late to stop her now. The door opened onto the garage and they looked around. There were several groups of people nearby, but it was impossible to know who was who and which way they were going. Then they spotted a Hummer limo with the motor running.

"Come on. We'll catch them when they pull out onto the street. You'll have to distract them for a second."

They walked fast toward the exit. The gate was lowered and the limo and a Mercedes SUV were taking a while maneuvering their way through the parking maze to get to it. They beat the vehicles there and got behind a massive pillar near the ticket booth.

"The limo has got to be second for this to work," Elias said, as the two vehicles approached the gate from different directions. But the limo got there first, and the Mercedes eased in behind it. They couldn't see inside the reflecting windows, but Elias was sure the Mason Dixon group was in the limo. There was no way he could attach the tracking device without being seen by whoever was behind them in the SUV.

Anna uttered a "fuck you" and tried to surge forward anyway but he caught her back. The limo driver was waved on through, then the Mercedes pulled up and the window went down. For a moment they could see the driver speak to the attendant.

It was Breedlove.

Elias said, "Walk in front of the car, quick, but don't let them see who you are. I need thirty seconds."

Anna jumped forward with her hood up and walked slowly between the Mercedes and the street just as the gate started up, carrying her backpack. Then it dropped upside down out of her hand spilling the contents onto the concrete. Thank God he had removed the .32. Instead of crouching down to pick it up, she bent from the waist in her tight low-rider Levis, and as her unzipped coat opened, she in effect exhibited her ass at point blank range. Elias couldn't be sure if she was mooning or teasing the men watching, but her actions had the desired effect. No one was looking behind the car.

He got down on his hands and knees and crawled behind the Mercedes, ducked his head under the rear bumper next to the tailpipe and managed to affix the small magnetic tracker to the inside of the fender. In no more than twenty seconds he was back at the pillar and looked just in time to see Anna pick up her pack and walk off, but not before turning halfway to the car and from behind her sunglasses ask, "Enjoy the show?" Then Breedlove gunned his engine and the underground rumbled with the noise. As Anna moved out onto the sidewalk, he peeled into the slushy street and Elias watched as the SL fishtailed a little and sped off, heading west on Franklin.

At Lombardy Franklin becomes Monument Avenue, and that was where Anna pulled the GPS up on his droid while Elias drove. They had run all the way back to Capitol Square. No sign of Mountain Justice. The main streets were clear and the traffic normal now at lunchtime. The road divided as they slowly circled the Jeb Stuart and Robert E. Lee monuments. Then Anna got a stationary signal; Breedlove must have parked, and it didn't look far off in front of them. As they passed the tall and elegant Jefferson Davis monument she was able to locate the position of the device exactly. It appeared to be coming from a large, three story brick home across the street, surrounded by a brick wall about six feet high. They couldn't see the Mercedes, and there was a gate across the driveway. The place was a fortress.

"I'm going to drive around the block and then park on a side street."

Once he found a space and cut the engine off, Elias turned to look at Anna and assess the situation. The sun had come out and was glinting off the snow, and the air in the Jeep was warm enough to open the window. It was an old tony neighborhood near downtown and the Virginia Museum. The narrow tree-lined street had attractive Colonial revival brick and wood framed houses on deep lots. There were a few children throwing snowballs, but mostly the area was quiet. Elias realized he was pretty exhausted; he hadn't slept, of course, as he said he would during the long trip. But underneath the fatigue was the incessant anxiety about what they were doing, and when it would stop.

Anna, on the other hand, did not seem in the least fatigued, except for the dark circles under her incandescent eyes. Her skin had a pallor that made her look completely Caucasian. She was fidgeting in the front seat, and it seemed to Elias like she didn't know what to do next either.

"Well, here we are," he asked. "Now what?"

"Now we look the devil in the face and tell him he has to pay his dues."

"Does that include ringing his doorbell, or are we just going to kick the door down?"

"Instead of being sarcastic why don't you tell me what you think we should do, since you obviously think you know what is best, as usual."

"If I thought you were objective and open-minded enough I would tell you what I sincerely think. I think we should go to the police with what we have."

She reached for the door handle but he caught her hand.

229

"Okay. We go to the door and maybe Breedlove himself answers. Then what?"

"What do you think? We tell him about the documents we have. We wave them in front of his ugly face. We tell him we have video of his son with a murdered girl just hours before she was killed. We let him know that we know he had my dogs lynched and my home burned down. That people he employs tried to kill us and are at this very moment spying on your house. We tell him we are taking all this evidence to the district attorney who is a personal friend of yours."

She paused.

"And then?"

"And then he gets scared and has us come in and probably will try to buy us off, and we record the whole conversation."

Elias thought about it for a moment.

"Actually, that doesn't sound like too bad of a plan." He was thinking of the conversation between George Clooney and Tilda Swinton at the end of *Michael Clayton*. "Unless he just calls the cops and we have to make a run for it."

"I've been running all my life; makes no difference to me." She reached down under the seat beside her, pulled out a little ceramic pipe and a lighter and nonchalantly took a hit.

"Anna, what the fuck?"

"It's just a one hitter. Chill out."

She put her stash in the glove box and they got out of the Jeep and walked down the block to Monument, then turned east until they got to the address. Elias could just see over the wall; there was no car out front, but there was a separate three car garage. The gate to the driveway was locked; so was another pedestrian gate. They looked up and down—there was no one on the sidewalk—then when there was a pause in traffic Elias offered Anna his cupped hands as

230

a foothold but she didn't wait and shinnied over the wall before he did.

Up close the house was imposing; a good 6,000 square feet, Elias thought, at least. It wasn't far to the door, the yard was almost all pavers, and they were halfway there when the barking dogs came around the corner from the backyard.

This time it was pit bulls, big ones. White and pink, like two of Satan's albino minions. Instantly Elias' mind was buzzing with possibilities: Did someone see them climb the wall and let them out? Did these dogs just roam the yard? There was no sign to warn people; they couldn't just allow vicious dogs loose in their front yard on Monument Avenue in the Fan district. They could kill someone. They would be liable. In the seconds he was thinking these things he instinctively looked for a weapon, a loose paver, anything. There was Anna's knife, strapped to the inside of her shin, but before he had time to ask for it she had moved toward the dogs and said something to them in that Melungeon language of hers, walking forward in the precise, slightly bowlegged way she had, like a ballerina who became a bareback rider in the circus, until she had somehow with a combination of soft talking and hand motions coaxed them into stopping, then lying down in the driveway. Two white pit bulls, like a couple of ceramic figures out front. One looked to be the mother of the other; she must have been sixty pounds, he maybe seventy. Anna stroked the female's head, got Elias to stroke the male, then sent them back to the backyard or the underworld with a single word and a point: "Gelida!"

"Nice dogs" was all she said as they walked up to the wide oak door and she knocked. Elias was still watching for them, but he remembered to reach into his shirt pocket and click on the voice recorder.

A woman answered. She was reasonably tall, with reddish black hair. It looked like she had put on too much

231

makeup; her skin was too pale, her eyes too shadowed. Her face was chiseled, like a woman in a German expressionist painting, with high cheekbones and a wide full mouth, but it was creased with wear and tear. She had what Anna sometimes derisively referred to as "poor face" when she was feeling malicious. One could have guessed she had lived a hard life, maybe even a mean one. But her eyes were a strikingly beautiful pale blue, like a rift in an overcast sky. And she was very well dressed, in a pricey skirt and blouse and a gold necklace and bracelets. She had a cocktail in her hand.

"Yes?" she asked, as if they were salesmen or Jehovah's Witnesses.

"We're here to see Mr. Breedlove," Anna said, firmly.

"Junior or senior?"

"Senior," Elias said.

"What do you want to see him for?"

"It's personal," Anna said. "He's trying to kill me."

"Oh. That I can imagine." Then she looked at Elias. "Did you go to UVA, or did you just buy the tie?"

He looked down. "I went there."

"My son is in law school. Maybe you know him."

"Yes, we've met."

"Ron," she yelled over her shoulder. "There are some people here to see you." Then she turned and let them into the foyer, which was enormous, with four chandeliers and twin staircases travelling up the back wall from both sides to a balcony above. It looked like a movie set; everything seemed a bit larger than life. There was a twenty foot Christmas tree in the middle of the marble floor with white lights, popcorn, and cranberries.

The door to a side room opened, and Ronald Breedlove Senior appeared in the suit he had been wearing earlier, but with his tie loosened.

"Who are you?" he asked as he walked up to them, sizing them up and glancing out the front windows. "And

232

how did you get in here? The gates are locked." Without taking his eyes off of them he said to his wife. "They must have climbed over the wall, Doris. They're trespassing. Call the police."

"This one says you're trying to murder her."

Breedlove stopped and looked at Anna more closely. "You're the girl who was showing her ass in the parking garage. Which means you must be part of that left-wing radical commune that calls itself Mountain Justice. They were protesting illegally at the board meeting."

"I have some pictures that you should look at," Anna said. "We're taking you down, fat ass, and your psycho son as well. He's in the video too."

Breedlove's tiny eyes downshifted from malevolent to baleful in a second.

"I was wrong," he said to his wife. "This isn't just another commie group breaking into our home. This is the bitch that tried to kill Ronnie, and the older guy, I suppose, is her sugar daddy pimp. Don't even bother calling the cops. Just go to my office and get me my nigger knocker in the corner."

Mrs. Breedlove apparently didn't respond fast enough.

"Get the fucking bat, Doris!"

She left the room and immediately Elias pulled the documents out of his inside pocket and thrust them in Breedlove's face.

"We have photographs of these documents taken from a murdered girl's cell phone, and video of her with your son right before she died. The documents are in your handwriting, written in code in the Saponi Indian language, and they detail transactions between your company and officials and politicians across the region. I don't think you want these made public, but that is exactly what's going to happen if you call the police."

233

Breedlove moved face to face with Elias. "I didn't say I was calling the police. I'm going to smash your head in with my bat and throw you off my property. Those documents don't mean shit. My lawyers will be all over them before you can get a hard on."

He was about Elias' height and standing close enough for Elias to smell the whiskey on his breath.

"I'm going to show you greeniacs once and for all what happens when you try to threaten somebody and his family. You have no idea who you're talking to. I've been in the coal business since I was fifteen and I've had to knock morons like you out of my way all the time. I can squash you like a mosquito and no one will ever know the difference," and he rubbed his fingers in the air like he was squeezing a bug between them.

The Kokoshka woman came back into the room with a two-foot billy club in the hand that wasn't holding the highball. Elias moved back to give himself some room and started looking around for a weapon or a way out. There was nothing in reach that wasn't nailed down except the tree. Breedlove was so focused on intimidating Elias that he had apparently forgotten about Anna, or didn't consider her a threat, but just as he held his hand out to his wife for the club Anna grabbed the back of his suit coat and pushed the tip of her newly unsheathed blade against his left kidney, and he stopped in midair.

"You killed my cousin and my dog, and burned down my house," she said calmly, "so do not think that you can pull any shit with me. I'm crazier than any miner you've ever known, and I've got nothing left to lose."

At that moment all four heard a car pull into the drive with the motor racing, then doors slamming. Three of them stood frozen in a kind of profane triptych, while Doris put the club on the windowsill and walked over to the door. When she opened it there he was. Ronnie. Dressed up like

234

Santa. And he had one of the Mason Dixon security men with him.

"Hi mom," he said as he sauntered through the door.

"We've got company," she said.

He recognized Elias but at first didn't see Anna hidden behind his father.

"The Jassey girl's come a courtin', Ronnie," Breedlove said. "The whore's got a knife in my back but otherwise I think she's glad to see you."

"You're damn right I'm glad to see him, so I can finish the job I started last time on the piece of shit that murdered my cousin."

"I'm confused," Mrs. Breedlove interrupted. "I thought you said Ron was trying to kill *you*. Well, who is it, you or your cousin?"

When the security guard realized that the voice coming from behind Breedlove's broad shoulders was attached to a knife, he pulled an automatic from a shoulder holster and aimed it in her direction.

"What do you want me to do, Mr. Breedlove?"

"Don't point that goddamn gun at me for starters."

"Anna," Elias said, "take the knife out of his back. We didn't come here to attack anybody; we just came to get some information, remember?" He moved beside her and put his hand over hers on the hilt. "The truth, remember? Just to confront them with the truth, not kill anybody."

She glanced at him sideways with a look that was almost impossible to interpret, except that Elias knew she was fighting a deep instinct to plunge her sanctified blade into the big man's flesh. If he had not been there with her, there would have been no question, he thought. Breedlove would have seven inches of surgical steel and Berlin Wall rebar honed to a samurai sharpness shoved through his left kidney and he would have died there on the marble within minutes. Perhaps the big man sensed this as well, because as Elias eased the blade away from him and moved Anna back,

235

he stepped away and turned on them with the pallor of a trussed pig who had just felt the life slowly drained out of its body.

First he took the papers that Elias still held in his hand and tore them up. Then he ordered the security man to hold his gun on them while he went through Elias' coat and trouser pockets, removing his droid and breaking it in two between his large white callused hands like it was a piece of coal and letting the pieces fall to the floor. Then he turned Anna's backpack upside down and everything clattered out. He smashed her cell with his heel, then he picked up and sniffed her glass pipe.

"She's a crackhead as well. We weren't far off when we torched her trailer," he said to no one in particular. He broke the pipe in his hands and crumbled it until the fine bits of glass drifted through his fingers like sand in an hourglass. "You tree huggers are all alike; you want to mess with other people's business, but you haven't got the will power to get what you want. You need to use this shit just to deal with reality."

"You're wrong," Elias interrupted, "if you think we're going away. It's coal that's going away. You're becoming an anachronism. You're a dead man walking. That's why you're selling out to the Chinese. Getting out while the getting's good."

Breedlove walked over to Elias and once again stood a few inches away. His eyes were saturated with such a deep suspicion and anger that they looked like the liquid inside had burned away many years ago and left just a tarry residue.

"The crack whore I can understand," he said. "She grew up in coal country and her father used to work for me. I see her kind every day of the week. But you, you're nothing but a fucking outsider. Even worse. You're a goddamn know-it-all professor. First it's the mines aren't safe enough; everybody's got the right to work in a safe mine. Maybe the men would like some couches and a TV set while they're working. Then when we started strip mining and got the miners out of the hole they say, 'You can't blow off the tops of these mountains, you're ruining our view.'" Ronnie Junior sniggered at the sissy voice his father used. "Shit, you don't even live here. You're just interfering with the thousands of good jobs that hard-working Christian people need to feed their families and keep a roof over their head. Now it's global warming, they say. The EPA says we got to stop all the carbon dioxide from going into the atmosphere, as if it was some poisonous chemical that we can't breathe. Hell, we breathe it every day of our lives and never get sick! But the EPA and Gore and Kennedy and Bono all say that it's bad for us. Wah wah wah. Well, you know what the EPA stands for, don't you?"

"Everybody's pussy agency," said Junior.

"You're goddamned right. I don't give a shit about the bats and the fucking fish; I care about the people in West Virginia and Kentucky who are unemployed and struggling to make ends meet. You faggots want to put them out of work. If you want the government to run your life, why don't you just move to China? They're going to take all the jobs we lose, and someday soon your kids will be atheists learning Chinese in school. Hell, your kids are probably already atheists." He turned away, then thought of something else. "The end of coal? What kind of asshole American are you? Coal is what made this country great, and it's going to stay great as long as people have the balls to stand up to idiots like you."

"Save the speech for the media," Elias said. "We don't believe a word of it."

Breedlove spat on Elias' shirt in response and turned to his wife.

"Now, what time is it?"

Doris, who had remained seemingly unperturbed by all the histrionics, as if they were an everyday occurrence, looked at her expensive watch. "Ten to one."

"Shit. We've got to go back to the Jefferson. Saul, keep them here and call the police. Ronnie, I'll see you this afternoon at the party. Don't be late, and don't do anything stupid, you hear me? And you shouldn't be driving around in that costume. You'll get it dirty."

He pulled his tie up, took the glass out of his wife's hand, and the two of them quickly left the room through a door between the staircases. Elias saw a tear in the back of his coat as they left where Anna had stuck her knife. He quickly sized up the situation, the gun still in Saul's lowered hand, the billy club still on the windowsill. What might these two be capable of now that the old man was gone? If he was going to act, he needed to do it now, suddenly, in the transition. But it was too dangerous, he reasoned. The window wasn't close enough, and the security guy looked like a dumb ass. He might shoot them just for trying to get out the door. The police were preferable to the coroner. But Anna still had her knife; for some reason Breedlove had never taken it.

"You two really are a couple of idiots," Ronnie said once his parents were gone. "What did you think you were going to accomplish coming here? Did you think you could intimidate us? Did you really think my father would be afraid of you? Did he look afraid? These fucking pictures you have …," he began, moving closer to them. "Hold the gun on them Saul, the girl is a freak. These pictures don't prove anything," he said, as he bent down to pick up the smashed cell phone, "though I would like to see old Sylvie one more time. I understand you had that last video she made of us. Did you get a good look at me fucking the shit out of her? We had some wild times together in this house. Too bad she had to go and die on us, the meth whore."

Elias was thinking how close Ronnie was to incriminating himself, but he was also dissociating a little from the whole scene because it seemed too incongruous, Ronnie in the Santa Claus suit with a pillow around his waist

238

talking to them in the entrance hall of a mansion on Monument Avenue. Not some dacha in Russia or the Central American jungle where Elias had honed his skills. He had to focus to take it seriously.

"You cocksucker," Anna shouted at him. "She only fucked you to get pictures of those documents in your father's desk. The whole time you thought she wanted you she was just using you to get to your dad. You were just a piece of shit to her."

"Just like you were faking when you sucked my dick in Charlottesville?"

"Like crap I sucked your dick. I'd cut it off as soon as touch it."

"But you can't stop thinking about it, can you? You and your cousin are just alike, like sisters. She wanted it, you want it, but you just can't admit it. You're just hot and nasty redneck bitches, like all the other local color. My daddy told me all about how back in the day they used to come around to the mining camps and make a killing fucking all the men. No wonder you told me you taught Sylvie all the sex tricks she knew; you probably supported yourself whoring after your daddy threw you out of the house. Oh yeah, I heard all about how you got knocked up at sixteen and married a man twice your age until he fucked you into the loony bin. You've got quite a history, you have."

Anna whipped her knife out from under her shirt where she had hidden it and lunged forward at Ronnie. He jumped back but he would have taken it full in the stomach if Elias hadn't seen it coming and grabbed her arm as she thrust so that the tip of the blade just nicked him. She yelled at Elias to let go just as Saul raised his automatic and threatened to shoot them.

"Damn she's quick," Ronnie said to Saul. "I told you she was wild. And where did she get that knife? Look at that thing; it's as big as she is."

239

Anna was beside herself. She kept trying to get the knife away from Elias who had her arm in a lock, screaming at him repeatedly to give it to her, then pulling her arm back so violently that she finally cut herself.

"You killed my sister, you fucking bastard, and I'm going to kill you for her sake. You killed her and then you raped her and mutilated her, and I'm going to make you pay. Let me go!"

"Goddamn but I'd like to fuck the piss out of this one," Ronnie yelled, "and smash her face in at the same time, just like I did Sylvie. But you got it wrong, sister. I off'ed the bitch *after* I fucked her, not before. What do you think I am, a perv?"

Anna went into a full frenzy. Elias had to pick her up from behind in a bear hug to restrain her, but she kept kicking him in the shins with her boots. He was thinking he might be able to just walk out the door with her, nobody would want to get near them, but Saul moved to block them and Ronnie pulled his cell out and punched in three numbers.

"Yes, I'd like to report a B & E at 3225 Monument Avenue. The home of Ronald Breedlove, CEO of Mason Dixon Energy. This is Ron Breedlove Junior. The criminals are still in the house; my pit bulls attacked them and they're pretty torn up. You better send an ambulance. Thanks."

He hung up and smiled. Saul looked anxious.

"Ronnie, remember what your father said. He just wanted them arrested."

"Fuck what he said. He isn't here and he doesn't tell me what to do," and he made his way to another door that apparently led to the kitchen, because Elias could see a paneled hallway and two double door stainless steel refrigerators at the end when he opened it. He whistled loudly. "Pluto, Vulcan! Come!"

Elias got nervous and Anna stopped squirming and slid down out of his embrace. They could hear the dogs

240

scraping their claws through a door and saw them as they rounded a corner and raced down the parquet of the hallway to where Ronnie was standing.

He turned to Elias and Anna, still grinning. "Say hello to my little friends. They're bred for fighting, and they do not like intruders." Then he shouted the two words Elias was afraid he would say: "Sic 'em!"

The dogs stared at Elias and Anna, showing their teeth. Then the younger one took a couple of tentative steps forward. The mother was growling but didn't move. Elias tried not to show any fear but he was already imagining planting a foot in the male's chest and putting him into a choke hold.

Then Anna dropped to her knees. She put her hand out in front of her and quietly spoke again in her language. "Biwa tsok," it sounded like she said. "Biwa tsok."

The male had gotten about ten feet, stopped and looked back at Ronnie and his mother like he was awaiting further instructions. A moment later the mom sat down, and then the son followed suit. They were wagging their cropped tails.

"What the fuck?" Ronnie said, then he ran over and kicked the male hard in the ass. "Get up and sic the bitch!" he yelled. "Sic her!"

"Biwa tsok, biwa tsok," Anna kept repeating softly. Her voice was unearthly, an alien thing, a voice out of *Green Mansions*.

The dogs still didn't move.

"Sonuvabitch!" Ronnie kicked the male again, viciously, and this time the dog yelped in pain. And within a second the mom turned on Ronnie, biting into his thigh and knocking him to the floor in her ferocity. He put up his arms to keep her from his face and starting kicking at her while he tried to regain his feet but then the male jumped on him and the two started savaging his arms. Saul ran to help but didn't seem to know what to do; he kept pointing his

241

gun like he was going to shoot but couldn't get a stable target in the confusion of thrashing white and red bodies and flying saliva. He kicked them. That didn't work either. Elias instinctively wanted to intervene; he had stopped a dogfight once by pulling them apart by their tails, but these animals had no tails. He and Anna stood there, momentarily transfixed by the body flailing on the floor under the snarling animals, watching Santa Claus get mauled, until Ronnie suddenly got to his feet and screaming obscenities and bleeding profusely from his face tried to run. But they caught him from behind before he could get to the door and all three crashed into the Christmas tree which seemed to pitch to the marble in slow motion, shattering a thousand lights and throwing rings of cranberries everywhere, and then they all disappeared into the urban forest of fir branches with Saul standing above still trying to get a clear shot.

"Come on," Elias said, tugging at Anna's arm.

They ran out the door and across the drive without looking back to see if Saul was following. Elias glanced once when they had gotten over the wall; the front door was still open, and then they heard a shot, and then two more. They kept running around the corner all the way to the Jeep and got in. When he got the car started and pulled away from the curb, he looked over at Anna. Her face was transfigured, enflamed from within and shot through with calm. He was caught between admiring her fearlessness and fearing for her sanity. She looked as if she had just walked offstage from a violent dream of teeth and blood in which she played the protagonist, a tragedy thousands of years in the making.

He hit the gas and the jeep accelerated into the slushy streets of Richmond.

Chapter 17

They couldn't go back to the house under Buffalo Mountain, at least not for long. It was too risky now. There were sure to be repercussions from Richmond. Elias assumed that Breedlove would accuse them of attacking them, maybe even of instigating the dogs, although how that could be explained beggared the imagination. Anna was a Native American who could command animals to rip into their owners? And there was no evidence that they had broken into the house, as Ronnie had indicated in his 911 call. But Anna was already wanted, and no matter what happened after they left, whether Ronnie was dead or only mauled, the authorities would be after her. Probably the security people stationed at his house had discovered by now how they had slipped by them, or maybe not. Maybe they had been asleep. Anyway, it was not safe to return unless they were to go to the law.

It took a while for the realization to sink in. They were maybe ten miles outside of Richmond, the landscape had gone from apartment complexes to farms, when Elias was confronted by the fact that Anna had been right all along. This was no drug violence. This was a conspiracy to silence her and her cousin for knowing something they shouldn't have. They just used the drug epidemic to cover it up.

"Play that recording back," he said.

It was eerie for both of them to hear—in the warming afternoon sunlight pouring through the closed windows as they fled through the forests and farmlands on the back roads of central Virginia—father and son incriminate themselves: Ron Senior said that he had "torched" Anna's trailer, and Ron Junior admitted to "offing" Sylvia. Whether that evidence would be good enough for a prosecutor, along with the documents they had on the cell phone, he couldn't say for sure. Was a surreptitious voice recording admissible evidence? But he thought that contacting Sigmon and running it all by him was the logical next move. And then there was the forensic evidence: if Ronnie did kill Sylvie, and there were certainly grounds for believing that now—it was no longer just a paranoid delusion fabricated in Anna's revenge-warped mind—then couldn't they exhume the body and collect DNA, if they hadn't already, and then compare it to Ronnie's? Of course his lawyers, and they would be good ones, would admit that he had had sex with her, but maybe the DNA would prove that he had inflicted the wounds that killed her. Elias was no legal expert, but he thought they had a case that could be brought forward and inevitably that would get Anna off the hook.

Then he remembered that Sylvie had been cremated, which fucked up everything. They should have taken a sample when they were in the funeral home.

Naturally Anna had other plans.

"I want to go home," she said apropos of nothing, at the end of a long silence, pulling hard on the last of a cigarette after they had listened twice to the conversation back on Monument.

"What do you mean home? Home where?"

"Home. Back to Grundy."

"Grundy?" Elias was surprised. She had only spoken of it as somewhere she escaped from. "Why Grundy? I thought you hated the place."

"I've got some business to take care of."

"What kind of business?"

"Personal business."

"What kind of personal business."

"Look, per-son-al"—she articulated each syllable—"means it's none of your fuck-ing business."

"Yeah, but I'm driving you and we're in this thing together."

244

"Well you can let me out right here if that's the way you feel," and she opened her side door as if she was going to step out at sixty miles an hour.

"Jesus, Anna," he said and slowed down so he could pull over to the side of the road. They were somewhere near Farmville and there was little to no traffic. He cut off the motor and she sat there staring straight ahead out the windshield at a billboard in the distance advertising that "Uranium Is Good for America." "I just wondered why you wanted to drive all the way to Grundy. Do you want to hide out there? Do you want to see your family? I can understand that if you want to. I can take you to Grundy and then go back to Floyd and get Sigmon to help us get the police involved. We can take these bastards to court now. Don't you see that we have a case now?" She didn't say a word. "Don't you? I'm on your side, Anna. I'm involved in this now no matter what happens."

Her response was to open the glove box and pull out her meth pipe. Elias sat there exasperated and suddenly very down, as if the whole weight of his years-long depression had caught up with him here on the edge of this cow pasture with a mad girl in the seat next to him. She lit it up, took a couple of drags in silence, then put it in her lap and turned in her seat to face him.

"I need to talk to my dad. Something happened back in Richmond; you probably didn't even notice on the recording. I can't explain it. And I've been having some bad flashbacks for a couple of weeks now, enough to make me feel that I'm more fucked up than I thought I was. And I think I know who's behind it."

"What didn't I notice?"

"I called Sylvie my sister."

It took Elias a moment to reconstruct the scene.

"Oh yeah. I remember. I figured you just misspoke from stress."

245

"I don't think that calling your cousin your sister is misspeaking."

"I don't know. Maybe." For some reason he reached over and took the pipe from her, then hit it. "What do you mean you're having flashbacks? You mean like drug experiences, or something else?"

"I'm seeing people tying me up and talking shit to me. I mean when I'm a little kid."

"Talking shit to you?"

"Crazy shit. Religious shit."

"And who are these people? Do you know?"

"If I knew I wouldn't have to go talk to my dad. He's got to know."

"And you feel like it's important enough that we should go there now, even in the midst of all this mess that we're in?"

"Like I said, it's my problem, not yours. You still haven't done anything. I can take care of my business on my own."

They sat there for a long minute listening to the engine ticking. The snow in the fields hadn't melted yet and the light was pretty dazzling, as if they had woken up in the middle of the night in the dark bedroom with the TV on to *Doctor Zhivago* or something. Elias rolled his window down to get some air.

"Okay. We're going to Grundy. I can call my neighbor and ask him to keep the dogs for a few days. And I can call Sigmon too and update him. Maybe he'll have some ideas." He reached over and took Anna's hand, brought it up to his mouth and kissed it. "You may be the most complicated woman I have ever known," he said, and started the car.

"I may be the most fucked up is what you mean."

They drove all afternoon, slowly winding through the peaceful countryside, the Friday commuters around Danville

246

and Martinsville, and over into the Blue Ridge, stopping at the Tastee Freeze for shakes and fries in Hillsville before descending into the New River Valley, crossing 81, and picking up 16 outside Marion, keeping to the two lane roads. Elias was having a difficult time concentrating after they hit the first switchbacked mountain, and he realized he hadn't slept in two days. He stopped and let Anna take over. When they finally ran into 460 after an hour and a half of hairpin turns, he felt comfortable their taking the thoroughfare the rest of the way. He nodded off on the straighter road and when he woke completely up it was after nine and Anna was speeding down the valley about ten miles out of Grundy. The moon was up and seemed to be following them west. Every mile or two the silver darkness was interrupted by the neon lights of another coal mine on the cliffside above them, its spider leg conveyor belts and girders over small strip malls with nail salons, karate studios and video stores, sometimes in the same space. There was kudzu everywhere. Winter dead, hanging hillsides of kudzu, like they had blundered into a time warp driving through this lonely canyon and emerged into a brown jungle. Anna said they used it for the erosion but it got out of control. Then they were in Grundy proper and she took a right up a holler. There were some nicer houses up the narrow road than Elias had seen the last time they were here. About a quarter mile up she turned into an asphalt drive and parked in front of a two story brick colonial, with chimneys at each corner. It was strange, but the house reminded him of the one in Richmond they had just left, only this one was much smaller, wedged into the side of a mountain. There were lights on upstairs, but not down. They got their gear out and walked uphill to the door.

"He's most likely in bed already," she said. "Old habits are hard to break."

"Maybe we should have called."

247

"Doesn't matter. He's not going to interrupt his routine for us. But his girlfriend will be up."

"See if we can park the car in the garage."

"What for?"

"In case someone comes looking for us."

Anna gave him a disgusted look and buzzed, and a half minute later a woman came to the door. In her forties, Elias thought, with blond hair and a ready smile. Her face was pleasant enough but creased with worry lines around her eyes and mouth, and her eyes had a strained, searching look like maybe she had cried herself to sleep too many times. She was wearing a robe but still had makeup on, and she had the ubiquitous cigarette in her hand.

She shooed the smoke out of the doorway and apologized. "My last one for the night. Can't smoke in the bedroom with the oxygen." Then she gave Anna a hug. She didn't seem the least bit surprised to see them at her door at 10 p.m. on a Friday night a week before Christmas.

"Nila, this is Elias. Elias, Nila."

"Pleased to meetcha."

"It's my pleasure." He held out his hand but she hugged him like he was her son, even though Elias had the years on her. She looked like a mother, a mother who had been forced to work hard all her life to raise her kids.

"Sorry to barge in on you like this. We were out driving and Anna wanted to visit her dad. I hope we're not disturbing you this late."

"Don't give it a second thought. Anna never lets us know when she's coming. She just shows up and she's always welcome. Come on in. You must be hungry. We've got ham in the fridge and some left over biscuits from supper. What can I make you?"

From the next room Elias heard Anna say, "How 'bout a poster of an old rodeo?"

She had already stretched out in one of the two Lazy Boy leather recliners positioned in front of the television, an

248

old floor model, with the remote in hand. The parlor, as Nila called it, was comfortably furnished with couches, a grandfather clock, and pictures on the mantel, but she took Elias directly into the dining room and sat him down at the table covered in a hand-stitched tablecloth while she continued into the adjoining kitchen.

"Would you like a soft drink, milk, or a beer?"

"A beer would be great if it's not too much trouble."

"I'll get it," Anna said, jumping up and moseying into the dining room.

Then Elias heard a man's voice calling down the stairs.

"Who's that down there? Nila, have you got company?" The voice was raspy and quiet, but strong in authority.

"It's me, daddy." Anna stuck her head around the corner of the dining room wall and spoke up the stairwell. "I've come to visit for the weekend. Me and my boyfriend. Merry Christmas."

"Diana, is that you? What's the matter, are you in trouble?"

"Me, in trouble? Whatever gave you that idea?"

"Well, get something to eat. You say you brought your boyfriend? Where is he? Do I know him?"

"No daddy. He's a new one." She motioned for Elias to come over and he got up from the table with the beer in hand that Nila had already brought him and stood by Anna.

He felt awkward and tried to look younger. "Good evening, Mr. Jassey. Sorry to bother you so late." He stared up at the top of the stairs but all he could see was a dark face in the shadows. A scruffy, rigid jaw and two large luminous eyes.

"I wasn't asleep." There was a pause. "Anna, get the young man a beer or something."

"I've got one," Elias said, and held up the can.

"All right, then," the voice said, and he disappeared down the upstairs hall and they heard a door close.

Nila brought out sliced ham, biscuits, and homegrown canned peaches, while Elias, realizing he no longer had a cell, used their phone to call Sigmon and leave him a voice mail on his office phone. The long drive and the cold night air made him hungrier than he thought he was, and he was thankful for the food. Anna didn't eat much, but he noticed she did drink a couple of beers. Nila asked a few questions of Elias about what he did and so on but when she turned to Anna and didn't get any long answers she excused herself and went off to bed, apparently leaving the sleeping arrangements to them.

"There's extra blankets in the closet," she said, as she headed up.

"I told Elias he can park his car in the garage. Is that okay?"

"Sure, honey. Good night."

"Are we sleeping in the same room?" Elias asked after she was gone.

Anna gave him a quizzical look. "I'm sure they don't approve, but nobody's going to say anything. They aren't married either."

Elias had wandered over to the pictures on the mantel. There were several of Anna, all when she was little. It was strange, as if she had died at puberty. He studied the girl. Anna jumping a horse. Anna at her middle school graduation. Anna holding a live raccoon with a group of men with guns. It looked like it was taken at night.

He pointed at it and then at her.

"I got to the coon before they did, and they couldn't shoot it while I was holding it."

"What about the dogs? Don't they use dogs to hunt coons?"

"Expensive dogs. But I raised that coon and knew where it was."

After Elias parked the jeep, she grabbed two more beers from the refrigerator and they re-slung their backpacks and slowly mounted the stairs.

The bedroom was small, with a narrow four poster and a vanity with a big ornate mirror and combs and brushes, pins and brooches laid out.

"This isn't your old room, is it?"

"Probably Nila's," she said. "In case she wants her own room. I've never lived here. We used to stay down by the river, right on the highway. Until I was fourteen."

"Then what happened?"

"I left town."

That was all he got, so he changed the subject. Later, when they had gotten naked under the covers and the hand-made quilt, he started thinking about how she had referred to him as her boyfriend. That was at least the second time.

"Have you had many other boyfriends, before me?"

"A few."

"How long ago was the last one?

There was a silence.

"Listen," she said. He listened. Anna had left the window cracked as she often did when she smoked. There was no wind. The curtain was parted and the moon was still up. The house was not creaking. He heard the clock downstairs ticking, he thought. Then there was another mechanical sound. The furnace? Maybe, but it was too rhythmical. He couldn't place it.

"His respirator. Can you hear it? Has to carry that bottle of oxygen everywhere he goes now. Down to the Piggly Wiggly sometimes you see two or three men in there with their bottles. Almost like they're back down in the mines."

Then she continued: "Three or four years ago. He was a musician."

"And what happened?"

"I caught him cheating."

251

"And then what happened?"

"I put a copperhead in him and his girlfriend's bed."

"Damn Anna! You're relentless. But isn't that a felony?"

"Class four misdemeanor. If you get caught." She snorted and curled up next to him.

"A copperhead bite can kill you, can't it?"

"Not normally. You can crush up some bloodroot on it."

"Where did you get the copperhead?"

"They're not hard to find in the mountains, love. Just look around on a sunny day."

"I know, but how did you get it into his bed?"

"Ain't you never heard of snake handlers? Lots of people around here can take up serpents without getting bit. It's a tradition. Not as many as there used to be, of course, but that's the case with everything."

"So you went to one of those Pentecostal churches?"

"Mountain Holiness. I expect I did a few times."

"But I thought you were Catholic."

"Well we were Catholic, at least my dad was. But when I was little my mother used to take me to the Oneness group. You got to remember there's a lot of communitying up here when it comes to religion. There's not many people in Grundy, in case you hadn't noticed, and church is a big thing. People often go to several churches, or the churches share the same places. Old Regular Baptists and Pentecostals and Methodists. Even daddy would get down with the Jesus Onlies if he didn't feel like driving all the way to Tazewell to mass."

"But you were just a little kid. That's got to be dangerous, handling snakes."

"I never minded." And she made a writhing motion under the covers with her arm, like she was attacking him. He grabbed her hand and threatened to cut it off if she didn't behave. She stopped and sat back up against the headboard.

"So what else do people do during those services?"

"The Holy Rollers? Well, I wouldn't call it a service. It's more like a family gathering. There's a sermon, and some foot washing. And they pass the snakes around to whoever feels like he's in the spirit. There's no pressure to touch them. Once in a while someone drinks some strychnine, but not too often. And of course there's a lot of speaking in tongues."

"Jesus, Anna. Poison? That's crazy. It makes me wonder how you turned out so well adjusted."

She punched him in the ribs. Hard. "It just seems natural when you grow up with it."

When he went to sleep he dreamed that she was a snake woman. Lamia. At first she scared him, with her serpent eyes and tongue. But then he felt sorry for her. She was an animal, but she was possessed with a human soul. How did she come to be a serpent? Was she a regular woman in the past? Had she been the victim of a spell, a curse? So he embraced her, and felt himself sexually drawn to her, but at the same time he was watching himself and contemplating how strange it was to make love to another species. Then he woke up and they really were having sex. Anna had turned her back to him so he couldn't see her eyes and his were only half open, but the tip of his cock was already inside her and she was moving her ass against it. Then he was fully in and she reached out each hand and grabbed the two posts at the head of the bed and seemed to half pull herself up from the covers with them like she was crawling out of the ocean onto a beach like some prehistoric fish climbing onto land by its flippers and he threw the bedclothes off and she was lying on the sandy sheets with just an uncurtained stripe of moonlight across her back like she had been branded with it while he slowly came and came into her and all the time he could never tell if her eyes were open. She never uttered a single word. She might have been asleep the whole time for all he knew. It was like a fairy tale. And the room was enchanted, with its ivory combs and tarnished mirror. And he didn't know if he wanted to wake up from it or not, but then he did awake some time shortly after to the sound of a toilet flushing somewhere in the house, and he looked at the phosphor and tritium-lit hands on his watch and it was 5:15 and once again he didn't know which life was real.

Daddy takes me in the Bronco down to Bluefield to see the priest. It's been months since momma went away and the snow ball plants are blue now the color of Sylvie's eyes. I stare out the window watching the train tracks and the cartoons on the cars along 460 I remember to put in my notebook when we get home while daddy smokes and coughs. It's just rained and there's turtles in the road. I say daddy let me out to put the turtle on the side but he pays no attention. I never understood why they always cross the road after a storm he says. They carry the world on their back I blurt out and he tries to cuff the side of my head but misses.

The man's older than my daddy and first he gives me some candy and then some scripture to read and he asks can she read and daddy says she reads good but I don't like this air conditioned room with no windows and all the crosses on the walls and I refuse to read correctly and then he splashes me with water from a weapon it stings not like the elders at the meeting place when they take you to Lake Moomaw in the summer and the water feels cool against your legs and the minnows swim up your dress but he makes me take it off and he touches me and I'm about to scratch him when my daddy says behave yourself Diana Leigh and then he says talk in that language like you been doing lately and I won't and he says talk that stuff your momma taught you when you used to visit up to Green Bank that devil's tongue and I won't and he says I'll beat it out of you willful child and the man says I've seen enough.

Daddy stands in my door and says I hear you talking to your momma she's not coming back but I pretend I am asleep and he just

254

stands there with the coal dust ironed into his skin so that his face looks like an old wallet. He is amazed when I know where his keys are that he put in the sugar bowl or how I can tell when it will rain from the wind blowing or a lottery number in a flight of geese.

Then the men come one night and tie me in the twisted branch rocking chair her mother made. They think that they will kill her in me but the ancient tree protects me while the man in purple calls to her in bad names saying she is unclean and he knows her true identity and presses pictures of Jesus against my forehead. Then the other man starts speaking in tongues hanamanashandamonhalaseradolamanhanda for a long time and while he's in the rapture another holds a rattlesnake to my cheek and moka comforts and kisses me and so I am happy momma and nuni are there with me and then he puts the snake back in the box and lies down on the floor and starts squirming around like he's the snake and the purple man bends down with his eyes bulging and says we know you are there we see through this disguise this poor child and nani untwists the branches and I pull my ankle loose and kick him right between the legs and then they get really angry and yell at me and I yell back at them and they take my from the chair and tie me down on the bed and then the words start coming out the curses fuck you goddamned sonsofbitches and the words momma learned me for the deer babosgo and the cat dalusgik frog hemo pig masgolo wolf ts ungiwe horse ts ungide white man miha ma gana ga like water flowing over rocks, like I am travelling down some meherrin I remember I have never been down before that never ends and I walk and walk backwards it seems all the way from that pentagon Fort Christanna until a gap in the green castle opens before me and then I am among the animal people my mother told me about who live in stick houses and they smile at me with their brown faces and dancing eyes we communicate with no words when the other man with the moustache puts the duct tape over my mouth all the while I can hear them from behind the hills a terrible shouting Go away seducer go back to the wilderness you came from be cast down from your infernal throne and they pray over and over that Jesus and the Pope will deliver me from the abomination that pours from my mouth they tell me I'm going to eternal damnation cast into a deep pit of smoke and fire with monsters that will devour my flesh from

255

the living body if I don't renounce the serpent within they cite scripture from heart for rebellion is the sin of witchcraft and stubbornness is iniquity and idolatry because thou hast rejected the word of the Lord First Samuel let the wicked forsake his way and the unrighteous man his thoughts and let him return unto the Lord and he will have mercy upon him Isaiah and rise and stand upon thy feet for I have appeared unto thee for this purpose to open their eyes and to turn them from darkness to light and from the power of Satan unto God Acts 26 and they strip the clothes from my body and throw water on me again my mouth my boobies my stomach my private places then they turn me over and sing hymns Jesus thou art the sinner's friend onward Christian soldiers and by now the sun has come up and they keep shouting and singing and praying and casting me out some leave and come back and finally I think they will never go away as long as I live they will haunt me I think I will hide a part of me here in the green holler of the animal people from these monsters who look like my father and will not leave me alone and then I will walk back into the black world and live there for a time because it is foretold that I must suffer because of something I have done being born or being born in the wrong time or being born to the wrong people or not realizing something all the other children realized or not forgetting something everyone else forgot and so I say goodbye to the animal people and they say not goodbye you are one of us and I walk downstream out of the holler in the rapids of the tears I have wept with their voices in my head back into Grundy where the rivers join but before I tell them yes, I will renounce Satan and all his words I lie facedown on a flat rock in the shreds of moonlight that have not been torn apart by their machinery and I stretch out my arms as far as they can reach as they untie me and I grasp the roots of the inverted tree in the water that holds the earth and I hold onto the earth so that I can awake as the men sing hymns of praise and shout hallelujahs and leave me alone with Elias ...

Chapter 18

In the morning Anna was sitting on the side of the bed smoking and coughing. She was naked from the waist up, her ribs visible through her pale brown skin like a birch bark canoe. You could watch them heave each time she took a drag. He came from the bathroom and got on his knees behind her and massaged her neck which was so dystonic with stress and long-term anti-psychotic medication he could barely press his fingers into it. She said it felt like she was in a permanent vise. When her jaw cracked she got up without a word and started getting dressed. It wasn't even 6:00. Still dark out.

"Did you sleep at all?" he asked as she buttoned up a flannel shirt they had found at Goodwill.

"An hour or two."

"Now what?"

"Now we confront the old man."

"What do you want me to do?"

She pulled on her tight jeans and gave him a defiant look while she zipped them up, then seemed to think better of it and said, with just a residue of irony, "You can be the voice of reason." She pulled on her boots without socks and sat on the bed again while he hurried to get dressed. Then they marched downstairs to the kitchen. Elias felt like he was going to a funeral.

Nila was at the stove cooking eggs. She turned to Elias.

"Coffee?"

"Absolutely, thank you."

She poured into cups with saucers and they all three sat down at the little wooden enamel-topped table and drank in silence for a moment, until Nila said, "Your father's in his office. But if you're fixing to ask him something serious you better wait 'til he's read the paper and finished his breakfast."

"I was fixing to *tell* him something serious."

"Oh, well, in that case you don't even need to wait."

But they waited. Nila fed them and when Anna offered to clean up said, "Don't bother; I'm just going to put it in the dishwasher." Then they went to the half-open door of the office on the other side of the house. Anna knocked and opened it.

"Can we come in and talk, daddy?"

"Sure, come on in. And close the door behind you."

It was a medium sized room with a desk and a couple of bookcases, a small red leather couch against one wall, and two east-facing windows that would have let in plenty of morning light if the sides of the holler weren't so steep, but it felt smaller with the three of them in it. Mr. Jassey sat at his desk with newspapers spread open before him. The TV in the corner was tuned to Fox News but the sound was low. There was a computer and fax on a side table. Behind the desk stood a metal coat rack on rollers which had a small oxygen tank attached, and a rubber hose and mask that dangled halfway to the floor. Despite his long illness, Jassey was still a large man, not fat but big boned and trim, and Elias's first reaction was how could Anna be so petite. He had a long jaw with some grey stubble, a large Gallic nose, prominent ears, piercing dark eyes like Anna's, and his left eyebrow seemed to stay quizzically or menacingly raised while he spoke. He had a moustache that partially covered his full upper lip, and very white teeth. Or maybe it was just the contrast with his skin, which was dark, but not by heredity, for his short cropped hair was still reddish, but almost as if it had been stained with tobacco juice or coal dust for so many decades that it had taken on the color of leather.

His sentences were often clipped from lack of breath and he occasionally wheezed when he spoke, but his voice still had volume and he never reached for the oxygen. Elias detected the traces of a hard East European accent partially buried under the soft, slow Southwest Virginia pronunciation.

Anna introduced Elias again and they sat down on the couch. Jassey leaned back in his chair and watched them and didn't say a word.

"I'm in some trouble and there's some things I need to know about," Anna said after a half minute of silence.

"Well, I didn't think you'd come for Christmas. You never were religious. Or family oriented."

Elias sensed that the last comment hurt, but she didn't visibly react.

"What family? There's just you and me."

"And Nila."

"Nila's okay, but she's not my mother."

"Always about your mother. But you get into some problems with the law and it's your father you come to."

"Who says I got problems with the law?"

"Well, we may be the last town in Bum Fuck, Egypt but 460 still runs all the way to Roanoke, last time I looked. I probably know more about what you're doing down there than you know yourself."

"What do you know?"

"I know you were arrested again for using meth. And you've been making accusations concerning the death of your cousin."

"That bastard Ronnie Breedlove killed her, and his father set me up for the drug bust and burned down my trailer. I could have been in it."

"From what I hear you got no evidence on either account."

"That's because all you hear gets filtered through your buddies in Richmond."

"And who am I supposed to believe, the people that run the biggest coal company in Appalachia or the little girl who does drugs and has been in a mental hospital more times than I can count?"

259

There was another silence.

"You should believe your daughter," Elias said. "She's right. Ron Breedlove and his son are behind Sylvie's death and all the problems that Anna is having. They've admitted it. The father will apparently do anything to protect his business, even if it means having people killed, and Ron Junior is a psychopath if I ever saw one. I hear this is not a new phenomenon in the history of Appalachia and the coal business, so I would think that you would have some experience with it."

Otto Jassey's expression changed when he heard Elias speak and the room seemed to darken, as if a cloud had suddenly obscured the narrow band of sky above the hollow. His eyes caught fire and he abruptly half stood up, knocking his oxygen rig back a foot. Then he appeared to compose himself, smiled and sat back down.

"And who the hell are you?" he asked, quietly. "You're not from around here, that's damn obvious. So what business of it is yours what happens to my daughter? 'Lessen you think that taking her side is going to get you into her pants."

"Daddy, shut up."

"What are you, twice her age? Did you think you could come up to Grundy to her father's house and badmouth my livelihood and she would become your girlfriend just like that? You don't know the half of it. She's always had men, older men too, and then she dumps them just like a load of coal once she changes her mind, which she does all the time. It's called manic depression, if you don't know. And she's had it since her mother spoiled her. Hell, the man she married when she was no more than fifteen was my age."

"Daddy, shut the fuck up. You've got no right to lie like that about me."

"Watch your language little girl. Who's lying? You've been a wild child since you were born. Nobody could do a thing with you once she filled your head with all that garbage."

"I think you're the one who made her sick," Elias interrupted.

Jassey acted like a man attacked on two fronts. "I made her sick? How do you figure that?"

"You did something to her."

"What are you talking about?"

"He's right, daddy. You did something bad to me after momma went away."

"Watch what you're saying, Diana."

"You hated me because I was like momma, and after she left you tried to force her out of me somehow. You and some other men tied me up, I remember."

"We never did no such thing, except you acted crazy and needed to be restrained."

"It was more than that. I've been in restraints before, but what you all did was worse. It was awful. Wrong. Evil. You tortured me and wouldn't leave me alone until you said I stopped talking like momma. You might as well have raped me."

He stood up again. "Diana, you talk like that to your father and as old and sick as I am I'll get out of this chair and beat some sense into you. Evil? You think I'm evil? Evil was what we had to dig out of you. You were possessed, girly girl! Talking that satanic language and saying things you had no business knowing. Practically living in the woods. Skipping school. We had to bring in the priest to drive the devil out of you!"

Anna started quietly crying during this harangue and Elias stood up from the couch and took a couple of steps toward the desk.

"Wait a minute. Are you saying that you performed an exorcism on her? Are you shitting me? A fucking exorcism? Why? Because she spoke a Native American

261

language? Because she had a pet raccoon? You must have been insane."

"She was the insane one. She was possessed. She was going to hell. She had that hardness deep down inside her; it took us all night to get it out, but we finally did. She was better after it was over. She was saved. We saved her."

"Saved? She wasn't saved. That's why she had to go to all those hospitals, right? Because she was so much better? Really she was worse. She had to live a lie. You had to brainwash her. It's like what you do to these mountains around here: you blow them up to get what you want out of them and then you think you can just smooth over the surface and everything goes back to normal? With the dirt you take off, the what do you call it? Anna, the dirt?"

"The overburden," Anna said, a small voice from off in the distance.

"The overburden. So you brought in a priest when what she needed was a social worker to protect her from you."

"Shit." He said it like an East European might, with a "z" in it. "You don't know what you're talking about. Her mother, if you can call her that, used to take her to the serpent church and she would play with the snakes while they had the rest of the service. Did she tell you that? A four year old girl, playing with rattlers! Her and her mother brought a bear cub home once. Wanted to keep it and raise it. Pitched a fit when I got rid of it. Did she tell you about how she could go all week without sleeping, and how when she walked in her sleep outside the house she talked to the moon? Or the birds? She had a pet crow up in her room! One time she took that clock in the parlor apart and left all the parts scattered across the floor. Cost me $350 to get it fixed. Her mother was just as crazy, and she was becoming more and more like her every day."

"My mother was not crazy!" Anna shouted through her sobbing. "She was sweet and loving and full of life.

262

Nothing like you. You're filled with darkness and hate. You hated me because I loved her. You couldn't stand it."

"She was crazy as any person can be. Couldn't stop talking for weeks, then she would shut up and not say a word for a year. Moody all the time. And she was not a good wife, neither. Not a coal miner's wife. You know what I mean. The less said the better." He was looking down, talking to the desk now as much as to them.

"Why did she go away?" Anna wanted to know.

"She had to go away. She was too sick to stay."

"You mean she was too difficult and wouldn't let you control her."

"I mean she was too sick. She tried to kill herself."

"I don't believe it," Anna said. "She would never do that to me."

"She did it."

"Why did she do it? You drove her to it, didn't you?"

"I did no such thing."

"You did. I know when you're lying. I can see it in you. I can look inside your mind and read your thoughts. I have special powers, you know that. And I know right now that you're lying."

There was a short silence, and then she said, "What did you do? Was there another woman?"

Jassey kept looking down. Elias had sat back down on the couch and watched.

"Well, what did you expect? I told you, she was no good as a wife."

"You had an affair, she found out, and that drove her to suicide. And I know who it was too."

"You don't and you never will."

"It was Sylvie's mom. I know it as surely as I know who you are."

He looked up. "How can you know that?"

263

"I know Sylvie was my sister. I've always known it. I just couldn't put it into words until recently. So, where did you put her? Which insane asylum?"

"She went to Staunton."

"And you never saw her again, did you?"

"No I did not," and Elias heard him half choke on these words. Then he put his head down on his hands and started crying softly into them.

"I knew it. I knew it," Anna kept repeating. Then she walked around behind the desk—Elias tensed, thinking maybe she was going to strangle him—and ran her hand through her father's hair. "And she died locked up in that old hospital and the folks from Green Bank buried her up there."

Otto stopped crying and opened a handkerchief he kept in his back pocket and blew his nose into it.

"She was a half breed," he said to Elias, after a moment. "They call them Melungeons. Half white and half Indian. Some people say they're Portuguese. I don't know. Didn't know a thing about it. I was working down in Wise County, near Big Stone Gap, and I met her at a restaurant. I had a thick accent back then and she liked that for some reason. She thought I was different, like her. She looked like the women back home. She never did tell me her background and I never asked. Should have, and she should have told me. I didn't meet her family until later, when she got pregnant and we had to get married. We had the priest in Bristol to marry us and I thought she had converted to Catholicism from whatever she was but she did not. Then after a while I discovered she was mostly Cherokee or some such tribe, and they had family up in Pocahontas. So she stayed up there much of the time and took Anna with her because I was managing coal mines by then and moving around a lot."

"You were ashamed of her, and of me, because we were Melungeon."

"I was. I'm not denying it. To me you were gypsies, just like we had back home. Lazy good for nothings who live off other people. She never did like me again after you were born, and we lived apart mostly, and I did see other women. I never had more children, no sons of my own to leave the business to. But you became just as stubborn, disobedient, and hard-hearted as her after a time, and I realized I had to do something about it."

"Anna is not hard-hearted," Elias said. "Just the opposite. She may have a broken heart from losing her mother but it is a wide-open heart, despite what she may say about herself. It's so wide open that it takes in the whole natural world. That's how she can communicate with other species and knows things we don't know. She's not walled off. In fact, she's too open for her own good. And that's why she scares people. They're afraid to be as open as she is. They're afraid of the freedom."

Anna was watching as he made this defense, but didn't speak. She seemed to have quieted down, even without lighting the obligatory cigarette in the oxygen-rich room.

"I don't know about that, but she has always been willful. She won't stop until she gets her way. You can put a mountain between her and what she's after and she will not stop. She's like a continuous miner; she just keeps ripping away at the seam and throwing everything behind her into the shuttle until she's got all the coal out. She should have worked in the mines. Lots of women do now. It would of been good for her."

"I have been working in the mines," Anna said, standing behind her father's desk and looking through the blinds.

"Well, she needs your help now because I'm telling you Breedlove has fixed it so the police think Anna is not only dealing meth, which she isn't, but because of a charge of attempted murder when all she was doing was protecting

265

herself from the son. Ronnie. They have already tried to have us killed at least once, and I suspect they are looking for us right now."

He was quiet for a minute. "It's a terrible thing," Jassey said, "the black lung. I've had it for twenty years. Everyone knows the risks, but some of the men still don't wear respirators because they're uncomfortable, and the dust you don't see gets picked up in your nose hairs anyway and you breathe it into your lungs where it makes little black nodules, little seams of coal that turn your lungs black. And then they send you to the company doctors, if you can call them that. They hire them sometimes without ever checking for a license, and if the one doctor says you ain't got it then you go back down. Of course the ventilation is much better now than it used to be, which was nothing when I started. It's too late for the oldtimers, but there's no reason to complain. Death comes to every man, and it don't scare me. The world is ugly and mean but it's what God gave us and we have to accept that."

Elias was trying to take it all in.

"He means he's too old to help us," Anna said from across the room. "Too old and sick. He ain't going to help us. Let's hit the road."

"I ain't saying that, little girl," Jassey spoke up and grabbed for Anna's arm which she moved out of his grasp. "I ain't saying that exactly. I am sick. I've had this goddamned bottle attached to me like I'm carrying a dead buddy on my back for twenty years. What do you want me to do? Kill somebody? Make a few phone calls and get the company goons to stop doing their job? If I could, I would. But these people are not going to listen to me. I'm retired, and I don't even know who some of them are anymore. Young lawyers and accountants from Ivy League schools."

"Well, you know Ron Breedlove. I've seen him in this very house before. Why don't you tell him to go fuck hisself."

266

"He used to be a friend. Fished together. Hunted. I spent several winters holed up in a camp in West Virginia with him. But no more. That was a long time ago."

"What happened?" Elias asked.

"Well, he ran me out of business is what happened. After managing some of his mines I saved up some money and bought my own. Was doing pretty good. But Ron didn't like it. Bought up all the land around me, hired away my workers, harassed me. I was forced to sell at a loss."

"He's Melungeon," Anna said abruptly.

"What?"

"He's a Ramp, just like me. He writes in Indian code and his son is Indian too but he don't know it."

"Don't use that word!" he yelled at her. "How did you find out he was Melungeon? Did your mother tell you that?"

"What, that she was related to the man you hated? What difference would it make, seeing as you already hated her by that time? Was it because she was Indian, or because she was Black?"

"Don't ever say that in this household. You know damn well she wasn't."

"Mr. Jassey," Elias interrupted, "maybe you could just tell the authorities that you suspect Mason Dixon Energy's CEO has been paying off politicians and the police to operate illegally, and even to cover up these illegal transactions by killing people. I'm sure you've still got some clout in this business. They'll believe you and start an investigation."

Jassey looked at Elias, grimaced and contorted his features and then started laughing so forcefully that he choked and couldn't get his breath. Anna gave him the oxygen mask but he didn't stop gasping for air and Nila came into the room with an inhaler when she heard the commotion but that didn't seem to help either. She went to the phone to call 911 but Jassey took the receiver from her.

267

"No," he managed to say. "No ambulance." He walked to the couch, still coughing and pulling his oxygen behind him, and lay down while they all stood around him waiting to see what he would do. His body was wracked with seizures of coughing and Elias could see now that his chest was caved in under his shirt and his legs were pitifully thin and mottled with bruises. After a few minutes though he seemed to settle down and was peaceful.

"Coal has run Appalachian politics for a hundred years. And that includes the sheriff," he managed to get out.

"We've got proof," Elias said. He switched on the voice recorder that he had in his pocket, and played the track of the altercation in Richmond. It was once again strange hearing it out of context in this room in Grundy, as if they had been pursued by ghosts, and Anna too seemed unnerved when Ronnie said he had killed Sylvie. But Jassey listened quietly.

When it was over he muttered, "I don't think the bastard can lie his way out of this one. But we'll see. Now I need to go to the ER and get a shot. My lungs are on fire." And without stopping to explain he grabbed a cane from the corner and started out the door with Nila right behind him.

"Daddy?" Anna shouted, but he went through the kitchen and the garage door and was gone, just like that. And they watched the Explorer drive off a minute later and wind its way out of sight down the narrow passage.

Chapter 19

They talked it over and decided that Anna would hide out in Grundy for a few days while Elias drove back to Floyd and checked things out. He could consult Sigmon, take care of the dogs, see what was going on at the house. Also buy a new cell. He was somewhat concerned for Anna staying there with her father, but they seemed to have vented enough already to live in the same house for the weekend without killing each other. Nila was a steadying influence. He knew by now that Anna was unpredictable, subject to intense mood swings, but he also knew that no one could control her but herself. He certainly couldn't.

They had been able to translate enough of the documents to establish a narrative of secret payoffs for services rendered, but who exactly was involved, when, and for what, was tricky to decipher. She would have to show them to her father when he got back from the hospital and see if he could piece together what the names and numbers meant. The last thing he did was get Anna to agree to take the Nano with her if she went out anywhere.

"Not in my bra again."

"Pocket's okay."

So in the afternoon he drove the three hours through Raven and Red Ash, Tazewell and Bluefield, the two tunnels, across 81 and up the mountain to the high plateau. It seemed to take longer without Anna talking beside him with her boots up on the dash. When he turned into his driveway about 6:00 p.m. and saw the house, he felt like he had been away a week instead of one night. There were tire tracks in the snow. Elias didn't believe in outside lights in the country—they blocked the stars—but the moon was almost full and he could see pretty well. They looked like they were from his neighbor's pickup, and he followed the footprints back to the kennel, but the dogs weren't there. He panicked and cursed himself for leaving them in such a vulnerable place, but when he unlocked the back door and called next door he found out they were there. His neighbor had picked them up yesterday morning. Elias decided to walk over and retrieve them, which would give him an opportunity to scout around the property for cars parked along the road or any other signs that they were still being spied on. He was standing in his kitchen wondering if he should change his boots before he crossed the fields when something made him stop what he was doing and listen. It was a voice inside his head. Was it still snowing here yesterday when he called Sam who said he was going right over to see about the dogs? It was definitely still snowing in Richmond, but the storm was moving east. Now that he thought about it, those tracks out front were too precise for a sunny day. They looked new. Had Sam come back over today to check on things? He hadn't said anything about it on the phone. But it was like him not to say anything. Maybe Elias was just being paranoid; it was a disease, and he was catching it. He looked down at his dripping boots, and then slowly followed with his eyes the wet path he had made on the hardwood from door to wall phone. Then he looked into the hall and he could just make out melting crinkles of slush going that way too into the living room. No dogs—no warning, he thought.

The smart thing would have been to just slip out the back door. Drive next door. Call the police. Whatever. But too much had happened for him to back up at this point. Elias was still angry about the exorcism, the fake cops, the hanging, the burning, the killing and torture. He could still see Ronnie Junior's smug face. Besides, he had built this house, his grandfather's house, and he didn't like the idea of leaving it in the hands of an intruder for even a second. They'd probably burn it down too before he got back.

He had turned on the kitchen light when he came in; otherwise the house was dark. And the shutters were pulled together so there was no moonlight. That gave him a slight advantage. He walked back to the door and switched off the overhead. Now it was almost pitch black, except for the digital clock on the microwave. He knew every floorboard, every measurement. He tried to remember if there was anything glowing in the living room. The printer? The iPod? He stood there for a long time, leaning against the counter, listening. Nothing. Maybe the intruder had come and gone. There was no car. It was cold inside; he had turned down the thermostat when they left. The ice wouldn't melt very fast. He waited some more. Nothing. So he started to move into the living room, his idea being to get to the katana on the mantel.

Before he took the first step he remembered something his sensei had taught him: to make no noise, don't move. He never really understood what that meant, logically: it sounded like he was saying don't do anything, or don't do anything aggressive, but he sensed there was more, or maybe less, to it than that. His sensei was generally so subtle that it was simple to mistake what he said. Now, his body started to not move. It was as if he wasn't thinking about moving, or doing anything. His mind was blank, but prescient. He didn't exist. He was not in the kitchen, the katana was not in the living room, because the two rooms were just part of one space. And in the dark, space didn't seem to matter anyway. He took maybe ten steps this way without thinking, automatically, aware but not aware of himself as a separate entity, turned the corner toward the fireplace, put his open hands up in front of his face and grabbed the scabbard and the tang right where they came apart at the tsuba. He was slowly lifting the katana out of its holder when several things happened all at once.

First, the room lit up. There were shadows everywhere, thrown against the walls by a powerful but diffused beam from a flashlight behind him. Elias saw a man and a gun out of the corner of his right eye.

271

Second, he drew the sword from the saya in one sweeping overhand arc through the air of the room, the curved 28 inch blade just missing the eight foot ceiling by an inch, and slicing through the man's right arm just above the wrist with almost no loss of speed.

Third, the man's hand, which had been holding a Smith and Wesson .32 caliber semi-automatic, fell toward the floor, still clutching the weapon which discharged in the air, as if the finger on the trigger had squeezed it on the way down, lodging a bullet in the wood box next to the fireplace.

All of this happened in a second. The flashlight in the man's left hand stayed motionless. Indeed, both Elias and the intruder, whom he recognized at once, despite the light in his face, as the younger of the two security guards who had come with the sheriff to the house, were motionless too, staring at the thick hand with the blood-spattered gun lying now on the floor, as if they were both trying to decide whether to pick it up, as if the katana, reputed to have once been owned by a member of the Japanese royal household and which Elias had spent a year's salary on, had severed it so cleanly that they were not even sure if it had actually been cut off, as if the owner had not even felt the loss and couldn't quite believe it. It seemed more likely to have a life of its own, this hand, as if it might raise the gun and shoot it again, and vivid scenes from 50's horror films flashed through Elias' consciousness which seemed to suddenly have perfect recall.

Then they both looked up at each other, and Elias, slowly raising the katana between them so that the tip was inches from the man's face, said in Japanese, reflexively, almost as an apology, "wari." And then when he got no reaction, shouted "zama miro!" and a split second later the man took off without his hand through the front door which he had obvious trouble opening. Elias calmly followed him outside, saw him hoofing it through the snow-covered stubble and into the woods down the hill toward the road,

272

where presumably there was someone waiting, or at least a car. He figured he could make it to Christiansburg, or maybe Roanoke, if he staunched the bleeding, the cut was so clean. The doctors could re-attach it.

He resisted the strong temptation to wipe the blood from the blade and return it to the scabbard, which he was still holding in his left hand, then walked back inside, turned on the lights, removed the gun from the hand, picked up the hand, which was surprisingly heavy, wrapped it in some clean dish towels, and put it in the refrigerator, which was set at 37 degrees. He figured that was cold enough. Then he called 911 and told the dispatcher what had happened. He had surprised an armed man in his home and the man had been wounded and fled. No, he was not armed now; in fact, the man's gun and his hand were still at the scene. He had to repeat the hand part. Then he poured himself a double shot of Jameson's on the rocks and sat down to wait. His mind had been perfectly clear and blank and brilliant for the last ten minutes; now he had time to think about what had just happened. He had killed people before in the military, but he thought he had resolved that a long time ago. He had seen his students and his wife gunned down senselessly. That was beyond horrible. But this time was different somehow. It made him anxious. Was it because Anna was in danger? Or was it because even though he was sure the man was not dead, and that he had meant to kill Elias, still there was something uncanny about severing someone's hand. It was almost as if just the part of his body was a reminder of something more terrifying than death.

The police, local and state, were on the scene in ten minutes, quickly, as if they had been hanging out nearby in case something else went down at his place. A couple of deputies searched the property: the blood line, clearly visible in the light from the ascending, almost full moon, ran straight down to where a car had been parked next to the road. Elias handed the hand to the state cop, Bondurant, who had been there before. He examined it gingerly. There were no tattoos or rings. The fingernails were long and dirty. Then he put it in a gallon-sized, plastic, multi-purpose storage bag with some ice which Elias gave him and passed it along to a deputy to take to headquarters. He picked up the gun with a pen from his shirt pocket, held it up so they both could look at it, and then it was evident they both had the same thought: did he really need to worry about fingerprints when he had the hand that had held it? But he placed it in another baggie before he and the deputy asked Elias the usual questions. When did he come home? About six. Where was he coming from? Willis. What was he doing in Willis? Getting gas. Was Miss Jassey on the premises now or when the perpetrator was here? No. Did he know where she was? No, he did not. Did he have any idea why this man was in his house? Yes. Why? He was spying on him. Why? Because he was working for a company that was trying to cover up crimes it had committed. So he knew the man? Yes, and so did they. What did he mean? "He was the security guy from Mason Dixon that you brought with you the last time you were here."

That effectively ended the interrogation, at least for the moment. Then Bondurant wanted to examine the sword which Elias had laid reverently on the kitchen table.

"This was on the mantel?"

He started to pick it up but Elias stopped him.

"It's a priceless antique, at least to me. It's also extremely sharp. So be careful how you handle it."

The lieutenant looked at Elias like he was an amateur talking to a professional; still, he was careful not to touch the blade when he grabbed the handle and held it up.

"It's light. Don't see how it could cut through the bone so clean."

"It's very well balanced. Here, let me show you." And Elias took the katana from him. "Can I wipe the blood off now?"

274

"Yeah. We already got a sample."

Elias pulled a Pampers baby wipe from a nearly full green plastic container on the kitchen counter while Bondurant raised an eyebrow. He fastidiously cleaned and polished the steel with it. "In feudal Japan," he said, "they used to test their blades on the bodies of criminals they had executed." Then he stepped into the middle of the room, took the box in his left hand, deftly threw it a few feet into the air, and sliced it in half with the blade in his right hand on the way down. The moist toilettes divided into two piles on the floor.

"Handy when you want to conserve paper," he said. He cleaned the sword again, put it into its scabbard, walked into the living room with the sheriff behind him, and put it back on the mantel.

"Yeah, but you ruined the box."

It was getting late by the time they concluded their investigation for the evening. More questions to come on Monday in downtown Floyd. Elias wasn't sure if Sigmon had put the state cops onto the case, or if this was routine, but he didn't ask. Frankly, his nerves were still on edge, despite the whiskey and the sword demo. He just wanted them to leave so he could get his dogs and lie in bed with them and think it all over, but it was too late even for that. He forgot he had told his neighbor he was on his way over hours ago. He also wanted to call Anna, but he was afraid he would just wake everyone up.

A window had been broken. That's how the guy got in. Apparently he hadn't taken anything; it appeared that he was just there waiting for Elias to come home, or someone, to murder them.

"Normally I would advise you to lock your doors and windows," the sergeant said outside as he was leaving, "as a precaution. But I don't think this feller is going to be back, unless he wants to look for his hand."

275

When he went back in and shut the door, the phone rang. It was Anna.

"You said you were going to call. Had a late night, did ya?" He could picture her sitting at her father's desk with her feet up smoking a cigarette and blowing rings across the room.

"You might say that." And he explained what had happened.

"The bastard almost shot you? And you actually cut his hand off?"

"You know what this means," he asked rhetorically. "They're out to get us, and they don't care anymore about making it look like a hunting accident or a house burning down with the people in it. They just flat out want to get rid of us, make us go away. I guess going to Richmond put Breedlove over the edge. He's reckless now, and that's dangerous even if …."

Before he had finished, he heard her coughing on the other end. Then it was choking, but really the beginning of soft but unmistakable sobbing, like thunder before a midsummer shower, more like she wanted to say something but couldn't speak, like every time she started to she gagged.

"What's the matter?"

"I don't know. I just don't seem to be able to stop. It's been twenty-four hours now. It's killing me."

"It's good to let your emotions out. It purges the system." He only half believed this, and the half was really for other people.

"You don't cry, except when a dog gets killed in a movie."

"I'm retarded."

She laughed. "If I let my emotions out, it wouldn't purge the system; it'd break it."

"No it wouldn't."

"You don't know me. I've lost too much already." She paused, then started sobbing more loudly. "He doesn't love me. He never did. He hated my mom and then he hated me. Why? What did I do? Just because I was mixed race? Because I was bipolar? Is that a reason to hate a child? A child can't defend herself?"

"He doesn't hate you. He's just ignorant. Prejudiced. He grew up in another time, a different country. He never was able to get beyond his own childhood."

He could hear her take a deep drag. "I feel like I'm at the edge of an enormous pit, looking down. It's like that engraving from Dante's Inferno showing the levels of hell, except there are no people in this pit, nothing, not even the dead. And it's like I'm being pushed in, something's pushing me into it, or I'm pushing myself in, or maybe I'm just afraid I'm going to jump. Who knows?" She paused to take a drag. "Fuck, I didn't mean to burden you with this. I'm crazy, you're not. It's just like an enormous emptiness, inside. ... What were you saying?"

"It's no burden. Really. I understand. I think we're all empty inside. But we repress it. We dread it. Then something happens that forces us to confront it. And the ego dies. And then the emptiness is turned inside out." He stopped. He couldn't think of anything more to say that wouldn't run the risk of sounding either too academic or too maudlin over the phone. He wasn't good with these emotions himself anyway. "What I was saying was that we don't have to cover up what's going on anymore. We can take it to the police. Let them handle it."

"You mean the state police. I wouldn't trust the local law anymore n' I'd trust a rattler not to bite me."

"But they don't bite you."

She didn't respond to this. Then a moment later she said blandly, "Daddy didn't come back from the hospital yet. They're keeping him overnight for observation."

He told her to stay safe and not to take any chances. She sniggered.

Before they hung up she said, "Elias? … I'm going to try to stop using when this is all over. Maybe you're right. I know it's making me worse. But right now I don't seem to be able to stop."

"That's the first step, isn't it? Powerlessness?"

"It is. But I have some philosophical issues with it."

"I know, Anna. It's up to you. You'll do what's right for yourself." He paused. "I don't think the Native Americans would use these man-made chemicals. Weed, mescaline, peyote: they used everything that grew for some purpose. But it was religious. A way to contact the spirit kingdom. It was holy. Speed's not natural; it's a byproduct of capitalism, you might say. To get stuff done."

"Shit. The Injuns smoked buffalo dung to get high."

They laughed and said goodnight. Elias turned out the light and rolled over onto his side to face the window. The naked trees were bathed in extraterrestrial silver, and he felt a chill before he pulled the blanket tight. He wondered if Anna felt it too.

Chapter 20

First thing in the morning Elias called Sam and walked over and got the dogs. Needless to say, they acted like they were insane. Even Gypsy, a little piece of Anna. All three started running in circles. What was the evolutionary reason for that?

He waited until afternoon, not knowing if Sigmon was a churchgoer, and called him at home. He answered on the first ring.

"Bobby, it's Elias. How're you doing?"

"Better than you, I think. I got your message."

"There's more. Last night when I got back there was a guy in my house. One of the Mason Dixon security men. He tried to shoot me."

"Goddamn, Elias. Are you okay?"

"Yeah. He missed. But he ran and I called the police. They were here until eleven, and I've got to go back Monday and talk to them some more."

"So, the shit is starting to hit the fan. Well, after you called me I checked with the Richmond police and near as I can tell there was no report filed of a breaking and entering at Breedlove's house. There was a 911 call, but the only thing the first responders got was a man mauled by a dog. The report says it was his own dog. Didn't say why it attacked him."

"Did it say what happened to him?"

"Just that they took him to the ER and he was admitted to MCV. Sounds to me like you are off the hook. And another thing turned up. The girl is no longer wanted for attempted murder. They dropped the charges. No explanation. Of course she still escaped from the psych ward, but under the circumstances, I don't think they are going to go looking for her."

"You mean the police?"

"Correct. The police. What did you mean?"

"Why would they drop everything? It sounds to me like they realize they're too implicated in it and so maybe instead of threatening us or trying to get us locked up they're just going to disappear us, like the Argentinians say."

"That's possible, of course, but it sounds a little Hollywood to me. More than likely they are just giving up trying to scare you and are going to let their lawyers handle any accusations you make. They can't afford any more publicity: this is pretty sensational stuff. They're going to let it drop."

"Then why was that guy in my house?"

"Maybe you surprised him. Maybe he was still collecting information. I don't know."

"The state police were here. Did you ask them to get involved?"

"I did. I have to be honest; as a former prosecutor I still have a hard time believing that there is a corporate conspiracy out to get you, but I can see how some individuals might take it upon themselves to silence a witness to something illegal they've done, whatever it may be. You know, this Breedlove family could be acting on their own. I'm still not ruling out the drug connection, but any way you slice it, you are in danger. You and the girl."

"I appreciate that. I'll forward the documents we found to you once Anna gets her father to look them over. Turns out he used to work for Mason Dixon. We're hoping he can pinpoint some of the payoffs Breedlove made. But he's sick; he's in the hospital right now. It may be next week before I can e-mail them."

"One thing I can say for sure. Too much has happened, too much really to explain away, and somebody is going to get charged with something. The cat is out of the bag, and it ain't going back in."

Sunday afternoon Elias thought of driving over to the only open Verizon shop he could think of, in the mall in

Roanoke, but then he remembered there were only six days until Christmas and it would be a madhouse. He hated crowds. So he put that off and spent the afternoon working around the house, cutting more firewood and laying it up, battening down the hatches for winter storms. He didn't return to school until the second week of January. It was normally a quiet month off. Not this year of course. There were a dozen contrails crisscrossing the sky from different directions, like a celestial spider web. Everyone headed home for the holidays.

While he was outside Anna called and left a message, in her usual laconic way, that now that her father was "knocking on heaven's door" he had actually been able to figure out who was named in the documents. That was it. She didn't give any details over the phone. In the early evening he made some vegetarian chili and wrote up a summary of everything he could think of that had happened in the last two months that the police and prosecutors would need to know. Somewhere in the middle of that he called Anna back but no one answered. He figured they were at the hospital. Then it got too late to call.

He had to be at the police station at 9 a.m. Bondurant was there, the sheriff, the deputy who had done the investigation, and a lawyer from the Floyd Commonwealth's Attorney's office. They sat around a metal table in a small conference room that looked out on the land that Elias' ancestors had once owned that became the town of Floyd, then called Jacksonville, some two hundred years ago. First, Bondurant told him they had not arrested anyone in the attack at his house; apparently the suspect was willing to lose his hand, which was still on ice at Roanoke Memorial Hospital, than risk being charged with attempted murder, although they knew who he was and had a warrant out for him. Then Elias gave them the report he had written. They spent some time reading it over and asked a few questions. They wanted to see Sylvie's cell phone, so he passed it

281

around, and gave them copies of the documents he had printed with some translations of the Saponi words. He also played the voice recording of the conversation in Breedlove's home. They kept everything for evidence, as they said, in the "continuing murder investigation of Sylvia Presley."

"So what do you think?" he finally asked the group.

They looked at each other, and settled on the lawyer to answer.

"The problem is that the crime against Miss Presley was committed in another part of the state. That's why Lieutenant Bondurant is here. We can only investigate the crimes that were committed here in the county: for example, the assault at your house on Saturday, and the wreck and the death from a few weeks ago. We clearly need to discuss these matters further, but at the moment the consensus is that Lieutenant Bondurant's office should take over the case. And I understand your concerns that there may have been some lack of proper police procedures on the part of the local law enforcement. We also can't move forward of course until the criminal investigation is completed on this end, and that could take some time, maybe months. But based on what we have so far, I would say that an exhumation of Miss Presley's body is definitely in order. If Lieutenant Bondurant is in agreement, a new autopsy and DNA collection would seem ...."

He had forgotten to include the cremation in the report.

Two hours later he was standing on Main Street thinking that the worst was over. Now that the cat was out of the bag, as Sigmon said, the violence would have to end. It was only a matter of time before it hit the media: the murder, arson, dog hanging, threats, not to mention the deaths of two of the energy company's employees and the mutilation of another. The meth charges against Anna would be dropped. And then the real circus would begin: the evidence that Mason Dixon had paid off police and politicians to get their way, played out every day on television and in the press. Really, this was just the calm before the storm. Elias decided to celebrate with lunch at Oddfellas.

But would the state police be able to make a case on Sylvie's homicide without a body, and could they make the other assaults and intimidations stick to Breedlove and son?

Then he stopped at the local communications store to get a new droid for himself and a cell for Anna.

When he got back to Buffalo Mountain and took the dogs out, he saw the message light was blinking on his land line. It was from Jassey, left on his voicemail at 8:30 a.m. His voice sounded hoarse and tired.

"Kraft, this is Otto Jassey. I wanted to let you know that Anna went to a meeting last night and didn't return. I see that you called about 9 p.m. but we had already gone to bed. I don't know if there is anything to be alarmed about. She is liable, as you probably know by now, to disappearing without telling anyone and sometimes stays away for days. But under the circumstances I thought you would want to be informed." That was it. No sense of concern. Just matter of fact, except for his difficulty breathing. The message seemed to end, but then it started up again. "By the way, I was able to piece together most of the names from those ledgers you left with me. There's several congressmen, from West Virginia, Virginia, and Kentucky that I recognize because they were always friends of coal, as we called them. And I also know at least one sheriff and one state police officer who are listed. That's all. Good night."

Elias checked his watch; it was now almost 4 p.m. He called Jassey back and got Nila. She said Anna had gone to a seven o'clock NA meeting. She wasn't sure where it was, but she would call around and find out. She got a ride with some friends but wasn't sure who they were either. Elias told her he thought she might be in trouble and to please find out anything she could, and to notify the police.

She said she would. Before he hung up he asked about Mr. Jassey. She said he was at home but not capable of speaking at the moment, his breathing was so labored.

The first thing he did was to log into his Nano account on his laptop and check to see if the Nano Anna had promised to take with her was working. He checked and double checked but could find no data from the tracker. Something was wrong. Then he logged into his other account and looked to see if the tracker he had attached to Breedlove's Mercedes was still working. It was. He was still in Richmond; Elias could see the car parked at MCV Hospital on the GPS map.

Then he called Bondurant. He was out but the woman who answered transferred him to his cell when he told her it was an emergency related to a case he had just been interviewed about that morning. Bondurant said he would contact the Division Four office of the state police in Wythe County and advise them, but he didn't think there was much they could do but relay the information to the local sheriff in Buchanan. Normally they wouldn't start looking for someone for forty-eight hours, unless it was a child. Elias had a sudden foreboding. What if the local law enforcement were involved? Or even the state cops? He decided not to relay the information Nila had given him until he could verify the name of the policeman himself.

"Maybe the state police can handle this on their own. What do you think?"

"We'll see," he said. "Give me your phone number and I'll get back to you."

Elias decided that he couldn't wait in Floyd if Anna was in danger, so he packed up everything he could think he might need: the pistols, the GPS tracker, a laser painter, flashlights, amphetamines, some energy bars, and as much cash as he had on hand. He unlocked the hidden closet behind the mantel, looked over everything in there, and removed an M110 with the Leupold 3.5 by 10 scope, a semi-automatic sniper's rifle, along with an AN/PVS-14 night sight and some ammunition. He downloaded some maps from Google Earth and printed them. He even threw his tent, sleeping bag, and some camouflage gear in the jeep. Then he closed the dogs in the kennel and told them he would be back as soon as he could. No more than a couple of days if he was lucky.

On the drive to Grundy he kept thinking of all the possibilities. Anna had gone to a meeting and stayed over with old friends and slept late. She had met people who were still using and went somewhere to party and get high. That was the likeliest scenario. Maybe they were still high and she was unaware of what time it was. Their car broke down. She had no cell so she couldn't call him, but wouldn't someone else have a phone? The service was good in town; it was only when you got deeper into the mountains that it stopped. But maybe the meeting wasn't in Grundy.

Then there was the other possibility: Breedlove had caught up with her. His thugs had tracked her down and grabbed her. They had probably talked in the parking lot after the meeting and then forced her into a vehicle when everyone else had gone. Quite possibly she was already dead. Her body would probably never be found. He cursed himself repeatedly for not making her wear the GPS device in her bra or somewhere it wouldn't be found at all times while they were apart. She had told him she'd use it. Of course, he couldn't make Anna do anything.

He was half way to Bluefield when he called Nila back on his new cell.

"Have you heard anything?"

"Well, I got aholt of the girl who drove her, Missy Deel. She and Anna was friends back in middle school. Real nice girl. The meeting was up to Hurley at the Pine Grove Church. Missy said Anna started talking to some fellahs there that she didn't know, Missy didn't know, like maybe it was their first meeting. Anyways, Missy had to get back to feed her baby and Anna said she'd get a ride. That was the last she saw of her."

"Did she say what these guys looked like?"

"Didn't ask. Want me to call her back?"

"That's all right. I'll be there in an hour. I'll talk to her myself. Hurley? Where is Hurley?"

"It's about ten miles up 83."

When he pulled up to the brick house in Grundy it was almost 8:45. Nila let him in and said there was no other word. Otto was in his office. Elias asked her where Missy Deel lived. She said she lived over in Kentucky, but she worked at the Rexall in town and they didn't close until nine for the holidays. He got directions and drove back out the holler.

It was just down the main drag from the funeral home. He had driven right past and not noticed it. Nila had described Missy: "Just look for the black girl."

She could have said, just look for the baby face. She was standing behind the checkout counter thumbing through *People* and looked about sixteen. Her eyes were guileless and direct and she was chewing gum, but she had a slightly mischievous smile. Her hair was pulled back and festooned with beads. Elias introduced himself and explained why he was there. She instantly assumed a more serious tone.

"You're Anna's boyfriend. She told me about you. Said you were a good man." Elias couldn't help but feel strange, like he was back in high school being addressed by someone who looked like a teenage Kerry Washington and was checking him out for a girlfriend.

"So, did you and Anna go to this meeting before?"

"When she was home, which ain't often."

"What about the guys she was talking to? You never saw them before?"

"First time. And they didn't look right to me. When I saw them say they was addicts I didn't believe it. I know what addicts look like, and they didn't look like it to me. I quit two and a half years ago when I got pregnant; my drug of choice back then was oxycodone. That and meth will account for ninety percent of the people who come to NA around here. These guys didn't look like no whitechip addicts."

"Why not?"

"Well, for one thing, I'd never seen them before, and I know everyone around here. Second, they looked too big. They looked too well fed. Meth heads are thin and the Lortab junkies look like zombies, with that glazed look in they eyes, you know what I'm saying? These were some good old boys all right in they dew rags and jeans, but to me they looked more like football players than miners. If it weren't for the tats I would have asked them flat out who they were, except for the anonymity of course.

"They had tattoos?"

"Both of them. On they hands and arms. And on the neck they had, you know that thing farmers use to throw hay up into the barn?"

"A pitchfork?"

"Right, a pitchfork, just like Satan carries."

When he got back to the house he ran up the stairs to the bedroom. The tracker was in the top drawer of the dresser, right next to her one hitter and a bunch of white poker chips. Reflexively he cursed, "God damn, Anna," then he put the device in his pocket. He went back downstairs to Jassey's office. The old man was sitting in the same place behind his desk with the oxygen tank. The light was bad, as if he was trying to save electricity. He looked even older than usual; death was catching up to him quickly, or maybe it was just past his bedtime. Elias lowered himself onto the couch, slouching like a truant son, and sighed heavily. He was already exhausted, and it was only just after nine.

"I have no idea where she is," he began. "I talked to her girlfriend, the one who was at the meeting with her, and she told me Anna was talking to a guy with a tattoo on his neck just like a couple of Mason Dixon security men I met. I'm guessing she went off with them, or they took her, but they could be anywhere at this point. Can you think of anywhere they might take her, somewhere safe, for them, where they could question her or God knows what? You worked for them. Where would you take someone who was a threat to the company?"

"An old mine." He said it like he had done it.

"Jesus," Elias said. "What are there, a hundred abandoned mines within ten miles of here?"

"More like a thousand."

"Why don't you ask Ron Breedlove?" said a voice from the doorway. Nila was standing in the shadows like a bottled-blonde-haired wraith. "Seems to me he's the one would know where she's at."

"What's he supposed to do, call him on his phone and ask to speak to Diana?" the old man grumbled and coughed.

"Well, Breedlove is an important man. Elias's got a better chance of finding out where he is than where Anna is. Somebody's got to know where he is. And if he finds him, then maybe he can find her. I saw something like that happen on TV."

"Damnation. He can't just call Ron Breedlove and ask him."

"No, but you could."

"I won't."

"Why won't you?"

"You know why."

"Because he robbed you of your business and forced you to work for him?"

"Because he's a lying sonuvabitch who ruined my life from the moment I wandered into this God-forsaken country forty-seven years ago."

"Because he did you a favor by getting your wife committed."

Jassey raised a baleful eye to his girlfriend. "You don't know what you're talking about."

"Actually," Elias said from the couch, "I already know where he is. He's in Richmond. A couple of days ago I put a tracking device under his car and I checked it on the way here." He paused. "At least his car is in Richmond." That realization worried him. Then he got up and leaned on the desk to look the old man right in the face. "Mr. Jassey, this is crazy. I realize you hate Ron Breedlove, but you're not calling him to ask him for a favor. He's abducted your daughter! He's a psychopath like his son. I've seen him up close; he has no regard for human life if it interferes with business. He has no conscience. He will kill her if he hasn't already. You have got to call him for Anna's sake. Just find out where he is. That's all I ask."

Jassey stared him back for a while without saying anything, but as an answer he pushed the oxygen cart far away from him, reached into his top desk drawer and pulled out a pack of cigarettes and a small leather address book. He lit up with a stainless steel flip top, took a deep inhale just like Anna always did, and started thumbing through the pages. Then he reached over for the phone, punched in the numbers, and sat back in his old wheeled wooden chair.

"Ron," he said after a moment. "This is Otto. I understand you may know what's happened to my daughter."

Nila walked across the carpet, reached across the desk and turned on the speaker phone.

"What happened to her?"

"She's gone missing. Went out last night and never came back."

"You're about six weeks late in calling me," said the voice on the other end. "The damage has already been done. We maybe could've worked things out back then, but now between that red-haired love child of yours and your insane daughter we've really got us a fucked up situation. You

289

should see what that bitch did to my boy. He's in the hospital right now with stitches all acrost his face."

It sounded to Elias like he was on the highway. He could hear it in the background engine hum and the way Breedlove sounded like he was making a speech to himself. He could imagine him nearby cutting through the cold night air in his SUV. He pulled out his droid and checked the Mercedes again. There it was, heading down 81 near Roanoke. He could even read the speed: 76 MPH. Maybe he would get pulled over.

"Ron, you've got no right to take her. You let the law handle whatever she's done. She can pay for any crimes she has committed. She's a tough girl. She can do the time."

"She's too tough for her own good, that's her problem. Doesn't know when to quit. Like her father. But I haven't got her, Otto. I don't know where she is. Maybe she decided to run away again. Maybe she's off screwing her middle-aged boyfriend.   Maybe she blowed her brains out. I really don't know and I can't say that I care."

Elias reached over and covered the phone in Jassey's hand. "Ask him to come here and talk to you. Maybe we can coerce him into telling us where she is."

Jassey pulled the phone back and cleared his throat. "God damn it, Ron. Can't we at least discuss this? Can't we work something out? Where are you now? Come on by the house or I'll meet you somewhere even if I have to bring my oxygen." He was starting to sound a little distraught.

"No, I'm not stopping in Grundy. I'm heading home and I've got business to take care of. Goodbye Otto. You stay out of my way." And the phone went dead.

"What does he mean he's heading home? Has he got a home anywhere near here?"

"He's got a big place over on the Kentucky border. A regular fortress. Bout an hour from here."

"What do you mean it's a fortress?"

"I mean he's got a wall around it and dogs and it sits up on a ridge all by itself."

"So if he's driving from Richmond, does he have to go through Grundy to get there?"

"There's several routes he could take. He could take 83 on over if he went through here, or he could take the interstate all the way to Abingdon and take 19."

Elias opened his droid and moved behind the desk beside the old man and brought up the map of the area from Google Earth, overlaid with the route the Mercedes was taking. "Show me here where his house is and the routes you mentioned.

Jassey opened a side drawer and pulled out a big magnifying glass and started poring over the map. It took him a moment to get oriented.

"Here's Grundy," Elias pointed.

"I know where Grundy is. Everything's just so goddamned small. Now, you just pick up 83 in Vansant, and take it on over to Haysi, and Clintwood, then at Pound it gets a little tricky, cause there's a bunch of roads coming through there, but you got to get over to 620, here," and he pointed a long, scarred finger at the map.

"Then the other way is from down here in Abingdon up to Norton. He lives near Norton. That's where he's from. Between Norton and Appalachia."

Elias looked at his watch. It was 9:50. If he left now he could be at Breedlove's place maybe by eleven. Then what? He could get the state police there; maybe Bondurant would send them. Or he could try to break into the "fortress" himself. He had done such things before, but it didn't sound likely. He was too old and didn't have all the equipment he needed. On the other hand, what if Anna wasn't there? In fact, she probably wasn't. Breedlove wasn't fool enough to take her to his home, fortress or not. More than likely she had been taken to some mine he owned. And he was on his way there.

"He said he wasn't stopping in Grundy. Is that right?"

"What?"

"He said on the phone he wasn't stopping in Grundy. He didn't say he wasn't going to detour to Grundy or go out of his way to come to Grundy. He said he wasn't stopping here. Right?"

Nila verified it. "That's what he said."

"So it stands to reason that he *is* taking this route. Really all we have to do is wait and watch. In thirty minutes he'll hit 77 and then we'll know if he's coming this way. If he is I'm going to drive to Vansant and park where 83 branches off. When he passes by I'll just follow him. "

Elias had an hour and a half if he was coming this way, and that was a big if. But it made sense. If Anna was taken just down the road in Hurley, they probably wouldn't transport her too far. The closer the better. Then he called Bondurant on his personal cell and talked to him for fifteen minutes. Bondurant had alerted the state police in the area about a possible abduction, and told them to keep everything out of the normal law enforcement loop for now. They were to report to their office only or call him directly and let him field any information they might have. Elias told him that Breedlove drove a white Mercedes SUV, but he didn't know the license number. Bondurant said he would get it and send out an alert to his officers. There was a field office in Vansant. He gave him the phone number and address. 1313 Lovers Gap Road. He could contact them himself or Bondurant would call for him. Of course Anna wouldn't be in the Mercedes. That was the problem. Stopping Breedlove really wouldn't do any good; in fact, it would tip him off to be more cautious. There wasn't enough other evidence to do a search of his house. All they could do was be on the lookout.

Bondurant seemed to believe him but there was nothing he could do because Anna was technically not even a missing person yet and no one had seen her being abducted. Elias realized it was up to him to find her. He couldn't get the state cops to pull over the Mercedes or even look for her without jeopardizing Anna. He didn't mention to them that he had put a tracking device on the Mercedes a few days before. He reasoned that if he could follow the car Breedlove would take him to Anna. Eventually. That would be safer than having the police involved, at this point anyway. If he was in fact driving the SUV; there was no way of knowing from the phone call, but it was highly probable. You had to go with the probabilities in an emergency. Or if Anna wasn't already dead and buried inside some mountain somewhere. Then he would find her corpse.

He made a couple of other calls to Virginia Beach. He had close friends in the military there, and he wanted to know if there was anything they could do for him. He had started formulating a plan during the ride over to Grundy. It was highly speculative, but he wanted to be able to use all his resources if he had to. He needed an edge.

The next time they checked the Nano the Mercedes was halfway up I-77 to Bluefield, heading their way. At the speed it was moving it would be in Vansant in an hour. Elias packed up his stuff, used the bathroom and hit the road. Before he left, Jassey stopped him in the hallway with a double barreled .12 gauge and a baggie full of birdshot shells. Without saying a word he took them and headed out into the 20 degree mountain air.

Chapter 21

When I see them I know this is the beginning and the end it's good that it should be that way symmetry is profound momma always said the universe moves in circles shoot a gun straight ahead of you and the bullet will wind up in the back of your skull. So I have one more coffee to go too bad it's not stronger I say I could use something like what they say like crystal well we know a place not far we can get some I need a ride anyway so I climb in between them and we double back on 650 and I'm where're we going and they say Haysi and I'm 83's shorter and they what difference does it make which is the law of life here for meth heads and anyone under thirty besides I have the tanto in my boot one pulls a jar out from under the seat and massages my thigh and then we get to Haysi and they it's just a little further and Fremont and Pound it's just a little further here have a hit off this shit and I'm playing the radio have to find some nigger music they call it and then we're off the road and there's a guard so it must be Red Onion or Rollins Ridge or Norton or maybe it's the final loony bin but it's not it's an active volcano with a construction trailer at the bottom and we get out and go in and lock the door there's a room in the back carpeted with a couch and a portable heater and party all night. Like they said I'm the onliest girl but the men keep changing every time the sun comes up and goes back down again they talk on the phone and to each other how's she doing she's fried like a bag of pork rinds and I don't care what you do just so's she can talk oh she ain't stopped talking since she got here and don't let her out of your sight and we'll keep her company but they don't know two things first the knife still sharp in my boot second the spirits who keep changing too every time the moon rises and sets a raven croaks outside the tiny window and strings my eye with his red bead. We are one and so too is Elias.

The second night Satan finally gets here and the party cranks up into high gear. The men will all make their cuts now management's arrived no jobs are on the line and they can prepare the body for the sacrifice later. He walks into the little room with his red hat and *wings and they leave me alone with him and an endless supply of drugs on the coffee table. He wants to know if I am ready to receive him and I say yes but first I have to tell him what I know about his business and the videos and the voice recordings and all the other nonsense that he says I think will break him. He asks me God's plan for me and when I do not know he tells me he will take me up because he knows I have been lost all my life and he is the propitiation for my sins. Then he makes me kneel before him and recites the catechism backwards: How does sin proliferate? Through the separation of man from God. No, it is through the separation of man from his own sinful nature and strikes me down. What is virtue? To obey God's commandments. No, to obey the needs of your own nature and strikes me down again. Why don't you have any virtue? Because I am fallen from grace with God. Yes. What is the relationship between grace and human freedom? Without grace I have the freedom to disobey. Yes. Why did your father send your mother away? Because she was not a good wife. What was wrong with her? She had fallen away from the church. Why doesn't your father love you? He has never loved me because I am sinful and without virtue. Why doesn't anyone love you? No one loves me because I have not done any good in the world. Why doesn't God love you? How can God love such a fuck up? God only loves the righteous, the pure, the industrious, the kind. How far can a daughter fall? A daughter can fall all the way to the bottom of the earth. Where are you now? I am in hell. No, you are at the bottom of the earth. Hell is yet to come. Why didn't you prevent your sister's death? Because I am too sick to help anyone and ready to receive my punishment. He finishes undressing me but not the boots I say why not because my feet are cold you're a crazy bitch but I can see why my boy wanted to get some of you and your cousin my sister and why he couldn't stop it's a weakness must run in the family until he started moonlighting until things got out of hand with those other girls but he's still my boy and now he's paid for it and now so will you kekog dagiku no he says metaugh, kihoe and I rise from the floor pulling the blade Muramasa from its sheath and stab Satan on the right side where his heart is supposed to be but the knife doesn't find its mark you goddamned cunt Elias was right I am not one with the tanto he laughs and takes it out of his own chest and pushes*

295

me back on the couch my head bangs against the wall and that is the end of my revenge I have done everything I could now it is finished . . .

By the time he got to the 83 turnoff in Vansant it was 10:30. Nila had made him a thermos of coffee and packed some sandwiches. Elias realized he hadn't eaten since breakfast. He crossed the river and pulled off the road into a small, almost empty strip mall parking lot, cut the lights, and sat with the engine running to stay warm while he ate ham for the second time in maybe twenty years. The smoke-cured, salty kind that he loved as a kid. Every now and then he would glance up at the droid which he had propped on the dash. Cedar Bluff. Richlands. Shortt Gap. Marvin. Then he began to worry. How long had this battery been used? He had put the tracker on Friday afternoon. Now it was Monday night. It had a life of 30 hours, motion-activated. How many hours, though, had Breedlove been driving since Friday afternoon? There was no way of knowing. Chances are he had stayed around Richmond, visiting the hospital. And this trip was no more than five or six hours. It must still be good. Then he got a spooky feeling, like the presence of someone creeping up on him. He looked around the car. There was almost no traffic on 83 while he waited. The town, such as it was, apparently shut down after dark. He dismissed the sensation as nerves and was just checking the radio to see if he could find a station when a car swung off the bridge and sped by the lot, going way over the speed limit. It went by fast, but he was pretty sure it was a white SUV. There was no time to think about it so he took off, holding the open thermos in one hand and the wheel in the other, flooring the Jeep as it bounced onto the road and fishtailed in what was left of the slush. The Mercedes, if it was the Mercedes, was already a half mile away. Elias accelerated quickly so as not to lose the taillights but the road started to bend and they were gone anyway, intermittently. He was doing 65 in no time on the

296

two lane road and didn't seem to be catching up, but he wasn't losing ground either. Elias felt momentarily elated: now here he was, the monster, right in front of him, taking him to Anna.

Elias knew the tracker could work anywhere, but he also knew from his military experience that signals sometimes got lost in these twisting, steep valleys. He didn't want to lose sight of the vehicle, but he also didn't want Breedlove to suspect anyone was following him, especially if he made a turn, so he kept back as far as he could without completely losing the lights. It was frustrating and scary, because this was his lifeline to Anna, and if he lost the Mercedes, then she was lost. Then he was lost. He felt as if that far red beacon and the electronic tracker became symbols of his longing, his attachment. Like that green one on the pier on Long Island.

He had studied the droid map on Jassey's desk in detail long enough to know it by heart without constantly checking the small lit screen. It was his old business, after all. In fifteen minutes they went through Haysi, with Elias hanging way back as the Mercedes finally slowed, then another fifteen they were in Fremont, then before ten they were going through Pound. After that it got confusing. Elias thought he had turned onto 619 but wasn't positive and didn't have time or the balance to check the map again. He lost some time following the route on the tracker as they maneuvered around Pound, and then when the Mercedes sped up again he was so far back he couldn't see it anymore. This threw him into a panic, but he fought it. It was a new feeling for him, this fear for a loved one. In all the dangerous places he had been in his life, he had of course often been concerned for others, very concerned: his squad, his friends. But this was different. He felt fear; so he thought, I must love her. He had a vision of her being held down by the security men he had met and then the picture morphed to Sylvie lying in her casket and then to his wife in her classroom and he had to shut it out. A sign flashed by that said they had entered the Jefferson National Forest. It was pretty in here in the dark; the trailers disappeared and the woods ran right up to the edge of the road.

And then all of a sudden there was no new signal. It had been more than a couple of minutes since the last update. What had happened? He kept driving and waiting for another. Nothing. His first instinct was to speed up, which he did for the next mile, but when he hit 85 for a minute and still no sign of taillights he slammed the brakes and pulled over to the side of the highway, opened the door and got out and looked around. Nothing but moonlight on snowy mountains. A large bird appeared in his headlights on the forested highway and almost crashed into the front of the car before he flapped away down the hillside into the dark. Elias remembered crossing the Pound River some ways back; he grabbed the Atlas he had thrown on the passenger's seat and found where he thought he was. It looked like he was already in Kentucky, but he didn't remember seeing a sign. He jumped back into the Jeep, made a 180, and punched the accelerator down heading east. A few miles back there was a gravel side road, but it wasn't on the Atlas or the droid. However, it looked well travelled. There were ruts that looked to have been made by heavy machinery. Then he saw the new tire tracks in the leftover snow in his headlights. Someone had just been here. He punched it again and had gone no more than a half mile when he got a new signal, like a heart monitor registering the resurrection of a dead patient. He slowed down and cut his lights. Then a little farther he passed a dirt turnoff with a sign on a post—Ajax Mining—with some numbers that looked like permits. There was a small guard booth nearby with a light on outside and a small gravel area around it, but that was it. Not much. But it looked like the Mercedes had turned in here. He drove ahead another hundred yards and didn't see anything so he looked for a level area to pull the

Jeep into, got off the road as far as he could without getting stuck in the snow drift, and waited for the next update. There it was, but the Nano map wasn't getting the details. The Mercedes was off road. So he switched to Google Earth. Still nothing. How often did they update these things? Every year, every five years? There was no road on Google, just 3-dimensional ridges covered with trees. It must be a new mine, he thought. The car had stopped moving, right at the top of a ridge it looked like. It was almost midnight. There was no way Breedlove would be driving to the top of a mountain at this hour on a Monday night unless he had some urgent business. It had to be Anna. She was up there. Probably still alive. There was no going back once he left the car; he could call the state police in Vansant, but only if he got confirmation that she was here. They might make it here in an hour. These people were very dangerous and he would probably not get more than one chance to rescue her, and more than likely somebody was not coming back down from this mountain. At least, not on his own power. These were all risks he was willing to take. The last fifteen years of his civilian life had vanished on the highway; his mind was 100% focused on the extraction.

He got out of the car and silently changed into the winter camouflage gear he had stowed in his backpack. Then he stashed the .32 in a side pocket. A thought struck him as he got the shotgun out of the back seat: it's still hunting season. Deer. Bear. People. He slung the M110 over his shoulder. With the 20 rounds and the tripod and scope it weighed about 15 pounds, but it would be worth it if he needed it. When he was in practice he could make a kill at 800 meters. He wasn't in practice now, but the semi-automatic gave him the diversity of an assault weapon as well. Last he double checked everything he needed, then he took off back down the road, staying in the shadows, keeping the .12 gauge in his hands as he walked.

When he got near the driveway to the mine he very cautiously struck off through the trees and made a circle around the guard booth, as wide as he could considering the woods were cleared out all around it. He could see a man inside. The problem was getting on up the road beyond without the man seeing him. The moon was completely full and the plants were so thinned out this time of year there wasn't much to hide behind. Everything cast a shadow. He decided to be on the safe side he would have to climb part of the ridge behind the booth and come back down once he was past. It would take time, but if he was seen now he probably would not have a chance getting to the top.

It took him a good ten minutes; the hillside was fairly steep but there was enough vegetation to hang onto so that he didn't slip much. When he thought he was in the clear he came back down onto the dirt drive, listened for any sounds, and started jogging up it. He was pretty sure he heard some machinery at the top. It was a long way up; the ridge, from the looks of it, was at least 300 feet above him, and since the road looked to switchback all the way up, he figured he had maybe a mile or two to go. The trees at the top were backlit by a glow of some kind, lights probably; he couldn't tell exactly what it was, but he could estimate their distance pretty well. The problem now was that as the road ascended the sides were stripped bare and there was nowhere to hide quickly unless he jumped off the cliff side of the road. He strained to hear anything coming down or up and looked for headlights flashing across the valley as a vehicle made its way through the hairpin turns. He figured with his camouflage he could lie down in the culvert and no one would notice him. It was a risk, but nobody came by, and in fifteen minutes he was almost at the top.

Now he faced another problem: he didn't know what was up there. It could be nothing, or it could be people. With a hundred yards to go he decided to get off the road and cut across the ridge, climbing as fast as he could in the clear cut until he got to the treeline. Once inside the woods he made his way up the last ascent until he reached level ground. Another half minute of walking and he pushed through the tangle of hardwoods and pines and scared some large birds out of the branches until he appeared to be coming to the edge of a cliff. A supernatural light blazed up from below, and suddenly he was left standing on the edge of the world.

We are all haunted by dreams that go back to childhood, even if we don't remember them. There was a dream Elias had been having repeatedly since he was a kid. He was wandering around his old neighborhood in Norfolk, but in the dream it suddenly opened out onto a vast, primeval wilderness that seemed to stretch out to infinity. It reminded him of a painting he had once seen of Daniel Boone standing on a cliff at Cumberland Gap, surveying the expanse of virgin forests that stretched from Kentucky all the way to the Mississippi. "Boone's First View of Kentucky" it was called. You can't see the woods, the paradise; it's out of the frame to the left, but the old pathfinder points to it, and the small group of explorers who stand with him have a dreamy, sublime air about them, as if their deepest wishes have been fulfilled. It's the heart of America off in the distance, the new frontier, unseen, never seen perhaps, because it is unreal, because it is the only real. It is already peopled of course with red men who have been there for thousands of years, but no matter; it is the promise that has always been America, not the reality. As a boy in the dream Elias was filled with both excitement and dread while gazing toward this western horizon; he was at the terminus, and he didn't know what lay beyond, but there was a wall somebody had built there on the border centuries before. To keep something in, or out, he had no idea, but he would climb a tree in the dream and look over the wall into the depths. Maybe it was Nietzsche's call and response from the abyss, or more likely it was some sublimated Skull Island of his own divided identity.

Whatever it represented, here it was again.

What Elias confronted at the ridgeline was his dream, but it was reversed, as if some alien life forms in a parallel universe had made a negative of it. Instead of lush forests that stretched as far as the eye could imagine, the mountaintop in front of him looked like it had been beaten with a giant club, pummeled by an idiot god, until there was nothing left but a dirty hole in the ground a couple of hundred feet deep. Between him and the far ridges a mile or two away there was no vegetation, except on a small clump of land absurdly spared in the middle of the pit. Down at the bottom prehistoric creatures were shoving the earth around, raking their claws through rock as they crawled along the moonscape, the whole inferno illuminated with a million watts of stadium lights. As he watched from above the dozers pushed tons of sediment and rock over the edge into an adjacent valley, filling it up so they could flatten it out. Cascades of debris slid down the ledge and boomed as they hit the bottom. It was destruction on a grand scale, man over machine over mountain, something befitting the new millennium. Unsatisfied with digging coal out of the deep seams, the global economy demanded that we bring the mountain to its knees.

But where was Anna in this hellish place? Once he adjusted his eyes to the unearthly glare, like a spectator at a football game emerging from a tunnel, he spotted a trailer a half mile away with some vehicles parked near it, and several other small buildings. There was a light on in the trailer. He pulled the M110 off his shoulder and looked through the scope. He counted five vehicles: three pickups, a van, and the Mercedes. That had to be where they were keeping her, if she were still alive. It was 1:17 a.m., and he estimated that Breedlove had about a 30 to 45 minute head start on him. He couldn't see anyone walking around; it seemed that the only people outside were on the machinery. He had to figure out a way to get her out of there without harm.

As he gazed out across the wasteland, momentarily hypnotized by the spectacle, something clawlike touched the base of his neck and he jumped aside, swinging the butt of the rifle around at the same time. There was nothing: just the blackness of the trees behind and over him and the wind moving through them. Pine branch. But it left an imprint on his back, like the prickly hand of a fortuneteller, preternaturally suffused with being. It gave him a chill which morphed into a sense of something uncanny happening, like the whole world was suddenly in danger, even though his focus was on that tiny trailer below, and his apprehension for Anna was so clear and intense that he thought he could actually hear her voice in his head. Not a complete sentence, just her saying his name, short and distinct, as if she were in the next room with the door closed.

Then he looked up, and above the human tragedy of life on earth he noticed something was wrong too in the heavens. It was the moon. As it was ascending through the eastern sky the upper left quarter was growing dark, was losing its brilliance, as if some night predator was eating away its rind. Clouds sailed across the inky firmament from west to east but none near enough to the moon to explain the phenomenon. What was happening? Then he remembered Anna's voice at the table. The lunar eclipse. This was the solstice; the eclipse was tonight. It must have just started as he was climbing the ridge. The shadow of the earth was crossing out the moon, blotting the reflected light of the sun. In an hour or two it would be completely dark, throwing the kingdoms below into consternation.

He thought about this: if he waited until the total, he could go for the transformers that powered the klieg lights; a couple of cartridges should do it. Then the whole place would be dark and he could pull Anna out. But they would know he was coming; they would panic and she would probably get killed in the process. Anyway, he didn't want to wait another minute. On the other hand, he couldn't just start shooting civilians; it would be relatively easy, even from this distance, to take out anyone in the open, but that would be mass murder. Out of the question. He hadn't even verified that she was there. And he was running out of time. The most rational approach would be to hit the trailer hard, get her out of there as quickly as possible, and then try to get back to cover. But the only ways out were the road or a climb back up onto the ridge where he was now, a steep ascent and completely exposed. If he shot up all their vehicles but one they might make it down, but there was still the guard at the bottom. It seemed like a viable alternative. Especially if he alerted the police once he got to Anna.

He started looking for a way down. The descent wasn't going to be easy: the cliff he was on was terraced all the way to the bottom where they had removed the overburden, layer by layer with explosives and cranes with buckets, but in some places the terraces were extremely narrow, with a ten or twenty foot drop between them, and in others the cliff had caved in, leaving a 50 or 60 degree angle of loose dirt and rock to negotiate. Still, getting down was going to be a piece of cake compared to climbing back out, if he were forced to go that route. He decided to ditch the tripod. He reached into his pants pocket and pulled out the tin of Dexedrine, crushed a few 5 milligram tabs in his hand, swallowed them, and jumped over the least steep incline he could find.

By working his way back and forth across the sloping face he was slowly able to traverse the cliff like a skier, losing his footing only once, and keeping as low a profile as possible. He figured the people on the ground were too engaged in what they were doing to notice a solitary figure on the hill above them, in camouflage. Besides, the lights were so bright in a confined work area that he was pretty sure they couldn't see beyond it. It was cold on the bare ground; the temperature was well into the teens at this elevation, but he was sweating from the exertion.

When he got to the bottom he quickly made his way across the flat to a parked dump truck and checked his watch: 1:52. Down here he could barely see the moon, much less notice the penumbra. He had re-slung the M110 and was holding the shotgun in his right hand. Moving from truck to dozer to the occasional boulder he slowly snuck up on the single wide and the cars parked around it, then stopped to listen. He thought he could hear voices, but the dozers and trucks that were working were enough to interfere with his hearing. He waited a few minutes to see if anyone would enter or leave, and when it seemed quiet enough, he ran the remaining fifty yards and flattened himself against the darkest side of the trailer. There were several windows, closed of course, and he quickly moved between them, listening at each in turn. At the last one on the far side he was startled to see a huge crow sitting on an air conditioning unit, but it flew off and when he got to the small window he could hear voices again. It was almost completely blocked, but there was a thin strip across the top he could look in once he pulled a cinderblock over to stand on. He couldn't see much, mostly a blank wall on the opposite side of the room, but when he pushed himself a little higher he could see two people from the knees down. One was a man. The other was a woman. He could see the cowboy boots.

Ten seconds later he tried the front door. It was unlocked. There was no one in the room. He entered, closed the door, and went to the next one and tried it. The knob wouldn't turn. So he backed up, and timing it to coincide with the next bucket of coal hitting the bottom of a dump truck, he kicked the door open and walked in with the shotgun leveled.

Anna was in there with Breedlove. He was sitting on a chair in his underwear and she was on a couch completely naked but for the boots, and apparently unconscious. There was blood on the floor and soaking through a large bandage Breedlove had wrapped around his chest. When he looked up and saw it was Elias he cursed.

He didn't seem particularly surprised or perturbed, however. "Mister, you've watched one too many movies if you think you or her is gonna get offa this job site alive," he said as he continued winding tape around his body. "My men will be on you like stink on shit." Then he noticed the sniper rifle and looked more closely at him. "That's a heavy duty piece of hardware you got there. Where'd you get it? Or better yet, what were you planning on doing with it?"

Elias ignored him, but not completely. He didn't appear to be a threat in his current condition, but he was a stout man and probably used to injuries. Elias was more concerned with Anna; if she was drugged he might have a tough time carrying her away. He went over to the couch and sat down beside her, keeping the shotgun pointed at Breedlove. He shook her but she didn't respond.

"What did you do to her?"

"The bitch hit her head on the wall is all," he answered, bit the end of the tape, finished it off, and starting pulling his long woolen undershirt back on, bloodstains and all.

Elias checked her head and found an abrasion on the back. It didn't look too bad. He shook her again and talked to her and she started to come around, but she was really woozy. The room was littered with beer cans and whiskey bottles, not to mention the smell of weed and chemicals in the stale air; he assumed she was too inebriated and high to walk. Meanwhile Breedlove pulled on his pants and finished dressing.

Elias found himself suddenly very angry and wanted to confront Breedlove. "What's all this for?"

"All what for?"

"All this shit. Hanging dogs. Burning down homes. Blowing up mountains. Polluting wells. Killing innocent people. All this. To get to a black seam?"

"Ain't no such thing as innocent people. Everyone who uses electricity is implicated in this."

"It's greed, pure and simple."

He grunted while he tied his boots and said, "It's the economy, stupid."

Elias couldn't stop himself. He kept shaking Anna periodically and buying time. "That's what you businessmen and politicians always say to rationalize your greed. You live in a corporate fantasy. What the fuck is the economy? It's just an abstraction."

"It's not an abstraction. It's jobs. You're the one who lives in a fantasy. It's people working and getting paid."

"Bullshit. The jobs are leaving and the miners are pawns. What does it take to blow up a mountain? Ten men? Compared to underground mining? And how much money is getting recycled into the region? The bulk of it goes to Richmond, to the stockholders and the executives like yourself. You can't spend it all. The excessive profit's the real overburden. There's no human dimension anymore in the exchange value."

"It's capitalism, where anyone can make as much money as they can. This is a free society. You sound like a communist."

Breedlove stood up, zipped his pants and fastened his belt. Then he took a thick jacket with the Mason Dixon logo on it off the back of another chair and casually put it on.

"You're not leaving," Elias said, and stood up too.

He laughed. "You're not going to stop me," he said. "You haven't got the guts to shoot an unarmed man. I'm going to walk out of here, call my men, and then we're going to throw you and the girl down a deep hole."

"You're right," Elias said. "I'm not going to shoot you." And he swung the butt of the shotgun into Breedlove's jaw, stunning him and knocking him to the floor. He took off the boss's jacket, got the tape and quickly tied his hands and feet like a calf before he could recover his wits, reached in the pocket and retrieved the keys to the Mercedes. Then he went over to the couch, put the jacket on Anna and zipped it up, grabbed her arms and lifted her onto his shoulder, picked up the shotgun and started for the trailer door.

It opened just as he reached for the knob, and two men stepped up into the room. There was nothing he could do with the shotgun in his other hand and Anna over his shoulder except instinctively kick the first man in the chest, sending him sprawling back into the second and both down and outside onto the hard pack. Then he shut and locked the door. The men started kicking it from the outside and it began to give immediately, the cheap metal frame bending and the screws pulling out of the hinges. When it burst open a moment later he fired both barrels from the 12 gauge and the doorway cleared. Then before he could reload, it filled again with more men who pushed him to the floor, held him down with Anna under him and beat him in the head with their fists and boots. The last thing he did before they pinned his arms was push the panic button on the Nano in his pocket.

"Get me out of this tape!" Breedlove bellowed from the next room.

Within a couple of minutes there were four men in the room with them. Two more were outside wounded and moaning in the back seat of the van, and another was behind the wheel getting ready to take them to the hospital. Besides Breedlove, Elias recognized the security man who had given him the tight handshake back at his house a week earlier. He had his knee in Elias' sternum and was holding a .45.

"Get them up and bring them outside," Breedlove ordered. They hauled them up and out the door into the frigid air. All the mining operations had stopped, the dust was settling, and it was preternaturally quiet.

Elias sized up the situation as they exited the trailer. Anna was semi-conscious now and still had the oversize Mason Dixon jacket on, but nothing else except her boots. One of the other men was holding the 110, but they had thrown the shotgun on a desk. They had taken everything out of his pockets, including the Jeep and the Mercedes keys and the Nano. With the van pulling off, it looked like he had four men to deal with. The security guy he figured would be the most difficult. The other two looked like miners: wiry and tough, but not professionals. Then there was Breedlove, who was at least Elias' age.

The Nano had sent two texts preprogrammed into it with his present GPS coordinates: one to the office of the Virginia State Police, Division 4 in Vansant, with the message: "Need assistance immediately." Bondurant had already alerted them to be on the lookout for him. If they were out on patrol he figured they would arrive within thirty or forty minutes. If he had that much time.

The second text went to Director of Flight Operations, CNIC Naval Air Station Oceana. Its message was short and to the point: "How low can you go?" The response time on this alert would be much faster: five to ten minutes.

"Get that goddamned jacket off her and put her clothes back on. If they ever find their bodies at the bottom of the valley fill I want them to look like another couple of greeniacs buried under the dirt they were trying to save."

They brought Anna her stuff and she put it on, shaking badly from the subfreezing temperature. She looked pitiful, white and thin under the glare of the work lights. She squeezed his hand when he took off his coat and handed it to her.

"Is it cold enough for you now, little girl?" Breedlove mocked. "Seventeen God damn degrees. Still believe in global warming?" All the men but the burly security guard laughed.

"This is the one who cut off my brother's hand," he said. "He needs to lose something for that."

"I don't care. Mess him up all you want. But no guns. I don't want no bullet holes in his corpse."

They had moved away from the trailer by now, out towards the middle of the plateau where the small hill and clump of trees was still standing in the pit. One lonely forested hump in the middle of Death Valley. No-neck had paused at one of the trucks as they went by and removed a couple of billy clubs and an aluminum baseball bat from the bed. Then the whole group stopped. Elias was searching the western horizon above the rim a couple of hundred feet above them.

"What's this?" he said, pointing to the acre or more of unstripped hill, still stalling.

"This," Breedlove answered, "belongs to the idiot who refused to sell his property. So we just mined around him. Sometimes he comes out here and watches, poor bastard. He's still got a right of way."

There were some fresh limbs on the ground where they were standing, probably shaken free by the incessant explosions and machinery. Elias saw one that looked the right size, straight and wrist-thick, about four feet long. Like someone had put it there for him. Now if it was only solid enough.

Then he looked up again and there they were: blinking red lights just over the western rim, coming in too fast to hear.

"Okay now, boss?" the big guy asked anxiously, tucking the .45 into his belt and raising the bat.

"Yeah, sure. Have some fun," and Breedlove took the rifle from the other miner.

310

"Now you're going to lose your head to pay for a hand," no-neck said to Elias, and handing the billies to the other two guys, the three of them spread out and began to close in on him.

At that moment, before they could even see the F-18s overhead, everyone suddenly became aware that something very loud was happening above them and they had to look up. Louder than the diesel engines on the cranes and dozers. Louder even than the explosions that rocked the site during the day, which lasted no longer than a few seconds. This mountain on the border of Kentucky was off the VFR; no jets flew low over here. But they were here now, and flying low, unbelievably low, only a hundred feet it seemed above the rim, as if they were going to land right on top of them on this flat mile of strip mine in the wilderness. Except they were going far too fast to land. Six hundred knots too fast.

The first impression you had was that they were on a bombing run and you were the target, screeching down from the sky straight at you like prehistoric birds. The cloven sky had opened into another dimension. Everyone reflexively ducked as the first one passed over, watching the cross of its shadow transfixing the puny humans below for a split second, its jet wash ripping the trees above them. That is, everyone but Elias ducked and watched. By the time the second variable wing jet hit ten seconds later, he had already unnoticed picked up the hardwood stick he had chosen and was quickly moving in on Casey with the bat.

The shiho-giri technique that Elias used was developed as a defense against four aggressors. He had learned it in Japan and spent many days banging heads with it. Of course he had to modify the pattern on the spot, because he didn't have a sword and neither did they. But the changes made little difference.

In the aftermath of the F-18s no one could hear anything for a few seconds and they seemed frozen in stop motion, like they needed a few seconds to collect their wits about them after the alien invasion. While they had fanned out and surrounded him with their clubs, he had taken several deep breaths and composed his mind. Now he quickly raised the smooth branch vertically above his head into jodan no kamae position and brought his right leg diagonally forward so that he turned slightly and faced the security guy. The beefy ex-jock seemed taken aback by the fact that Elias was coming at him with a weapon in his hand, and he gripped the bat tighter and started to swing it viciously. But he was too late reacting. On the first swing Elias adroitly stepped in and brought the branch down hard on his left hand, breaking it and causing him to drop the Louisville Slugger. Without stopping he looked left and turned, pivoting on his right foot so that he faced Breedlove behind him, simultaneously bringing the makeshift bokken down and flat against his own chest, and then, sliding both feet forward, thrust the point of the branch into the Mason Dixon CEO's solar plexus, keeping his weight centered and fixed in the earth. With no interruption in the fluid motion he next pivoted to the right and went after Casey again who was still temporarily immobilized with pain and shock, his pistol still in his belt, bringing the wood down hard this time onto his forehead from jodan. Then another pivot to the right and another makko to the third aggressor's skull, and a last pivot to the left to face his final opponent in left jodan. As he slid forward the fourth man looked like he wanted to flee but couldn't, the billy club frozen in his fist. Elias brought the bokken down an inch above the center of his forehead, and just barely touched the place where his third eye would open someday, probably in another body, and the guy took off, running across the flat like he had been born again. Afterward Elias pulled his right leg back and resumed hidari jodan no kamae, surveyed the scene and, by force of habit and ritual, brought his feet together and bowed slightly from the waist facing shomen to his left. The whole seitei-gata took maybe five seconds.

The two men he had struck on the head were on the ground, dead or unconscious, their skulls no doubt fractured. Breedlove was on his knees and bent double, but he still had the 110 in his hands. Elias walked over to him, took the rifle away, re-slung it, then kicked the dropped handgun over toward Anna and went to her. She was sitting on the ground twenty feet away with her legs crossed under her, almost as if she were meditating, and looking up into the sky with wide, uncomprehending eyes. She still seemed to be under the effects of all the meth she had done even though she was nearly clear of the concussion. He knelt down beside her and checked her head again.

"Anna, how're you doing? You got knocked out for a while. Are you okay? Can you walk?"

She pointed up into the western sky. "I saw them," she said, "the space ships that fly over the mountains and come down to rescue us from the human beings. Ezekiel's chariots. There were flames shooting out of them and the thunder of a heavenly host."

"Those were no space ships, sweetie. But do you think you can walk? We need to get out of here. I can carry you if you can't." And he pulled her up.

"I can walk on my own," she said, pulling her arm away. Then she asked, "Why is that man running?"

Elias whirled around and saw Breedlove hoofing it surprisingly fast across the pit for an old man, already almost to the trailer. He cursed and thought first that he was just running away, but instead of getting in his SUV he went into the trailer, only to emerge a moment later and head off in a different direction, toward the mining machinery that had been abandoned when the fight began. Elias's immediate reaction was to pull up the 110 and try to stop him in his tracks, but he quickly realized he wasn't going to have time to hit a moving target before it reached its destination, and sure enough, ten seconds later he saw him climb up a ladder into what looked like a huge excavator. Elias had no keys for any of the vehicles, the police were still probably miles away, if they could find the place at all, and if he and Anna hid in the trailer until they got there, Breedlove could probably crush it with his machine. It was enormous.

"Come on," he shouted and grabbed Anna's hand, and they took off in the opposite direction. He heard the deep chugging of the diesel split the silence across the site as they ran side by side to the far edge of the pit where an inclined roadway gave them a chance of climbing to safety. They started up it, ran to the end of the first switchback, and stopped to look back. The excavator was clanking across the work site full speed, maybe five or six miles an hour, as fast as someone could jog, on level ground. It was a monstrous thing some three stories high with tank treads instead of tires and an enormous backhoe bucket on hydraulic lifts that extended another thirty or forty feet in front. The driver's cockpit was positioned on top to the left side in front of the motor and behind the bucket, and in black on its yellow boom was the name Komatsu and the number 5500 below the cab. Elias raised the sniper rifle and looked through the scope. Breedlove was at the controls but there was no clear shot at him as long as he kept the bucket low. There was also a slight overhang above him which made it difficult to shoot down at him. At the speed he was going, he would catch up with them in a minute, unless they got to higher ground.

He swung the rifle toward the klieg lights and found a transformer at the bottom of a pole. On the first round it crackled and exploded and half the lights went out. Then he managed the same thing with two shots on another bank of lights and they blacked out. Now the place was darker except for the headlights on the moving Komatsu, which appeared to have eight or more. Breathing deeply and taking his time, he had to squeeze off ten rounds to extinguish the

314

main ones; but there were still small lights all around the platform. Ten plus three equaled thirteen: he had seven rounds left in the magazine. He put three of them into the front end without any success, then three more into a rear side panel, but the damn thing didn't die, it just coughed up some black smoke. Inexorably it kept clanking forward, like some kind of doomsday weapon that couldn't stop once it had been set in motion.

When he lowered the rifle and looked around, it was definitely darker, but it was far from pitch black. The moon was full, though almost completely in eclipse now. Instead of white gold winter moonlight washing the mountain in an ethereal haze, a strange red glow was beginning to saturate the work site, almost as if it were emanating from below. He held his hands out in front of him and they turned red, as if they had been dipped in gore.

"It's the blood moon," Anna said. She was standing there in her ripped shirt and jacket and her ragged dirty jeans looking at him like it was all her fault. "It's time to pay Satan for all my sins. You're going to have to die too. "

"Nobody's going to die. We can climb out of this," he said, and they began their ascent again.

They had gotten to the middle of the second switchback up the ridge when the excavator caught up with them. It stopped at the bottom of the pit, some forty feet below, and began to extend its arm up and out toward them, the hydraulics a modern marvel. It was an unearthly machine, something made to scavenge Mars. Then the bucket, wide enough for two men to lie down in, moved forward rapidly and like an open mouth sank its five metal teeth into the ground just in front of them, gouging a Volkswagen-sized hole in the side of the road. They couldn't go forward anymore.

"We've got to go up right here," Elias said and moved over to the cliff wall. It was solid but not nearly vertical, with shale and other rocks sticking out to use as hand and foot holds. A mountain goat could scale it, he thought, and so could they. They rapidly pulled themselves up six feet while the bucket was getting ready to take another swing at them. Breedlove had extended the hydraulics farther and it reached up over the road and tore into the base of the cliff where they had just been standing seconds before, shaking the ground under their hands. For a moment Elias thought the whole thing was going to give way and they would be caught in the slide and buried alive at Breedlove's feet. Then it looked like he was trying to leverage the arm higher but by the time he did they were another six feet up and again out of reach. They heard the diesel suck in more fuel and the Komatsu backed up and then lurched forward up the incline they had just climbed. Elias could just see the next switchback thirty feet above them. They were about ten feet in the air now and climbing steadily, their mostly frozen fingers digging tenaciously into the hard dirt. He almost dumped the 110; it was heavy and he was starting to feel the weight. But he still had a single round left and might need it. Anna was breathing heavily but she was an agile climber, faster than he was, even in the cowboy boots.

They could hear the treads clanking below just as they made it to the next switchback. Elias looked down in time to see the bucket ascending like a shark propelling itself out of a red sea, mouth agape and ravenous, to fasten on his right leg as he pulled it over the edge just in time. It scraped against his boot and clamped down on another twenty thousand pounds of dirt and debris and pulled them back down with it as it descended. Then it shot back up and reached forward across the road, tearing a long groove in the ground in front of them.

They started climbing again. This time Elias thought he could see the top of the pit, but the cliff was steeper and they weren't making much progress. Some of the shale was so porous it was giving way beneath their feet. They stopped

316

to take a breather on a ten inch ridge that marked the line between one strata of rock in the cliff and another, and looked at each other hanging onto the side like trapeze artists in a Kafka story.

Anna was coughing like crazy. "I need to stop smoking," she said at last.

"Me too. Maybe we should go back down and take our chances on the road. I still have a cartridge in the gun, and that thing can't move any faster than we can run. I don't like being stuck out here in the open."

"I can see the top," she said. Just one more climb and that monster can't reach us. Come on."

So they continued up, and so did the excavator. But when it got to the switchback just below them and out of reach this time it didn't stop. Instead, it kept going to the end, turned, and clanked up the last steep incline in a race with them for the top. It was unnerving to calculate the speed and distance while they were climbing, but in the next sixty seconds it became clear to Elias, and then to Anna, that they were not going to win this race. They were stuck, fifteen feet from the top and thirty feet from the bottom, when they heard the diesel pounding on the cliff up above them. Then they looked up and saw the front row of the treads just over the edge.

They started down but it was too late. The extended arm had already swung out and over the lip and was making a blind grab for them below. Breedlove's problem was he couldn't go far enough forward to see where they were. The bucket banged against the cliff below them and to the side, tearing out tons of the cliff at a time and throwing huge chunks of dirt into the air while they flattened against the face. Again and again the metal mouth bit into the rock, sending cascades of debris to the bottom, but they kept moving to avoid the next assault, predicting where it would be. For a while they thought he would slowly dig the hill out from under them, but suddenly the giant arm stopped, and a

317

moment later they saw him standing on the tread overhanging the lip with a flashlight, searching until he saw their heads.

"I'm sending you straight to hell!" he yelled down at them. "Stay still." Then disappeared.

Then he tried to flatten the arm against the wall and scrape them off like a windshield wiper squashing bugs, but they had found a narrow niche in the solid wall and were too close to the top for the mechanical thing to straighten out that much. Instead, the arm passed just inches behind them as they clung to the rocks and each other; they could feel the wind from its passing raise the hairs on the back of their necks. They couldn't move now without risking getting hit. Once, twice, three times the giant arm swung by them, gouging the rock below in its arc, throwing chunks of granite into them, one large stone right into Elias' ribs. And each time it seemed like they couldn't take it much more. It was going to eventually knock them off the cliff, or the cliff itself was going to give way. Then the bucket stopped again and they moved down and over to the right. Breedlove appeared above the rim and cursed. Then they heard the diesel chug, and the clanking, and the excavator moved forward another six feet out over the edge to get a better angle.

The move also gave Elias a better angle on the cockpit. He unslung the rifle with his right hand and was able to look almost straight up through the scope while he rested it on the cliff face above him. It was going to be a tough shot; the cockpit was in the shadows and seemed to have steel bars over the windows, and the arm was still partly in the way. He didn't have the night scope anymore. Then, as he focused on the possible soft flesh within that steel cage, he heard Anna say something that changed everything.

"It's coming down."

He took his eye from the scope, and he could see it, hear it too. The groan and rumbling of mountain giving way. The Kobatsu had reached too far, its giant arm and

318

bucket's weight too much for the counterweight to stop it now that the platform itself had moved forward, and the ground was crumbling underneath the treads. It was tipping over, slowly but surely, pitching forward into the darkness below. They had no time to move, not even to scream, for though the monster's fall registered in their adrenalin-soaked consciousness for what seemed a lifetime, tumbling in slow motion fifty feet to the switchback below, long enough for them to see Breedlove's maniacal face in the cab window as it passed by twenty feet away, the pope's terrified face in the painting by Francis Bacon, long enough for the bucket to take a stab at the moon as it went by—in fact the whole thing surely took no more than ten seconds. The excavator struck the edge of the switchback below, cartwheeled again down the next slope and crashed finally to the bottom of the pit. Then they felt the earth moving under them, and as they frantically ascended the last ten feet, the whole cliff began to give way and surge down the hill in a landslide of rock and dirt to the bottom.

Elias scrambled to the top before Anna, reached over and grabbed her by the wrist and pulled her onto solid ground just as there was no more. They backed away from the edge quickly and stood there in each other's arms long enough for her to stop shaking, from cold or fear, then they turned and looked back down into the pit they had climbed out of. The dust from the slide was clearing, blood red in the lunar light. The excavator was completely covered but for its arm, which reached out of the overburden like a giant's, its bucket a ragged claw at the end, grasping shreds of moonlight.

There was no more noise; the night had been returned to other sentient beings. Oaks creaking in the breeze. Birds cawing in the distance. When they looked up again they could see the far ridges outlined with trees, and farther still, the lights from a small town huddled in a hollow. They had no idea which direction they were looking;

it could have been Kentucky they saw, it could have been Virginia. Then in the direction of the highway they saw a ruby light flashing through the forest. Elias looked at his watch. It was 3:52. By the time they heard the sirens coming up the mountain, the full eclipse had ended, and the golden orb began to appear again from behind her veil.

The state cops were first. Two cars showed up, followed in the next hour and a half by a fire truck, three ambulances, more police, the local sheriff, a forensics unit, and later still, people from Mason Dixon and the media. By that time Elias and Anna were long gone. The second rescue squad wanted to take her, but she refused to go without Elias, and he was still answering questions. They wanted to know everything of course, especially about the sniper rifle, which was military issue and not registered in their databanks, but somehow the presence of the F-18s never got mentioned in the repeated storytelling. Anna was questioned too, and she would be lucid for a while, then burst into a rave with English and Saponi words all jumbled together like she was speaking in tongues. She hadn't slept in several days and appeared to be decompensating now that the present ordeal had ended. The authorities didn't seem to know how to take her. Then she started sleepwalking around the trailer, re-enacting some scenes from her life in the headlights of the assembled public vehicles while a female EMS walked beside her, like Lady MacBeth and her doctor. But before she and Elias climbed into the back of the ambulance and collapsed on the narrow stretcher together in exhaustion, he borrowed a flashlight from the sheriff and went off to find the branch he had used to fight their way out of their execution. He thought he should save it as a souvenir.

"Lemme see that," the sheriff said when Elias walked back with the four foot weapon in his hand. A middle aged man born and bred in Wise County, he was standing with one boot up on the front bumper of his cruiser chewing

320

tobacco. Elias hadn't had time to examine it before he used it: in the car lights the bark was smooth and grainy, a warm brown; the whole length felt solid and heavy and limber. Stronger than a man's cranium.

The sheriff looked it over. "If I don't miss my guess, I reckon that's a piece of chesnut," he said. "You don't see hit very much anymore; the blight's killed almost all the chestnuts in Appalachia. It's a real pretty wood. Hard too. People up here used to make furniture with hit. Must be a tree up on top of that ridge they left." And he handed it back to Elias. "You take care of that chesnut," he said. "People say they're making a comeback."

"I will," Elias said.

Chapter 22

March 20, 2011.

He's dressed in a corduroy jacket and khakis, apple green shirt that matches his eyes, and the Indy boots he never expected I bought him out of the J. Crew catalogue. What the hell four hundred and fifty dollars on my credit card I'll have to pay off when I get out in a couple of weeks. He's worth it. Gives me a kiss on the cheek as I sign out on a day pass we're taking over to Green Bank to see momma. Comes every weekend for the three months they've kept me locked up while the lawyers argue. No one's gone to court yet of course. He says "It's such a tangled web it'll take them years to figure it out and by then no one will care who's guilty and who's innocent. Except us." And the people who got poisoned and who died in childbirth and who got their land took away. Nobody's going to shut down the power plants anytime soon it's the same old same old out with the old boss but I'm not supposed to think too much about it got to keep focused on my own program. I'm on step four skipped one through three can't handle the powerless stuff and the god shit yet but a searching and fearless moral inventory seems in order considering what's happened especially with my father and being baptized by Satan and all. I still see things that ain't there demons sometimes human faces sometimes but I can tell a hawk from a handsaw when I want to. When I ask Elias about the spaceships saving us all he does is gives me a wink and says deus ex machina. That's his comic answer but I believe there is a god behind the spaceships and even small events that can't be explained maybe from another dimension they just appear and disappear we can't track them a dimension of good not evil that opened in 1961 when the telescopes appeared to counteract the destructive force called human. Do you think god intervenes in human affairs like those spaceships or was it just a coincidence they were planes he says well do you think it was fate that night at the Waffle House or just coincidence everything is connected he says we step and do not step into the same river as we go the ripples spread in all directions throughout the universe. If I had a dollar for every mysticism he makes I'd be rich and buy my own psychiatrist instead of the one the state gave me. One day I'll get inside his head and see what he for sure thinks.

I was in the real hospital for a week before they transferred me to Best Western, my home away from. The lawyer says it's the best idea. Sometimes I see momma's ghost walking down the same corridors I'm walking in the same washed out green gown palming a cigarette housekeeping slipped her. Did these leather restraints stained with sweat hold her wrists and ankles down twenty years ago? No wonder she died Indians can't be confined. Sometimes I see Ron Junior looking in the window I know he's not there but it's hard to get used to. It took a long time to believe the docs about the pregnancy even when they had me look in the mirror alien babies don't grow the same you can't expect me to get that fat. Of course they say I've been addicted to meth for so long I have become delusional and they send me to NA with the regular customers but I don't have a sponsor because I don't know if I'll go back to the meth have to decide that when the time comes.

Two fifty west through Churchville, West Augusta, Head Waters, McDowell, Monterey, High Town a place I can say I've been to more than oncet, and then we're in West by God and take 28 South at Thornwood. Now we're in the spiritual kingdom where the forces of good and evil battle for our souls it's always been right here right under our feet and up up in the tear in the sky that's why they put the telescopes in Green Bank because it's hallowed ground it's where the spaceships home in it's where people know the exact time of day they were saved. We're in the 13,000 square mile quiet zone now I tell him what's that shhhhh no talking I say and touch his lips he has a scruffy beard just like an English prof then whisper so's there's no radio interference for the telescopes they're searching for extraterrestrial life intelligent life he says good luck and I they met in 1961 the scientists did and came up with the Drake Equation the what the number of possible civilizations in the Milky Way equals the average rate of stars being born times the number of stars that have planets times the average number of planets that could support life times the possible number that could actually go on to produce life times the number that produce intelligent life times the fraction of civilizations that could give off

323

detectable signs times the length of time it takes to have a civilization which gives off these signs of course it's been modified many times since then. He looks at me for a while does he think I'm a freak idiot savant shakes his head you just never know he says it's the part about civilized life that's problematic he says maybe civilization always ends up destroying itself something in the DNA or in Darwin or Descartes then reaches in his shirt pocket for the cigarettes which are not there anymore damn so I dig one out of my bag what about the crow he asks what crow the crow I saw outside the trailer did you know it was there I'd rather not talk about it Jesus I'm sorry that was an idiotic thing to bring up it wasn't a crow a raven your father said you had one as a child that's the only reason I asked my father remembered that well I guess he would he found it in my bedroom talking to me more than once they're smarter than parrots try speaking to them sometime …*

"Didn't I just read somewhere that the SETI project lost its funding? After fifty years. What's that all about?"

Turn left here we cross the North Fork that's where my aunt lives the geese gliding down do you want to stop we can on the way back first we'll go to the cemetery it's on the other side of the valley I just wanted to show you not all my relatives are rednecks. They've given up searching means we're left alone with the demons to our own devices no more divine intervention. When we get there I see at the top of the hill there's a little girl with my angry face playing under an oak and thirty juncos feeding in the snow melt around the graves we are all kin here there is no separation anymore all things merge into the oneness

Some of the stones are so weathered that they have merged with the words. She runs her finger along the grooves and reconstructs the texts. "Like a thief in the night death stole the infant son of ...." "Beloved wife of Samuel, the angels took her from us but she will wake an … an something … on that golden shore."

"She will wake anon, again, sometime soon."

You're the Vanna White of Green Bank he says I you're so full of shit let's eat I'm starving all they feed us is meat and potatoes cooked in lard look at how fat I've gotten and open my coat you could never be fat touching my stomach he says he means I could never not be

324

a maniac and he doesn't know yet about the baby inside me but he's made shrimp fried rice and miso and for dessert ice cream with waffle cones in a special compartment in the cooler in honor of Waffle House and so I let him go on about how he wants me to move in with him when I'm discharged you could go back to Hollins or Tech or wherever you want and in the summer we could go abroad yeah you speak five languages what am I going to speak hillbilly he says but how many people can speak a dead one? Green circles in the grass are a message I know some being left here for me to decipher

"What are these circles?" she asked. "They're everywhere."

"I don't know. Probably some kind of fungus in the ground that travels in circles. Maybe they're where mushrooms grow. Fairy circles, I think they call them."

and he pulls my boots off on the blanket it's been an early spring in Appalachia almost sixty degrees and rubs my feet see what kind of perks you'll get and I laugh it tickles so what's the number he says what number the Drake number what's the possibility of intelligent life in our universe?

"Anywhere from 1 to 10 is the best estimate."

"At least one."

"Probably at least one."

"Then I think we should live together. For a while anyway. Until you figure out what you want to do next."

"You still have no idea how sick I am," she says after a long while. "A girlfriend is supposed to make your life less stressful, not more."

"I don't see how it could possibly get any more stressful than it already has been. And here we are."

She hit him.

"Do you find me attractive?"

"Get real."

"Do you really, really desire me?"

"Of course I do."

"Well then you're an idiot," she said and walked away into the newer section. He found her sitting on her mother's tombstone, flat and half buried in the earth, as if she could remove the lid from inside, stand up and leave if she wanted. The inscription read

Latona B. Jassey, 1962-1999, beloved daughter, sister, and mother, wa gilida she went home. I want that on my grave, she spoke, *if I am buried here most likely not some vacant lot some garbage dump maybe but not in Grundy*

"What's the B. stand for," he asked. "Breedlove." *Breedlove, he repeats, as if he didn't hear* her name was Breedlove *and then he looks around and everywhere he looks there it is Sarah and Michael and Mosnukky and Gabriel and Orion and Christanna all Breedloves and Powers and Hales and Denhams and Ridleys and it's like*

It's like they're at the beginning *and end* of everything *Elias was thinki*ng here in this green valley with the giant saucers that search the sky for meaning under these mountains that were the last thing God created *before he departed ...*

www.ingramcontent.com/pod-product-compliance
Lightning Source LLC
Chambersburg PA
CBHW070211260626
47160CB00002B/517